FANG

VOLUME 8

Edited by Ashe Valisca

FANG Volume 8

Production copyright FurPlanet Productions © 2017
Cover artwork copyright © 2017 by Jack Rohn

Published by FurPlanet Productions
Dallas, Texas
www.FurPlanet.com

Print ISBN 978-1-61450-387-3

Printed in the United States of America
First Edition Trade Paperback July 2017

In loving memory of Bandit

All Dogs go to Heaven

Table of Contents

Introduction

by Ashe Valisca

Putting the Fang collection together each year is always a mix of frustration and joy. The sorrow of telling people they did not get in juxtaposed with the joy of accepting works into the final collection. But one thing is always difficult, coming up with the theme is one of the hardest parts. For this year. Fang and Roar are sharing a theme – Paradise. But reading stories that are pictures of perfection would get boring. So I opened it up to allow the authors to explore, paradise lost, paradise gained, paradise earned, and the paradise created by settling or letting go. While I can tell you that there are erotic elements in every story, I cannot promise you that everything has a happy ending.

Serenity in Blue

by Al Song

What's the point of life? I thought to myself standing on the roof of the administration building. I stared out at the rainbow constellations of lights spattered on the small city before me, and then eased my way toward the edge of the rooftop following the bright yellow anti-slip mats so I wouldn't stomp a hole through the top floor's ceiling.

The night looked like a fusion between a Van Gogh and a Pollock painting when I took my glasses off and gazed into the void of consumerism and high-class living. I knew it had better things to do than gaze back into me. I thought one day I'd be a part of that world, but at the moment I was only serving them.

I unlocked a small storage closet using my worn master key with its logo as faded as my company granted, cornflower blue uniform, and found a stepstool. I propped it up against the shallow wall of the roof, climbed it, and then hoisted my chubby body onto the chilled, glossy, painted ledge. The icy wind clawed through my facial fur as I witnessed an even grander view. The streets below struck my mind with a dizzying sense of vertigo making me feel nauseous, and my stomach wanted to leap from my throat. I dangled my legs over the side and took my phone out.

I started looking through my photos and stared at an image of myself in the screen. I smiled at the handsome fennec fox who grinned back at me. It was only a year ago when I was a senior in college, but that still felt like it had been another lifetime. I took a selfie of myself and frowned at the ugly fennec grimacing at what I had become. The handsome fox was hard-working, intelligent, and had so much drive and ambition. He had friends, a boyfriend, and actually got laid. The fox I looked at now was worthless, and lacked any energy in his thick body and mussed up face. He barely had anyone, and his chances of ever having sex again plummeted below rock bottom. I deleted the repulsive fox from my phone.

I scrolled to an image of myself in my cap and gown holding my diploma. I should've celebrated even harder that day, since it was the zenith of when I felt such a sense of glowing achievement. It was like I was shining brighter than the sun in the cerulean sky that day.

After I graduated I struggled to find a job, and it seemed like everyone else had their lives in order. They were either going to grad school or they had internships with companies that made millions by the minute. I double majored in English and philosophy hoping to work with books, but instead I became a security officer for a company that didn't give a damn about me.

The security job dropped into my lap after my friend suggested that I apply. I was unsure about how a short guy with extra pounds and no experience with self-defense would get such a job, but they asked like five yes-no questions, and then asked if I could work in Schoenblick, it was nowhere near as big as Seattle, but it was definitely a place for the upper crust to rise and it was close to home.

The job itself wasn't very difficult and emergencies didn't really ever happen. I walked around the offices during my patrols, and when I wasn't wandering I sat in the security office as the other officer roved the site. I had a shiny badge which meant I had some sort of authority, kind of, but it was losing its luster and had a little rook symbol on it so no one took me seriously. 'Fortitude Protection Services,' the company I worked for had placed me in a position at 'Acedia Mattresses.' The mattress company only rented out a couple floors worth of offices in their administrative center, so the building itself had its own security patrolling the rest of it including the outside block. I guess I was pretty lucky, since I had been told there were other sites that come with more stress and incidents. I mostly answered emails, checked guests in, and made sure there weren't any shady characters skulking about in the offices. 'Acedia Mattresses' didn't pay me, since I was in contract security, which meant I made a little over minimum wage from 'Fortitude Protection,' and the client could treat me like garbage.

My freshman year of college I worked in fast food, and I thought my degree would get me out of being an emotional punching bag, but that wasn't the case whatsoever.

I knew no one was around me, but I still double-checked my surroundings. I went to my private pictures and looked at a photo of a handsome red fox with exquisite emerald eyes modelling for me. He was lounging on an indigo love seat with a salacious smile and a throw pillow covering his groin. I swiped to the next pic, which had the same fox in the same position, except the pillow was now gone. I bit my lip and felt a stirring under my zipper as I zoomed into his plump sheath and an exposed tip along with his sensuous sac resting on the cushions below.

I then heard a splash of static from my hip and almost dropped my phone a dozen stories. The radio announced in a low baritone, "Holt, do you think you could head back to the office? I haven't had my lunch break yet, and it's close to the end of our shift. Over."

It was my supervisor, Irvine. He was a tall, handsome coyote with a belly, which I had nothing against, and honestly I wouldn't mind having it against me. I had a crush on him when I first met him, since he was kind of the older 'daddy' type of guy, but I learned the hard way not to fall for straight guys. I was thankful that I had stumbled upon a gay porn star that roughly looked like Irv, except the actor was on the leaner side, and had hazel eyes instead of my supervisor's blue ones.

The two of us worked the swing shift together on weekdays unless he had to go to meetings with the managers. He usually took his meal break later in the shift to simulate dinner, whereas I stayed up late at night so it'd be my lunch and sometimes naptime when Irv let me. We'd eat in the security office unless I wanted to sleep then I would doze off in an unoccupied conference room.

I snatched the radio from my hip and said, "Copy that, I'll be on my way back. Over."

Sluggishly I slid back onto the rooftop, put my glasses back on, stored the stepstool away, and sauntered back into the top floor's elevator. I could have taken the stairs and jogged down, which could've been faster, but that would've required more energy than I wanted to spend, and at that point of the night my effort ATM was already overdrawn.

I exited the elevator car and quickly poked my head into a few of the offices to make sure only employees were in them. It seemed like everything was fine so I walked directly to the security office.

"Hey, Irv anything happen while I was gone?" I asked the coyote as he typed out a lengthy email.

"Everything's been quiet on this end. How's it going out there?" Irv asked and turned to me with a calm expression on his face. I knew that meant he got a stressful phone call or email from someone and had to put out a fire.

"It's been calm. No one's on the roof, and there are just a few IT employees still working."

"That's good to know. How are you doing, bud?" he asked kindly.

"I'm okay," I said as I stretched and yawned. "It's been an easy day for me, and those are always nice."

Irv nodded and turned his attention back to the computer screen. He exhaled sharply as he typed.

"Are things actually okay?" I asked when he finished the email.

"It's just another instance where bureaucracy prevents itself from running smoothly," the large coyote sighed and rubbed his temples, which made his tall, pointed ears rotate a bit. He then logged off the computer and took out a paper bag from his backpack.

I hopped onto the swivel chair and logged into my account as the cyan background appeared. I opened up a few programs and started typing in my logs on the activity report. I guess in a way I was using my degrees since I wrote every day, which I had done for my English classes. I was working with ethics, which was a branch of philosophy. *Yeah, lying to yourself will definitely get you out of this job and into greener pastures with bluer skies.* I really hated myself sometimes.

"What's for dinner today?" I asked Irv as I finished writing that there was nothing to report, but in a more eloquent and professional manner.

"Sandwich, granola bar, and protein shake," the coyote said after a gulp of what smelled like a bitter chocolate milk substance.

"That's even less food than yesterday," I said and frowned. I felt my big ears drop and my tail falter at the news.

"Well, I'm still trying to lose weight and add some muscle," he said nonchalantly and glanced into the bottle.

"Come on, you look fine," I said with a smile. I tried not to worry straight guys into thinking that I was hitting on them even if I liked them, and I wanted to reassure him that I didn't see anything wrong with his appearance. "In my book I don't think there's anything wrong with bigger guys. I just wish that the freshman fifteen and the senior sixteen didn't team up on me."

"There's always exercise," he suggested kindly and then grimaced after taking another swig of the viscous drink.

"I guess so," I sighed and looked down at my belly.

After our repeat of health class we chatted about indie films, anime, and manga. Irv kept telling me of ones I should check out. Time went by quickly when we talked, and it always made work pleasant.

* * *

When I got home I tossed my uniform onto the bathroom floor and quickly showered. My parents were already asleep since they both worked during the day and they left me some takeout on the counter. I diverted the water flow back down to the faucet and plugged the bathtub. I wiped my paws on the bathmat and grabbed a jar candle from under the sink and a gray bath bomb in the shape of a star. I lit the aquamarine candle which was labelled with "Ocean Breeze" on the lustrous jar along with a picture of a bungalow situated on a beach with the open sea and sky blending into one another.

The steam from the shower fogged up the mirror so I wouldn't have to look at the sad, dripping, disappointing fennec fox through the clear curtain and feel even more frustrated and upset.

After I got the grime out of my fur and set up the accoutrements I lowered myself into the bath letting the water envelop and flood over me. I reached for the bath bomb on the edge of the tub and dropped it in. The gray star fizzled as electric blue leaked from it like a tiny, toppled inkwell spilling its contents.

The smell of 'Ocean Breeze' was Oliver's favorite scent. It relaxed him, and he always had it lit in his room. He gave me the same candle that sat on his desk before he left for New York. The smell hit a 'play' button in my brain and the memories of the handsome red fox flooded my mind.

He was tall and lithe with deep green eyes that commanded attention when he was above me. He could wrap himself around me like a creamy orange sheet, whether to warm me on cold Seattle nights or when life had me down.

Under the hot water I felt my sheath becoming plump. I started gently massaging the tip out and caressing it with my thumb as the memories leaked from my emotionally stormy mind. The photos on my phone of him drifted through my thoughts fueling the fire in my body.

Oliver was the first (and to be honest was the only) person I ever had sex with. He filled our days full of joy and elation during my college career. He was incredibly smart and kind, but most importantly he was there for me, well, until the end at least.

It was a few days after graduation. Oliver and I sat naked on his indigo patterned sheets as I nuzzled his fluffy chest. We watched "Aoi Sora," an anime about college students with superpowers, who also had to deal with the drama and struggles of everyday life as well as saving their town from being destroyed.

Aoi, the leader of the group had the power of flight and his best friend, Tsukuru had super strength. Oliver and I shipped them together, and we even wrote a little fanfic of the two.

After streaming the second season finale the red fox rubbed my chest and stomach. The sensation overflowed my mind with euphoric ecstasy as I felt my tongue flop out.

"You want me to be your big, strong Tsukuru?" he asked flexing his arms and legs at me. His muscled thighs flanked his swollen sheath and his shapely balls.

"Sure," I said as I reached my hands out to massage his powerful legs as I worked my way up to his fuzzy chest.

He gently spread my thighs as he stood on his knees smirking at me.

I remember staring up at him and thinking how lucky I was to have such a wonderful fox like him as my boyfriend.

He leaned down to kiss me as I fell back on the pillows. Our tongues caressed as I moaned into his muzzle. He then lowered his stiff groin onto mine. Our mouths and balls were warm against each other's.

I mewled as he reached down, stroking our cocks roughly against each other's, and snickered at the noises that elicited from my throat. He then suddenly yanked our knots out of our sheaths. I yipped as my plug was suddenly released from its warm pouch.

These memories of intimacy made my heart and mind race in the warm bath. My shaft emerged from my sheath as I rubbed my tip more vigorously. The steamy water felt incredibly pleasant as it enveloped my member.

In my memory Oliver then nibbled on my neck leaving little nips down my collar, running over my chest, and finally down to my stomach. I shuddered as his hot breath left a trail along my body.

He leered down at me with his vibrant verdigris gaze as he reached underneath my waist and groped my rump.

"Just wait a sec, hon," he said and kissed me on the forehead. He maneuvered himself over to his nightstand to retrieve a bottle of lube from the top drawer as his arousal bobbed along the way. He squeezed a dollop out and started rubbing his paws together.

Oliver started stroking his shaft and gave me a little show as he humped his paws. His balls swung back and forth, smacking his knuckles and sinewy thighs as he gave me a grin. He smeared more on his swollen knot and then applied some to my aching erection. Lastly, he coated my ring with a slick finger and let out a little chuckle. The red fox probed me with another digit and started massaging my prostate. With his other paw he stroked me as my hips bucked, and I whimpered under the intense pleasure. I humped his tight grip as he leered sadistically above me and chuckled at my whines and moans. I tried my best to hold back and not to finish all over my boyfriend too early, but he wasn't going easy on me whatsoever.

I eased my sheath back to expose my knot in the warm tub water. I played with my balls and fondled them gently as I rolled them back and forth. I wasn't well endowed like the adult actors I watched, but I did enjoy the size of my pair which rested beneath.

After what felt like a million strokes, but in actually was just a couple moments, he loomed over me and whispered in my large drooping ear, "You ready for the main event, hon?"

"Yeah," I replied breathlessly, and it almost seemed like I could hear my own heartbeat pulsing in my head.

He lifted my haunches up as he placed a pillow beneath my lower back.

I felt his tip enter me slowly as I then wrapped my legs around the red fox. His large, fluffy tail wagged like a metronome as he slid in all the way up to his knot, and then hastened the pace of his thrusts. His face was filled with a furious form of lust as his eyes were screwed tightly shut and his teeth were bared and gritted. Oliver's hot breath was like fire against my muzzle as my breathing became shallow and staccato under the frantic rutting fox.

I remembered trying to stroke myself to the frenetic rhythm of his bucks and feeling euphoric pleasure envelop my being. The gentle thuds of his balls against my tail, the electricity emanating from my groin and the intense pressure against my prostate altogether clouded my mind in a sensuous state of ecstasy.

In the bathtub I started panting and whining as my fingers danced across my member faster. My memories drowned me in blissful elation as water splashed around me. The choppy waves were originating from my frantic paw as my shaft sent electricity to my overstimulated mind.

On the plush, pillow top mattress the pressure towered in my groin as I felt my balls draw up and my muscles tighten.

"I'm close," I squeaked to him.

"Me too," he growled back at me, and with one big thrust the red fox buried his knot deep inside me. He plugged me so fast and hard, that I gasped, and felt a searing burn underneath me.

I whimpered as Oliver hastily snarled and panted above me.

"Fuck, Holt, I'm coming," he shouted violently at me as he filled me with his hot sticky seed.

I burst as milky strings of my essence covered my belly fur.

Oliver then fell atop me with his tongue lolling out and the two of us sandwiching my come between us.

As the present mirrored the past I stroked by cock faster as I made a ring with my thumb and index finger, and gripped tightly under my engorged knot.

I ran the scene through my head and wanted to relive those memories so badly. Oliver's wonderful cock inside me and his sexy plump sac smacking against me; the thoughts pushed me over the edge. I moaned and felt my swollen, sensitive balls draw up as I pictured us coming together.

"Oh, fuck, Oliver," I groaned in the tub as I blew a nice load on my chubby belly. I counted three spurts escaping my tip and landing onto my torso.

I let out a pleasurable sigh and let my thoughts drift back to the red fox.

After the red fox and I made loved we cuddled in a tranquil, warm embrace swaddled in soft sheets. He held me so tightly and kissed me on the forehead as our bodies were tied into one being crafted from love and bliss. Oliver cupped my bottom and caressed it gently as I nuzzled his fluffy chest and inhaled his familiar, musky scent. The cozy indigo island was where I felt safe and at peace. It was where the stresses of life couldn't reach me and do me harm. A bit later the two of us watched a few movies together. We were having a relaxing day with each other in his apartment, and he kindly made blueberry pancakes along with hot chocolate for us. At the end of the day he said to me, "I need to talk to you about something."

"What's up, hon?" I asked and scooted towards him.

He put an arm around me and said, "I made it into Sapphire University with a scholarship." Oliver then gave a little sigh.

"That's awesome!" I exclaimed and hugged him tightly. "I'm so happy for you. They'll help you become the greatest journalist ever."

"It's great, but it's also kind of terrible," he said rubbing my back and holding me close.

"Why's that?" I asked as confusion and worry tangoed through my tight throat.

"You're moving back in with your parents, and I'll need to be in student housing for my scholarship to count," he said grimly.

"Okay, we'll go long distance," I blurted.

"No, when I moved to Seattle I tried going long distance with my boyfriend from high school, and it wasn't working, so I had to break it off with him," he sighed and immediately went silent.

I felt tears dampen my facial fur and then I started weeping harder and louder.

"You're so sweet, and I love you so much, and you make me so happy, but long distance relationships don't work for me," he said and started to sniff and tear up himself. His emerald eyes and the ruby red cracks emanating from them broke my heart even further. "I'm going to miss you, and I'm going to hate the fact that I won't be able to hug and kiss guys that are right there in front of me, who like me, and then I'm going to resent you for that, and I don't want to fall into that spiral again."

We both cried in our nest of sheets and pillows decorated in confusing indigo lines and shapes. I ran my fingers through his russet fur and nuzzled his creamy chest.

We spent as much time as we could together those next few weeks, but it was bittersweet knowing our relationship had an expiration date firmly stamped on it.

We helped each other pack up and move during that sore and aching time. I was so unmotivated to put his belongings in boxes since it felt like I was packing little caskets and sarcophagi with parts of his life. All the little knick-knacks and tchotchkes brought back happy memories, but they would all turn to sad ones as soon as we were no longer together.

I dropped him off at the airport and kissed him gently. He stared at me with his smaragdine irises and gave me a deeper kiss.

Oliver held my paw and said, "I'll call you when I land in New York."

"I'll be waiting for it," I replied.

We kissed again and he shut the door. I then drove to the nearest free parking lot and bawled my eyes out. I remember getting into the back seat, lying down, and then crying into a faded turquoise pillow.

I was there for a couple hours, and then I got the call from Oliver. He calmed me down and then I went into a grocery store and bought some 'Birthday Explosion' ice cream. It was a baby blue and white ice cream with cake pieces and sprinkles tossed in. I ate about half the pint and drove back home to Kirschland. I locked myself in my room for a couple days after that episode.

If Oliver ever wanted to fuck me again I wouldn't refuse the offer, and if he ever wanted me to be his boyfriend again it would make my year. I didn't care if it made me desperate. I just wanted him back, but I knew it would never happen. Even the novels from my literature classes usually had sad endings, so I knew that life liked to imitate art more than I actually wanted it to do so.

"Doubt thou the stars are water," I whispered to myself and inhaled the scent of blueberry pie mixing with the 'Ocean Breeze' candle. I then submerged my body under the murky blue depths of the tub. The warmth engulfed me as I held my breath and closed my eyes. I felt my creamy, yellow fur and my whiskers dance in the water like seaweed waving in the subaquatic currents. Little bubbles escaped my muzzle as I tried to keep all of my body still, especially my tail, ears, and brain. My chest, throat, and head felt pain increasing exponentially. They all started burning and soon

I sat upright and coughed violently. My lungs gasped desperately for air. Whenever I tried that it never worked.

I hugged my knees to my chest… well they were close to my chest. My stupid fat belly and thighs were in the way as I quietly cursed them. Soon the water cooled down and I unplugged the tub.

I snuffed the candle with its lid and turned on the ceiling dryer after I toweled off the excess water. My fur fluffed out and I strode towards my room. My parents would throw my clothes in the hamper for me.

My fur was significantly less damp and I got in my bed with my laptop and chatted with a few friends who were online late at night, and there was a message from Oliver. Our current conversations usually went something like this:

"Hi, how are you?" he'd ask.

"I'm good. How are you?" I'd ask back.

"I'm good too, but I have a lot of homework, and I'm so busy," he'd say.

"That sounds rough," I'd reply.

Talking to him was never the same as when we were dating.

As I chatted with friends I watched mindless videos and scrolled though memes and funny pictures online.

I supported vicarious vacations, foods, and fun as I stared into the laptop screen. I wasn't even watching films or television shows like before. If I actually watched those then I could discuss them with friends and people at work.

Looking at my bookshelf I noticed the 'to read' pile I had stacked up horizontally on the edge of the shelf. The only issue was that novels required effort from my unmotivated mind.

I turned my gaze toward the 'teach yourself this new skill' set of books I had on the bottom shelf and felt the same way about those.

My mind and body were feeling drained so I wished my friends a good night and shut my laptop. As I lay my head on the pillow the sandman quickly smothered me into a temporary death.

My alarm woke me up at around noon so I got about nine and half hours of sleep. I showered and had some breakfast my dad made me before he went to work. I then got in my azure two-door car and drove to Schoenblick. It was only about fifteen minutes away and I was always glad that I didn't have to drive during rush hour.

Rinse and repeat for a few more days until the weekend hit. I would then go on the internet some more and maybe call some people. Sometimes I'd go out to eat or shop a little, but that was a rare occasion for me, since I didn't like dealing with long lines, nor did I want to sit in traffic and worry about the reckless drivers around me.

I watched an internet celebrity going on tour through the US, and she was also a fennec fox. In different videos she talked about her struggles growing up without very much, and how people kept saying she wasn't an American even though she was born in the mid-west, and her parents were already in the US for a decade before they had her. She did comedy videos and even had a book out along with a CD of her standup comedy. *What are you doing with your life?* I thought to myself.

That Saturday my parents asked if I could pick up a couple items from the grocery store. I wasn't a fan of doing work on my days off, but they also gave me extra cash to buy myself whatever I wanted so I complied with their request. I threw on a plain t-shirt along with a light jacket, and stepped into my dark blue jeans. The knees were worn and the ends were frayed but they were comfortable. I was voted best dressed in high school and now I was wearing some pretty nondescript clothes because it was easy and quick, and maybe people wouldn't recognize me without a tie or blazer on.

It was later in the evening so there were fewer customers around, which meant fewer awkward shopping cart dances where people avoided bumping into one another. There were still a couple people in line so I just stood there staring at the candy and magazines illuminated by the fluorescent lights hanging from the high ceilings. A pop song ended and then a bluegrass song rained down from the speakers with frantic strings being plucked back and forth ferociously. I watched the clerk, who was a tall, skinny otter swiping groceries quickly across the scanner and typing in numbers for the produce like his life depended on it. It seemed so stressful. I could never do a job like that.

The speedy otter scanned all the food and miscellaneous items faster than I could get my debit card out and put it into the chip reader.

The last stop in the store was the pharmacy. I saw a perky weasel behind the counter and told her that I was picking up medication for my parents.

"Alright, sir, you're lucky, we're about to close in ten minutes," she said and then looked up at me and squealed. "Holt, is that you?"

"Oh, Wendy, uh, hey," I said back to her. She was a friend of mine back in high school. We shared a couple classes, and she was a year ahead of me back then. She received her associate's degree when she graduated high school since she was doing the 'College During High School' program, and took classes during summer quarter so she could finish undergrad sooner.

"It's been so long. Do you have time to talk? I'm off work in ten," she said rapidly.

"Sure, I'll put my groceries in the car and then I'll be at the café," I said and Wendy quickly gave me my parents meds.

I sat at one of the creaky wooden tables and stared out at the cloudy skies. I sipped some hot chocolate from the compostable blue cup with the store's logo on it. I looked up from the drink and saw Wendy walking towards me gleefully.

"How's it going Holt?" Wendy said with excitement coating her voice.

"I'm okay. You know, just picking stuff up for my parents," I said trying not to reveal that I was a complete failure, while also trying not to show that I was afraid of someone who knew a lot of people in my past and could reveal the truth about where I was in life to said people.

"I could've bought the drink for you. I've got a store discount," the cheerful weasel said kindly.

"Thank you, but it is okay. It's just hot chocolate. It only costs like two dollars," I said rolling the cup between my fingers.

"What've you been up to these days?"

"Nothing much. I'm working as security in Schoenblick," I admitted. I knew Wendy wouldn't go around talking about me. She just wasn't that type of person.

"That's cool. My dad's a security officer too. He works at the city hall in Schoenblick," she said smiling.

That knowledge made me relax a bit. I responded with, "Yeah, my job probably isn't as difficult as doing security at a federal building. I work in a business office."

"But it's still important," Wendy said, maybe a bit loud for the chill café area. "It's not like there aren't corporate spies out there. People have to watch out in the healthcare industry too. I have to be careful even though I have a wall of plastic in front of me when I'm working."

"Congrats on becoming a pharmacist," I said, and she got up to give me a hug. "I know it was your dream

"Thank you. I'm actually a pharmacy technician, which means the pharmacist is my boss. I was working in Seattle, but my roommates had to leave for grad school and moved. I didn't want all my paycheck to go to rent so I moved back home."

"Yeah, something like that happened to me."

"You okay?" she asked. "Your ears are drooping."

At that moment I realized that I was frowning, and said, "Yeah, no I'm okay." *You could have fooled me.* I wished my brain would just shut up.

"Really?" she asked raising a brow.

"No, it's just. Seeing you achieve your dreams and becoming what you wanted makes me really happy for you, but now I feel like I don't have my life together. I remember the times you talked about aspiring to be a pharmacist and now you're working in a pharmacy. I was in all the advanced classes, and I was in all the clubs, and I did tennis for all four years of high school, and then I went to the University of the Pacific Northwest, and I double majored, and I was in all the clubs, and I went to my professor's office hours, and I graduated with honors, and now I'm living at home, and I'm making a little over minimum wage working as a security officer," I confessed spilling out all that was stewing inside of me.

"Holt, there's no shame in living with your parents. I'm doing that right now instead of living in a rundown apartment complex," she said with a sigh. "But it would be nice to live with Chad."

"Chemistry Chad?" I asked astonished at this news.

Wendy nodded with a wry smirk.

"You and him are together?" I asked. We didn't always get to choose who we were partnered up with in chemistry class, and those two always seemed at each other's throats. Wendy thought Chad was a good for nothing slacker, and he thought she was a ruthless dictator. "I thought you hated him."

"Yeah, he's different now. People change. He lost his job a few weeks ago, so moving out and living together isn't really an option right now, and it might not be for a while."

"Yeah, my boyfriend broke up with me last summer," I said with a sigh. Great, everyone else had someone to screw besides me. I was both a failure in the realm of relationships and in the workforce.

"Aw, I'm sorry for bringing boyfriends up. I know you and I know you'll get a career and a guy who makes you happy. You always find a way. You have a roof over your head and you have a full time job. It's not the end of the world," she said with a bright smile.

"Thanks, Wendy."

"No prob, Holt. We should hang out more now that we're both in Kirschland."

"That'd be fun."

* * *

A few weeks later at work Irvine sat down in the little security office with me as the morning shift guys were in the lobby.

"So, Holt," the tall coyote said and paused. "I know you don't like to cover shifts, but this week I really need you to work Saturday, Sunday, and I'll need you to come in four hours early on Monday."

"No, I'm sorry, but no," I replied. I didn't like disappointing Irv, but this was one of the things I hated doing. "That's going to wreck my sleep schedule, and I'm gonna be tired."

"I need you to do this," he begged. "The floaters are already working at the music festival in Seattle, Jake is on vacation, Iris has finals this week, and I've already done sixty hours of work and we're supposed to work more than that per week."

"But, I really don't want to do this."

"I know you don't, but others really need you to step up for them."

I looked up at him with my face covered in indignant anguish as he looked down at me with exasperated desperation pouring from his steely cool eyes.

He then sighed and said, "Alright, how about this? If you do this for the team then you can have Friday off in two weeks."

I exhaled though my nostrils audibly and relented to this damn, diffident, Seattleite standoff.

"Fine, Officer Salvatore," I said and the coyote smiled back at me. This was going to suck.

"Thank you, bud," he said and gave me a one armed hug. "Weekends are even easier. There are barely any employees around besides a few in the IT department and normally they don't have visitors with them."

I usually slept in on weekends and I was not looking forward to waking up four hours earlier on Monday.

Saturday and Sunday afternoon I worked with Chad, an older wolf. He filled in for Irv once in a while and was a really nice guy, but we didn't have very much to talk about with one another so I spent a good amount of time on the computer reading articles.

On Sunday night I still wanted to watch a few videos before I went to sleep. As I was viewing a music video that had a couple badgers on a road trip I realized that traffic would be chaotic Monday morning. So I went to bed unable to fall asleep and worrying about snoozing past my alarm clock's buzzing. I turned on my phone and set an alarm on that as well and set it on the shelf on the other side of the room so I couldn't turn it off easily. I had it so that it would go off five minutes later just in case the first alarm didn't do its job. I really hated it when my sleep schedule changed.

I think I fell asleep about an hour before my usual bedtime and when I woke up at eight it felt like a bus had hit me.

The shower helped wake me up a bit and I ate a hardier breakfast since adding four hours to my work day only garnered me an extra ten minute break. There was more traffic on the road but I still made it to work on time. I kept telling myself not to fall asleep at the wheel, and I think the fear of slipping into slumber and getting into a painfully deadly collision kept me awake.

At work I met up with Eli, a round moose and relieved a very tired looking vixen named Julia, who worked all nightshift and did the extra four hours in the morning.

I tried drinking some coffee to wake myself up, but I hated the taste so much that I couldn't stomach it. Irv brought in a bottle of sweetened green tea for me when swing shift rolled around. I had explained to Eli my predicament and asked if I could sleep during my break and he was cool with it. I also asked Irv when he came in and he didn't like it but he allowed it since I was doing everyone a big favor. The ten minute naps didn't really help and the half hour nap during lunch left me tired and hungry.

Near the end of my shift I kept trying to keep myself awake by walking around the lobby and the security office, but I also had a couple emails that I needed to answer. As I typed and proofread what I had written I felt my eyelids growing heavy and I started slouching.

The next thing I heard was Irv's voice. I jumped up and looked around me uncertain of what was taking place.

"Holt, can you hear me? Are you there?" he asked upset and confused. His words surrounded by static and desperation.

I picked up the radio from my hip and said, "Yes, Irv, I'm here at the office. Uh, over."

"Who were the people who left thought the lobby in the last twenty minutes? Did any of them carry a teal handbag? Did any of them look like they were concealing a bag?"

"Uh, I don't know. I was… uh," I muttered still unsure of what to say. Fuck, why couldn't I think of what to say? Dammit. I hated everything at this moment.

"What?"

"I don't know," I confessed. Why the fuck didn't I say anything else?

I panicked and worried as I saw on the clock I only had fifteen minutes left on my shift. I slept for about forty-five minutes while Irv was on patrol. A few minutes later I saw him in the lobby as his presence exuded exasperation as he headed into the security office with a serious expression.

"What were you doing that distracted you from monitoring the flow of traffic through the lobby?" he asked sternly.

"I fell asleep," I admitted and looked down at my fingers clasping on to one another tightly.

"The CFO said her purse had been stolen," he said coldly, and I felt my ears drop and a wave of guilt splash over me. "She brought it to work and couldn't find it. I asked you who left through the lobby, and you said you didn't know while I was on the radio with you standing right in front of the CFO, and you not only made me look bad, but also all the officers here."

"I'm sorry," I said. "I really messed up." I bit my lip and told myself not to cry.

"I'm going to check the cameras to see who left using the stairwells," Irv said quietly. "Maybe we do need a security camera in the lobby too."

That last comment stung harder than anything else I had heard him or anyone else at work say to me. I tried to do my best at this job which wasn't very difficult, but I still managed to screw up big time. I didn't want to disappoint Irv, since he was such a nice supervisor, and he wanted all of us to be happy. He always took care of problems right away for us too. He did little things for us like always having paw sanitizer on the desk, and he dealt with the bigger issues as well like when a former employee was homophobic towards me.

The front door had a badge reader on it so employees needed to use their employee IDs to get into the offices and this included the stairwells that led to the garages. Besides watching cameras, patrolling, and responding to emails we had to check in guests when the receptionist wasn't working, and we had to make sure people weren't keeping the front door open for those who didn't check in.

I put my radio and keys on the desk, clocked out on the computer, and then wandered to my car. There was a drafty chill in the parking garage which froze my spine and limbs. My movements were stilted, and articulating my joints felt like such a struggle as I made my way to my automobile.

I cried as I drove home through the desolate streets and I almost took the wrong exit. I put on the jazz station to see if it could calm me down, but a blues song played with a solemn, lonely sax wailing in a sea of percussion. When I got home I parked and then quickly noticed that I left the car in neutral and fixed the problem.

When I got into the shower I sat down and wailed into my paws as I rocked myself back and forth. I dried my fur a little, crawled into my bed and cried into my pillow. I went to sleep without talking to my friends or watching any videos. My stomach was running on nothing and it was punishing me for not eating.

Why was I such a fuck up? I didn't know if I would be written up or if I'd get fired. If I got canned I wouldn't know what to do to get a new job, since I wouldn't be able to list this job on my resume, since I'd have to tell the interviewer that I got fired, and they would never hire me. If I couldn't find a new job then I wouldn't be able to pay for my student loans and I couldn't help my parents with the bills, and they'd get mad at me, and then maybe they'd kick me out, and then I really wouldn't know what to do.

It was so stressful and hopeless. I didn't want to deal with problems anymore. I was worthless. My parents worked so hard to give me a happy life, and I just turned out to be a stupid disappointment, who didn't matter whatsoever to this world, which had so many opportunities. Nothing I did ever mattered until it affected others negatively, then I would be relentlessly punished by those I've hurt, even when my actions bore no ill intent. I was complete garbage that deserved to be incinerated into nothingness. I hated myself so much. People kept asking me why I was working security if I had a degree and I would never have a good answer and it's actually because I was a scared, lazy loser who quickly became complacent.

* * *

The next day at work I went into the security office early and clocked in on the computer. I went down to 'Officers' and then clicked on 'Holt Szalay.' It popped up with a message thanking me for checking in early/ on-time. Eli handed me the keys and radio, and then I started my patrol before I could have any chance of running into Irv. I turned off my radio and unlocked the door to the roof. Without even thinking about it I had the stepstool from the storage room propped up against the wall. I took the three little steps and climbed onto the ledge. There I stood and blankly stared at the sky. My brain did away with the concepts of breathing and blinking at the bustling scene before me. It was a sunny day in Western Washington, and the sky was a terrific turquois stretching out infinitely. Below me people hurried across black and white patterns as impatient drivers angrily blared their hedonistic horns and irritably revved their tumultuous engines. There were shoppers carrying dozens of sparkling pastel shopping bags with brand names branded on their chests and bellies as they flaunted their promotional status symbols, while ignoring the people near them begging for their next meal. The silvery towers jutting from the streets of tar and grayed pavement reflected one another along with the scenes below in an aberrant, spectral version of its own reality.

The world was full of beauty, yet there was so much pain and anguish spread throughout it. Life was a sea of cruelty and torment in which kindness and peace were constantly drowning as they struggled to survive. Why did things have to be this way? Why couldn't everything be just and fair? There needed to be less malice and terror. The world was disgusting and putrid, and it didn't need another shitty person like me in it.

I set my glasses down on the ledge and closed my eyes. I didn't want to think about the reasons why I shouldn't do this. Images of my parents, friends, and coworkers flashed in my mind's eye. I opened my eyes and felt tears running down my cheeks. I wanted the beautiful blue sky above me to be my resting place.

I heard the door violently burst open behind me as I waved my arms in front of me to keep my balance.

"No, stop, don't jump!" Irv cried.

I turned to meet his gaze and he looked so distraught and in pain.

"I'm begging you. Please don't do this!" he pled as he fell to his knees and started weeping.

My heart broke into irreparable pieces at that. I'd never seen him in such a manner before. I guess I'd never seen anyone in my life look so drained of hope, and so distressed and dejected. The only person that I could remember looking like that was myself, whenever I stared into a mirror or a picture. Watching him sob I realized that I'd be hurting more than myself if I had leapt.

I climbed down and walked toward him. He ran to me and scooped me up in his arms panting and coughing in pain.

"I'm so sorry for everything. I'm so sorry about yesterday. I messed up so badly," I said as he held me tightly.

"No, I screwed up," he said squeezing me securely as we shook. "I was going to tell you that the CFO called and said that she left her purse in the trunk of her car that day and found it when she got home. She didn't bother emailing me until this morning."

What he said made me feel like I was a complete idiot. I was going to kill myself due to someone misplacing something. What the fuck was wrong with me?

"You're not getting in trouble. I shouldn't have made you work so much. You wouldn't have been tired if it weren't for me. I'm to blame for this. I'm just so happy you're alright," he said hastily to me.

I turned my gaze to look at him and his beautiful cobalt eyes. They were like two slabs of illuminated lapis lazuli beaming at me. We stared into each other, and I felt a peacefulness wash over my mind and my being. He looked at me the same way Oliver would, and I smiled longingly at him, then he gave me a quick gentle kiss. It was the happiest I had been in the last nine months. Even though it only lasted a second in my mind it felt like an eternity of bliss.

"You like guys?" I asked as I turned my gaze downward and felt him hug me even closer.

"And women. I almost never tell anyone at work, and I've liked you for a while. It's just that I wanted to keep this professional, and I didn't want to weird you out since I'm almost a decade older than you."

"I don't care if you're thirty-one and I'm twenty-two, and I'll be twenty-three soon," I said and gave him a kiss. His ears perked up at that and his lacquered, lovely eyes shone bright in the afternoon light. "How did you know I was up here?"

"The building security officers called and said a fennec fox was on the ledge of the roof and you weren't answering the radio so I presumed it was you," he said and stroked my back.

"That makes sense," I said and smiled tiredly up at the handsome coyote.

We nuzzled each other again and Irv said, "Come on. Let's talk downstairs so we don't worry the receptionists."

In the office I explained to Irv how I felt like a useless failure and how I kept making mistakes in life and pretty much all that I had told Wendy the weekend before.

"What do you want to do as a career?" he asked.

"I don't know. Maybe work with books?" I answered and even I caught the uncertainty in my own voice.

I told him how I was rejected when I applied to higher positions within the library systems and how I wasn't used to rejection.

"What about an entry level position there? Usually companies like to hire within. Maybe it's the same with the library, and they might help with paying for a master's degree in library science or they might know about scholarships, and then you could become a librarian after climbing the ranks," he suggested.

"Well, I checked the hiring page on their website and it said that pages only get fifteen hours a week at minimum wage and I can't afford to pay my student loans and my cellphone bill and give money to my parents to help with other expenses with that amount of money, and the schedule changes every month," I said and sulked.

"You're allowed to have another job as an employee of 'Fortitude Security,' so I can talk to HR and help you get a part time position as a floater if you'd like. I mean the hours will be strange but you're allowed to say no to sites if you feel like you're working too many hours or if it interferes with your library position. We might be able to change your hours here too."

"Okay, that doesn't seem too bad. I guess I'll have to work hard to get what I want. Ugh, everyone seems to say that," I sighed, and then grimaced at the thought.

"Also, we're technically allowed to go out since there's not a policy against it. I mean they never made one because our company mostly has men and they think men would never date each other. I'm sorry I'm rambling. I really do like you, and I want to help you," he said the last part with a small smile.

"Going out with you sounds amazing," I responded and saw his brilliant, blue eyes light up at that.

"And another thing," he said quickly. "This company helps pay for therapy, and I can help you find someone who could help you."

"That sounds good too," I said and I could see even more relief in his handsome face.

We smiled at each other and it felt like the world had stopped. The stormy turmoil in my mind cleared into a calm, island paradise where the gusty winds diminished into soft breezes caressing my whiskers and cheeks, along with a radiant sun entering its zenith embracing my body with warmth, and clear, ultramarine waters lapping lightly at my toes. Those blue eyes made me feel serenity in its purest form.

* * *

After my shift on Friday I changed into the clothes I brought from home in one of the men's restrooms, and packed away my uniform in my old periwinkle gym bag. I had to search for it in my room since the last time I used it was in high school.

I wore a plain dress shirt with khakis and a celeste bowtie with stretchy suspenders to match.

"You ready?" Irv asked as I walked into the lobby. He wore a blue flannel shirt and a pair of plain, denim jeans.

We waved goodbye to the officers starting the nightshift and headed to the garage. I put my belongings in the trunk of my car then Irv and I headed out into the downtown core.

"You look cute by the way," the coyote said.

"Aw, thanks, Irv," I replied and felt my cheeks warming up.

"I'm sorry I didn't say that earlier. I didn't want to reveal my *preferences* in front of the other employees," he explained. "I kind of still don't want them knowing that I'm… you know."

"I understand. There were definitely times in my life when I didn't want people knowing about that part of my life. You look really handsome," I said beaming up at him.

"I'm flattered, but this took like two seconds to put together. I'm not all dolled up like you."

"This didn't actually take very much effort. The bowtie took a few tries, but it wasn't a big deal," I said messing with the knot around my neck. "Where are we going? Aren't most things closed at ten around here?"

"Some of the restaurants stay open until eleven, and let's just say we're going to have some fun at the mall," the coyote said with a mischievous grin.

After a few blocks we made it to 'Blick Square,' the mall at the center of downtown, one of the few malls I knew that could only expand upward.

We entered the shopping structure, and I noticed that most the stores were closed except for the restaurants we passed by, and a few franchised coffee shops.

The hallway forked at a bubble tea shop, and we took a turn to the left. At the end of the hall there was an azure haze of light emanating from a cave of cacophonic rings, beeps, and other electronic sounds.

An iridescent sign shone proudly above the glowing entrance, which read, 'Rakuen One.' A chibi version of Tenchi, the tennis-playing raccoon videogame character leaned against the capitalize 'R' and gave a thumbs-up.

"Ah, here we are," Irv announced.

"An arcade?" I asked.

"Yeah, this is one of the places I go to blow off some steam," the coyote explained excitedly. "Their grand opening was just a few months ago, and it beats having to drive down to Rentown to play arcade games. After nine at night anyone under twenty-one has to leave since they start serving alcohol, and they stay open until two in the morning."

I crossed the threshold with the coyote and stared in wonder at flashing lights and musical whimsy of the electronic games beaming at me for attention as we wandered towards a help counter. It was years since I had been to an arcade and everything seemed so different, yet so familiar. Instead of children yowling and shrieking in delight I mostly saw adults crowded around various games as they laughed and chatted.

"I'd like to reload twenty-five dollars on this card, and I'd like a new card for my friend here," Irv said to the doe behind the counter.

"How much should I add to the card, sir?" she asked retrieving a card from a drawer.

"The same amount," he beamed.

"Oh, Irv, I can pay for myself," I said placing a paw on his forearm.

"Hey, I insist," he protested.

"Aw, thank you very much," I said smiling up at him.

"No problem!" he declared and pulled me into a side hug. "What do you want to do first?"

"I have no idea," I responded looking around at all the flashing lights and cacophonic noise surrounding me.

"Let's check out the cabinets," he suggested.

"Sure," I replied with a smile.

In one of the corners sat a few rows of short, glossy white arcade cabinets. I looked around and suddenly gasped.

"Is that an 'Aoi Sora' videogame?" I asked and looked up at the coyote.

"Yeah, did you watch that show?" he asked.

"I did. I finished the second season last summer."

"Did you know that they're making a third season?"

"Really? That's awesome," I said feeling excitement run through me.

"So, for this we can do a two player game. I can play Tsukuru, and you can be Aoi if you'd like," he offered.

"Sure, that sounds great."

Irv explained the controls to me and the basics of how to play. As Aoi I was battling robots in the sky, and the coyote controlled Tsukuru as he mowed the mechanical guys down on the streets. We stood near each other as we played and cheered each other on, and the closeness warmed my heart.

We made the leaderboard, and then we decided to head to an area consisting of claw machines gathered in clusters. There were many plush and boxed vinyl toys piled on top of one another trapped behind their glass prisons begging to be freed. I saw a Captain Coyote plush in one of the machines where it was on a glass pedestal, but the claw only had two prongs, unlike the three pronged ones I usually saw at grocery stores. I explained to Irv that I loved the show, since it always emphasized the importance of teamwork, and I always thought the ship captain was hot. Ever since I was young I wanted him to bang me like a bass drum. I tried for the toy a few times but failed each time, and Irv tried for it once and got it. I hugged both coyotes and thanked Irv about a dozen times. He explained that it was less about skill and that success was usually dependent the payout rate.

After we tried a few other claw machines we focused on playing games that granted us tickets. We tried out a mini bowling game together and Irv managed to get a jackpot on it as well as a couple other games. He said that the tickets get loaded onto our cards since each game started up after we swiped them through little readers jutting out of the machines.

Irv and I pooled our tickets together, and I learned that he had a couple thousand tickets on his card compared to my few hundred.

"You can get whatever you want," he said and smiled at me.

"Really? Most of the tickets are yours."

"I can win more," he said matter-of-factly. "Is there anything you'd like?"

I looked around in the prize room, and there were items that ranged from candy to plush toys to electronics and many other things. I didn't want to get something that cost too much since Irv probably spent a good amount of money acquiring his tickets. I did spot an 'Aoi Sora' poster on display behind a few action figures for one thousand tickets and purchased it.

I thanked Irv again and we walked out into the chill of the midnight air since the mall entrance was blocked off.

"That was really fun and thank you again for everything," I said with a cheerful grin.

"No prob," he replied and gave me a tight hug with both arms. "It's nice going to the arcade with someone else, and it's a lot more fun with another person. Are you hungry?"

"Yeah, I could use some food. Is anything actually open at this time?"

"I know of one place and it's really good."

We walked down a block and took a left turn. I saw restaurant with its lights on and a few people wearing business attire chatting together while walking into the establishment. The restaurant was called "Parahn Bada" with the Hangeul above it in a blocky, aquamarine font. When we entered the restaurant the world came back to life. The décor consisted of a cartoonish nautical theme. One of the television screens showed a k-pop music video as the speakers played a slow but catchy song.

A kangaroo seated us and gave us two menus. He then said that he would be back soon to take our orders.

"Do you like Korean food?" Irv asked.

"Yeah, I've had soondubu jjigae before in downtown Seattle," I replied. "Anything you recommend here?"

"Their bibimbap is really good. It's basically rice with veggies and an egg. I know it sounds basic, but they make it really well here."

"I haven't had it before, but it sounds good."

"Would you like to get the dolsot version? It comes in a hot stone bowl and it makes the rice warm and crispy."

"Sure, that sounds even more delicious."

After a bit the kangaroo came back to take our drink orders. Irv ordered green tea and a mango smoothie, and I just stuck with water.

"So, how's the night going for you?" the coyote asked and scratched the back of his neck.

"It's going great. I'm having a lot of fun and you won me these," I said and gestured to the rolled up poster and the plush toy on the table.

"Hey, *we* won those together," he said giving me a cheesy grin.

"*You* did most of the work," I replied giving him a knowing look.

"It was a team effort. So, how's the week been for you?"

"It's been better," I said and took a moment to think about the events that transpired, and tried to stick to positive things in my mind. "I worked on my resume, and I called the wellness center from my university to see if they could help me find a gay or lesbian therapist in the area. The receptionist was really helpful, and our headquarters said that my dad's insurance would help cover most of the costs for one I found."

"That's great," Irv cheered and went around the table to give me a big hug. The embrace warmed my face since I wasn't sure if anyone was staring, but it also filled me with a strong sense of elation.

The kangaroo smiled at us as he set down a ceramic cup and the mango smoothie in front of Irv. He then set down a large blue glass for me and filled it with water and a couple ice cubes.

"I'm trying to do a little every day."

"That's a lot of work in less than a week," he said happily.

"I just don't want you to worry too much about me," I admitted to the big coyote. "I've noticed that you've been nervous at work ever since that day."

"I really appreciate it," he said with relief in his voice as he sat back and relaxed his shoulders. "I really want you to be happy."

"You make me really happy. I guess I still have a fear that I'll never be successful and that college was a waste of my life. It's so frustrating. I worked so hard in high school and I burnt myself out to get into college and then I burned myself out even more just to make a little over minimum wage. I could have just taken it easy that entire time and I would have still been in the same place," I said and sulked into the glass of water. My reflection stared back at me in hues of blue.

"Hey, it's alright," he said and gave me a warm smile. "I know you'll find your dream job. You're a competent employee, and I don't hear any complaints about you. You work harder than a lot of other security officers I know."

"Well, the job isn't that tough," I said swirling the water in my glass.

"But that's the thing. Our site isn't very difficult, but people become more and more complacent and lazy. Simple tasks become a thirteenth labor and whenever I ask you to do something you actually do it, and I don't even need to ask you to do patrols or to take care of inventorying the keys."

"It's a lot easier than writing an essay about some straight, old guy's novel complaining about ennui," I said and smirked at the coyote.

Irv gave a small chuckle and kept his kind smile directed at me as he said, "That's another thing about you. I mean you find these tasks not to be very appealing, but you do them and, you do them well. My cousin was the same way. He worked really hard, and after he graduated college he was jobless for about four years then he worked retail for three more, and then he landed an office job for an online retailer. He's happy now, but it took a lot of time. It was a similar story for one of my closest friends, who worked in a diner for years before he got a job in marketing. I didn't start college until I was twenty-three and at times I do feel like I haven't received much from studying criminal justice, but I know this won't be my job forever, and I know that you'll find a job that makes you happy one day."

"Thanks, Irv," I said after a sip of water. I let myself relax into the seat and looked into his stunning, stark blue eyes.

"No prob. Things take effort, but they also take time," he said gently.

A couple minutes later the boomer brought out our dishes. Two black bowls with little round trays underneath were set down in front of us. Irv explained not to touch the bowls themselves since they were fiery hot, and to mix the rice and vegetables, but to leave the bottom layer of rice touching the bowl alone so that it would get crispy.

I added some red pepper sauce to the mixture of veggies, rice, and the fried egg and stirred it up a bit. I took a bite and it was delightful. The greens and tofu complimented each other as the pepper sauce added a sweet and spicy zing to the warm saucy egg. The crispy rice gave a nice crunchy depth to the other soft ingredients.

It was wonderful sharing such a nice meal vis-a-vis with such a handsome coyote. The music was relatively quiet, and the other diners weren't being noisy and disruptive. Irv caught me looking at him and he smiled back. He asked me how the food was and I told him it was perfect.

When the check arrived I offered to pay since he spent so much at the arcade, but Holt kept the check to himself and wouldn't let me see the cost.

After dinner we walked back to the building we worked at, and retrieved our cars. Irv gave me his address, and I tried to follow him the best I could. He drove a bit under the speed limit so I would have less of an issue getting to his apartment.

About fifteen minutes later I managed to arrive at the coyote's place, and I parked in one of the guest spots. He walked me to his front door and unlocked it.

"This is my home," he said with a grin as he let me in.

A tall moose sat at a desk next to a flat screen television set, and looked up at us.

"Hey, Kai, this is Holt, and Holt this is Kai, my roommate."

"It's very nice to meet you," I said and shook the moose's hand.

"Nice meeting you too," he said. "I guess it's my cue to get going. I'll see you in a few days." Kai packed up his laptop in a backpack, grabbed a suitcase and left into the night. "Have fun, you two."

Irv and Kai waved at each other as the moose walked into the chill of the night.

The coyote and I sat down on his bed as I nuzzled him, and he held me tightly. I felt his large biceps as he flexed for me and I groped his muscled pecs in delight. I'd love for him to bench press me sometime this weekend. I looked up at him as he granted me a gentle kiss. It warmed me up as I felt him undoing the buttons on my shirt.

I pulled him down into a deeper kiss, and then I undid my bowtie, and let it drop on the carpet. Irv's tongue ran along my own as he caressed it deeply. I started unbuttoning his flannel with his assistance. We threw off our shirts along with our undershirts as we held each other tightly. I rubbed his belly as he made joyful noises at the base of his throat, and noticed a slight throbbing in the bulge of his pants as I felt a stir in my own groin.

"You wanna undo them?" he asked.

"Yeah," I said nodding as I reached down to cup his maleness. It was warm, and Irv let out a gentle moan at the touch. Excitedly I unbuttoned his fly and unzipped his pants as his bulge emerged from his jeans. A pair of navy blue briefs hugged his large package. I nosed the swelling groin and kissed it. I thought I had a hefty set of balls, but his were even bigger.

He then stood up to shake off his pants as I stared down at his crotch. I turned around, lifted my tail, and dropped my khakis, revealing my rump framed by a turquoise jockstrap.

"You wore a jockstrap to work? You kinky little fox," Irv said as he sidled up to me cupping a cheek in his massive paw.

"I thought you might like it," I replied looking back at him with a delighted grin.

"You're full of surprises. It looks like the jockstrap's pretty full too," the big coyote said as he caressed my stiff package in his other paw. He pulled me into a tight embrace from the back and pressed his groin between my cheeks as he gently humped me with his bulge.

"You're the one getting me excited," I said as he maneuvered his thumbs under the elastic around my waist as he slowly kneeled and gently pulled down my jockstrap. My boner sprung up as it was freed.

"Nice balls," he said when he stood back up and looked down over my shoulder as he started stroking my fuzzy sac in his warm palm.

"I bet yours are bigger," I said grinding my rump against his bulge. I then turned around to face him and fondled his package. I knelt as I slid down his briefs exposing his stiff cock and his large, shapely balls.

His crotch was in my face as I cupped the pendulous nuts in one palm and stroked his shaft in the other. The coyote's voluptuous orbs were warm and the furry sac they rested in was sensuously soft. The considerable pair complimented his admirable cock well.

Irv's throbbing maleness was about the average length, maybe an inch or so longer than mine, but boy was he thick. The coyote's girth was incredible, and I was eager to have his swollen cock inside me.

The shaft was a heavy weight in my grip. Irv pulled his sheath back revealing his swollen knot which looked almost as big as a baseball.

I nuzzled his package as I huffed the aroma of his intoxicating musk.

A drop of pre formed on his warm member as I lapped it and wrapped my muzzle around the pointed tip and maneuvered my lips back and forth slowly along the girthy length. This elicited a sigh from the big coyote.

"That's really nice," he said and pet me on the head. "I haven't felt this good in years."

He hadn't had sex in years? I knew he was single ever since I started working with him, but I thought that he'd get with someone now and then. The news made me feel special, like I had something Irv liked that others didn't possess.

At that knowledge I started bobbing faster as I gently massed his balls and spurts of pre jetted from his pulsing tip more frequently.

After a few more minutes I was able to kiss his gorgeous knot as the tip banged against the back of my throat.

His moans became louder as his hips bucked and trembled.

"Gonna come," he groaned. "Keep going."

I made a ring with my thumb and index finger and placed it behind his knot.

"Oh, yeah, foxy," he shouted. "You know what feels good."

He cried out one last moan, and then howled as his essence pulsed from his cock, and filled my muzzle with his lightly sweetened nectar.

He smiled tiredly down at me as I lapped up his creamy load.

"Does it taste good?" he asked and caressed my cheek.

"Yeah, it's sweet," I said and smiled up to him.

"I thought you might like it. I've been eating and drinking a lot of fruit this week to make my come taste better for you."

"Aw," I said, and gave him a big hug. He held me tightly, then lifted my chin up and gave me a deep kiss.

"Dang, you weren't kidding about how sweet I tasted," he said smacking his lips.

"I really enjoyed it," I said and gripped his cock again. "Need some time before we do more?"

"Heh, I still feel pent up even after that, and I could definitely go for another round. Is there anything you want to do? Want me to jerk you off or do you want to frot or something?" he asked caressing my rump while stroking my back with the other paw.

"Are you cool with topping me?" I asked looking up to him with a lascivious grin; eager for his authorization on my salacious request.

"Oh, are you sure?" he asked with concern in his voice as he held me close. "I'm kind of thick. I don't want to hurt you."

"Well, I've been prepping myself. I've been playing with my toys, and my biggest one is about as large as you," I said giving his shaft a gentle squeeze.

"Sure, if you'd like to," he said and kissed me on my nose. Irv went to his closet to grab a small box. "I bought some condoms this week and wasn't sure which ones you'd like."

The container had an assortment of extra-large condoms. Some were ribbed and others were glow in the dark. I dug through the selection and pulled out a turquoise latex sheath in a transparent package.

"I like this one," I said and gave it to Irv.

"Do you want to do the honors?" he asked.

"Sure," I replied and opened up the clear square. I pulled out the condom and Irv handed me a bottle of lube. I put a drop on the inside and rolled it along the length of the thick coyote cock. I put some lube on my paws and stroked the shaft a couple times, which elicited a few moans from the bigger guy above me, and I added extra to his engorged knot. I generously greased up my ass giving the large canine a little show.

Irv put a towel on the bed and I hopped on and flagged my tail. The bed creaked as the ravenous coyote summited it and I looked back to grin at him.

"Mm, nice pucker," he said and groped my cheeks.

"Glad you like it," I replied and pushed my haunches up.

"There are a lot of things I like back here," he said and fondled my balls. With his other paw he started stroking my back. "Relax, Holt. I'll go slow."

I felt Irv's tip against my rear, and I felt him push in a bit. I squeezed a little on his tip.

"Unh," he moaned at the pressure. "So good. You doing okay, cutie?"

"Yeah," I replied and gave another squeeze.

He moaned again and pushed in slowly. It was sweet of him to care so much about my safety, and the fact that he cared more about not wanting to hurt me than his own pleasure melted my heart. I then pushed back against him engulfing his shaft right up until his knot.

He elicited a more guttural groan as he sighed, "Oh, foxy."

"I told you I've been prepping," I said. I didn't actually know he'd be this thick, but I worked my way up to my biggest toy just in case.

He rocked his hips back and forth as he rolled over my prostate, and I felt pre dripping from my cock in long, viscous strands.

"You doing okay, cutie?" he panted.

"Yeah, oh, you feel so big in me," I muttered under all the pleasure.

After a bit he slowed down and I wanted to collapse onto the bed, but I also felt the urge to keep going for Irv no matter how tired my limbs were. I wanted him to feel as much pleasure as he could. I wanted to do something nice for someone who was incredibly sweet to me.

Soon the coyote's thrusts became faster as he started grunting. I felt his knot banging against my hole as I bit my lip at the pain and pleasure mixing inside me. I drew sharp breaths through my nose and exhaled moans under Irv's warm body and powerful hips.

He reached a paw under me and started stroking my shaft to the pace of his thrusts.

His bucking became erratic as he grunted, "I'm close."

"Me too," I groaned. "Knot me."

"Really?"

"Please," I begged.

"Okay," he said and ground his massive knot into my pucker. He slowly pushed his way into me letting my body adjust. It felt like I was being stretched apart as he entered me little by little. I drew in a sharp breath at the pain, and then he suddenly slipped completely inside me.

Irv gripped me behind my knot and clasped tight as I squeezed around him.

It was all too much; the giant knot mashing up against my prostate, the tight fingers behind my knot, and the snarling coyote above me.

I felt a towering azure wave crash against me as I shot my hot seed into the indigo towel beneath me shivering and shouting in the process. The intensity and ecstasy within the world around me funneled through my groin leaving me limp in the arms of serenity.

"Foxy," he howled as he shuddered filling the turquoise condom with his milky essence.

We both fell to our sides, spent, as the bulky coyote spooned me.

I leaned into his fluffy body as he held me tightly with his massive arms. We chatted and complemented one another. I told him how much fun the night was.

Irv stroked my belly and I moaned at the sensation running through my torso. His fingers combed through the fluff of my chest as he hummed and gentle tune into my ear and explored the curves of my body.

After about twenty minutes his knot subsided and Irv took my glasses off, and then lifted me up and carried me to the bathroom. He sat me down on the edge of the bathtub and removed the drooping condom off of his member. Despite being glasses-less I could still see there was so much of his seed contained within it and we grinned at one another at the sight of how much he produced in one load. He tied off the end and disposed of it. The coyote turned on the hot water and we showered together. We soaped each other up as I memorized his body with my excited paws. He pecked me on the forehead and told me how adorable I looked. We then shared a deeper kiss as his whiskers brushed mine and our tongues danced.

Irv tossed the come-laden towel along with the ones we used to dry off with into his hamper. We cuddled up in bed surrounded by soft, cerulean sheets as I leaned my head against his warm chest and listened to the gentle rhythm of his heartbeat. The last thing I remembered was giving the coyote a gentle kiss and looking up at his cobalt blue eyes, which chased away my troubles, and ushered me into the utmost sublime state of serenity.

For Metal Do I Bleed

by NightEyes DaySpring

"You're wearing that to the Nighthowl concert?"

Evie paused by the front door and turned to look at his mother. She wore the look of disapproval she gave when she didn't like something. As a teenager, it was often directed at him. Now that he was older, he would go weeks sometimes without seeing it.

"Yeah. Do you have a problem with it?"

"Honey," said his mother with a polite cough, "I can see your nipple piercings."

Evie knew the silver of his nipple piercings and belly button ring were visible under his purple fishnet shirt; they glinted against his black fur when they caught the light. "That's the point, mom." Tight ripped jeans completed the ensemble.

She sighed. "Stevie Johnson Williams, did I not raise you right? I know I wasn't always there for you. With your father gone—"

"I'm twenty-two," Evie interrupted. "Anyway, I'll be with Shawn."

His mother flicked her ears. She didn't like Shawn that much, but he was a wolf too, unlike most of Evie's friends. They worked at the local food co-op together. For months they planned this concert, and Evie carefully selected his outfit for tonight.

"I thought you were past the Goth phase," his mother responded. Now that he paid half the rent on their little apartment, she didn't have the leverage over him she did back when he was in high school. For the last year, she had been focusing her parenting efforts on getting him to go back to school. So far, he was just taking night classes, but the guilt trip about enrolling in a four-year institution was coming.

"Mom, its Nighthowl. The lead singer dyes his fur black."

She drew herself to her full height, her black and gray pelt standing out against the tan couch. "That doesn't mean you have to dress like this. I'm not going to fuss about the spiked collar, but at least wear a t-shirt."

"Fine," he sighed, turning to go back to his room. She knew he would just take it off in the car, but sometimes you just had to humor your parents.

He grabbed the Nighthowl t-shirt he wore yesterday from on top of the hamper and pulled it over his fishnet shirt. When he walked backed into the living room, his mom relaxed. Evie told his mother not to wait up, and after giving her the insisted upon cheek kiss, he was free for the night.

* * *

A few minutes later, he was in the back of Jasper's car with Shawn.

"Next stop, the Westwood Amphitheater," said the jaguar, as she shifted the compact car into gear. "Everyone has their tickets right?"

Evie checked. His ticket sat safe and sound in his pants' pocket. "Oh yeah."

"Hey Evie, I thought you were wearing your fishnet shirt to the show," Carrie remarked, from the front seat, the hyena turning so she could look at him.

Evie grinned and pulled off his t-shirt. "I got it," he said, with a grin. "Mom wanted to make sure I was dressed appropriately for the show."

Carrie rolled her eyes. "Really? It's not like anyone is going to care. I'm surprised you haven't moved out yet."

"Since the divorce, she doesn't get out much," said Evie softly. "It's tough on her, and she's still getting over it."

Shawn chimed in. "I think my folks stay together because of the fear of being stigmatized." The tan and white wolf was resting his hand on Evie's knee and squeezed it to reassure him. "But your mom is really cool, Evie. She can find someone else if she looks."

"I don't think she wants to. Her and dad were married twenty years."

"Does he still call you?" asked Jasper, from the front.

"It's been a month," said Evie. "He's doing okay. Last time we talked, he said he is dating a bear. He likes the change."

"It makes sense," the jaguar remarked, "if he doesn't want to have any more kids. No pregnancy risk."

Evie agreed, and they lapsed into silence. Jasper picked up her phone, and without even looking tapped the screen. The car was flooded suddenly with Nighthowl's music.

"No howling in the back of the car now!" yelled Jasper, over a crunching metal riff.

46

Shawn laughed and leaned forward. "It's instinctual!"

"So is my fist to your face," replied the Jaguar, keeping an eye on the road. Carrie laughed and Shawn sat back.

"Lesbians," he remarked to Evie. He would have whispered it, but he couldn't over the music.

"Hey, that just means more boys for us," laughed Evie, punching Shawn in the shoulder. They both grinned, tails wagging in the confines of the back seat. Over the speakers of the car, the vocalist for Nighthowl came on.

"*Run with me, run with me to the moon, and you'll be mine.*"

"Moon Run" was one of Evie's favorite songs. It was about a couple falling in love, and it always got him jumping. He glanced over at Shawn, who had settled back into his seat to listen with his eyes closed. Maybe tonight would be the night he would finally get to take his own moon run with Shawn. It would be the perfect capstone on the evening.

Carefully he leaned over so he could rub his shoulder against Shawn. A tan arm wrapped itself around Evie, and he settled down to enjoy the ride to the concert. After the show, he would make his move.

* * *

The Westwood was a small arena that spent most of its time hosting college basketball games. When they arrived, they managed to snag one of the parking spots in the main lot. Already a number of fans were there tailgating before the concert.

Nighthowl's original albums contained a strong wolven theme, but the band had started to finally break out beyond that market. Five years ago, when the initial base guitarist, Crusher, had a falling out with the band, they brought in an arctic fox to replace him. The arrival of Ice Spear had broadened the band's appeal. Not only that, his song writing skills had pushed Nighthowl in a new direction. There still were a lot of wolves at the shows, but they were part of a mixed species crowd now.

"Evie, you need to stop hopping from paw to paw. Save some of that energy for the show," remarked Carrie, rummaging through the small cooler in the trunk they had for drinks. Her dark shirt and loose black pants, stood out against the light gray of the car and her sandy colored fur.

"I've been dreaming of seeing these guys since I was sixteen and my parents separated," said Evie, trying to contain the wagging of his tail.

The hyena nodded and pulled a beer out of the cooler. She opened the can with a satisfying snap. "I'm thrilled to share this experience with you. Thanks for inviting Jasper and I along. She seems to be having fun so far."

Carrie pointed to Shawn and Jasper, who were talking to a group of foxes and wolves two cars over, swapping stories about the band's music. One of the wolves, Janice, was a fellow student at Jasper's community college.

Evie grinned. "Thank you for coming. I know you're more into electronic body music than metal."

She shrugged and took a sip of her beer. "I'm not that picky," she remarked. "Anything that gets Jasper dancing I enjoy."

"I meant to ask, how is the new place working out?"

"Good. When you aren't working, you should come over and drink with us. Shawn came by last weekend."

"Sorry. With work and night classes, I just haven't had time since helping you guys move," said the black wolf.

She nodded and leaned against the back of the car. Evie wasn't short, but next to Carrie, he felt small. The tips of her ears were four inches higher than his, and she had broad shoulders. "Yeah, that's what being an adult seems to entail."

Evie shrugged. "At least we're here."

She smiled and held up a beer. "Yup! And look at those goofs over there." Shawn was making funny faces with a fox, obviously in some type of contest.

Evie chuckled. "Want to walk back over?"

"The beer is over here," said the hyena as she pulled out her phone. "Did you want another one? They open the doors in fifteen minutes."

"Nah. I don't want to have to go find a tree before we get our seats."

She laughed and closed the cooler and car trunk. "Good point. Let's go collect everyone and get in line. They can keep making faces on the way to our seats."

* * *

Security did a quick check of everyone going in, but no one blinked at Evie's collar or choice of shirt. He wasn't the only one who had dressed up for the concert. He saw a number of people wearing collars and arm warmers. Black was the most frequent color, but purple and reds also were common in the crowd.

They had to part with Jasper's friends once they got inside. Evie had gotten tickets closer to the stage, and while Jasper's friends went to the upper level, Evie and the gang headed for the lower.

"Oh man, they're a hoot, Jasper. Where did you find these people?" laughed Shawn, as they walked down the aisle behind an usher.

"Janice? She's in my English class. Richard, the shorter wolf, is her boyfriend. The others I don't know well."

"That fox with Janice, Iggy, was kind of hot," whispered Shawn to Evie.

Evie stopped dead in his tracks. This wasn't something he wanted to hear. "Do you think you have a chance with him?"

The other wolf shrugged. "Who knows. I noticed he kept checking you out though."

Evie could feel his ears reddening. "Me?"

"Yeah you, looking all sexy in your fishnet," said Shawn tugging at the shirt gently.

"Hey, stop touching him and get over here." called Carrie, from three rows down.

Carrie's interruption couldn't suppress the giddy feeling Evie had as he followed Shawn down to their row where the usher showed them to their seats. Shawn had called him sexy, and that made his heart stop for a moment.

They had snagged centerline seats a few rows up above the floor. The stage was placed in the middle of the basketball court to give a more intimate feel. Below them, was the stadium floor. They considered getting tickets down there, but it was standing room only. Evie had wanted to mosh, but Jasper had told him she didn't want drunken people touching her. Since they managed to get good seats, Evie was happy.

They talked until the opening band started the show. The lights went down and a hush fell over the amphitheater as Danger Box, an up and coming act with a female lead vocalist, opened the concert. Like a wave, everyone was on their feet. Jasper and Carrie knew Danger Box's songs well, so they both sang along to the guitar and vocal work.

After Danger Box went off, there was a brief intermission, and a second band called Splat took the stage. Splat wasn't a favorite of Evie's, but they were high energy. The drummer for Splat was a blur of motion, and the guitar work dark and moody.

When Splat went off, there was an intermission while the stage hands changed out the sound equipment for the main act. Evie had trouble staying still, but his friends made him sit down and wait. Shawn had to pin Evie's tail against the chair to keep it from hitting him, and the fact Shawn had to hold it down made it even harder for Evie to keep his tail still.

Finally the lights went down again, plunging the arena back into darkness. Evie sprang up from his chair.

"They're coming on!" he screamed in excitement.

It started with a low machine gun drumming in the darkness, and then a brilliant pillar of light pierced the darkened stage as Ice Spear stepped out and started crunching to the rhythm. A second pillar of light struck the stage as the lead guitarist, Gray Tail, joined in.

The stage lights blazed on, as the lead singer, Mistake, started singing.

"Into the night I go, into the woods I roam…"

Evie screamed in excitement. They were playing "Forest Walk" as their opening song. He'd listened to that so many times when his parents had started having marital problems he could sing it by heart.

"…Oh don't forget me, but I need to go now…"

This had to be one of the best moments of his life. He was jumping up and down so much it took both Carrie and Shawn to keep him from accidentally launching himself into the row of seats below. This was his favorite band, and in the sea of guitars and powerful vocals, he was in heaven. Everything was going to work out. He was going to get that moon run with Shawn tonight. He mother was going to finally start dating, and everything was going to be good.

* * *

After two hours, and one euphoric intermission, Evie glowed with energy and excitement. His tail couldn't stay still; Nighthowl had played all of his favorite songs, and some of their new stuff.

"It was amazing!" he said, grabbing Jasper's paw as they were walking out.

The jaguar gave him a well-practiced eye roll but smiled. "Not enough eye candy for me. I wanted to see more of Lady Smoke and her drums and less of Mistake eating up the crowd's attention."

"That's what he does though! He keeps the crowd engaged."

"As if anyone couldn't be excited by a show like that," laughed Jasper. "Did you want to wait and see if you can get an autograph, Evie?"

"How would we do that? The meet and greet was before the concert, and it was too expensive."

"If we are lucky we can pull it off."

Evie grinned, showing all his teeth. "That would be awesome, but I didn't bring anything for them to sign."

"If you want to splurge, they'll sell you a CD," said Carrie, pointing over to the merchandise booth.

Twenty dollars later, Evie had a brand new copy of Nighthowl's latest album, *Perpetual Motion*, clutched tightly in his paws.

They waited down by the loading dock where the stage hands were loading up equipment. They weren't the only fans who had thought of this.

More than once a roadie or two tried to usher them away, but as long as they stayed to the side they were ignored.

After a while, the crowd thinned, and Evie and Shawn were one of the few guys hanging out. His friends just talked amongst themselves, but Evie had picked up that most of the fans waiting were female.

"Jasper, you put us with the groupies," whispered Evie.

"Yeah, so? We just want a signature. They're looking for something else. I think we can land it."

Evie shivered and sidled closer to Shawn, forcing the tan and white wolf to wrap an arm around him. The temperature had dropped and the cooler air of the night breeze ruffled Evie's fur through the purple fishnet shirt. While he wasn't comfortable, the excitement in his stomach kept him warm, and he felt content against Shawn. Any minute now, his heroes would come out of the arena.

After an hour of waiting, while Carrie was telling a story about her brother the bouncer, a shout went up through the crowd.

"It's them!" "Hey!" "Over here!"

Shawn twisted his head around. "Hey, look!"

Walking down from the loading dock was the entire Nighthowl crew. They were out of costume now in their street clothes, but they looked like they were walking out of promotional photo. At the front was Mistake, black fur silhouetted against the loading dock's lights. He had ripped jeans and a dark gray t-shirt with the band's logo printed on it. Most of the roadies scattered but one of them came over, and quickly talked to him. After an exchange of words, the roadie nodded, and he moved to help control the crowd.

"Ladies, I'm flattered, but it's been a long night," remarked Mistake to the crowd.

A group of female fans tried to mob the lead singer, but two wolf roadies jumped in. "He can sign stuff, and that's it," huffed one of them.

Evie wanted to get a signature from Mistake, but he wasn't going to be able to get through the crowd. Gray Tail had gone off to the side, and had an equally impressive group of fans crowding him. Instead, he walked over to where Ice Spear and Lady Smoke were milling about talking to fans.

"I love you Lady Smoke," said a leopardess, standing next to the black and gray wolf.

Lady Smoke smiled and flashed a pen across a CD cover. "We love you too," she said, with practiced ease and waved to another fan.

"Hey, can you sign my CD?" asked Evie to Ice Spear, who had just finished hugging a female fox fan.

The white fox turned and caught sight of Evie. His piercing blue eyes looked him over him over appreciatively, and he gave a smirk as Evie walked up and held out his CD. The arctic fox took it and pulled out a pen. To the side of him, Evie could see Shawn fishing out his cell phone to take a picture.

"Who do I make this out to?" he asked Evie.

"Evie, E-v-i-e," said the wolf sheepishly.

The fox nodded and quickly popped open the CD and signed it. They posed for a quick pic by Shawn before the fox handed the CD back to Evie. "Nice piercings," he remarked.

"Oh." The wolf's ears reddened. "Thanks," he said, and he turned to go.

"Is that the only thing you have pierced?" asked Ice Spear.

Evie stopped and turned back. "Uh, yeah. Just the nipples and my belly button."

"I've got something else that could pierce you."

Evie's mind went blank then. He must have made a questioning sound, because the fox said something affirmative. A couple of female fans nearby murmured their surprise, and then Shawn was by his side saying, "Go," gently pushing Evie toward Ice Spear.

"What?" asked Evie, confused. He didn't want to sleep with Ice Spear. He wanted to sleep with Shawn!

"This is a once in a lifetime chance," said the other wolf. He gently pushed Evie toward the fox again, who wordlessly turned and started walking away. Evie wanted to say something in protest, but Shawn made a shooing motion, so Evie followed Ice Spear. When a bear roadie walked up to Ice Spear, the fox just pointed at Evie. The bear nodded knowingly and let Evie walk past him.

As he reached the stairs by the loading dock, Evie turned to look back. Shawn and Jasper were talking, and Jasper did not look happy. The jaguar had her hands up and her fangs out. Carrie was getting in between the two, and the hyena had a surprised look on her face. Her gaze met Evie's and she nodded to him.

"Hey, come on," called Ice Spear.

He took a deep breath to still his raging mind, and turned to follow Ice Spear up the stairs.

* * *

In a daze, Evie followed the tail of the white fox through the back corridors of the arena. Ice Spear led Evie around the maze to where the dressing rooms were. Along the way, they passed staff, and one of the members of Splat who gave Evie a glance and fist bumped Ice Spear with a, "You go fox!" comment.

Now back in the dressing room, Ice Spear turned to Evie. His powerful frame made Evie feel small next to the bassist, and his tight pants didn't hide his interest in the wolf. "The tour bus won't pull out for another hour. Would you like something to drink?"

"Sure," Evie said, with butterflies fluttering in his stomach. He was still in shock at being plucked from the crowd, and he couldn't believe Shawn had pushed him off either. Had the other wolf not realized Evie was into him?

The fox walked over to the table and pulled out two red solo cups. Into each, he poured in a generous portion of whiskey. While he did that, Evie looked around at the dressing room. There was a table of ravaged snacks and alcohol to the side. A dozen empty beer bottles were lined up to one side. Across the room, an empty rack for costumes sat, the outfits obviously already packed up. The room smelled of stale sweat and food.

"Here," said Ice Spear, handing Evie the cup. Evie took it, still holding his signed CD in the other hand.

"Cheers," said the black wolf holding up his drink and taking a big gulp. The burning sensation helped settle his nerves.

The fox took a gulp, and looked over Evie with a hunger. "How long have you been a fan of the band?"

"Since high school. You guys have helped me get through a lot of bad spots in my life."

The fox's ears flicked. "That's nice," he said, tilted back the solo cup and downing the rest of the whiskey. "Oh that burns good," he mumbled, tossing the empty cup into the trash. It bounced off the full can and came to rest on the floor. Ice Spear got closer to Evie and reached up to start playing with one of his pierced nipples, gently massaging the nub of flesh and fur through the fishnet shirt. "So, are you going to show me how much you appreciate the music?"

"I uh… sure," mumbled the black wolf. Carefully he put his drink and CD down on the table.

Ice Spear leaned in to nip gently at the side of the wolf's face and then at his neck. Sharp vulpine teeth dug into his flesh. "Good," growled the fox.

All Evie could do was paw at the fox, as he was held in the bite. When the fox released his neck, the pressure on his shoulders told him exactly what the bassist wanted.

Evie knelt down and the fox shoved the bulge in his jeans against Evie's muzzle. The scent of soap from recently washing was drowned out by a strong fox musk. Hesitantly he reached up to fumble with the belt.

"Come on, don't be shy," remarked the fox, pushing away Evie's hands so he could unbuckle and unzip. He pushed his jeans and underwear down, and then grabbed Evie by the back of the head to rub his shaft against the wolf's lips.

Evie wanted to say something but the tip of the cock was shoved into his muzzle. He lapped at it, getting used to the taste of fox. If he imagined, it was just like he was sucking Shawn off, and for a moment he thought he might be, but then Ice Spear shifted and the smell of his musk reminded Evie he was servicing a fox, not a wolf.

"Yes," hissed Ice Spear. "Such a sweet muzzle, I could tell when I saw you, you knew how to blow a guy."

Evie glanced up at the fox, who licked his muzzle and growled happily, thrusting in and out of Evie's muzzle.

Ice Spear kept at it for a bit, but then he broke off. "I could fuck you all night, but we don't have long," said the fox, pulling out.

"Is that it?" asked Evie, letting himself fall back so he could brace himself against the ground.

The fox laughed. "Not before I get a taste of that sweet ass."

Evie pulled off his tight jeans and tossed them across the floor. His cock was hard with anticipation. There wasn't a bed in the room, and all the chairs were cheap folding affairs, so the wolf rolled over and got on all fours.

Ice Spear got behind him and jacked up Evie's tail. The wolf heard the pop of a bottle top and then felt the drizzle of lube against his rump. Ice Spear let go of his tail to smear it around. Then Evie heard the sound of a wrapper being opened as the fox put on a condom. When he was done, he grabbed Evie's tail and pushed himself into the black wolf.

Some people take their time, letting you loosen up. Ice Spear pushed in until Evie yelped. He pulled back, just a little, waiting only for a moment before pushing on. He seemed to be in a hurry, and Evie was along for the ride. Each thrust was needy, each motion more urgent then the next.

There came a knock on the door. "Ulrick, you in there? We've got to get on the bus." Evie recognized the voice as that of Mistake.

The fox grunted, pushed Evie all the way down onto the ground. "Give me a minute."

"Dude, are you fucking that wolf? I thought you just wanted to land a blow job."

"Fuck off, Lars," he panted, grabbing Evie's sides, digging his claws into his fur, and plowing himself in. "I'll be there in a minute."

Evie squeaked, and there came a grunt from the other side of the door. With practiced ease, Ice Spear kicked it up into high gear to make his conquest of the black wolf complete. He gripped the wolf tightly, claws digging in to prick at Evie's skin. Ice Spear steam-rolled his way through the final motions and pulled out before he tied with the wolf.

Evie panted and collapsed against the floor, his own need unsatisfied and aching. Only some pre had leaked out. The fox hadn't even touched his shaft once this whole time. Ice Spear peeled off the condom and tossed it onto the ground. It made a splat sound as it fell next to Evie.

The arctic fox then got up and picked his pants up off the floor. Evie rolled over onto his back, looking up at the back of the fox. That was it? The fox wasn't going to finish him off? His erection flagging against his stomach.

Ice Spear turned around to look at Evie. "I've got to go," he said. "We need to get the tour bus on the road."

Disappointed, Evie just nodded.

The arctic fox came over and knelt next to Evie. "I ripped your shirt."

Evie glanced down. His fishnet shirt was torn where the fox's claws had scrapped his sides. "It's not a big deal."

The fox fished into his pockets and pulled out a fifty-dollar bill. "For the shirt, and if you need a cab ride home."

Evie didn't want to take the money, so he didn't reach for it. "I'm not going to see you again, am I?"

The fox slumped. "No, of course not." He paused. "You thought you would?"

The black wolf shook his head.

Ice Spear got up, still holding the fifty-dollar bill and walked over to where the CD case was. He opened it, pulled out a pen to write something else in it, and then closed the case, leaving the money on top.

"Don't forget your CD," he said, walking over to the door.

Evie nodded to himself, and the fox opened the door to leave. He paused in the doorway. "Have a goodnight," Ice Spear said and then closed the door, leaving Evie alone in the empty dressing room.

* * *

A few minutes later, one of the convention center staff came to the dressing room, while Evie was pulling his pants up. The jackal waited for Evie to finishing dressing, and then led him out of the labyrinth of corridors. Already the buzz that had been there only thirty minutes ago was gone. People were clearing out for the night. The jackal didn't say anything except to ask if he need to call Evie a cab. The black wolf had checked his phone, and found a text message from Jasper saying she was taking everyone home, but to call her if he needed a ride.

"Yeah," said the wolf, not wanting to bother Jasper. He needed to process what just happened before he talked to her or Carrie.

The jackal waited with Evie out on the Westwood Amphitheater's steps until a cab pulled up, and Evie got in. The driver, a raccoon adjusted his mirror to look back as his charge.

"Where to?" he asked.

"43rd West 54th, over in Green Hills."

He nodded and wrinkled his nose. He could smell the sex on Evie. "Rough night?" asked the cab driver.

Evie's ears lowered, "Yeah."

The raccoon gave him an appraising look, possibly noticing the tears in Evie's fishnet shirt in the automatically dimming cabin lights before he pulled off. He had the decency though not to comment about Evie's collar or choice of attire.

Evie pulled out his phone. It read 2:37 am. He had to be at work in a little over seven hours for his shift with Shawn.

He pulled up Shawn's contact information. *You still awake?* he typed into the phone and hit send.

Less than a minute later, the phone buzzed. *Yeah. Got home fifteen minutes ago. How was it?* read the response.

He considered. *A little weird. I'll tell you the details at work* he typed and hit send.

The response came back quickly. *I'm so jealous man. I can't land someone like that.*

Evie blinked at the phone. It felt like a sword had been stabbed straight into his heart. Did Shawn wish he had been in Evie's place? *It wasn't as good as you think it would be,* he managed to type out.

A few minutes later, another message came in. *No?*

Yeah, he responded, and then, before he could stop himself, *Shawn, why haven't we ever hooked up?*

It took a while before the phone buzzed again, and by then he was halfway home.

It would be awkward.

Evie stared at the message. What the fuck? He tossed the phone onto the seat next to himself with a low growl. It bounced against the CD case. He stared out the window, not seeing the darkened city roll by. What had he done with himself tonight? He was no closer to getting Shawn, and instead of making a move on the wolf, he let Shawn push him into fucking someone else.

He wanted to cry, but he didn't want to do that in the cab. The driver would notice.

His phone buzzed again, and he picked it up. *I'm sorry if you thought I was interested in you, but I'm not into you like that* read the latest message from his friend.

"Fuck you, Shawn," growled Evie. This was not how tonight was supposed to end.

"You okay back there?" asked the raccoon from up front.

"Yeah," he sniffed. "I just need some sleep."

He hands hovered over the screen for a minute trying to think what he should say. Maybe he should call out tomorrow. He didn't think he could stand Shawn's presence right now. He managed to tap out a quick *Okay* and put the phone back down.

His hand brushed against the CD and he picked up the case. He popped open the CD case and looked to see what Ice Spear had written. He had to turn the phone back on to read the words. Neatly written with a flourish on the back of the art book it said, *"Evie, Keep rocking on! Ice Spear."* Below that, in the same handwriting was printed a phone number.

He shook his head and closed the CD. That wasn't happening again. The fox was vapid in person. He just wanted to get his rocks off and move on. He wasn't someone Evie could have. What was he going to do, be some call boy for the next time the band swung through the area?

The lyrics to one of the songs on the CD he held, "Dark Quest," came to him then.

"I know, it won't be easy, but I go forth, to meet my fate, meet me, on the forest path tonight, and together, we can fight as one."

Evie cried the rest of the way home.

Reflections

by TJ Minde

Waves crashed on the pristine beach as a rabbit and raccoon walked side by side, both in swim trunks and t-shirts.

Lacing his fingers behind his head, the rabbit took a breath. "I got one, Jared: like, how long have you done art?"

"Man, Derrick, took a while to come up with that." The raccoon grinned. "I guess I've always done it." He put a paw to his chin. "Since elementary school, at least. And once I got to college, I had the chance to take better classes. Two years later, I figured I might as well declare it as my major. And that was about a year ago."

"Did you, like, ever think it would get you where you are now?"

Jared scoffed. "You mean in debt?" He ran a brown paw through the fur atop his head. "Shoot, just about anyone can get in if they have the money."

"But, oh my gosh, how many people can say they've taken classes in the Bahamas?" The rabbit wrapped his arm around Jared's side.

"The people who live here?" he joked.

"*Girl*, please."

Jared rolled his eyes. "Oh, don't *girl* me, Derrick—you say that to everyone." He pressed a brown ear to the rabbit's shoulder. "Can I at least be you're only *hunny?*"

"You got it, *hunny*." He tapped the raccoon on the nose and turned away from the beach, sliding his paw along Jared's back before it dropped to his side. The two meandered towards the tree line. "But, like, art got me closer to you."

"Aww." Jared wrapped his arm around the rabbit's back and squeezed his hip. "Well, I'm happy for that."

The rabbit smiled. "Your turn."

"Hmm." A devilish grin split across Jared muzzle as they crossed the tree line. "Oh, I got one: what's the longest you've gone without sex?"

The rabbit's ears perked in surprise as he looked from the raccoon and back to the path. "Heh. And here I was thinking *I* would be the one to start the sex-questions."

"Are you the only one in this relationship allowed to have dirty thoughts?" Jared raised an eyebrow with a flirty grin.

Derrick scoffed. "As if." The rabbit stopped and leaned against the thick trunk of a palm tree, putting a paw to his chin in thought. "Well, let's see. Not counting the first seventeen years," he winked, "I'd say... like, three months or so?"

"Three months?" Jared jaw gaped.

Derrick gave a sly smile. "You know what they say about rabbits. Besides, I've never heard you complain." He eyed the raccoon up and down as he licked his lips.

Jared couldn't keep his eyes on Derrick as he was gawked at like a piece of meat. "Stop that, you tease." His ears warmed again in a blush and a smile crept across his muzzle. "Your turn again."

Derrick hooked an arm around Jared's and pulled him along the path. "Don't worry, hunny, I'm not gonna do anything here." The rabbit pecked the raccoon cheek. "Now that we have our minds in the gutter, what's the biggest dick you've seen?"

"What?" Jared stumbled at the unexpected question. "Why are you asking that?"

"You, like, so started asking about my sex life, now I get to ask about yours." He bumped the raccoon with his hip. "Tell the truth."

Jared sighed. "Really?" He looked to Derrick, then at his footing. "Well, there was this guy I saw a few videos of. It was years ago, but he had this, like, twelve inch dick. That thing was a freaking monster. But, while I wanted to watch, I couldn't stand his personality. He would go on and on about how—" the raccoon raised his paws in air quotes, "—'alpha' he was." Jared rolled his eyes. "He was obnoxious.

"But," he pulled the fur along the back of his head, "in real life, you're kinda the only guy I've ever seen. Outside of a locker room or art class, but that never counts."

"Wait-wait-wait," Derrick stopped the raccoon with a paw. "You mean I was your first?"

Jared nodded. "That's not a bad thing, is it?"

"No." Derrick shook his head. "Of course not, hunny. It's just surprising. Like, I didn't realize I was taking your v-card." He shrugged. "I mean, I've gotten used to hearing everyone around me talk about getting laid. Friends in high school. Other friends in college. It's, like, so different hearing the opposite for once. And dating someone who doesn't have a lot of experience."

The rabbit curled an arm around Jared's hip. "Besides, it makes me happy to know I'm your first." He pulled the raccoon along the path a few more steps. "Your turn again."

"Well, now you have me curious." Jared paused, ears against his head and eyes down.

"That's, like, the point of the game: to get answers to those burning questions." Derrick squeezed Jared's hip, encouraging him along. "Besides, eyes up or you'll run into a tree."

As if on cue, a leafy branch bumped into the raccoon and he jumped, flailing his arms around. The rabbit couldn't help but laugh.

"You could have warned me." He brushed an errant leaf from his shirt.

"Oh, hunny." Derrick braced a paw against his knee as he calmed down. "But it pulled you back to the present." He chuckled again. "Now, come on, dish. What's on your mind?"

Jared sighed. "Well, you know how many people I've been intimate with. What about you?"

"You mean how many guys have I slept with?" Derrick smiled. "Honestly, I'm not sure." The rabbit stretched and laced his paws behind his head again. "Like, maybe one or two a year, but I don't quite remember. There've also been a few one night stands. And condoms were used every time it wasn't serious, don't worry." He waved his fingers to Jared. "I mean, if I had to guess, maybe, like, about seven or so guys."

"Really?" Jared's head sank lower and his shoulder slumped.

"Hey, you don't want to get attacked by another tree, do you?" Derrick joked.

The raccoon's head shot up, expecting another branch. When nothing was there, he stopped. "You're right." With a shake of his head and a breath, Jared forced a smile on his muzzle and walked, on looking ahead.

Derrick grabbed his shoulder. "Hey, no, wait. I can see the fakeness there. What's wrong?"

Jared turned around with a huff. "It's stupid."

"Well, now I so want to know. Do I have to make it my turn?" Derrick crossed his arms and leaned in toward the mopey raccoon.

"I guess…" Jared's shoulders slumped. "I'm worried I'm not enough."

"Hunny, why'd you think that?" The concern was clear in the rabbit's voice as he pressed his forehead against the raccoon's, setting his white paws on his shoulders.

"I mean you have all this experience. Maybe I'm not good enough for you." Jared closed his eyes as more worry sank in.

"Baby, come on." Derrick wrapped his arms around the raccoon and held him tight. "Don't say that. I haven't complained yet, right? And it doesn't matter in the grand scheme of things." The rabbit rubbed his lover's back.

"I know, but," Jared sighed. "Hell, I don't know. I care about you, but I also wonder what else is out there. Not that I want to leave you or anything. It just makes me curious." He looked away from the rabbit.

Derrick chuckled. "Hunny, will you take a chill pill? Everything's going to be all right." He wrapped his arms around the raccoon.

Jared sighed and pressed his head back against the rabbit's "Thank you."

"For what?"

"Being here for me. In all my weird neuroses."

The rabbit chuckled. "Hunny, you aren't crazy. I've heard of other couples with similar issues. We'll be okay." He slid his paws into the raccoon's and squeezed. "Let's go." He led them on, side by side.

No further words crossed between them as they walked through the forest. The trees grew tighter together, blocking out more and more of the sunlight. As the path exited the forest, the sun was too bright to see past. They left the trees behind them, raising a paw to block the sun from their eyes. Once they adjusted, their jaws dropped.

The small grove led them to another beach, but unlike every other one they saw on the trip, the sand was covered—not with people—but with trash. Mammals of all types were working together in an attempt to clean the beach up.

* * *

"It was crazy, Charlie," the raccoon said. "Bottles, balloons. The plastic that holds a six pack together. It was all just lying there on the beach. And we had to be there for at least an hour, right?" He turned to Derrick.

"And, *girl*, let me tell you," Derrick pointed his fork at the fox across the table, "even though we helped fill, like, five massive trash bags, it looked just the same as when we got there."

The raccoon pushed the last bit of food on his plate. "It was like errant paint on a clean canvas. Just... no." Jared sighed. "Like a corruption of paradise."

"You guys don't know about the shitty garbage patches?" Charlie. The other two shook their heads. "Well, now you've had first paw experience with the one in the Atlantic."

"So it's a big floating trash heap that lands on shore?" Jared's tail puffed up in agitation.

The fox sighed. "Pretty much."

"Maybe if people stopped dumping their trash wherever they wanted…" the raccoon grumbled.

"Jare, it's not that easy. You can't go yellin' at people to stop fuckin' shit up." The fox crossed his arms in front of him with a sigh.

"Hunny, Charlie's right." Derrick set a paw on his partner's shoulder and rest atop it.

The raccoon slumped as his anger cooled, until once he realized the rabbit was leaning against him. Jared looked from the rabbit to the fox and back.

"What's wrong, dude?" The worry was obvious in Charlie's voice.

Jared moved his paws under the table, twiddling his thumbs. "I mean… I just…"

"What? Don't like Derrick leanin' on you?" Charlie asked.

"No, no," Jared shook his head. "I just don't want to make you uncomfortable."

Charlie laughed. "No shit? Man, we've been drawin' naked dudes together for three years. Why would I care if one hugs you?"

Derrick scoffed. "I'd so hope you don't."

The raccoon looked up to the rabbit. "And what's that supposed to mean?"

"Like, he was one of the guys I was telling you about before." Derrick pointed to the orange fox. "I mean, he doesn't fit the stereotypes, but he knows how to please a guy."

"And what stereotypes are those?" Charlie asked with an innocent tone.

"*Girl*, please. You're not a sub," Derrick said. "Don't get me wrong; you're, like, *so* smart, and sly as hell. But you are way more verse' than a lot of other foxes I know." He crossed his arms in front of him and leaned forward. "You're not your standard tail-raiser."

"Bitch, that's speciest." Charlie crossed his arms.

Derrick sat up. "Again - *girl* please." He spoke the two words as one with a tilt of his head.

Jared stared from the fox, to the rabbit and back. "Guys, really?"

"Quit pickin' fights before you get hurt," Charlie said as he curled his paw into a fist.

"Woah, woah." Jared leaned forward, trying to put himself between them. "Will you two cut this crap out?"

Charlie and Derrick stares turned to glares before they each closed their eyes and turned away from the other.

The raccoon sighed. "What's the matter with you two? We're in public for Christ's sake." He crossed his arms.

The silence between the two carried on, and, a moment later, Charlie's chest heaved and air spat through Derrick's muzzle. They lost all composure, doubling over in laughter.

"Do you two feel better?" The raccoon asked.

Charlie waved a paw. "It's fun making you squirm."

"And any others around." Derrick planted a quick peck on the raccoon's cheek.

Jared shrunk into his seat, ears flat and tail wrapped around himself. "Do you always have to make a scene?"

"I'm sorry, hunny." Wrapping his arms around the raccoon's shoulders, Derrick rested his head on Jared again.

"Damn," Charlie sighed. "You two really are a cute couple." The fox rested his chin on a brown paw. "But, really, why the hell were you all the way out there? Looking for a quiet place to fuck?" He smirked at Derrick.

"Just going for a walk," Jared answered. "You know, taking in the island. How many times are we going to be able to be here?"

Charlie leaned forward. "But you said you were talkin' 'bout me before." He spoke to both of them, but the comment was directed to the rabbit.

Derrick mimicked the fox, leaning and stage whispering. "Playing Truths."

"You still do that? Shit." The fox sat back with a chuckle. As he looked from the smiling rabbit to the raccoon, his eyes lit up. "Wait a minute, that's why we stopped fuckin' around." The fox pointed a claw at the raccoon. "Well, 'he's' the reason."

"And what's that supposed to mean?" Jared pressed his paws to the table.

"Hunny, calm down. He didn't mean anything by it." He rubbed Jared's arm, working his way up, and leaned closer to the raccoon's ear. "Take a breath, baby. Remember that night in the studio?" He added a seductive huskiness to his voice. "Our first time *together*?"

As the rabbit rubbed, Jared relaxed little by little. His eyebrows rose and ears flicked in surprised understanding and he cleared his throat. "Yeah."

"Well, like, before that night, Charlie and I might help each other... *relax* a little. Here and there." He blew into Jared's ear, driving a sigh of passion from the raccoon.

"So you two slept together?"

"Not a lot," Charlie said. "Just when one of us needed it."

"What do you mean 'needed it?'"

The rabbit sat back down, ears drooping, and rested his head on his balled up fist. "Like, have you ever had a day where you were so *totally* pent up, all you can think about is sex?" He grinned, eyes half-closed, whispering as he continued. "Every cute guy you saw you undress with your eyes? And every nice ass, you just want to take a bite out of?

Jared nodded as he lowered his ears, trying to hide the blush that was forming.

"And once you *can* get fuckin' off your mind," Charlie picked up with an equally flirtatious tone, "it's like a long drink of water after a hard workout. And then you can think clearly again beyond your dick."

"I mean, he's totally an attractive fox, isn't he?" Derrick pointed his palm to Charlie.

Jared swallowed. "Uh, y-yeah."

"And, you have an attractive rabbit," Charlie added. "It never meant nothin' beyond a release." The fox sat up, lacing his fingers behind his head. "Though I'll admit, I never would have guessed Derrick would be your type."

"What do you mean?" Jared crossed his arms.

Charlie met the raccoon's gaze with a grin. "Dude, we've shared four or five different art classes together. When you are focusing on work, you have a great artist's eye for what you're seein'. But just before that happens, you gawk at the model."

"I do?" The raccoon looked down, his blush more evident.

Charlie nodded "It's fun seeing the switch from gawkin' to focus. But it always happened with a few of the more masculine models."

"I am masculine, thank you very much," Derrick crossed his arm and put on a fake scowl.

"Yeah," Charlie answered. "But you don't have the muscles of a toned wolf. Or horse."

"Or, like, maybe a certain fox?" Derrick bobbed his head with a raised eyebrow. "Well, masc' and muscled are totes not the same thing," the rabbit said with another nod.

Charlie chuckled. "And that wasn't effeminate at all."

"Well, he's still cute." Jared said. "Derrick's nice, and always willing to help. I mean, he modeled for me last semester. And he's smart, funny. A great person to talk to. And he knows what to say when I'm upset."

"Aww, baby." Derrick leaned over and pecked the raccoon again before resting his head on Jared's shoulder.

With a smile on his face, Jared reached an arm around the rabbit.

"You two are just too *fuckin'* cute," Charlie said. "Now I can't ask." He smiled as he stood.

"What?" Jared and Derrick asked at the same time.

"Well…" Charlie looked away and his ears fell. "When I heard Derrick was gonna be our model here, I was thinkin' I might get a hook up. But I can't ask now. I won't be a wedge."

"That's actually a totally great idea." Derrick jumped over the table and hugged the fox.

"What?" Jared's jaw fell as the rabbit hugged Charlie.

"I'm with Jared on this one, dude," the fox said. "Whatcha mean?"

Derrick nodded. "Well, like, not you and me, but maybe you and Jared." He looked over to the raccoon. "I mean, we were talking earlier about how he was worried he didn't have enough experience with other guys. And I know how you work," he squeezed the fox, "so you're safe. And, like we've been saying, it's just a release."

As the rabbit explained, Charlie relaxed and met the raccoon's gaze. "Well, I wouldn't complain." He licked his chops.

Jared looked away. "I don't know how I feel about it." He stole a glance at the fox. Standing beside Derrick, he was a little shorter, but bulkier with the body of a guy that hits the gym all the time. Jared tried to picture him without a shirt, with that long tail up, inviting him. For a moment, he thought of it against his chest as he pressed himself into Charlie.

"And that's the gawkin' gaze he gives models," the fox staged whispered to Derrick.

"Shut up." The raccoon shook his head with a smirk. "If Derrick thinks it'll get me over my hang-ups, we can try it."

"Well, then, it's settled." Derrick let go of the fox and leaned across the table and planted a kiss square on the raccoon's muzzle. "I'll leave you two to, like, get better acquainted, then."

"And what the hell are you gonna do?" Charlie asked.

The rabbit shrugged. "I might get a drink. Hit the pool. I have options." He hugged the fox again before grabbing the remaining plates. "I'll take these; you two go have fun." He walked away, shaking his hips all the while.

As Derrick vanished from sight, Charlie sat down again. "A beer don't sound too bad. Wanna grab one first?"

Jared swallowed. "I think I could use it."

* * *

The fox held the door to his room open. "After you."

"Thanks." Jared walked in and the subtle scent of fox permeated the air. He moved to the small couch, placed in the same position as the one in the room he and Derrick shared a floor down. Everything was identical: two beds, a nightstand between them, a writing desk in the corner, and a connected bathroom.

The fox slid onto the cushion beside the raccoon with a smile. "Do you wanna shower first?"

Jared shook his head. "No, I think I'm okay. Unless you'd rather me take one?"

"Nah. You're fine, Jare." He set a paw on the raccoon's thigh. "So, just to make sure we're clear, no kissin' and a condom is a must. Any other rules?"

"Do you mind if I top?" Jared mumbled.

Charlie lowered his voice. "Just the itch I'm lookin' to scratch." He stood and moved towards the bathroom. "I think I'll take a shower. Don't want you smellin' *too much* like fox afterward." He turned on the light and started to close the door before turning back. "Relax and get comfortable."

Once the door closed, Jared started to squirm. *Get comfortable?* he thought. A moment later, the shower started. He looked toward the door. *Do I take my shirt off? Lay on the bed?* He sighed, and the scent of fox filled his nose again. *I haven't smelled this much of him before. He certainly isn't Derrick. But he's still good looking.*

The raccoon leaned forward and pulled his shirt over his head. Folding it in half, then in half again, he tossed it over the arm of the couch. *Comfortable? Shit, I don't know.* He stood up, grabbed the shirt and put it back on before pacing around the room. *Derrick wants me to do this, right?* He nodded to himself. *Right. He isn't just trying to push me away. He wants me to do this. He's slept with lots of guys.*

And, again, he wants me to do this.

Jared continued to pace as he became more and more lost in his thoughts.

The shower stopped, but Jared didn't hear it.

You're allowed. We've checked out guys together before. This is about the same.

"Jare?" Charlie called.

The raccoon whipped around, surprised. The fox stood in the doorway of the bathroom in just a towel. He had a more muscular build than

Derrick, and it showed in his chest and arms. While he kept his fur short, he looked puffier, still, than his rabbit did.

Charlie hooked his thumb onto the towel around his hips. "You doin' okay, man?"

Jared's eyes walked up and down the fox. *He really looks good.* He met Charlie's gaze and nodded. "Yeah. Just nervous."

The fox grinned. "Nervous? Derrick talked like you weren't a virgin."

"I'm not." Jared shook his head. "I've just never had sex with anyone besides him."

"Ah, so I'm your first one night stand?" Charlie took the few steps needed to meet the raccoon. "Do you need some help undressin'?" He tugged at the hem of Jared's shirt. "Or maybe some *other* encouragement?" Charlie took the raccoon's paw and set it over his crotch. "Won't take long to get going."

As he groped the fox, Jared closed his eyes. *Doesn't feel too much different from Derrick. A little thicker. Maybe I can pretend?* He took a slow, deep breath and the scent of the fox flooded his nose.

Jared sighed and took a step back. "I'm sorry. I can't."

Charlie's brow furrowed. "What's wrong? It's just sex?"

"I know." The raccoon held on to his elbow, finger playing with the hem of the sleeve. "It just… doesn't feel right."

Charlie's ears fell. "Did I do somethin'?"

Jared shook his head. "No, not at all." He reached a paw out. "I just don't think I'm quite ready to sleep with another person."

Charlie sighed. "Well, I ain't gonna force you. Go on and give Derrick a call; I'll get dressed and we can watch TV while we wait."

Before Jared could respond, Charlie turned away and opened the top drawer of the dresser. With fresh clothes in his paws, he slipped into the bathroom again.

When he was sure the fox wasn't coming back, Jared fished his phone from his pocket and call the rabbit. One ring. Then two. *What are you up to?* The phone rang a fourth time and the voicemail picked up. Before Derrick's voice was done telling him to leave a message, he ended the call. He send a short and simple text instead.

Room 403. Please come.

Jared had no idea what the rabbit was doing or how long he'd be. Sitting on the couch, elbows on his knees and muzzle down, the raccoon pondered the situation. *I hope he isn't mad…*

The bathroom door opened and Charlie walked out in a plane tee shirt and sweatpants. Jared lowered his gaze and listened as Charlie flopped onto the bed.

"You care what we watch?" the fox asked.

Jared looked up at Charlie. Some pain was in the fox's eyes, but he hid it well.

The raccoon shook his head. "No, you pick."

"Okay." He laid back and pointed the remote at the TV. "Home improvement shit it is."

Jared stayed on the couch, and Charlie, the bed, and the two waited for Derrick to show up.

After about an episode and a half, a soft knock came from the door. The fox rose and made his way over.

As Charlie cracked it open, Jared perked his ears as best a raccoon can.

"Hey, I got Jared's message. Everything okay?" Worry was in the rabbit's voice.

The fox nodded. "Yeah. We're fine. Come on in." Charlie looked over his shoulder at the raccoon and back. "I'm gonna to take a walk. I'll be back later." He held the door open for Derrick and slid past him as the rabbit entered the room.

Jared lowered his head again and his shoulders slumped.

"Hunny, what's wrong?" Derrick sat beside the raccoon and draped an arm around his shoulder.

"I… couldn't do it."

A white paw touched Jared's thigh. "What do you mean? What happened?"

The raccoon shook his head. "Nothing, and that's the problem, isn't it? I mean, after you left, we were having a good time. We got a drink or two and talked about sex. About how we each met you." He raised a brown paw towards the rabbit. "When we came here, he was eager—totally willing. I was fine with using the condom, and he was okay with me topping. And, Charlie's a good looking guy…"

Jared finally looked the rabbit in the eye. "But he's not you. The smell was wrong, his muscles were wrong. It just felt… *wrong*. I really wanted to, but I just couldn't.

Derrick hugged the raccoon. "Hunny," he cooed. "It's all right."

Jared wrapped his arms around the rabbit's middle and buried his nose against his neck. "*This* is right."

"But what about trying new things? I, like, don't want you to feel as if you missed out."

Jared closed his eyes and thought about being intimate with the fox and the idea was still pleasant. But now, with the scent of rabbit closer, it felt more okay.

"Well, I have a thought," Jared said.

Derrick let out an inquisitive grunt.

"Would you stay—if Charlie was okay with it, of course?"

The rabbit grinned. "Oh, hunny, I don't think he'll mind at all. Wouldn't be the first time he's put on a show."

And, as if on cue, the lock disengaged and Charlie opened the door. The fox walked into the room, muzzle down and ears low, until he caught sight of the two on the couch. He put on a more neutral expression. "The hell you two still doing here?"

"Maybe we're, like, waiting for you," Derrick said putting a balled paw on his hip.

"Why, you lookin' to mug me?" Charlie held up his fist as if to defend himself, though his muzzle had a joking expression. "You wanna fight?"

Derrick scoffed. "Why don't you tell him, hunny?"

The raccoon looked to the floor again. "Do you, uh, want to maybe have another go?"

"Another go?" Charlie repeated.

"I'd understand if I upset you, and if you don't want to now."

Charlie took another step into the room, letting the door close behind him. "What changed?" He shoved his paws into his pockets.

Jared met the fox's eye. "I've only been with one person, and the idea of sleeping with another felt wrong to me."

"Even though Derrick gave you permission?" Charlie looked from the raccoon to Derrick, and the rabbit nodded.

"I know," Jared continued. "But you two may be used to something like this; I'm not. It's not that you aren't attractive—you are. I just felt like I was cheating."

"But how would that change now?" Charlie asked.

Jared looked to Derrick.

"Go on," the rabbit said. "Your request, so you ask."

Jared closed his eyes and took a breath before looking at the fox again. "Would you mind if Derrick stayed?"

Charlie's eyes went wide.

Jared pressed on. "Not like a three way, but more like he just watches. Just giving moral support."

The fox gave Derrick a sly look. "And that's your play, you fuckin' voyeur."

The rabbit shook his head with a grin. "*Girl*, it's totally his idea. I just get the bonus of watching two hot guys fuck."

Charlie relaxed more. "Same rules?"

"Are you okay with Derrick being close?" Jared looked away in embarrassment. "And me kissing him and stuff?" He forced his ears up, listening for an answer.

Silence fell over the room as he waited for a response. A moment later, a white paw tilted his muzzle up toward Derrick.

Before the raccoon's head was all the way up, the rabbit leaned in and pressed his lips to Jared's. A quick kiss at first.

"I know he won't mind," Derrick said.

Jared looked to the fox for confirmation. Charlie stood there with a smile and nodded his head.

Derrick set a paw on Jared's thigh and their eyes met. Before another word was said, the rabbit leaned in for another kiss, opening his muzzle. Jared did the same and their tongues dancing together.

With his eyes closed, the raccoon felt Derrick's fingers slide from his thigh and moved between his legs, giving a light squeeze. Letting out a small moan into the kiss, Jared leaned back, allowing the rabbit better access.

Derrick moved with him, focusing more on the swelling length of Jared's shaft. As the passion of their kiss grew, so did the bulge in the raccoon's shorts.

When the rabbit broke this kiss, a huff escaped from him. "Well," he squeezed Jared's cock, "that didn't take long."

"You know the quickest ways to get it there," the raccoon said with a sheepish grin.

Derrick leaned in again. "Hunny, do I," he whispered, kissing the raccoon again.

Jared closed his eyes and focused on the sensations: Derrick's soft tongue as is ran across his, the rabbit's short muzzle pressed close, and the confident paw rubbing him through his shorts.

The raccoon slid his arm around Derrick's side, rubbing the short fur along his back. His light frame felt malleable in his paws, but he knew how strong the rabbit was. Those thoughts—of the rabbit and him in tight spaces and soft beds—drove his excitement further.

Derrick's paw left his tenting shorts, and Jared let out a whimper. He broke the kiss to question, but the rabbit pressed back. Jared's belt clattered and a paw undid his button, and a moment later, his shaft was freed from its cloth prison.

Derrick pressed his tongue into the rabbit's muzzle, trying to gain control. About the same time, soft pads gripped his shaft and stroked it up and down. The raccoon moaned again. The first direct touch always turned him on further. The firm grip, the confident stroke, the warm breath.

Wait, breath?

Just as Jared completed the thought, a soft tongue brushed across his tip, and he shivered.

Derrick broke the kiss with a chuckle, resting his arm against Jared's chest. "I think he liked that."

The raccoon finally opened his eyes and looked down. Charlie was there with his paw around Jared's thick cock and his tongue out.

"Bet he'll like this shit more." The fox bent lower and licked from the base to the tip of the raccoon's dick again. When he reached the top, the fox swung his head over and slid the raccoon into his muzzle.

Jared moaned again and laid his head back, taking in the new sensations. Charlie's muzzle was longer than Derricks, allowing more of his shaft to slide in. And the fox had palate ridges that were more pronounced, adding a different texture from his tongue.

Charlie made as much of a seal with his lips as he could before sliding back up the raccoon's shaft. The fox created a steady pace, sliding half of the raccoon's cock in and out of his muzzle at a time.

Jared huffed out a breath and placed a paw on the back of the fox's head, then raised it as he looked to the rabbit for permission.

Derrick shook his head. "Don't ask me. You can totally do whatever you want, and he'll let you know if you go too far. Besides, he has, like, some really sharp teeth around your dick; I don't think you'll try to piss him off."

Charlie reached forward for Jared's arm and slid along to his wrist. Once he found the raccoon's paw, he placed it on his head. He pulled against his arm, urging him.

"That's a good sign," Derrick said.

Charlie grunted in affirmation from around the shaft in his muzzle. With a nervous nod, the raccoon pushed the fox down. With each press, Charlie dipped lower and lower, until, without any trouble, Charlie's nose met Jared's pelvis. "Oh, damn." He rubbed the fox's ears in pleasured praise.

"And he can chill there pretty long," Derrick added.

Jared looked from the rabbit to Charlie. "*Really?*"

In response, the fox ran his tongue along the underside of the raccoon's shaft.

Jared closed his eyes. "Oh, *damn*. That's definitely not what I'm used to." The raccoon moved his paws to the side of his head, each ear between the gap of his thumb and index and lifted him up. And just before Charlie slid off, he pulled the fox back down. Moving up and down the full length of his shaft, Jared began a rhythm.

"Better than me?" Derrick set a paw on the raccoon's shoulder.

Opening his eyes, Jared watched as the fox slid up and down. "No." He stopped pushing the fox, but Charlie kept up the speed. "Just different. He's able to get more of me in at once and it's less of a challenge. His teeth aren't as large."

Derrick chuckled. "Did I mention he, like, totally enjoys giving head?"

Jared picked up the pace. And with each push of the fox's head, Charlie let out another moan of pleasure. "I can tell."

The rabbit leaned closer to Jared. "He also likes it when the guy he's going down on takes control."

Charlie grunted in agreement as he worked the raccoon's shaft.

When the fox was half way down, Jared moved a paw to the back of his head and lifted his hips, pressing his pelvis to Charlie's nose before sliding back down. He thrust in again, and Charlie let out another moan.

As Jared set a new, faster pace, the musky scent of fox became stronger. The raccoon looked down and saw, while he humped into Charlie, the fox's arm was working below the edge of the couch.

Jared stopped thrusting and relaxed his paw. "Do you just want me to finish here?"

Charlie slid off with a loud slurp and shook his head. "I told you already: I wanna get fucked. This," he moved his arm in a familiar way, "is just getting me going. Cause you're hot, gettin' all into this and shit." A snap of elastic came from out of sight and Charlie stood. "Wanna move to the bed?"

The obvious tent in the fox's sweatpants pulled at Jared's attention before the question registered.

He nodded.

"Well, come on." Charlie extended a paw to the raccoon.

Moving his gaze from the bulge in front of him to the fox's outstretched paw, Jared accepted the offer. As their grips met, Charlie hauled him to his feet, and Jared let out a surprised yelp.

The fox braced himself, catching the raccoon. "Oh shit. You okay, dude?"

"Yeah." Jared panted as he held on to his shoulder. "Just wasn't expecting that." He looked up to the fox. "You're stronger than you look. "

"I get that a lot." Charlie grinned. "But I think pokin' me like that's uncomfortable." He pointed down between them.

Jared looked; his dick pressed against the fox's leg, bending upward. "Oh." He took a step back. "Not really." He shuffled in place, trying to hide himself.

"You need to relax, Jared," the rabbit said, rising from the couch. "Here, hunny, let me help you." He set a paw on the raccoons back before sliding it down, hooking his shorts with his fingers and tugging them to his ankles.

"You just want to see me squirm, don't you?" Jared asked the rabbit at his feet.

Derrick smiled back. "I just want to see you have fun. Can't do that comfortably with your shorts around your knees; we've tried, remember?" He winked at the raccoon.

Charlie let go of Jared's shoulders and slipped off his shirt as he made his way to the bed. Dropping the cloth on the floor, he flopped back on the plush comforter and rested an arm under his head. He curled a finger, calling the raccoon over. "Why don't you take off your shirt and come here?"

Jared looked from the fox to the rabbit still at his feet.

Derrick stood, grabbing the hem of his lover's shirt and pulling it over his brown ears. "He's asking for you, hunny, not me." He wrapped a white paw around Jared's shaft. "And it seems you're still interested."

Jared looked back at the fox with a nod. Charlie's arms had more muscle than Derrick's, and the fur on his chest was thicker, too. But the tent in his sweats is what caught Jared's attention the most, and he licked his lips. After a firm nudge from Derrick, Jared made his way to the bed and stopped about a half-step from where the fox laid.

The raccoon continued to stare at Charlie all the while.

The rabbit slid up behind Jared and reached around to his shaft again. "You like what you see?" He whispered into the raccoon's ear as he stroked him.

Jared stuttered out another breath and nodded.

Keeping a paw on his cock, Derrick guided the raccoon to Charlie's pronounced bulge. "How's he feel?"

"F-firm." The raccoon swallowed. "Large."

With a chuckle, Charlie made his dick twitch. "About your size, eh?" He tilted his head, watching the raccoon explore.

"Jared's totally bigger," the rabbit said.

"Well," Charlie tugged at the elastic of his pants, eyes still on the raccoon, "how about don't you take these off and let's compare." The fox's cock jumped again.

With a nervous smile, Jared moved his paws to the fox's hips and slid the fabric down, catching on Charlie's shaft. He skimmed his fingers around the front, lifting the fabric free, and Charlie's flesh smack against his middle with a soft thud.

Jared's eyes were locked on the fox's dick as he pulled his sweats down. The elastic of the pants brought Charlie's knees together, pressing them

74

to the raccoon's stomach. Without a care, Jared moved his paws back to Charlie's hips, staring at the fox's shaft. The musky scent he caught before was stronger now. His jaw went slack.

The fox's dick bounced again.

Licking his lips, he sighed at the sight. Charlie was thicker than he was used to, something that would fit well in a paw.

Or muzzle.

Jared's breath caught at his own thought. Sliding his fingers along the fox's hips and middle, the raccoon brought his body forward, licking Charlie's cock from base to tip, coating his tongue in salty pre.

Charlie scritched the raccoon's head. "Getting more adventurous."

Jared smiled at the praise. Cradling Charlie's shaft with his fingers, the raccoon dragged his tongue across the fox's cock again. As he slid up, he angled Charlie's shaft closer and closer to himself. Once he reached the tip, Jared licked around it and slid his muzzle down the full length.

"Oh, fuck." Charlie closed his eyes, and let the raccoon work.

Bobbing his head, Jared took the fox's entire shaft into his muzzle, feeling the thickness of it against his tongue. Up and down he moved, like the slow pace of an ocean tide, listening to Charlie's moans all the while. And almost as fast as he started Jared pulled off with a smack of his lips.

"God above." Charlie panted. "Does he go at it like that all the time?" he asked the rabbit, still standing behind Jared.

Derrick grinned. "*Girl*, when he knows what he wants, he'll go for it. He just, like, happens to have a big muzzle and *totally* enjoys giving head, just about as much as you do." The rabbit ran a paw against the fur on the raccoon's back, getting his attention. "Why don't you do that a bit more?"

"Well, he said he wasn't quite looking for this," Jared answered over his shoulder. "I don't want him to finish."

Charlie chuckled and cupped the raccoon's cheek-ruffs. "I'm not gonna bust yet, if you wanna keep going."

"There you go." Derrick patted the raccoon's hip. "If you take his pants off the rest of the way first, I bet you'll both be more comfortable."

Jared looked up at Charlie for a moment before he wiggled back to a knee and, a moment later, the fox was as naked as the raccoon. Setting a paw on each of Charlie's leg, Jared spread them apart.

He stared at Charlie's sack for a moment before leaning forward. He pressed his nose to the white fur below the fox's shaft. The scent of arousal was strong, as was the heady scent of male fox. Jared reached his tongue out and licked.

"Ah," Charlie called. "Be careful there."

Jared didn't stop. His tongue lapped at his sack, feeling the weight contained within. He reached his paw back up and gripped the fox's shaft, teasing the sensitive skin there. Tilting his head, the raccoon leaned forward, allowing Charlie's balls to rest in his muzzle.

The fox huffed out a breath. "I don't needa worry about your teeth, right?"

Derrick chucked. "Trust me, he's had practice, and I'm still intact." The rabbit pulled off his shirt as he walked beside the bed. "Condoms and lube in the normal place?"

Jared let the fuzzy package slip from his muzzle as he worked his way up and took Charlie's cock back into his muzzle.

"Oh, yeah," Charlie said in both answer and pleasure. He grabbed the raccoon's ears as Jared bobbed up and down again.

"Good to know some things haven't changed," Derrick said, taking off his pants and adding them to the pile of discarded clothes among the floor. He slid open the drawer and grabbed a condom from the box and the small container of lube.

With prizes in hand, he walked back behind the raccoon and watched his lover work. As Jared rose and sunk around the fox's shaft, Charlie had his eyes closed and a leg wrapped around the raccoon's shoulder, both to get more leverage and his tail from under him.

"Okay Charlie, let him go." Derrick patted the raccoon's shoulder. "And I need you to stand up for me, hunny."

With a sigh, Charlie lowered his leg. As Jared pulled off with another loud slurp, the fox rested more on his hip. "Damn, you have a great muzzle, dude." He smiled at Jared.

"Well, you make it easy for me to work with." Jared pushed himself back and stood again at his full height. As he moved to turn, the rabbit leaned forward, reaching both arms around him. "What are you doing?"

"Helping," Derrick answered. "Now stop moving." He pinched the tip of the condom with one paw and rolled it along Jared's shaft. "There we are. Now we still need to compare." He pushed at Jared's back. "Get on up there."

"W-wait, compare?" The raccoon looked from Charlie's cock to his. "Does it matter?"

The fox chuckled. "Nope. Just fun."

Derrick nudged Jared on to the bed. "Come on, don't be shy." With a little cajoling, Jared climbed on the bed between the fox's legs. As Derrick walked around the side, Jared set his wrapped dick against Charlie's unwrapped one.

"And what's the ver-*dick*, judge?" Charlie asked the rabbit.

"Balls touching?" Derrick asked, first looking at Jared, then Charlie. Jared looked away.

Charlie pressed his hips up, and Jared squeaked in surprise. "Yes sir," he said with a grin.

"Good." Derrick leaned in, one paw behind his back, the other around his own shaft, starting to give it attention. He looked as if it was an actual competition. "So, from what I can tell..." He paused for dramatic effect, looking back and forth between the two before smiling at the fox. "We were both right," he pointed to Jared, "you're thicker," then to Charlie, "but you're a bit longer."

He stood up straight and pulled the bottle of lube from behind his back and squeezed some over both shafts. "But you're both larger than me."

Without complaint, Charlie reached between them and stroked both cocks. "Gotta get these ready, right?"

"Y-yeah." Jared swallowed again. "But I think I can get myself."

Charlie nodded with a smile. "But isn't this hot?"

Jared coughed. "Y-yeah."

"*Girl*, stop teasing him." Derrick moved back to the foot of the bed. "Come on, hunny."

Once Charlie let both of their shafts go, Jared slid back to the floor. "Can I get some more lube?" He held a paw out to Derrick. Without a word, the rabbit squeezed some into his paw. He looked back to the fox. "Should I stretch you out first?"

Charlie shook his head. "Just lube yourself up enough and I'll be good."

"Okay." He slid the liquid along his shaft, watching as the fox did the same.

"Relax. We'll have fun." Charlie smiled. "It's just fuckin'."

Jared nodded and reached down for the fox's leg and rested it against his shoulder. "You ready?"

"Yeah. Need any help getting in?" Charlie asked.

"The bed looks tall enough," Jared said, pulling the fox closer and nudged his tip into place.

"Yeah, right fuckin' there," Charlie sighed.

Still holding on to his shaft, Derrick stood and positioned his own cock against the raccoon's tail and hip. "All you need to do now, hunny," he said with one paw on Jared's side, "is push." As he said the last words, he pressed his hips against the raccoon's, and Jared did the same. "Come on. You know what to do. And Charlie can take it. Just push." Derrick pressed his hips with more force and Jared mimicked the rabbit.

While the raccoon pushed, Charlie relaxed more and his muscles loosened. And a second later, Jared's tip slid in.

"There we go." Charlie said with a sigh. "Now, take my leg and go to town." He tossed an arm over his eyes and smiled.

"You sure?" Jared asked, pushing in little by little.

"Fuck yeah," the fox answered.

With a nod, Jared grabbed tighter to Charlie's thigh, slid back then thrust forward, pulling on the fox's leg and sliding half of his cock in one thrust.

"Ahh, again," Charlie begged. "But don't fuckin' stop."

"You sure?"

Charlie nodded.

Derrick leaned closer to his lover's ear. "I've seen him take two guys at once with less lube. He can take it, don't worry."

Jared did as the fox asked. He pulled back again and pressed forward. Again, he was stopped, but he let the momentum carry and pulled back again. In and out, the raccoon moved at a steady pace.

"Yeah, that's great," Charlie moaned. "Can you go deeper?"

Without responding, Jared pulled the fox closer, laid a knee on the bed and slammed forward again. Each thrust getting him deeper into the moaning fox.

As hips started meeting hips, Derrick sat on the couch and watched, stroking himself again. With each thrust from Jared, Charlie's cock bounced this way and that. And seeing the raccoon thrust into the fox, hearing him huff as he worked, got him going more.

"Fuck, ain't going to take me long," Charlie said.

"Yeah." Jared nodded. "I'm getting close, too."

"Well in that case..." The fox let the thought hang in the air and he moved his paw down to his own needy shaft. "I just want you to cum first."

With that, Jared picked up the pace. He slid half his shaft from the fox, then slammed it all back in. Again and again, he thrusted his hip as he got closer to the edge. With each smack of their hips, Jared huffed and moaned.

"Oh shit, Jared. Just like that," Charlie said, stroking himself faster. "How close are you?"

The raccoon panted again. "Oh fuck, I'm real close."

"Ah, dammit." Charlie moaned in his own foxy way as he felt the raccoon's shaft pound into him. "I don't think I can wait."

"It's fine." Jared replied. "I want to see you finish."

Charlie's paw worked at a frantic pace, stroking as fast as he could. He moaned louder and louder as he got closer to the edge until his climax washed over him. With a long cry, the first shot of seed flew from his cock and splattered on the comforter. Then another.

Watching cum fly from the fox's shaft pushed him further along. Feeling the tightness around his cock, Jared tried to match his thrusts with it, slowing down his pace.

As the scent of musk hit the air, Jared looked over to Derrick. The rabbit sat back on the couch, stroking himself in frantic time with the raccoon. With each smack of his hips against the fox, Derrick's paw reached the base of his shaft.

The rabbit's muzzle was open as he panted and squeaked out in pleasure as he watched Jared work. As they locked eyes, Derrick broke Jared's pace as he let out a long, soft moan, and a few strokes later, the first shot of seed painted his stomach.

And that was the last bit of permission he needed.

Jared's pace became more and more frantic with each thrust. "So close." He wrenched his eyes shut, trying to slam in further with each pound. "Here it comes!"

As his climax hit, the raccoon thrusted his cock as deep into Charlie as it could go.

"Fuck yeah, there you go." Charlie moaned along as Jared's dick swelled with each shot of seed.

Derrick slouched where he sat as he watched the two spent men, Charlie with his paw and bed covered in white streaks and Jared as he pressed his hips into the fox, still trying to get deeper, knowing that his lover just finished in another guy. "Damn, that's hot, guys."

When Jared's climax had waned, he looked over to Derrick, white seed lost in his white fur. A tired chuckle escaped him. "Guessing you enjoyed the show?"

Derrick sighed. "God, yeah."

When the raccoon's cock stopped twitching, Charlie pulled forward, sliding him out from inside. "He likes a good performance. And by the strong smell of sex in the air right now, it was a fuckin' great one."

Jared carefully took the condom off and tied a knot in it. "Trash can?"

Charlie chuckled and held one up to the raccoon. "And how was it? Havin' sex with someone other than Derrick?"

Jared's eyes traveled down between the fox's legs and back. "Different. Not good or bad. Just different." He set his paw on the fox's hip and sat on the bed.

"And how are you feeling, hunny?" Derrick asked as he sat up.

The raccoon looked from the rabbit, to Charlie and back. "Relaxed." He chuckled. "Not quite what I expected."

Charlie scooted back along the bed. "And what were you expecting?"

Jared shrugged. "I don't know. Maybe stronger feelings for you? A want to leave Derrick?"

The rabbit laughed. "And do you now?"

"No. That was… fun. And certainly different." Jared patted Charlie's leg. "I appreciate the opportunity. But I don't know if I want to do it again soon."

Charlie nodded. "Nice change of pace, if you ask me. If you two want to hit the shower, feel free. I'll take care of myself after. Not that I'm trying to rush you out."

"I don't think a shower's a bad idea," Derrick said as he stood. "What about you?"

The raccoon looked to Charlie. "You don't mind us using the extra towels?"

The fox shook his head. "No problem at all."

"Thanks." With a nod to the rabbit, Jared and Derrick made their way to the bathroom, then into the shower.

As the water warmed, Derrick wrapped his arms around the raccoon. "Did you really enjoy yourself?"

Jared scoffed. "I came, didn't I?"

"That's so not what I meant." Derrick sighed and tested the water. "We can get in." He stepped into the stream

The raccoon was right behind him and pressed against the rabbit's back, letting the water run over them. They stood in silence as the water flow.

Jared sighed. "Yeah, I got off. And he was hot. But… in the end, it still didn't quite feel… quite right. Better, but still not right."

"What do you mean?"

Jared tightened his grip around the rabbit. "I love you. And having sex with someone that wasn't you felt odd. Being with you means so much more." He rested his head on the rabbit's shoulder. "I was able to finish. But it still wasn't the same."

"I thought you were, like, upset about how much more experience I had?" Derrick closed his eyes and wrapped his arm around the raccoon's neck.

Jared nuzzled the rabbit. "Well, now I've had all the experience I'd want with other people." He took a breath. "Look at it like the island; what we have is beautiful. My love for you is special and I've never felt this way about other person before. But there's this other thing, this small blemish. My lack of experience is my… what did Charlie call it? A garbage patch?"

"Yeah." Derrick nodded. "So you think it will never go away? You're feeling of inadequacy?"

Jared shook his head. "I think after tonight it will be easier to deal with. It's something that may never be cleared up, but could still be overcome."

Derrick turned around and kissed the raccoon. "I get that." He wrapped his arms around the raccoon's neck. "Not everyone can, like, sleep around easily. And that's not a bad thing." He pressed his pink nose to the raccoon's black one. "I don't care if you've been with other guys. If you do something I don't like, or something that I do like, I'll tell you."

"But, just because I may have slept around," the rabbit continued, "doesn't mean I hold it against you."

"I know," Jared replied. "I like what we have. Just another part of my paradise with you." He clasped his paw to the rabbit's. "Are there things that could be different or better? Sure. But isn't that every relationship?"

Derrick chuckled. "You're so right."

"I'm not saying what happened tonight was right or wrong," Jared continued. "It was purely an experience. One that I was happy to have."

"Looked like you totally had fun." Derrick chuckled.

"I did." Jared wrapped his arms around the rabbit. "Thank you for talking me into it."

"Looking forward to the next time?"

Jared scoffed and shook his head. "We'll see."

A Night Out

by Jaden Drackus

"What the hell am I doing here?" Captain Kerry Cooper, recently reinstated United States Army, asked no one in particular. The "here" was the city of Paris, where the pilot found himself on leave after a recent incident. His former British commanding officer suggested he might enjoy Paris. He'd even go so far as to suggest it might be a paradise—something which sounded like wishful thinking to Cooper.

The red fox was unsure if he would classify Paris as a "paradise." He'd been pointed to the Pigalle District the center of Parisian nightlife, with its cabarets, bars, and ladies of the night—or so the boys back at the aerodrome had said. The adjoining Montmartre District was supposed to be just as lovely. Looking around, Cooper couldn't see it: maybe he was just too old to see the appeal. He sniffed the air, his sensitive canine nose picking up the myriad of scents in the big city air. The smell of warm metal, the gas and burning mantles from the remaining gas lights, the acrid scent of cigarette smoke, the odors of a multitude of species and the various scent neutralizers they used, and the pungent smell of alcohol.

While his nose was filtering aromas, his ears were sorting through the soundscape. Music poured out of almost every door on the street with the subtle metallic clinks of player pianos, voices filled the air, the quiet hum of the new neon lighted signs, and the occasional rumble of the underground Metro trains all filled his ears. Every now and again, he could hear a car backfire and once or twice a siren rose over the background noise of the street.

Cooper had to admit that it was quite different from the aerodrome with its rumble of airplane engines and occasional thunder of distant artillery fire. But the pilot wasn't sure if he liked the change. Still, it was a rather nice evening for mid-April, and the general mood of the city was more upbeat then the officer would have expected. His CO seemed to be right when he said the city would be celebrating the American entry into the war. Most of the music in the air had a distinct American flavor to it as Cooper thought he recognized ragtime melodies that had been becoming popular when he'd left the States. Occasionally the fox's ears would prick up as the US national anthem, or "Stars and Stripes Forever" played— both to cheers from the crowd.

Cooper smiled at each of the outbursts and adjusted his uniform as he walked. It felt wrong to be wearing it when he was off duty, but he remembered seeing women unknowingly pin white flowers on soldiers out of uniform on leave in London to shame them as cowards, so he'd decided to play it safe. He passed by another cabaret door, and caught a whiff of burning fabric. Flames rose unbidden before his eyes and he suppressed a shiver. No, he would not think about that—how close he'd come to the edge. He'd come on this leave to forget the war a while. With a sigh and a shake of his head to force the memories away, the fox padded down the street, focusing on trying to decide just what the hell to do with his evening.

He had already decided that he wasn't a fan of the main cabarets. Not even the city itself might be for him. There was something off to the fox about to the city. It wasn't a scent, or sound, or sight—it was just a feeling. Cooper could feel it at the edge of everything: it filled the air, tinted the lights and posters, and deadened the music—a clinging, clawing, desperate attempt to pretend that everything was somehow normal. But there was no way that in the middle of a war that had engulfed the world, which left millions of individuals of all species dead, and much of the French landscape devastated anything, could be normal. Blakely was wrong—this wasn't paradise, it was a cut-rate imitation of it, and it showed. It was all an act, and he wasn't buying it.

"Do you like them *monsieur?*" A voice snapped Cooper out of his meditations.

He turned to find himself face to face with a vixen in a frilly red and black dress that reached only to her mid-thighs. That fact, combined with her wearing shoes told him that she was a performer in one of the cabarets out on the street to advertise a show. Cooper winced at failing to notice her behind him, but reminded himself that with the crowds, it was difficult to keep track of any one individual without focusing on them.

His head swept around, trying to determine which "them" she was referring to. He finally saw the poster he was staring at. "They're, interesting. But, uh, I don't smoke."

The look she gave him made it extremely clear that the cigarette advertisements on the wall he had been facing were not the subject of her question. It was only then that he noticed that she was topless, with only what looked like paper flowers covering her nipples. His ears fell back and his tail went still as he felt a rush of heat to his cheeks. He bit back his initial comment, reminding himself of his last trip to London where he'd seen many such displays when his host insisted they visit some of the seedier areas of the city—what they'd called "slumming." Paris, apparently, had similar rebellions against normal standards of dress and Cooper had traveled enough to know that the rest of the world didn't have the same conventions as the States. His ears twitched as he took a breath to steady himself.

"Err. They're quite lovely," he tried again.

The vixen chuckled at him. "Is it your first visit in Paris?"

"First of length," he said with a wave of his paw. "Passed through on my way to the front. Your English is excellent by the way. But how'd you know I wasn't French?"

"*Merci*. It helped you are wearing your uniform, but you don't walk like a French soldier." She smiled. "From your accent, I would say you are an American."

"*Oui*. I've been serving as an observer; just returned to duty."

"It is a good night to be an American soldier in Paris. You could see all ze shows free. And your glass will never be empty."

"Most kind, but…"

"You do not know what you wish to see?" There was something in her tone that worried Cooper.

"Something like that," he stammered. "It's all a bit, well, too much. Too bright, too loud, and too many people."

"*Ah. Je vois*," the vixen mused. "Somezin darker, quieter? Less crowded?"

"That might be best," Cooper agreed.

The vixen looked around, causing Cooper to do the same. He caught that she was looking for the couple other females in identical skirts that were mingling with other pedestrians. None seemed to be looking in their direction. Certain that they were unobserved; she produced a card from somewhere and passed it to the captain.

"Here *monsieur*. In Montmartre zere is a cabaret called *Le Terrier du Renard*. It is small and apart from ze other cabarets and taverns. Perhaps zey will have what you are looking for," she said with a sly wink.

With that, she strolled off and began speaking to a middle aged ferret before Cooper could ask any questions or even thank her. The aviator looked down at the card, which had the name of the cabaret and the address on it, then looked back up at the dancer. It was clear from the way she was purposefully ignoring him that their business was finished. He pocketed the card, looked up to orient himself towards the church at the top of Montmartre hill, and wandered off down the street.

Cooper strolled the avenues for over an hour before he found the painted sign of a well-dressed vulpine, complete with top hat, which announced the establishment to be *Le Terrier du Renard*. Like most of the buildings in the district it was a block covered in white plaster with nothing save the sign to announce that it was anything special. It was tucked away at the end of a small cobblestone side street at the bottom of the hill which gave its name to the district. The fox wasn't sure what to make of that other than the place did fit the bill for quieter and less crowded. Cooper let out a quiet sigh and approached the older looking fox standing behind a lectern next to the cabaret door. The fox greeted him, reached under the lectern to retrieve two menus, and gestured for Cooper to follow him inside. As the pilot entered, he noticed a scent that seemed familiar though he couldn't quite place it.

The interior of *Le Terrier du Renard* was sparsely lit, but as a descendant of nocturnal mammals, the fox could see just fine. The main room of the cabaret was a semicircle with an elevated platform on the flat side. The floor was filled with circular tables, arranged in arcs facing the stage. The walls were painted a pale color that wasn't white, but it was difficult to tell more in the dark. The light in the room was provided only by a series of widely spaced electric bulbs along the back wall, and a candle enclosed in a glass jar on each table. The air was filled with the scents of other species, and the greasy, dirty odors that never quite left those in industrial trades. One other oddity struck Cooper as the host led him across the floor—the clientele was almost exclusively males. That put the fox on edge, as if he sensed an enemy plane behind him, but shrugged it off as the rest of the crowd hadn't arrived yet.

The host took him to a table against the back wall, with a booth bench around two thirds of it and took a seat. Cooper took a look at the menu, which was rather sparse—unsurprising, given the food rationing going on. The wine and liquor list was much longer, but given that it was in French the American knew he was going to need help with it. He sighed, set the wine list down, and again allowed himself to regret that his command of French was still rudimentary at best. For whatever reason he just didn't have the gift for it, and it had turned out that most of the Frenchmen at the aerodrome spoke fairly decent English anyway. And those here in Paris, as the host had also addressed him in English. Cooper stared at the empty stage and wondered just what it was that marked him as not French, before he remembered he was in uniform—his U.S. Army uniform. He was still cursing himself when he noticed the server approaching his table.

He was a lion, the first that Cooper could recall seeing in the city since his arrival. Like most lions he was a head taller than the fox, with a closely trimmed mane of dark brown that contrasted nicely with his tawny fur. He wore a bland black tuxedo with white shirt, red bow tie, and matching cummerbund. The outfit was well cared for, but showed the little bits of fraying that told Cooper it was heavily used. The lion had been muscular, though he'd lost some tone—probably due to rationing, or due to whatever caused him to limp as he approached the table. Cooper winced. There was no doubt: the lion was making a concerted effort to put as little weight as he could on his left leg. The server caught Cooper's gaze and smiled warmly.

"*Bonsoir monsieur*," he greeted in a deep rumble. "How are you this evening? I noticed that you were having difficulty with the wine list. Would you like some suggestions?"

"Does this entire fucking country speak better English than I do French?" Cooper grumbled under his breath. The lion heard him and laughed which that caused Cooper's heart to flutter. He'd forgotten that the lion likely had better hearing than he did.

"*Monsieur* has been very fortunate in his encounters. Alas no, it does not. I have passed since three years as a liaison to our British allies before my discharge."

"Ah." Cooper breathed, feeling a bond form between them. He'd been correct: the lion was a former soldier. "Well, yes. I could use some help."

"Certainly, I am *Monsieur* Gee, and it will be my pleasure to assist you."

Cooper gave his own name, gave a brief summary of his evening including his encounter with the vixen, and invited the server to sit while they spent several minutes pouring over the menu and the wine list before eventually settling on a chicken dish and a white wine to go with it. Gee took the menus.

"It will be a while before the dinner is ready," Gee said. He paused for a moment, and Cooper caught the nervous expression on his face. It was like he was having an internal debate. "The meal is served during the performances. I will be back with the wine shortly."

Cooper nodded in response and watched the lion depart; taking a special note of the way the tuxedo hugged his rump nicely. The fox's eyes went wide. He shook his head, and flicked his attention to the dormouse that was approaching the piano next to the stage before anyone could notice that he was looking at another male's rear.

Cooper made the effort to keep his fur from bristling. It had been months since he'd had any urges, and he wasn't going to backslide now. Not that he was terribly ashamed of his attraction to other males, not anymore after living with the knowledge for over a decade, but in his personal opinion society as a whole wasn't ready to acknowledge his desires as "normal", at least not in the States. The fox sighed and put on a smile as Gee returned with the wine. The server gave a smile of his own, one that left Cooper with the distinct impression that whatever debate he'd been holding with himself was resolved, and leaned in just enough that Cooper got a good whiff of his scent.

It was warm: dry and grassy, reminding the fox of the wheat farms just outside his home city of Dayton, Ohio. Over it was the lighter odors of musk and amber that Cooper assumed were the lion's scenting powder. He was rather pleased to find someone that understood restraint when it came to powder—to a canine's nose, a little went a long way. Cooper sniffed a few times before Gee withdrew slowly with a broad smile. The fox frowned and stuck his muzzle in his wine glass, letting the floral bouquet and sharp alcohol purge the lion's scent from his nose. But it lingered in his memory. The lights above the stage lit up, and the first act of the evening began.

The first two shows composed of single males singing to the accompaniment of the dormouse on the slightly out-of-tune piano. The fox sipped his wine and focused on trying not to think about when Gee would reappear to refill his glass. The lion and the third act arrived together.

There was a pause in the show after the second performer left as a small orchestra joined the piano player. The break allowed Cooper to sweep his eyes over the room. The crowd had grown a little bit since the fox had been seated, but not by a great deal. He noted that the audience remained predominately male, with only a few females scattered about. That was curious. Given that the all the acts had also been male, Cooper expected a larger female audience. They seemed to be a fairly broad sample of people from France, and the military fox quickly picked up on the scent of chemicals and coal dust. Factory workers then, the fox thought—though here or there he noticed one or two fellow soldiers. Like Gee, who was hobbling towards him with a wine bottle in his paws. The server reached the table just as the band struck up.

The song was a higher energy piece, a bit louder than the other acts previously that night and the curtain parted to reveal a line of mustelid dancers. Cooper let out a short laugh: the dancers wore frilly skirts that reached down almost to their ankles, despite the fact that even from where the fox sat in the back of the large room, it was clear the performers were all males. There was no attempt hide this fact either, as all of the dancers were bare-chested. Cooper assumed that it was a farcical performance, and the failing at being females was supposed to be obvious for comedic effect. The music picked up and the quartet began to spin and gesture enough for the fox to recognize that they were performing the cancan. Gee finally reached the table and slowly began to refill Cooper's glass as the dancers formed a line for what he now knew would be the high kicks that had given the dance a somewhat scandalous reputation. The otter, weasel, and a pair of martens went at it with admirable gusto, kicking so high that paws almost reached their heads.

Revealing that none of the dancers were wearing undergarments of any kind.

Cooper's muzzle dropped open as they performed another series of kicks. Sure enough, four sheaths and four scrotums were on full display. That sequence done they spun around, lifted their tails, and ran their paws over their exposed rumps to the delight cheers of the small crowd. The fox's mind froze and he could do nothing but stare until the dancers took a bow and left the stage to applause from the entire crowd. He stared at the stage, even as the lights went down until a chuckle brought his attention back to the table and the very amused Gee standing there.

"Did the *Capitaine* believe he was the only one in Paris?"

The lion limped away, leaving Cooper to process that. The fox couldn't believe that a place like this existed so openly—yes it was tucked in the back of the district, but back in Ohio it would be hidden down some dirt country road where no one who didn't know about it would ever find it. He looked around, and was just overwhelmed: at one table an ibex and a stag held paws as they laughed at some joke, at another a pair of martens nuzzled each other's noses, and the dormouse on the piano was kissing the weasel dancer. All of them acting like it was perfectly normal, none of them showing the slightest bit of concern that they were out in public doing so.

Cooper leaned back in the booth and stared at the candle in the middle of the table. Ever since he'd discovered that he was different, he'd worked to hide that difference. When he'd joined the army, he'd learned that in some cases the ability to hide that difference could be the difference between life and death. For over a decade, he'd buried that part of him, and to see others indulging so freely in what he thought he never would have stirred a whirlwind of thoughts and feelings in him. It had to be a trick or a trap. Just like that lone German scout plane had been. For a long time, he stared at the candle, desperately trying to figure out what to do, what to think as the remembered smell of burning fur filled his nose.

"If I may be so bold *monsieur*," a familiar voice startled the fox. He looked up to find Gee had returned.

Cooper blinked. Had he been lost so long in his thoughts that it was time for him to be served again? Or had Gee come back so soon? The look of concern on the lion's face faded into a smile.

"I would offer you the advice that the owner gave to me. He told me that this place was special. That here we didn't have to hide. This is a place we can be ourselves. He told me to think of this place as paradise."

With that, the lion withdrew, leaving Cooper with the thought. The fox pondered the comment. A paradise? What other name could a place where he didn't have to hide part of who he was have? A place where he wouldn't be shunned for his attraction to males, a place where he could be himself, and it occurred to him that he wasn't the kind of person that would make another suffer to bring him luxuries. His head snapped up.

"*Monsieur* Gee," he called after the lion. "I'm not a youngster any more. I don't need my glass always full. Especially if your leg bothering you."

"Perhaps," the lion replied with a smile. "But perhaps it is worth the temporary discomfort. And please, call me Claude."

The lion departed, limping in the direction of what Cooper assumed was the kitchen. He disappeared through the door, and Cooper felt his tail bristle with shock. *Son of a bitch*, Cooper thought. *No, it can't be. No one has in... ten years. That can't be right.* But the more he thought about it, he realized that there was no other explanation: Claude was interested in him. Why else would he give Cooper his first name? The shock of the revelation sent a shudder through him, and the fox was sure his exposed fur was standing on end. It didn't go down, for as soon as he had registered Claude's intentions he realized that he returned them.

"Shit," he breathed, feeling a stirring in his loins. He wanted the lion. The lion wanted him. And no one would care—hell, they'd probably even celebrate it. The only thing that would prevent it was in Cooper's own head. The fox breathed, feeling all the old arguments rise to the surface, feeling the walls come up, feeling the shame return. He looked up and saw Claude returning.

He met the golden eyes of the lion and he remembered himself. He was a fighter pilot and despite his recent mishap, he was a damn good one. And the biggest part of being a fighter pilot was assessing a situation, deciding a course of action, and acting on in it in an instant. Doing that kept you alive. Cooper looked towards the doorway that led back to the entrance. He felt the energy gather in his legs. He could leave, run, try staying at the cabaret another day. He slid around the table, ready to spring. Better to be thought a fool than be caught in whatever this trick was to get him to expose his largest secret.

But as that thought materialized, he felt the predator in him rise—the part of him that knew this was no time to run. He hadn't felt it since being shot down and the fox realized that he'd thought it died in the crash. He settled back down and his eyes went to the ceiling. It wasn't just his instincts that had died: he'd been dead as well, and Life had been a bad dream. It dawned on him that he was awake now, and very much alive. He took a deep steadying breath, leaned forward, locked eyes with the approaching server, and spoke.

"Claude. If you need to rest between your other tables, please feel free to sit with me. There's plenty of room." He gestured toward the booth.

"*Merci Capitaine*," he said with a smile. His eyes swept the room, and Cooper followed his gaze. "But you are my only table."

The fox quickly confirmed the lion's statement: there were an unusually large number of people dressed in similar manner to Claude, and to say that each was seeing to only one table did seem to be the case. A moment ago, this information would have left him shocked—but he was back in pilot mode, and quickly rolled with the change.

"I told *monsieur* that *Le Terrier* is a paradise. The staff willingly spends their nights here," Claude put in before Cooper could respond.

Fuck it, the fox finally thought. He'd seen hell for the past year: the brown blasted lands cut by the black lines of the trenches that spawned only misery. If there was any chance of tasting paradise—even for just one night, he should pounce on it. He'd come this far and he was locked on target—he wasn't about to break off now.

"Then, would you join me for dinner?" he asked as he spread his paws in front of him.

"I was beginning to worry that *monsieur* would never ask." Claude answered with a smile that covered his entire muzzle.

The lion sat down after producing another wine glass from somewhere and filling it. The next act went on as Claude pressed close to Cooper: a play performed by an otter and a beaver. It was in French, so Cooper didn't catch what it was about other than it involved the pair comically losing their clothes as the performance went on. Claude tried to whisper a running commentary, but his occasional need to search for the proper English word and the laughter from the audience quickly made it impossible for Cooper to follow. Instead, he just leaned in close and focused on the lion himself.

Fighting against all the instincts that still screamed at him to hide his true self, Cooper pressed his nose into the lion's mane and sniffed to memorize his scent. Claude, seemingly aware of what was going on, casually draped his arm around the fox. Cooper let go of his last bit of reservation and sighed contentedly. This felt right—to be here, pressed against this warm lion, having a drink and taking in a show. Cooper could almost believe that this was paradise.

"How'd you know?" Cooper asked between acts. "That I was, um, the kind of person that needed here?"

"*Monsieur* failed to notice the resemblance between the lovely dancer and the host of *Le Terrier?*" Claude chuckled before explaining that the vixen Cooper had encountered was the sister of the host. Which still didn't answer the question, Cooper noted.

The rest of the show passed in a blur for Cooper, he remembered only that Claude got up between the fifth and sixth acts to retrieve the dinner from the kitchen after giving the fox's nose a lick. The lion's absence turned Cooper's memories to the single time in his life that he had acted on his love of other males—which he did not have fond memories of. The fox shuddered as his thoughts turned dark again and his eyes focused on the candle—the flame filling his vision; the stench of burning fur, canvas, and wood filling his nostrils, the scream of a wind and a dying rotary engine filling his ears. The clatter of plates on the table signaled the return of the lion with their dinner and broke Cooper out of the memory. Cooper smiled at the lion as he sat down. The lights dimmed as the next act began.

The remaining five acts of the night passed with the fox noting only that they increased in lewdness as they went on. Cooper looked up at the last act to see the performers engaged in what he could only describe as a full body kiss—nude, their shafts poking teasingly from their sheaths as the crowd cheered in delight. But mostly, the American's attention was on his dinner. Or rather his companion, since the dinner itself as bland as one would expect given the wartime rationing. The pair exchanged stories: Claude told tales of the cabaret, of the people that came and went, and of the escapades of employees and patrons that had occurred.

Cooper (after revealing that he was a pilot) told stories of the places he had been. Claude seemed fascinated by the fox's tales of flying, of London and New York, of the trip across the Atlantic, and especially of Ohio. The lion made him go over descriptions of his childhood home, and listened with rapt attention. But in their conversation, the topic of the war, and their parts in it, was studiously ignored.

They continued talking until long after the stage acts had ended, the lights had gone down, and most of the patrons had departed the main room. A few stood around chatting while the staff began to clean the tables. Cooper looked around as the conversation paused and realized that he had run out of things to say. The fox stood up, suddenly unsure of how to proceed when a tawny paw settled on his wrist.

"I do not wish to part just yet *Capitaine*," Claude purred up at the fox, his tail slapping against Cooper's hind paws.

"What else is there to do?" Cooper replied, realizing the answer as soon as the words left his muzzle. The toothy smile on the lion's face confirmed it. Claude got to his paws and pulled the fox to him, leaving the pilot's cap in the booth.

"This way," he said as he led Cooper through a doorway on the stage wall of the room.

That led to a long corridor with four rooms at various intervals. Cooper was surprised to see that none of them were adjacent. They hurried down the hallway as fast as Claude's limp would allow. In the tighter confines, there was no doubt about his intentions as the smell of lion arousal filled the fox's nostrils. The fox was wagging, though a lingering doubt crept into his mind as they reached the room farthest from the main area. Claude opened the door and dragged the fox inside before locking it behind them.

The pilot found himself in what appeared to be a hotel room complete with bed, night table, desk, dresser, and bathroom. The furnishings were all fairly plain, with the only thing catching the fox's eye being the lack of blankets on the bed. He had just finished his survey of the room when a warm, heavy weight settled on him. He moaned and shuddered as the lion's rough tongue ran along his ear from base to point. Claude chuckled and released Cooper so the fox could spin around to face him.

The lion had stripped down to his underwear which hugged his crotch tight enough that Cooper could see the outline of his sheath. His mane poured over his neck, giving a V-shape to his pectoral muscles, but did not continue down his torso like Cooper had seen in medical drawings. The lion's tawny fur lightened a shade on his front, and like the mane was trimmed close—closely enough for Cooper to see the outline of his still fairly prominent muscles. Powerful yet graceful, Claude was as close to the ideal male that Cooper had ever seen. Behind him, his feline tail flicked back and forth as the lion studied him.

"I, uh…" the fox huffed as he pointed in the general direction of his rump. "I'm not ready. I didn't think…"

Claude was on him in one move, snatching the fox from his paws and pressing him against the wall. The lion growled before pressing his muzzle into Cooper's ear. The raspy, warm, wetness of the feline's tongue slid in and sent shocks of pleasure through the fox that made his fur stand on end. Cooper let out a chittering purr as the lion withdrew his muzzle.

"But I am ready," the lion whispered as he guided Cooper's paw to his own rear. Cluade chuckled as the fox let out a little yip of surprise. He held his paw on his rear as they kissed again.

Claude broke the kiss, pulled Cooper off the wall, and carried him to the bed. He sat the fox down and undid the Army officer's tie with practiced fingers. Cooper didn't see where it went; he was too caught up in watching the lion undo the buttons on his shirt. Cooper pressed his nose into Claude's mane and inhaled the lion's warm scent as the Frenchman pulled the American's shirt off and went to work on the fox's belt. A moment later, Cooper pushed his rump off the bed for Claude to pull his pants and underwear off in one motion. As he dropped the American's pants, Claude stood up to get a look at the fox.

Cooper felt the heat rush to his cheeks he realized what he must look like to the big lion: he had the almost stereotypical red orange fur of his species, complete with white chin and belly fur, and black socks and ear tips. But the fox's most defining feature was his build: despite almost a decade of military service, Cooper was extremely thin compared to other foxes- almost effeminate, especially compared to the bulky lion in front of him. But what occurred to him were the large patches of fur, especially on his cheeks and tail where his fur was still growing back from the crash. He whimpered and tried to put paws in front of himself until he saw the server's face.

The lion was licking his muzzle, his eyes tracing up and down the fox's body in admiration. Cooper's paws drifted to his sides and he felt his sheath begin to swell as his pride and arousal returned. The woody, leafy scent of fox musk mingled with the warm grassy smell of the lion.

"Bel homme," Claude breathed as he slid his underwear to the floor, "Truly beautiful."

Cooper licked his own muzzle as he stared at the lion's equipment: the large balls in a tan furred sac, the massive sheath, and the reddish-pink shaft emerging from it. Claude smiled and stepped closer.

"You like?" he asked.

"Yes," Cooper replied. He had never seen a feline cock in person.

"I am glad," the lion said as he reached out towards the fox. "Beinvenue au paradis, Capitaine Cooper."

Cooper only managed to pick out and translate "paradise" before Claude's muzzle met his. The lion kissed him deeply, taking the fox's longer, narrower muzzle into his own as Claude's tongue slipped between Cooper's lips. Cooper let out a small moan as he pressed back against the lion. They broke the kiss only to breathe before launching into another. Cooper wrapped his arms around Claude's neck as the lion moved from kissing to lapping and nipping at his check fur. He could only hold on, moaning and yipping as the lion's rough tongue moved down his neck to his chest. He buried his nose in the lion's ear and tried to press his tongue inside as Claude had done, but it didn't quite fit in the feline's smaller ear. Claude growled appreciatively none the less, and Cooper switched to nipping at the mane on the back of the lion's head as Claude began showering attention on the fox's lean stomach.

Cooper let out a yip of pleasure and surprise as the warmth of lion breath flowed over his shaft. The yip changed to a low moan as Claude's rough tongue ran up his throbbing cock. The lion gave a rumbling purr of his own as he continued run his tongue up and down the fox's member, chuckling as the pointed shaft fully emerged from the white furred sheath. Cooper gasped as the lion took his cock into his muzzle, enveloping it in a wonderful warm wetness.

Claude bobbed on the fox's shaft, his tongue rubbing the underside and provoking shudders from the pilot as his cock throbbed in the lion's muzzle. He yipped and moaned, already feeling the pressure in his loins and the swelling at the base of his shaft as his knot fully formed. Claude released him with a slurp and stood up smiling and licking his lips. He whispered something in French that Cooper didn't quite catch, but before the lion could translate (if he was going to) Cooper remembered something that the boys back at the aerodrome had reminded him of before he'd left.

"Um, Claude, I don't want to ruin the mood. But you wouldn't have a rubber would you?" He asked, his tail coming up between his legs in embarrassment. He hadn't brought any himself, as he'd been sure sex wouldn't be something he'd have on this trip.

"Only a feline one," Claude shook his head and wrinkled his nose. His ears swiveled back in embarrassment. "It is very old."

Of course, on a server's salary, the lion couldn't afford to have a stockpile. Meanwhile, Cooper's eyes were drawn to the lion's erection, and he immediately took note of why Claude had made the distinction. Unlike Cooper's member, the lion had a blunt head to his shaft crowned by a ring of just barely visible barbs, which became a row that traced a ridge down the underside of his shaft, disappearing into his sheath. Cooper licked his lips, wondering just what those barbs would feel like. And of course, the lion had no knot. It was clear a condom made for felines wouldn't work for him.

"Do you feel we need one?" Claude asked, giving Cooper the distinct impression that he would get dressed and go find one if the answer was in the affirmative. At that moment, Cooper's member throbbed and the fox felt a bead of pre-cum form on his tip.

"Haven't been with anyone in years," he sighed. "If I had anything, I'd know by now. You?"

"Much the same," the lion shook his maned head.

"What?" Cooper asked, incredulous. "You? You're working around willing partners every night. How aren't you having sex whenever you want it?"

"I am much too professional for that, monsieur." Claude said, with a huff and a smile that told Cooper he was half joking.

"And what about me made you break that?"

The lion slinked on to the bed, pressing Cooper down to the mattress. As he crawled up the fox, his paws passed over the burned patches, caressing them. Claude kissed him again, a seemingly urgent desperation in the act that Cooper felt his body react to. The time for words was over.

They kissed and licked, nipped at cheeks, and growled playfully into ears as paws explored lover's bodies. The question Cooper asked was answered by the lion's paws tracing over the patches of fur left short by the crash, while his own paws located the canyon-like scar in the lion's left thigh. That was the answer: Claude had seen a kindred spirit, someone else that knew first-hand the hell of The War and had been left forever changed by it. A revelation came to Cooper then: in trying to forget how close he'd come to dying, he'd forgotten how to live. Somehow, Claude could tell, and in this place had given him permission to remember how to live and live well.

The lion broke off the kiss and moved up to straddle Cooper's chest. He leaned over to open the night table drawer, but the fox didn't see what he was looking for—his attention was firmly on the lion cock, now in his reach of his paws for the first time. Cooper grasped the shaft and tentatively began to stroke it, marveling at the feel of the barbs against his pads. It was so different from own, or the coyote's cock, the only other one he'd ever touched. He rubbed the shaft, and ran his thumb along the nubby ridge and around the crown of barbs, exploring them with utter fascination. It was so much thicker than his own, except for his knot, and a bit longer as well. So deep in his explorations was he that he barely heard the chuckle above him as he leaned forward to bring his head closer to that wonderful shaft. Cooper closed his eyes, leaned in and gave it a tentative lick. The warm taste of lion musk played over his tongue, causing the fox to salivate as he continued to nuzzle the lion's shaft. Suddenly he was pulled away from it by a firm paw on his shoulder.

"Another time for that *Capitaine*," Claude said. "For now, it is time for this."

The lion's paw left Cooper's neck and the fox opened his eyes to find Claude opening a small bottle and pouring a liquid in to his paw. The faint smell of olives reached his nose through the twin scents of their arousal. Claude smiled and reached behind himself and rubbed the oil on the fox's shaft, causing Cooper to gasp at the cool sensation. The lion reached under his tail and treated himself with the liquid before setting the bottle down on the night table.

"Has *monsieur* done this before?"

"Once. Long ago. Wasn't that great."

"Well. We shall do better then. For now just lie down and relax."

Claude reached back, took gentle hold of Cooper's erection, and slowly lowered himself on to it. They gasped in tandem as the tip entered the lion's waiting rear. Claude purred and moaned as he took more of the fox's length. Cooper did as he'd been instructed and just relaxed, groaning himself at the wonderful feeling of the lion around his shaft. Then Claude began to ride, working his hips to slide himself up and down the fox's cock, taking just a bit more of it with each move. He set a smooth pace, moaning as he rocked, keeping an eye on the fox.

Cooper was in ecstasy, his claws tracing little lines in Claude's fur as his paws clenched the lion's hips each time the lion's balls touched his stomach. The feel of the powerful lion on top of him, the wonderful sensation of his insides pressing against his cock, the sounds that Claude made each time his rump reached the fox's rapidly swelling knot were all unlike anything he had ever experienced before. Cooper let out a series of huffing yips as he felt the pressure beginning to build deep in his loins. Claude apparently had enough experience with foxes to know what that meant. He paused for a moment and smiled up at Cooper.

"*Bein?* Close?"

"Yes." Cooper hissed in pleasure.

The lion purred and resumed his riding, picking up his pace until Cooper was reduced to a constant state of moaning. The pressure built and built inside the fox, and he felt himself rapidly climbing towards climax.

He was almost there when Claude winced and sat down, whimpering. Cooper's eyes snapped wide open in concern, and he desperately tried to pull out of the lion.

"I'm sorry! I didn't—"

"It is not you, *Capitaine*." Claude sighed and looked accusingly at his injured leg. He muttered something in French that sounded like a curse. "It never fully healed."

Cooper felt the mood slipping and quickly made his decision. He reached up and took the lion's wrist in his right paw while he caressed Claude's hip with the other.

"Let me, then."

Claude looked at him for a moment—then nodded. The fighter pilot wasted no more time. He gently pushed the lion, indicating he wanted to roll to his right. With Claude's help, much giggling, a few false starts, and several muttered directions Cooper managed to get the lion's back onto the mattress with him now on top. Claude giggled and then purred. Cooper couldn't tell if the laughter was of pure enjoyment, or amusement at the fox's attempts to move the much bigger lion around against his will. He decided he didn't care. Claude had played along, and that was all that mattered now. Cooper stroked himself back to full hardness and positioned himself with the lion's rear before a thought occurred to him.

"I, uh, haven't done it this way before," he said.

"I know you will do just fine, *mon capitaine*," Claude assured him as he reached down and caressed the fox's cheek.

Cooper took a steadying breath, and slowly slid his tip into the waiting lion. Again, Claude gasped as he was entered, a sound which rapidly changed to a moan of pleasure as the fox pushed deeper into the warm confines of his insides. The fox groaned himself as he began to swing his hips to work the lion's rump. His thrusts were tentative at first, and he slid out once after pulling back too far, but with some reassurance from the lion, he finally found a rhythm. He slid out again, and cursed himself. But Claude rolled underneath him, Cooper guessed to get weight off his bad hip, and suddenly the fox felt the pressure of a leg wrapped around his hip. He went to work again, and the leg prevented him from pulling too far back again. Eventually he was thrusting deep into the lion and feeling himself climb steadily towards his peak. His eyes alternated between his groin and the lion's face, trying to make sure Claude was enjoying this as much as he was. If the contented smile was anything to go by, Claude was.

Cooper huffed and yapped as he thrusted, spurred on by the moans and purrs from the lion underneath him until he felt his knot against Claude's hole. The fox paused, suddenly aware of his knot, the memory of how it felt to take one, and the horror that the lion might not have thought of that. He looked up at the lion as he continued to work his rear.

"Want me to tie you?" Cooper grunted. The coyote hadn't been so considerate with him.

"*Oui, Oui,*" Claude panted, his tongue lolling out in ecstasy. "*Attachez-moi monsieur, s'il tu plaît!*"

Cooper wasn't in the frame of mind to properly translate what the lion had said, but he knew "Yes" when he heard it. He leaned forward and shoved his hips against the lion's rear. For a moment, Claude's hole resisted, but then the knot slipped in with an audible pop. It would have been hard to hear it over the lion's gasp, and Cooper bucked his hips rapidly as they both panted and groaned. The fox put one paw on the mattress next to Claude's hip to support himself, and reached the other up to stroke the lion's own cock. Or at least he tried to—the best he managed to do was form a ring with his fingers for his thrusts to pass the lion's shaft through.

It was only a moment after he tied the lion that Cooper felt the pressure in his loins reach its peak. The fox let out a sound that was half groan and half low howl as he thrust one final time, and reached his climax, pumping his seed deep inside his feline lover. He shuddered with his release, but maintained enough awareness to keep stroking Claude's cock until he let out a throaty growl. The lion's own shaft throbbed in the fox's paw, letting loose spurt after spurt of his seed over his belly. Finally, Cooper's energy gave out, and he flopped down on Claude's stomach. The lion panted and wrapped his arms around the fox. For a long time they lay there completely content.

It took about half an hour for Cooper's knot to go down enough for him to pull out of Claude's rear with minimal effort. After that, the fox slid into a more comfortable position and they fell asleep. There they stayed: sticky, fur matted from strange licks, reeking of sex, and happy for the rest of the night. The fox woke only once, momentarily startled by the strong arm of the lion wrapping around him. Claude leaned in, wrapping himself around Cooper and whispering something that sounded reassuring into his ear. The fox settled back down, and pressed himself into the warmth of the lion's embrace. He slept the rest of the night, untroubled by the nightmares that had plagued him since the crash.

From long habit, Cooper awoke a few hours before dawn. He extracted himself from his feline blanket and headed into the bathroom for a shower. He stepped out and was moderately surprised the former soldier had no drying powder—so the fox came out of the bathroom still toweling his fur off to find Claude sitting on the edge of the bed. Their eyes met, and the lion smiled.

"*Bonjour mon cher Capitiane.* Does duty call you back so soon?" Claude's smile turned sad. "Well. I would like to thank you, and assure you this was not something I do all the time. I am grateful for our night."

Cooper studied the lion, assessing his emotions as he did so. Yes it had been wonderful—and while he would be content with one good lay, he was older now and appreciated something more. Claude seemed willing to give that. *What the hell*, Cooper thought with a sigh. *Why not?*

"Want another?"

"What?"

"Want another night? I'm on leave for a week, and I can't think of a better place to spend it. And no one better to spend it with then you."

Claude's smile smiled broadly.

"There's one thing I'd like to know," Cooper said as his mind finally translated the establishment's name. "Why's this place called 'The Foxhole?'"

The lion paused before laughing long and loudly at that. Cooper frowned, sensing some joke that might have been at his expense, but shook his head. It didn't matter. He would stay with the lion for the week and spend the money he'd brought in the club. He would enjoy their time together, and perhaps even find out what those barbs felt like on the inside. The war and the hell it brought would still be there in a week.

Antisocial Paradise

by Miriam "Camio" Curzon

Mina's soft, uncut cock slid along my tongue as the genet's legs trembled on either side of me, his weight supported with help from his locked elbows, claws gripping to the marker tray beneath a dry erase board smeared with Marxist rhetoric and illustrations. Echoes of a broken accordion and ukulele melded with the familiar received pronunciation drone of the BBC News. I held Mina's open fly and loose boxers below his plump package, the dark spots in his coat melting into the brown-tan underbelly fur in the corner of my eye. He was a nerd, the Computer Science undergrad type who wore loose clothing and thin-frame glasses, hotness hidden in poorly fitted clothes and accessories. His tail he couldn't hide, ringed in bands of black fur it was as long has he was tall, more tail than I could imagine dealing with. He volunteered to run tech for the camp of protesters and the embedded journalists currently occupying the main foyer of the administration building.

I tasted him; my tongue swirled around the skin tight against his tapered head. My free paw traveled underneath his shirt, his stomach was soft and squishy, a deceitfully prominent stomach. His chest was just as doughy, not much muscle build up between the satiny short fur and breastbone. Mina's shaft jerked, pre-cum leaked out on my tongue as blood filled the flesh in my muzzle. It was nice that he was responding, and the weight and girth suggested a good mouthful. He gasped, his head and chest falling forward. A chain brushed against my fingertips, sign of hidden faith, though his dick gave away more than a hidden Coptic cross. I jerked my paw away out of reflex. Virgins and the faithful I tended to keep a wide berth from, sexually speaking.

"I-I don't know... how long I can—" Mina's legs were wobbling even more, and he had sunk enough that I could feel the weight of his sac in my palm.

Pulling back, I teased his tip as he slipped from my muzzle and down the wall. His thin muzzle was parted, his tongue pressed against his lips as he panted. I switched to one paw, kneeling beside him and rubbing and squeezing the thick base of his cock. "Ever done this before?" I asked, burying my reservation beneath a gravely growl.

"Not in the middle of a bloody public classroom."

I doubted he seriously minded too much, his balls certainly didn't as they jerked a heavy drop from his tip. "Get much tourist action?" The indescribable flavor of cock skin and pre was still prominent on my tongue and in my throat.

The genet growled a laugh in response. "I was too terrified. The clubs would get raided, we'd be imprisoned, and that tourist would be going home."

I fiddled with my own pants.

"I came to England for uni prep, and partied for the first year."

"Availed yourself of our delicate young males, did you?" Pants opened I leaned into his warm body. It was awkward, that was the nature of this little coupling, I settled for straddling one of his legs unable to slip between or over his legs. We were both larger folk.

"Hardly." He accepted my advance, his knee pressing up between my thighs. "Do I look like clubbing is something I do? Nah, just fucking casual shit. Got old quick. Not the casual, just the scene." Mina grabbed my hip, claws curling around the waist and belt loops of my jeans.

"Glad to hear it." I pressed my canid muzzle into his neck. "Wouldn't want to ruin the moment with a proposal and meet the parents' invitation." My ears flicked. Shouts and cheers sounded from the common room. Nipping at his neck, I pulled his length against mine.

"Yo, Landon, you in'ere?" Tix appeared in the open-door frame looking as disheveled as usual, his white t-shirt was looking a little gray, but the noose around 'Tories' was still very clear. "Hey, Landon!" the red squirrel sauntered up to our little pile of two large guys on the floor. "And... stranger." He seemed to notice that he'd walked in on me and someone not of our community of misfits.

As calm as Tix was, Mina was quite the opposite. His amber eyes seemed to vibrate between wide-eyed embarrassment and slit-eyed shame. I stroked his cock to keep him focused, and from freaking out anymore. "I'm Tix," he held out his paw, "Pleasure to meet you..." His paw hung there for a moment, fur caked in different forms of paint: acrylic, oil, and gouache.

I licked up the side of Mina's neck and along the underside of his jaw. "Shake the nice squirrel's paw and introduce yourself."

"Mina." His voice wobbled slightly as he shook Tix's paw; I squeezed as they shook, to see the bug out expression on his face.

"Nice to meet you Mina," Tix paw fell to his side, while the genet's just hung there.

"He's a hugger," I said to reassure Mina.

"On account of all the dicks out I figured I'd get the hugs in later. Now, Landon are you and h… What pronouns?"

I could feel his discomfort growing in the void left in my paw as he started to soften. "He's a cute boy I found from Egypt." Not wanting to lose more of his mood, I wrapped myself around him. My one arm snaked behind him as I stroked his dripping, but soften cock, now hidden by my body.

"Well, anyway, to the point so you two can get to the point, bunch of school kids are heading to Parliament."

"School kids are always visiting Parliament…"

"These are college and secondary kids, under 18 variety, protesting tuition hikes."

"You're not planning on hijacking it?"

"I hijack fuck all. We're picking some representatives, don't want the police to catch us snoozing and stop our occupation early. I'm climbing over to the theater in ten minutes if you want to come."

"We can try…"

Tix patted both of us on the shoulder. I could see his discreet glance and sly smile at Mina's reawakened arousal before jogging out of the room. The squirrel was generally jogging somewhere.

"Sorry," I said, "Tix tends to be rather brash. Parental issues, mainly." Looking down, my own arousal jerked at the glistening shaft in my paw. "Now, I thought you folk were routinely circumcised over there…" Mina bit his lip as I toyed with his covered tip, much like my own. It didn't really matter to me. I slipped down and pressed my nose to the base of his frenulum. I had a curious itch I wanted to scratch, but it wasn't about to stop me from blowing him.

* * *

I jogged ahead, pulling Mina along, the taste of his seed lingering in my throat and tongue. My pants were tight and a little damp, but there wasn't time for that at this time. We reached the top floor of the administration building. There was one of the old, tall windows that opened out onto the back roof. Tix was standing by the opened window, alone. "The others went on ahead, took my impromptu banner, too," he explained, black ink smudged across the fur of his forehead.

The squirrel ducked through the window, at home with these heights. I had snuck my way into several buildings from the third or fourth floor. That was how most of us were coming and going without the auspices of press credentials. Not that all who had them were journalists, undercover security, and of course Mina. The genet hung back even as I pulled him out onto the roof despite the protests. By the time we made it half way between the window and the back of the theater, Tix was already jumping down to the theater's roof. The slow going was starting to get at my vertigo as Mina inched along, pressed into the pitched copper roof long since oxidized. The roof was crenelated with the same old stone as the rest of the building, but Mina didn't seem to trust it. I was getting to the point of following suit, fortunately the rain had held off despite the overhanging clouds. It would be nice to say the view was great, that I could see all of London from up there, but I certainly wasn't paying attention.

Of course the crossing wasn't the worst to deal with. The back roof of the theater was three feet lower, but was flush with the taller building that our school building backs onto. I had done the jump several times already, both recently and as an undergrad. It was intimidating, small guys like Tix could use the exposed bricks and utility boxes and lines to cross the gap, but big guys like Mina and me needed a bit more dedication. "You should go first," I said, sliding across the genet's front. "Just go up to wall and ease yourself over."

"You're fucking nuts."

"Come on, you're one with heights, aren't you?" I answered, "Just go up to the edge and jump over. It's barely a foot away." I hooked my claws around his waistband as he inched to the corner. It was, in all honesty, a minuscule gap, just the angle and height difference made it easy to psyche yourself out. "You got this, just jump." His fur was on edge, catlike tail whipping in the wind.

Tix appeared around the blind corner. "Come on. You don't wanna get caught up there."

"Oi, shut the fuck up!" I shouted and Tix ducked around, back out of sight. I bend my head to his ear and stroked his hip. "You ready?"

Mina's eyes were closed and his muzzle was moving. Then he leapt, my fingers sliding free of his waist as he flew from my grasp. It was windy up on the roof, but he landed with ease, and I followed. Bumping into his back I hugged him. "See? Easy." It hadn't been easy; I could hear his heart pounding and his tail hung in a languid arc.

Tix was sitting half in, half out of the window of the theater, brushing flakes of paint and glue out of his tail. "We should hurry," he said, as he pushed himself off the window sill into the building.

We hurried after the large tail, breathing heavily to catch up with the swift squirrel. "Should I mention that I'm here on a visa?" Mina said as we pushed into a stairwell.

"And?" Tix called back over his shoulders as he skipped down steps, our progress echoing in the concrete brick tower.

"They'll kick me outta school, the country, back to Egypt to marry some Coptic girl, from there everything falls apart."

"About a third of my roommates are ex-students with expired visas," Tix began as he jumped the last few steps down. "They have no plans on leaving."

"See," I said, as we paused on the first-floor landing, "You can move in with Tix."

Tix started down the final stairway to the ground floor, "We got one bedroom, one shower, one toilet and a trench outback… at least until they shut off the water or force us out."

"Are you serious?" Mina asked, following Tix just ahead of me.

"It's really nice!" Tix insisted.

"Certainly better than the foreclosed warehouse you all were in before," I echoed.

The heavy metal exit door clanged shut behind us as we pushed out of the ground floor stairwell. It was hard to imagine this primly dressed genet showing up to live among an anarchist artists commune squatting in an abandoned building or empty Russian oligarch's flat. We danced between the cardboard and rubbish piles along the cobblestone alley, and dodged by puddles of filthy water to the empty street that ran along the back of the university and ran through the center of central London's higher education. We snuck by the back entrance, staffed more by construction workers than security, and veered around Senate House. Today was not a day to pay respect to where the University of London Union died.

Our goal was first to reach Piccadilly Circus where we saw the remnants of the unexpected tidal wave. The chill in the late fall air was hard to stand, but the mass of bodies we were heading to should help assuage the presence of cold. Piccadilly should be bustling, it normally is at all hours, but this mid-afternoon day it was scattered with more coffee cups and newspapers than onlookers or tourists. The number of pedestrians was noticeably low, although not as deserted as an hour after last call, after the tube stops and only night buses run.

It can be difficult to catch up to a protest already moving. They tend to proceed rather fast to get to the rally point before the police block it off because they don't like how we look or too many. When we start seeing people with their phones or cameras out ambling in the opposite direction I know we're getting close. While mildly inconvenienced by protests, the very least they could do was get a good photograph to show off the ungrateful blighters.

* * *

The stragglers were next and we blended into the crowd. Tix was off, his size making it impossible to follow in most crowds, too short to spot, and so small he can fit through the littlest cracks. I kept hold of Mina's paw. "Look, if we get separated," I began pulling him in close so he would definitely be able to hear over the rising street noise. "Do whatever you can to get out, look for the small side streets."

"What about them?" he asked, eyes darting to the line of police on either side of the march.

"Don't mind them, you're not breaking any laws, they've no reason to detain you for just being here."

"What about you?" His fingers tightened around my paw.

"Meet back at the university."

We dodged through more of the scattered rear guard. The chill of November was already starting to fade from the concentration of bodies. "What about Tix?" Mina asked, the red squirrel long gone.

I laughed, pushing in between a group of wolves with anti-Tory placards. "Tix is practically untouchable. Small, quick, and climbs."

The further we pushed through the marching crowd they seemed to grow younger and smaller. Tix was right, these were mostly children. There was a young rabbit, she didn't look over fifteen, prancing down Whitehall waving a sign as tall as her. This crowd was filled with hundreds like her. How many of them could have possibly been to a march before? I couldn't imagine they knew what they were doing. It was exciting, it made my heart race, this demonstration of raw emotion. As we pushed further into the crowd I wanted to join in the poorly synchronized shouts. Of course to join in anything more than gibberish would mean I could translate the variety of slurred phrases ringing through the air.

When the closed street opened up on Parliament Square it was a madhouse with rows of police three lines deep blocking off the south and east side of the park to protect Westminster. For a moment we stood still as streams of children pressed into the park. "Crazy, en'it?" I asked Mina, his amber eyes wide. The streets were mostly empty, most of the demonstration living within the confines of the park. "Mind your tail," I said, wondering what one could possibly do with six feet of tail in a crowd like this.

The crowd divided into small groups talking, dancing, smoking, drinking, shouting. All of us were here to be seen and heard, our sheer number the rhetorical message. Tix was likely ringside, fearlessly facing down the police guards in riot gear. As exhilarating as that could be, I doubt Mina was ready for it. Today we were along for the ride and I pulled Mina toward the climb that preceded the first drop and spike of adrenaline. In among the smokers and stoners, hippies, students and socialists, ukuleles and vuvuzelas, the sounds and smells were overwhelming: pot and cigarettes, sweat and stale beer and coffee, cum. My pants tightened. Mina wrestled with a scent bottle, dabbing just below his pointy nose. "Too much?" I asked. He nodded, stashing the small bottle in his hip pocket. "You'll get used to it. Though you gotta start using the scents less."

"How do you do it?" he asked as we passed by a drum circle.

"Practice," I answered, "And some desensitizing. Things tend to smell less shitty if you hang around houses with backed up septic systems and mold. Smell of life is much better in comparison."

"I—uhh—think I'll pass on that."

I threw an arm around his shoulder and brought my muzzle in close to his cheek. "I'll let you know if you miss something."

The hour grew later, but the crowd only grew. November can get chilly and temperature can be hard with all these hot bodies in one place and the biting wind of approaching winter. With time and density growth, order declines. I could smell the trouble starting. The acrid odor of burning wood, plastic, and chemical sealant. Smoke rose out of the middle of the park. I waited with a paw on Mina's shoulder.

"What's going on?"

"A fire." Fires weren't rare, especially when it's cold and no one's moving. This smelled more like property damage. "Watch out, things might get dicey," I warned. "They're burning a bench or something. They come when property is damaged." 'They' were the mounted unit, and they appeared riot helmets affixed to their heads rising three feet above the crowd; they had the power to part. "We should start backing away," I began just before a stone bounced off one of the officer's shielded face.

"Knock it off!" Mina shouted into the crowd, his voice dying in the overwhelming collection of shouted slurs, whistles piercing over top.

"I don't think they're gonna stop, Mina," I said. "It's too late anyway." The sun was already below the roof line.

We started fracturing, the crowd not sure just which way to go. Some headed straight for the mounted unit, others to the rows of riot police, some for any exit they could find. With more police streaming around the park from fire and flung objects, the scene was loudly and quickly devolving. Holding tight to Mina, I pulled him with me toward the northwest corner of Parliament Square. St. James Park was a quick hop away, the open space made it hard for the police to kettle us. On the outskirts of the park a group of protesters, muzzles covered, swarmed the treasury building as another contingent appropriated several eight foot sections of portable chain link fence, virtually blocking access. The glass windows splintered, but did not shatter, the reinforced glass far stronger than a mob armed with rocks and bits of discarded building materials.

The line of fences blocking off Great George Street to the east was falling in on itself, the barricade propped up by the bodies of experienced protesters failing. Outside of the square, groups lined the rim of the treasury, a small lip a foot or two above the sidewalk providing greater sight lines around the square. Others had climbed street lamps and traffic lights; a group was hanging a crudely painted anti-capitalist sign across the mouth to the square.

As the streets were getting darker, I climbed a concrete bollard to see if the way out to St. James Park was clear. Another riot squad was jogging down Great George Street. "Shit," I said, jumping back to the pavement. They were likely going to try to block off our escape route and kettle all of us in here and we were still within the perimeter.

"What about down there?" Mina asked, pointing to sunken area between the building and the sidewalk along the south side of the street.

With the other chaos, we could hide from the initial wave and sneak away after I figured. Pulling Mina along I ran for the doorway half down the block and we leapt over the stone railing into the private sunken path. Our heads came up just high enough to peek out street level. We followed the path until it curved around, and found a path out half a block later and bolted south. Fuck the park, the Met would likely be increasing their presence around it and the fancy shops near the northern edge of the park. We disappeared amongst the streets and alleys until I jumped and climbed a set of scaffoldings against a building. From the roof, we could see Parliament Square as the police over rode the protest. The groups on the outskirts around the treasury were a splintered mess.

"What's going to happen?" Mina asked.

"They'll be there for several hours," I answered with a shiver. The cold on top of the building overwhelming me for the first time.

"But they're just kids..."

"Not all of them, most, and it doesn't matter. Some will be arrested, only some will be charged, some hospitalized, some will get away just fine." Someone out there had started a fire in the middle of the park, this time more for warmth, probably. The police were enclosing around the park and the square. Power to the people, anarchy in the UK in the middle of a crusade led by children.

* * *

My pulse was racing and I was shivering. We should head back to the college, get out of the chilly November weather. Certainly, we should not be hanging out on top of a building with the wind. Neither one of us wanted to look away. The glow of lamps and fire, sirens and a few helicopters, news or police, couldn't tell which. I was wide awake, the adrenalin serving as a direct injection of caffeine. "We got out, at least."

"What now?" Mina asked, shivering just a bit.

I kissed him. It occurred to me that we really hadn't done that yet. I was pushing things beyond the bit of fun we'd already had to something more serious. He gasped as my tongue slipped against his. It didn't occur to me that this could be his first kiss either, having revealed his sexual history, I didn't think this was the one thing he may not have done. I pulled back, both of us breathing heavily, his paws had gotten tangled in my braids. He pulled me back until my larger muzzle was pressed against his thinner one, his tongue returning with force to roam against my teeth and tongue. Our bodies melded into one another, my groin a hardened mass of fire from the teasing attention I'd given it earlier.

Mina slid to his knees, claws sliding against my trouser waist and button as he zeroed in on his goal. I swore his hot breath was melting through the layers of my clothes. My pants clanged to the roof around my ankles and my tight compression trunks slid partway down my thighs. He sucked me into his muzzle, pulling me in until his nostrils flared against fur. Even the slight bulge at the base of my shaft throbbed behind his lips. Using his tongue for all the work, his paws wrapped around the back of my upper thighs, fingertips teasing me beneath my tail.

As quiet and shy as he seemed, his muzzle told a different story as he slurped, suckled, and salivated with a salacious smile all the while. Chills rocked my body, but not from the cold, which was distant and forgotten. He pulled off, whiskers twitching as pre dribbled on his chin.

"Turn around," he instructed and I wasn't going deny him. He bent me over the roof ledge and his tongue slid along my taint. I groaned as his tongue pressed into me.

Closing my eyes to the ongoing confrontation below us a mile to the northeast, I pressed against his muzzle. My cock throbbed against my stomach, my shirt and fur growing damp. "Hurry up," I moaned.

He scrambled up behind me and his length slid beneath mine. With a teasing touch, he rubbed my pre and saliva slickened shaft with a light brush of fingers, spreading a growing mixture of fluids around his cock. I gasped as the warmth of him against me retreated and pressed against my spit slicked hole. It fucking hurt, I gritted my teeth, no amount of relaxing making the intrusion easier. With some effort, I rocked my hips back against him, adjusting until the hurt subsided into the dull ache of cock filled ass. Rocking into me at a swift and steady pace, he felt so much different than I'd imagined. I imagined him sweeter with this, more fumbling, maybe even in my position, but his thrusts came with precision and the pain was more manageable than a bumbling virgin with too much lube and no skill.

Braced against the sturdy rampart, I arched up against him. One of his big arms wrapped up around my chest as he purred a rumbling growl into the nape of my neck. Beneath us order was returning. He fumbled a bit, reaching for my shaft, something I'd always found awkward. One of the unexpected hardest things of fucking like this was managing the reach around. His paw found my shaft and gripped me almost painfully tight, stroking me in short rapid bursts. Out in the park most of the protest had diminished into sitting and group huddles. A few skirmishes continued along the police line, the standoff would continue until they all were allowed to leave or arrested.

Through half lidded eyes, I recalled the exhilaration of the moment, throwing myself over into the shouting and fighting back the disillusionment of our government. I snarled in frustration as he pulled out, rapidly turning until he caught me in another kiss. Hot seed splashed against my cock, his essence boiling into me as his orgasm subsided. Without stopping for a moment, he returned to where he'd started with my length pressing down toward his throat. I clutched at his cheeks, ears, and whatever else I could grasp taking my turn to fuck his muzzle. "I-I'm close," I whimpered, legs starting to shake.

Mina pulled back until just my tip remained between his lips, his tongue toying with my foreskin. His fingers slipped around the base of my shaft and he stroked until my seed was flooding his mouth.

Sure, our walk back to the university was sore and uncomfortable, at least for me, but it'd been fun. We strolled through Piccadilly as the streets returned to normal. The bourgeois rich cats were hitting the clubs in their fancy chauffeured limos and Lamborghinis. My fur was dirty and matted, my walk of shame covering the few miles between King's Cross and the Thames and several hours embarrassingly early. Mina was quiet and I hadn't much to say. The recollection of our passions lingered in our noses. We avoided passing too close to others on the street and would dash across the street if we noticed an adroit muzzle coming too close. Some guys I'd been with didn't understand the need for discretion, but Mina shared an implicit understanding that just because we had this country's law and culture was on our side, our dark continent heritage was more unpredictable.

We arrived back at the college a little after midnight. The cold November air was starting to get to me and the cum caked fur rubbed uncomfortably against my jeans. Hopping the wall was easy enough. After hours, they liked to keep the central campus locked down to discourage any off-color pranks or political artwork. Few years ago, Tix tagged one of the statues with blood red spray paint and the school was less than pleased to see a distinguished alum and benefactor called a pig. The school couldn't do much since the statue was of Tix's own patrilineal great-grandfather. I'd never asked why Tix had such a bone for Dr. Morris.

As the hour was considerably later than we'd normally try to get back into the administration wing, we couldn't use the theater shortcut. Instead we had to do a little hopping and climbing. Mina seemed more comfortable despite his earlier hesitation. Maybe our little rooftop fuck cured him of some of his fear of heights.

Everyone was clustered in the little IT station listening to the news. I paused at the doorway, ears perked for the latest from BBC or SKY, but Mina pushed me toward the washroom. Like any other washroom, there wasn't a whole lot we could do with just fur dryers, toilets, and sinks. Mina locked the door and started stripping.

"Here?" I approached him as his shirt fell to the ground. "I liked the office better." His trousers fell to the ground. I reached for his loose boxers, the fly gaping tantalizingly open. My head was clouded by the outpouring of pheromones of our unwashed post-penetration state. "My turn?" I asked, slipping my claws beneath waistband along his hips.

Mina paused for a second. Even the sway of his long tail halted mid swing. There was a sparkled in his eye as he butted up against my muzzle with his. I eased the waistband down until his pants joined his trousers. "Stop." He huffed, breathing hard into my parted muzzle. He didn't pull away very far, just enough that he could dodge my attempt to re-engage. Even his cock jerked hard against my thigh.

Whining, I asked, "What's wrong?" My ears drooped involuntarily as though I were drunk. "You could do me again, if you're not into bottoming..."

Then he was gone, the coolness of florescent lights and neutral tile filled the gulf his retreat formed. "It's not that... we should wash up, get some sleep." His eyes seemed to search me for a reply, reminding me that we were essentially strangers, not familiar enough for silent communication.

"That's fine," I said with a shrug, off playing the disappointment my cock was experiencing. "I feel kind of icky anyway."

Mina bent down, his tail swinging in the air. How I'd love to feel that tail as he is moaning... I bit my lip, starting to undo my pants. The genet stood straight again, boxers in paw, cock bobbing. "Fine with sharing?" he asked, running the boxers underneath the sink tap.

"Huh?" My pants hit the floor despite having to clear my boner.

"Rag," he answered, soaping up his drawers.

Looking down I realized my briefs were look worse for wear, not quite up to wiping off the cum. "Better do," I answered, pulling down my underwear and tossing them in the garbage.

He patted both of us down with the soapy cloth, paying attention to my problems areas until I thought he'd pull the fur out. I wished he'd do more than wipe up and down my body, barely lingering along my hardness. We both left the lavatory hard and our underwear was in the garbage. Knowing he was not wearing underwear would haunt me, the bagginess of his trousers perfect for defining his bulge.

Unable to deny exhaustion, we headed to the "bunk" room and curled up in a corner. I hated being horned up before bed, too tired to get off and too horny to sleep well. Morning was likely going to suck.

* * *

Morning sucked. It came with shrill whistles and heavy banging. "Fuck." I rubbed the drowsiness from my eyes. My head pounded like a fifteen-day binge and of course my phone had died, no charger in sight. And the whistling and pounding persisted.

Mina let out a large yawn, his tongue flexing out as his fangs glistened. His open maw reminded me of the fun we'd had. Cute as he was, though, my mood was sour, my back stiff, my lips chapped.

Max, a big bull of a cow, appeared in the doorway. She'd been one of Tix's girlfriends from before Tix was Tix. The large dyke ran our circus.

"We gotta clear out." Her accent as thick as blood pudding as red as her fur. Despite her Scottish tongue, Tix assured me she was quite good at feminine linguistics.

"What's it?" I snapped as she turned to leave.

"We gone and pissed off the chancellor. Now we have'ta piss off or it's bondage night with unfriendly folk."

"That's it?" I asked with a groan.

"Ass up, Landon," she grunted as she disappeared into the hallway.

"Eat it," I shouted back, but she was gone and ignoring me. Now Mina was looking at me, his head cocked to the side. "Don't worry about it Mina." Resisting the urge to curl back up into him and the faint desire to reacquaint myself with his uncut cock, I stretched my limbs. My ass hurt.

"You okay?" Mina asked, standing with surprising ease.

"Yeah," I answered, rubbing at the ruffled fur on my cheeks. "We should get moving, though." I stood up, bones cracking. "But first some painkillers. And a piss."

We were greeted by zombies staggering around the wing. Clearly, I was not the only one surprised. Our removal was happening way too fucking early and that meant the coffee machine was being packed up rather than pumping out disposable cups of rejuvenating heartburn. Outside it was so early that the chill of an early sun still clung to the air. Mina was an exception. Acting completely unzombified, he stood out on the sidewalk like it was a fucking bright sunny noontime summer day. His crew was busy leaving with their arms filled with their networking gadgetry. Our little sit in occupation fizzled as the Marxist name Wi-Fi trotted away. I spat at the flagstone sidewalk. We just followed the rules, after all, whether they were stated or a reasonable understanding of our underlives. Actual transgression wasn't possible here, not when a knowing hand of the powerful institution come out in "symbolic support" drawing attention to what involved and bright students they had. I sighed.

"Tesco's?"

"Ugh!" My exasperation bittered my tongue. "I need a cigarette." Something to chase off this unfeeling taste in my mouth.

"I didn't know you smoked…" Mina's words came with that familiar 'it's bad for your health, I can't believe you'd do this to yourself' look.

Damn it! "I don't," I sighed. I didn't mean I don't in the same way I don't do heroin or some shit like that; more that I don't do it often or regularly. "I have one here or there." The look faded as though it hadn't actually been there. I could deal without a cigarette for now, I decided. Tesco was nearby and they'd be able to fix me. At the very least it was something to do and

I could do with water and caffeine at the least. "Too bad they don't make caffeinated water," I said, "Just water, caffeine, and nothing else."

"Are you sure you're okay?" Mina came in close, proximity driving me to kiss him.

PDA was not a thing I did. Sometimes fucking, sometimes groping, but this kiss was very much affectionate, so much so that my jeans didn't tighten around my free hanging package.

"Fag?" Tix jogged into view pulling out his trashy pack of crappy budget cigarettes even though everyone knew he could afford the fancy shite.

"You're looking awfully clean," I observed, noting the white t-shirt and flawless jeans, the scent of high-end fur cleaner wafting from his exposed red fur.

"Got picked up," he slurred as he lit his cigarette.

"What'd you do?" The smell of burning tobacco made my stomach rumble.

"Punched one."

"Okay..." I looked at Mina and noticed he had the same puzzled expression on his face as me.

"You know that whole bourgeois MP affluenza shite?" Tix asked, blowing out another cloud as Mina stepped out of the wind. "True."

"Shit."

"They held me in an interrogation until Minister Morris showed up this morning to collect their ungrateful little scion who used his communion dress to burn the rest of his pretty girly dresses. Took a shower, changed, and buggered right off in thanks to the lecture."

"Hey, Tix!" The red squirrel turned around as his name was called.

"Hey, Maryam!" Tix waved over a hyena in a bright rainbow headscarf. "Guys, this is Maryam, Maryam this is Landon and Mina."

She greeted us with a kiss to both cheek. "It's good to meet you," she said with a smile and accent thicker than Mina's. When she retreated from greeting us she stayed close to Tix. They were nearly the same height, but the natural huskiness of hyena blood made her wider.

"What you guys up to?" Tix asked, his arm slipping around Maryam's waist.

"We were heading to the market," Mina answered.

"Yeah, the early hour's eviction really sucked."

"Better that you were there," Tix laughed. "Getting evicted in absentia really sucked. Lost a whole bag of my shit that way."

"There's still time before the pre-pre-march assembly, what are you planning to do?" I asked.

The squirrel looked down to Maryam. "Kentish place, I think."

"See you," I said and they took off. Watching them go, I wondered if she was as good with her tongue as Max. Tix's ass, at least what was visible beyond the bush, swayed fine.

* * *

Mina stayed with me. Through the market run and the little cafe and the used bookstores along Charing Cross, he kept me company. Waters felt a little rocky as they did when a hook up or one night stand hints toward something a little more formal and permanent. I can't say I always ran in those situations, but me and relationships were never too jolly. Usually the younger ones hung around until dismissed without ever really stating their desires or opinions. Older knew to go once shit was done, and they usually retreated right quick. I didn't feel like dismissing Mina mostly because I couldn't deny something was there to make me want to keep him around. Not that I felt he would go, at least not without backfiring my dismissal. He'd say something like 'Why? We're both waiting for the march so why do you want me to go? Having feelings for me causing some problems for you? Can't concentrate?'

Yawning, I sipped my third espresso as Mina and I made our way to assembly point at Torrington Square. The square was one of the feeder spots, situated in the center of the Bloomsbury based collection of universities. Longer than it was wide, schools flanked the park on all sides. We got there a little early and the square was already filling up. Unlike yesterday there was miasma of anger, not a ukulele to be seen.

My hackles bristled with adrenaline as I soaked in the atmosphere. The need to rip something apart with my jaws ground my teeth. Mina appeared more confused or observant than participatory, gazing at the crowd with wide eyes. "This doesn't get your blood moving, your hackles quivering?" I asked as we intermingled with the various organizations. I could see Max to one side with a mobile cradled to her head.

"It's new and honestly kind of scary..."

"Not as much as in Tahrir Square," I answered.

"I wasn't there..."

"You missed out, probably. I can't imagine a people's protest actually causing a revolution."

Mina pulled me to a stop, forcing us eye to eye. "Then why do you do this?" he asked, eyes locked with mine. "If your goal is not revolution, if you do not even believe this has meaning, why do it?"

"Because if I don't, they don't, no one does, the government won't recognize the pain they're causing. They'll assume us compliant and they'll cut shit more and more until none of us can afford a glass of water let alone a degree." I pushed away and continued moving toward Max. Mina fell in step with me, which sort of surprised me. "Max," I called out with a wave. She returned a blank stare as we approached.

"Have you seen Tix anywhere?" she asked, holding the receiver part of the mobile to her paw.

"Not for a few hours." I chose not to spoil her mood more by sharing Tix's new friend.

"Fuck, okay..." Max turned around and went back to talking on the phone. When she finished, she rubbed her rusted furred forehead. "They've locked us out of Parliament Square."

"So, where we going?" I asked.

"At least they didn't pull our permits after last night's shit show." She sighed. "No one has a definitive answer so we're in a holding pattern."

"There's always HQ." Tix slid out of the crowd with the casualness of a summoned ghost. His shirt was a little dirtier and his fur less combed. Max's nostrils flared.

"Where's your friend?" I asked.

"Maryam's hooked up with the Fractionals. Now," he turned to Max, "let's go for Millbank."

"Tix..." Max started, gnawing on her lip, "That's only going to cause more trouble, marching thousands right up to Tory HQ."

The squirrel shrugged. "After last night, I'm out of fucks to care; they kneeled children for hours, arrested, and hospitalized us for speaking up."

"Why do you even plan?" Mina asked, silencing the discussion. "It's clear last night was chaos. Today will be chaos, too. Why not just go with it without a plan?"

"He has a point," Max said, a slight smile forming on her large muzzle. "Whatever we did we're headed the same direction. Just no assaulting royalty or Downing."

Tix and Max set out to talk with the other organizers. Mina and I just perched against a wrought iron gate over a basement access ramp. "You don't have to come you know," I said. Even my words were weird, like I was breaking up with him. Or at least giving him the space to leave me. Instead of leaving or replying he kissed my cheek and pivoted so he had me pinned to the gate.

I became increasingly aware of the lack of underwear on either of us. Brushing the spot warmed by his kiss, he said, "I like being with you."

"Is that it?" I asked, trying to avoid thinking about the bulge I could feel pressing into me. "You don't have to stay here for me." I hooked my fingers into his belt loops, one on either hip.

"No, I want to do this," he said as he pressed his lips to mine.

The crowd grew louder, our numbers starting to burst onto building steps and walls. Mina turned to the crowd, everyone starting to shuffle around as the mass surged forward a few steps. We fell in steps as the pace steadied. Without a real formal organization or banner, we just floated in the mass together in between Maryam's Fractionals for Fair Pay and the SWP student chapter. With no concern for destination we headed at a steady pace toward the Thames, past flats and semi-detached homes, museums and shop windows.

As we came to St. James Park, our only real access to the areas around Parliament, it was clear our numbers were too large. The Met would be panicking. Neon coats ran fast to try and catch the mass before they barreled through the Parliament Square barricades. The main column didn't branch off, and I could guess they were heading for Millbank screaming chants with the power of our voices.

Passing streets aiming to Parliament, we could see the flood of our fellows swarming over fences to take over the green outside the castle. The square wouldn't fit all of us, and the police were rapidly working to block off access with vans and riot gear. Our column skirted Parliament and Westminster as our number shrank and then reinforced with a group from across the Thames. The Millbank Tower grew into view.

Already the Met was focused on trying to contain us. A police van was swarmed and now firmly within our tide. The police were too late. When Mina and I arrived in the concourse outside the tower housing the Conservative Party, the lobby was smashed through, the glass doors and windows shattered. Our chants melded with the crunching of glass under paw.

There was a group on the roof, a series of canvas banners waved from the top of the tower. We craned our necks to see them up there, waving and shouting. I was breathless. My heart pounded, my tail wagged. I squeezed Mina's paw tight. This was the closest I've seen us come to revolution. This was a step beyond trashing police vehicles or destroying property. This was the seat of political power, or at least symbolic.

We weren't getting closer to the lobby. The police were pushing in between the demonstrators reluctant to trespass and the tower, their diverse muzzles covered by riot visors. They poised with their backs to the now empty lobby. Whatever demonstrators had been there had run up to the roof, or were busy ransacking the offices. Shouts echoed from our column. A louder, more raucous and impossible to decipher symphony than last night. They lambasted the government, the education cuts, police culpability and brutality, standard rhetoric inherent in our leftist discourse. I joined in and I think Mina did, but my ears were tuned to the collective.

At some point, Mina extricated his paw from my tight grip. While the natural jostle of the crowd pushed us around, the genet stayed tight to my side, his tail in his paws. It was too late when I noticed we were in the front row, my shouts screaming straight into the row of armored officers. The front row was not the place I wanted Mina to be, not the place I wanted me to be. I was older and had gone through my fair share of daring officers to knock me with a baton. These officers all had their shields planted between us and them, baton drawn in their free paws. Fear hung heavy in the air with a layer of anger.

I reached for Mina's arm to try and fade back into the faceless mob. Usually there were bold and eager protesters all too willing to step on others to get to the front. There was confusion and the row behind me seemed to be trying to get away, and behind them another group was pushing towards us. There was no place to go. If or when they decide to start pushing, shoving, and striking we'd be screwed. Squeezing Mina's arm, I leaned into his ear and said, "We need to move back." The trouble was the only space to move was the two-foot demilitarized zone between us and the batons.

"Don't throw anything!" Someone was screaming over the others.

In earnest, I started moving sideways as I could, careful to not step too close. Step too close and it is a sign of aggression. Inching our way along the front was hard, but not as impossible as trying to push into the too thick current behind us. Then I lost touch with Mina, my grasp failing. The genet stumbled in our awkward shuffle, or was pushed, or jostled, but he fell toward the row of batons and shield ready to strike. I reached for him, but he was too far to grab. The lunge agitated the officers he fell towards. They yelled, "Move Back."

One raised their baton, a fairly small wolf, I could sense their fear. I lunged as the baton came down toward Mina's back and neck. My stomach lurched as the pain sparked in my arm. Paws were grabbing at me as I fell on top of him. Tears burned the side of my face. Something cracked against my he-

* * *

Safe to say I don't remember when I woke up. All I know is that at some point I realized I was awake and in a hospital, although I was told

I had been awake several times before. My arm had already been set and cast, but my concussion was worse than my arm. Of course, my folks came, none too happy. I'd been handcuffed to the bed for the first twelve hours until no charges were filed. Mina met my folks, likely without planning to. I, of course, blissfully unaware between head trauma and drugs.

When thoughts became solid again I was at my parents' place in the outskirts of Reading. Everything I had was in my childhood bedroom with three beds. I required observation and no amount of cajoling would convince my folks otherwise. Effects of the concussion could last a month or more. My arm would need at least that to start to mend with periodic x-Ray checks to make sure the bones were healing as intended.

I was looking at nearly six months of total recovery time, in Reading. So instead of being in the action out in central London and joining in egging the Prince of Wales' Rolls-Royce, I got too busy myself with catching up on six months of law books. After all, even at one class a semester it shouldn't be taking me this long to earn my LL.M, unless I wasn't taking myself seriously. At least my folks took an interest in me after my elder sister moved to Nigeria and changed her name, older brother went in jail for embezzling money and younger trying to balance being a daddy with his sixteen-year-old baby mama and college. Out of the four of us I wondered if I was the biggest disappointment because of their time invested.

So, for six months I spent exiled in Reading. Suburbia. I barely had contact with the outside world. Mina would visit, but Tix and the others would only send a text or something. Of course, my parents loved Mina. Must've been something with his wholesome nature or just how he feels more normal than my normal crowd. My twenty-four-hour date had exploded into a relationship, blown completely past the meet the parents phase, all because I flung myself in front of a police baton. Nothing I regretted, he had more to lose, far more than me.

After progressing well in physical therapy after my cast was removed my half year recovery came to a celebratory end. By celebratory I mean my parents invited Mina together and were leaving us alone for the night. With a sigh, I changed from the comfort footy shorts to a nice pair of stuffy slacks, deflection from parental nagging.

I greeted Mina at the door, an uncomfortable affair made awkward by the presence of my parents. He went for my muzzle and I for his cheek. I blamed the desync on the circumstances. That didn't happen in greeting Mr. and Mrs. Elison. A smile lighting up his diminutive muzzle, he grasped my father's paw and shook with a, "How are you doing, sir?" My ears burned, sir was not an acceptable word in my vocabulary. The hierarchical construction of such honorary speech nauseated me. Mina followed his impeccable manners by embracing my mother and a kiss to the cheek, telling her, "Thank you for inviting me to dinner, ma'am."

It's not like I'm Tix or something, I don't hold my parents in contempt. I respect them; I just don't see them as magically endowed as my parents. Mina was quite striking in his trim, semi-formal dress coat and neatly tied bow-tie. Sitting down to dinner, I wondered if the drugs were still lingering in my system. As I watched Mina laugh and converse with my parents I didn't see the same Mina I did before the hospital. It didn't help that after six months I'd yet to figure out exactly what he was to me. He wouldn't have stuck around for six months of a sexless relationship if he were sticking around just out of obligation.

As Mina helped Mother clear the table, wash the dishes, make the tea, it seemed unknowingly, unwillingly I had a boyfriend.

"Something wrong?" Mina asked in my bedroom a little after my parents left.

I lay on the bed that was too small to share. "Just eager to get back into things," I answered closing my eyes. I flexed my right arm, rotating my wrist, enjoying the freedom.

Mina unbuttoned his shirt. "How are you feeling?" Mina asked. My ears flicked at the sound of his trousers falling, belt and all, to the floor.

"Fine, like I said."

"That's… not quite what I meant." The bed creaked and the mattress shifted, protesting the weight of two adult males more than it cared to handle. "I meant…" Mina slid on top of me, pressing his muzzle to my neck. "It's been half a year, I still owe you for that one night." His hardness pressed against me.

My chest lurched and my stomach somersaulted. "Is that what this is?" I asked, pushing him up. "An obligation for taking a beating?"

Mina drew back, ears flattening to his skull. Settling back on his knees, there was a look in his eyes that made me think back to the time by the fence among the punks and ASBOs that the Tories wasted no time in defusing, starting with our identity. "I-I'm just saying," he stumbled over words, tongue catching on his fangs, "you said it was your turn… and I know you've been drugged up. I thought now would be good…"

I flushed, blood burning my cheeks. "Look, Mina," I said pushing myself up with my arms. My right arm protested at the strain, but Mina's body anchored my legs. "I'm sorry. It's been a long time and being here is driving me crazy." I reached out with my formerly broken arm and brushed his cheek, I rubbed my muzzle along his. "If you want," my voice just above a whisper, "maybe I'm a little pent up." Time, I figured time heals lots of things. I had an attractive younger guy sitting in my lap, asking, begging, me to fuck him. He'd already won the approval of my parents, whatever that is worth. In time, I should heal and feel normal with him.

The genet's arms were strong and warm. He laid me down like I was a glass flower that would shatter if I fell too hard against the mattress beneath us. Mina did not observe the same difference as he assaulted my muzzle. Claws slid up and down my chest beneath my shirt. Memories of how he'd blindsided me on the roof, bending me over and leaving me in the dust as he took me without any sign of thoughts or reservations. Even before his claws trailed over my trousers, I was hard. He pressed and teased over the bulge. Arousal warmed my blood. Mina undid my trousers, pulling the fly as wide as it could open. Sharp teeth plucked at my chin.

My cock ached at Mina's touch. He fished my shaft from my underwear, teasing my foreskin. "Aren't you going to do some prep?" I asked, my hips shifting against his weight.

"I've practiced. Besides—" I hissed as cold liquid spread along my shaft and between my skin and cock tip. "—we have lube this time."

Mina shifted and the bed shuddered. It'd be a miracle if my bed survived this. A decade of a fourteen plus stone African Wild Dog slugging one out once or more a day followed by a decade of rest and almost thirty stone would be rocking the thirty-year-old frame. The entry was hot and tight, but slippery. Mina slid down until his balls and cock pressed against my fur. Hugging him tight, I fought the urge to come, biting into his shoulder. The months of pent up borderline impotence retreating in a flood of eager surges in my abdomen. I came after a few seconds. "Fuck," I sighed, his hips preventing me from moving.

"Oh, God," Mina groaned as he rode the flood of seed.

"I'm sorry," I said as the genet slowed.

"It's so odd," he murmured, sitting up. He rocked on my cock with soft swivels of his hips, stroking his own erect length.

"I couldn't pull out with your thighs locked around me."

"That's... what I wanted," he said between deep breaths. His forehead creased and he closed his eyes. He rubbed his cock against my fur, his stomach flexed and rippled. Ropes of his burning semen shot up my chest and shirt.

My bed survived. Thinking on this little miracle I relaxed, the remnants of my erection fading, still trapped in Mina's tight embrace.

"One more?" Mina asked, wiping his cum covered paw on the sheets.

My cock pulsed at the thought. "I was thinking how great that night was..." I shook my head. "No, I need to pack, but we should do that again."

"Go? Again?" Mina asked. "You're going keep going out there?"

"Why wouldn't I? Why wouldn't you?" I asked, my voice rising. "If we don't fight tuition is going to keep rising. Only the rich offspring of the fucking Tory cunts will be going to school. Our entire educational system will be reduced to some ruling class finishing school mockery!"

The genet got off me, seed seeping down the inside of his thighs. "It's dangerous and fucking terrifying." He hugged himself, keeping his thighs locked together.

I propped myself up on my elbows. "It's necessary. If we don't go out of fear than they'll just keep doing what they're doing and their powers will grow. My friends all believe this, all go..."

"And get arrested, beaten..."

"Okay." I sat up, resting my arms on my knees. "You don't have to go if you don't fucking want to. Does that make you feel better? I was never forcing you to."

"That's not it." Mina's voice crescendoed to match mine. I'd never heard him reach this level.

"What is it, then?" I balled the sheet beside my knees in tight fists.

"You fucking scared me." His eyes were wet and he was breathing hard. "I'm going to go shower," he said, his voice dropping several decibels. Amber eyes lingered on my before he ducked out for the bathroom.

I scared him? As his tail disappeared, snaking behind him on the floor, I was left alone on the bed. Had we a normal relationship I may have followed him into the shower. We weren't normal. Our relationship was a crazy twenty-four hours and then six months of dates like grammar school sweethearts. I rubbed my head. The time since I was hospitalized was a blur of routine, dulled by drugs. No well-formed or defined memories existed. Kisses and movie nights jumbled in my head.

The pipes rattled as Mina turned on the shower. I guess he could've formed a crush as I blew him or something. He didn't exactly need to be crushing on me to bend me over on a rooftop. Maybe that crush, seeded by our experience outside Millbank, had grown into something else while I was recovering?

I looked up at the lame room I grew up in. The posters of a childhood embracing the sweet world of capitalism with fast cars, big tits, and Coca-mother-fucking-Cola. Mina was asking me to give it up. Although, I suppose he only really didn't want me joining the protests. Was that something I could do? Flopping back, I stared up at the sparkling popcorn ceiling. The shower squealed to a stop.

Even dripping, Mina was cute. His fur matted and spiked, his long tail in his paws, too heavy to keep from dragging along the floor.

"So, no more marches?" I asked, swallowing hard. It was worth a shot, I supposed.

It was like he deflated, the sopping wet genet sunk to his knees.

"You're wet and your cum is all over my chest. You collapse and I can't help you."

"Then go take a shower," Mina said, "cunt. And... Landon? I love you."

I brushed his shoulder as I went to shower.

* * *

Everything was okay for awhile. Mina never pushed for an answer after my silence. Can one know what love is anyway? I played the boyfriend, waiting to feel like I imagined he did. We went out together on dates, just the two of us. We fucked one another in turn in my new tiny studio flat. We even hung out with Tix and my old crew despite my retreat from the active duty roster of ASBOs. Although Tix was an asshole about it at first, he eventually stopped most of his belligerent badgering, but only after I assured him Tories were scum and I wasn't about to go join the might neoliberal forces of the grandmaster Capitalism.

Everything should be perfect, but it wasn't. There was something haunting me. My heart would race with anxiety when Mina and I shared a bed, wondering if he was enjoying it, and if I enjoyed it. Nothing compared to the first span of time we spent together. At least not for me, but I was anxious that he didn't feel the same. Our desync seemed utterly complete.

"What's wrong?" Mina asked as we sat in some odd art-nouveau restaurant.

The number of times he'd asked that question over the last few weeks was uncountable. The answer was already prepared and on the tip of my tongue, but I froze it was a long sip of ice water. "Nothing, just tired I guess." I stirred the ice around in my glass.

Mina dabbed the side of his muzzle with his white linen napkin. His eyes were down on his empty plate. I waited, expecting some acknowledgment, or even an argument from his slanted posture. Nothing, though. No push, just silence.

"So, have anything in mind for after dinner?" I asked, resting my silverware on my plate with a small clink of metal on china. Maybe a shift in topic could push us out of this envelope of awkward silence. That wasn't how we were supposed to be, right?

Mina's whiskers twitched and he looked up with just his eyes. "We could... try a club or something?"

"Which one?" There weren't too many left. There were almost as many bathhouses in London as good queer clubs; a testament to the priorities of sex over parties. The ones I frequented in the past had shuttered from years of rising rents and housing inflation, and with the queers finding greater acceptance in conventional clubs and pubs meant they didn't have to be bothered by loud drunken drag queens anymore.

The genet looked down at his plate again, stirring the saucy remnants of his meal with a knife. He usually was more chipper. All I could think was this was me, I was bringing him down. "Want to try—" I leaned in, wanting to whisper the rest. "—taking me to a bathhouse?"

His tail swayed, peeking up from beneath the table. Even his ears perked up. I'd reasoned the atmosphere of a bathhouse might beat both of our moods. I for one did not enjoy the dour feeling that seemed to be internalized within me for the last several months. Interrupting the routine with the variables of sex and encounters should do something. Sitting back, I said, "Guess you're interested, then?"

"It… could be fun," he said after a moment, his ears flicked. "I… umm… that's how I practiced, during your recovery…" His eyes shifted to the side.

I shrugged. "Ready to go?" I asked.

"That's it?"

I nodded. "I blew you after meeting you for like five minutes, you really think my moral compass is that disparate that I would object to you going and playing around?" I had never considered any sort of relationship I had ever been in as conservative monogamy. Us, sitting there in the restaurant, the scene was unnerving.

Mina led under my request, with his greater knowledge of the scene we were entering. It was early afternoon in the middle of the week, an off-peak time for most traffic. As we arranged entrance I wondered if this had already contributed to making things better. We never really discussed or set parameters, never communicated our views on relationships. It very well could be a fuck up that we didn't need to live with for over half a year. Mina certainly seemed excited, a little more than I'd seen recently. His ears were erect and his tail bounced with the graceful, exaggerated sway of his hips. If the prospect of public sex potentially involving strangers motivated him, maybe I would finally feel the same as him. After all, it's not like I was private before, blowing Mina in an open office was hardly my first bit of passive exhibitionism.

Crossing my fingers, I wished for the experience to work as I followed Mina's long tail through the maze-like hallway in a west London bathhouse. It was quiet, which was a mixed bag for excitement and comfort. We were doing, well I was doing this, hoping for a thrill, a shock, and that required participants and witnesses. I adjusted the thin towel wrapped uncomfortably tight around my waist, present more out of erotic decorum than practicality. The lights were cheesily dim.

Mina led me to the showers, a large open wet room, and perfect for public shows. When he turned the shower on, he started his show. It was clear with how exacting his paws moved with his hips and swaying tail he was into this for more than just washing. He was here to give a show even if just one elderly elk and I were here. As paws slid from his abdomen to my hip and down around beneath my tail, I was pulled into his sensual dance of soap and water. He enjoyed this, far more than he enjoyed the blowjob in the office with the door open. This space was special, where acts of sexual openness were encouraged rather than punished. Here he showed no reservations about himself or his sexuality, no problem with sliding a finger up my bum as he kissed my neck. As skillful as ever, his touch was arousing, but the spark wasn't igniting yet.

Gay bathhouses function primarily as a place for hooking up for sex. No worry for lost connections or mixed signals. It was a safe place for bonding outside the realm of homophobia. Mina showed me the meatheads' gym, little better than a cheap hotel's. There was also a sauna and steam room, cafe and hot tub, and a host of specifically sexual spaces. Mina assured me we would enjoy most of what was on offer with a playfulness that belied the last few weeks.

Sweating in the sauna resulted in unflattering fur conditions. We were both bred for sweltering temperatures, although I was born with longer fur than my native African cousins. The Asiatic lion who joined didn't seem to mind. Sex in the heat seemed almost absurd. Nevertheless, the chubby lion toyed with himself when he walked in after us. His eyes were drawn into thin slits darting from me to Mina and back again.

Mina opened his legs inviting him over with a nod. The lion knelt and nuzzled into his fuzzy balls, likely sweating as much as mine. I observed the genet, trying to get a handle on how communication and the scene worked. In turn, Mina gripped my thigh, the lion lapping at his hardening shaft. His paw sank into my lap, gripping my soft cock moist with sweat. Taking the hint, I spread my legs and the lion found his way to mine. He switched between us, and pulled one hind paw from each of us into his lap. The heat of his cock was more than apparent. This lasted until the heat became too much.

Gasping we sought out water for our dry muzzles and a cold show, our nameless friend disappeared into a dark tunnel along the way. Sex in a sauna was indeed a chore, and likely impossible for any northern species not used to the dry heat. I was starting to get into it. My hard-on persisted through the cold shower and into the hot tub.

Flanked by two slim Thai felines, it wasn't long before our laps were occupied. They looked identical, but they assured us it was only coincidence, their accents differed significantly. Mine purred higher than the other, almost squeaking when my cock pulsed against his hole from the thought of Mina and I taking the "brothers" in tandem. They bid us goodbye before long, their slim erections bobbing as they climbed dripping from the water to follow a well-endowed wolf to the showers.

"It's not always like this," Mina said, floating onto my lap until my pointed shaft was pressed against his. "When it's crowded, things tend to happen less." He shifted rising until his uncut tip pierced the surface and my cock pressed against his hole. "But those times, when things happen they really happen." He sank down a centimeter and then launched himself up and forward. Genet cock bobbed in front of muzzle, the length glistening from water and the viscous pre leaking from his tip.

Leading me into the steam room we were greeted by a huge Arabian horse. He eyed me up with an aggressive stare. My legs squeezed shut at the sight of a broad-shouldered horse, at least seven feet tall, with a cock that looked large on him. After a minute of him gazing at me, he asked me to bend over. The request came off as a demand and I stood up and moved to leave, but Mina insisted I stay. My heart stopped as the horse approached my rear. I scrunched my eyes, bracing myself against Mina. His whiskers bristled against my cheek. The horse pushed my legs apart forcing one up onto the bench. I then received the best tongue bath of all time. As long fingers gripped the cheeks of my ass holding them apart to expose my hole, his tongue snaked all around and in my hole. The experience was overwhelming, my hard cock spurted a loads worth of precum. Still, I found myself slipping out of the experience, there wasn't a spark of spiritual pleasure grounding me in the physicality of this.

Mina, cradling my head, provided an emotional connection. He was fantastic about it, stroking my ears and braids as I sucked his cock in the humid steam, providing both emotional and physical pleasure. Something still felt empty that constantly had me slipping in and out of our time together. Later, when he slid into me in the dark room, flanked by a number of faceless others, it felt good. I couldn't deny the amount of arousal we'd shared. It blew almost everything we'd done recently out of the water. The pleasure was pure, nothing I could imagine was purer. When I finally came, I did not feel the same as that first day. As Mina pounded into me, muzzle full of some fennec's cock, I held what I could of him and cried.

* * *

I didn't tell my parents about the break up. It was easier to just dump everything and disappear. Our relationship had gone on as long as it could. A few days beyond the bathhouse and I couldn't justify staying. Of course, my parents probably knew about it already. They probably invited Mina to dinner. They'd always been very supportive in that way. Rather than dwell on the absence in my life, I skipped out on my studio flat with one bag of my books and one bag of clothing.

Tix had moved from his old squat in Kentish Town to a partially finished old factory conversion, the project abandoned in the recession. I moved in with him and his transient artist friends. He and Max were on friendlier terms and seemed equally taken with Maryam. There were nights of music, bathtub gin, pot, and cheap cigarettes. Midst the queer artists, the dirt grime lifestyle of living in a building we had every right to, but no legal recognition, felt more like home than ever.

In our fight, the last one we'd had, Mina asked, his voice drowning in quivering anger, "What's the point? If you torch everything, what happens? What do you do when you win?"

There is no winning, if we win we also lose. With Tix and Max and all the rest I felt that was implicitly understood, the bond we recognized in one another. Mina repressed or locked away that spark. I'd seen it that night, but no amount of love, romance, or physical pleasure would substitute. That small period I'd felt a spark, but the cops arrested and defused it before it ignited.

I didn't sleep the first few nights. Shitty gin and cigarettes with little food can only knock me out so many times. Instead I just stared up at the lights of London reflecting through the negligent skylights. I had a pack of Tix's cigarettes beside me, nothing or no one to stop me. I could smoke one stick or a whole pack. One night the squirrel joined me, setting out his paints and makeshift canvas and easel.

"How are you? He asked, laying out brushes and paint tubes.

"You know." I sighed and lay down on the rough cement floor.

The silence sang and we focused our attentions on our individual activities, mine to fight the futile search for stars.

"I was hoping you'd come back," Tix said, looking up from his canvas. "I missed having you around." He switched brushes, the scent of paint growing in the room. "Wasn't the same."

"No," I agreed. "Can we talk about something else?" The ragged metal roof, rebar jutting from crumbling concrete, as desecrated as it was here, it was a welcome change. The aesthetic was perfect.

"Gonna stick around?" Tix threw the brush against the canvas, splashing color just out of sight.

"Yeah, not planning on running anywhere just yet," I answer, running my thumb along my claws of either paw.

"Well there's a PLO and JVP march coming up if you fancy. Shouldn't be as hot as last time."

I laughed, but cringed at the memory, "Only if you take the hit instead."

"Sorry..." Tix started, his voice faltering. "I thought you were cute together. Sucks it didn't work out."

"Tix..."

Tix put down his brush, tail twitching in the air. "Sorry, Landon." With a sigh, he crawled off his concrete bench and lay down beside me, his head by my hind paws.

"How're the girls?" I asked.

"Seems like they like each other just a bit more than they like me."

"Welcome to the patriarchy," I joked.

"It's sexist jokes like that which contribute to your boys only club."

"Sarcasm."

"A lot of it," Tix pushed himself up on his elbows. "Pass the fags?"

I tossed the pack to the squirrel and we both settled on our backs again. The familiar scent of shit cheap tobacco started a few moments later mixing with the acetonic paint fumes. "You have a nice ass."

Tix coughed, a large pool of dark smoke expelled from his throat, but succeeded on the next drag.

"Figured I should share," I said, "Mina... Mina agreed."

"Well I'd fucking hope so. Glad to know my ass is highly appreciated."

"Seriously though—"

"Be careful with how you continue," Tix interrupted.

"Just saying. Anyway, best sex I ever had was Mina fucking my brains out on this random rooftop the night of the children's crusade."

Tix grunted and shuffled beside me. "That sounds hot."

I tilted my head, but Tix was just casually sucking on his cigarette. The squirrel had this habit of ambivalent tones, obscuring his true intentions. "It was, fancy a turn?" I asked, but his shoulders arched in a shrug.

"Maybe, if Max and Maryam are fine with it. Just the right time and place."

"Serious?" This conversation was going unexpected places. I wanted a cigarette. "Thought you stuck to the ladies..." I adjusted myself in my jeans.

"Paws up!" Tix commanded.

"Come on, it's normal for guys to jerk off together."

"Landon Elison, don't lecture me on what guys do or do not do together. Sitting in a circle jerk is not every guy's idea of a good time."

"Throw me the cigarettes. And a lighter."

"You took my cigarettes and not a lighter?" Tix chastised as he tossed the pack and a lighter in a small arc.

"Don't tease," I said, lighting one of his budget cigarettes. "If you aren't serious and get me riled up I'll have to go take care of it all by myself."

"Heaven forbid the recently single faggot would have to go take care of anything himself. There plenty of big cocks and tights asses out there to get your rocks off with," Tix flicked his cigarette away.

I contemplated me and Tix, allowing my cigarette to burn until ash fell down my paw. "Which M is better?"

"A gentleman doesn't answer questions about his ladies." Tix sat up and stretched his legs. "For the record, me."

"That is the most democratic answer."

"Fuck. This shitty gin has been getting to me. I could go for some nice shit." He jumped up and started pacing between me and his paints.

"And where does one get a bottle of gin at this hour?" I asked, rolling to my side.

"There's my folks' flat in Fitzrovia. They can't possibly drink enough to empty their spare house of liquor."

"It would be nice, in the least," I answered. Shuffling to my feet, my spent cigarette joined Tix's on the ground covered in concrete dust.

I waited outside, Tix taking a moment to talk to Maryam before taking off into the night. Fitzrovia was an hour walk through quiet streets and over the Thames. Tix had grabbed a spliff from Max and we partook to make the miles seem less daunting.

With the tingly sensation of THC and tobacco bubbling in our veins our tongues vibrated. Tix's parents just didn't have a flat in Fitzrovia, they had a bleeding building. When we arrived, I'd expected Tix to pull out a set of keys, or pick up an idiotic rock with a key taped to the bottom. Instead he sprinted at the wrought iron gate locking off the rear garden access. He clambered over it with enough clanging the whole neighborhood would wake up, if anyone actually lived in the land of million dollar flats. "Give me ten minutes, walk around the block or something," he said through the bars.

I shrugged, "And then?"

"Knock or something." The red tail flitted down to the dark alley until he disappeared.

A quick walk around the block wasn't much, certainly better than a grungy African Wild Dog standing outside a fancy flat owned by a conservative MP. Not by much. Despite my inherited privilege, it was nothing in the eyes of this crust.

Completing my circuit, I knocked on the door, my knuckles producing nothing but dead silence in the faux wood reinforced iron. The door opened slowly with a hydraulic hiss. Tix's porcelain white teeth glinted in a crooked smile. Imagining the tiny squirrel trying to move the bomb proof door was a quest of absurdity.

I followed him through rooms and halls of overindulgent Tory excesses, wishing I could just reach out and smash the ornate vases on carved solid mahogany tables beneath gold gilded mirrors with perfect roses, lilies, or carnations. A wet bar straddled the living room and a large sun room enclosed completely in glass with a little 8' by 8' courtyard in the middle. That door was open. Tix had climbed up the side of the glass room and walked on the ceiling to the courtyard. Smudges covered his point of entrance. "Why not the chimney?" I asked.

"Fucking scotch, scotch, whiskey, vodka... an African Wild Cunt..." Glass clinked as Tix thumbed through his parents untouched collection. "Here!" His hand retreated with a tall, skinny bottle, popping the sealed cork. "Cheers." Tix tipped the bottle to his muzzle and held it for a healthy amount of time, air bubbles erupting as the bottle became less than full.

"Don't hog all the gin," I said, holding out a paw. "Shouldn't we think about leaving?"

Tix passed the bottle to me and I took a sip, followed by a long drink. I don't care what anybody says, even fancy gin offended my tongue.

"First a thank you for my parents and their offerings." Tix was back fingering through bottles until he found a bottle of seventy proof bourbon. "For their American friends." The squirrel grabbed all the towels and tossed them in the sink. He tilted the bottle into the sink, the amber colored liquid seeping into the fabric, filling the air with a surprisingly sweet burning alcohol scent.

"You're not..."

In response Tix pulled out a lighter as he let the emptied bottle shatter in the sink. "Won't be much, but at least a wakeup call, EU kitchen safety standards." He lit the alcohol soaked rags.

They wouldn't burn long and the stainless steel and stone left nothing for the flames to jump to. "Now we should be leaving," I said, heading for the front door with our prize gin bottle.

Tix tarried behind, watching the flames lick the sides of sink. It took the alarms a few moments to detect the burning alcohol and then Tix joined me at the front door. I fumbled with the door until Tix worked his magic and it hissed open. We bolted out into the street, the door swinging closed behind us. The squirrel was laughing. He ripped the bottle of gin from my grip downing several ounces in one go. "It's not London, but it's something," he commented, wiping his gin moistened muzzle across the back of his paw.

"Fancy burning it all?"

"Only if I'm there in the middle of it all with the best view," Tix pulled out a cigarette, tossing the gin back to me.

"Save me a seat?"

"Or you could just be my seat. You're big enough."

"As long as you aren't offended when I react to a cute boy in my lap."

"You can count on it, and my punishment will be swift."

My ears picked up the siren before the flickering lights appeared behind us. Tix turned back and looked, his cigarette hanging lopsided out of his smiling muzzle. His paws were shoved deep in his trouser pockets. Blood pumped to my groin. The combination of chemicals rushing various hormones through my nerves. "Gin."

"Please?"

"Cunt."

Tix held the bottle just out of my grasp. "You did ask politely."

Grabbing Tix, the squirrel couldn't escape and his shorter arms couldn't prevent me from grabbing the bottle. But then he kissed me. We found a small alley, the kind that leads to the rear gardens of different houses. Unlit and out of the way I fiddled with my jeans, Tix with his. I drank more of the botanical liquor. Tix climbed onto me, claws digging into my sides and shoulders as the agile squirrel wrapped his legs around my waist. "Max and Maryam okay with this?" I asked, shivering as my length slid along the light squirrel.

"They'd want to watch." Tix kissed me, my tongue picking up the bitter sweet aftertaste of gin and cigarettes. His fur had traces of burnt bourbon.

I pressed into him, his hips and paw guiding me. His back pressed into the wood fence attached to the brick stone wall. Tix nursed the bottle of gin in between moans and kisses and bites, sharing the gin with me. My stomach burned, balls aching. "Fuck," Tix grunted, throwing the half-spent bottle down the alley. The glass exploded on impact.

With paws freed, Tix shoved himself against me. His body rocked, the compact muscle of the tiny climber flexing as his hips rose with ease and speed. "Next time, you're on bottom," he breathed into my cheek.

My tail wagged at the prospect of a next time, insides already starting to twist and tighten. "I'm always ready." I bit his ear and grabbed a bony shoulder, pushing against his thrusts, flattening him to the wall.

Tix gripped me, claws prickling along my back as he slammed against me. Chest heaving, fur damp from sweating, his gasps beat like his thundering heart in my ears. Our voices crescendo, anyone around would be able to hear or smell our combined intimacies if their windows were opened.

The walls around my length spasmed. "Fuck," Tix grunted, teeth grinding as his essence flooded the space between us. "Fucking cum, you bitch." He gnawed on my chin. "And you better clean up your own mess."

With the stamina greater than any power bottom I'd ever seen, the squirrel rocked through his orgasm. Thirst hit my tongue, a moment of remorse for the wasted gin. I detached Tix from chin and sucked at his muzzle. My load sprayed into his passage so hard my muscles clenched painfully tight. His thrusting rocked to a slow, relaxed pattern.

"That was fun," he gasped. "Now to get you up to speed in linguistics." He gripped what bit of my shaft was exposed, covered in the mixture of our fluids and raised his paw to muzzle level. My first taste of a new language. We tasted of fire.

Cause No Trouble

by NightEyes DaySpring

The sound of the door to the integration room opening caused Ivan to look up. The military police officer who had arrested him came in. Even though they were inside, the officer still wore his greatcoat.

"Let's get started," said the husky sitting down, placing a manila folder in front of him. "These are yours?" the husky asked, pointing to the set of books placed on the table along with the rest of the contents of Ivan's bag. The officer smiled, an amused expression on his muzzle as he waited for the snow leopard's response.

Ivan felt his stomach twist in knots. If he denied he purchased the contraband, it would incite deep suspicion; the books had been in his bag when he was stopped. Even if he was able to talk his way out of this, the government would monitor him carefully from now on. To claim them would instead bring immediate condemnation, but he might be able to explain it away as a moment of weakness.

"Yes," he said finally.

The husky smirked and quirked up an eyebrow. "You do know these are outlawed, yes? Such capitalist propaganda is not allowed in this country, citizen."

The two children's books were popular overseas, but unknown here. They could possibly be dangerous to the glorious state of Klechnia, but that felt silly. The book on macroeconomics, that Ivan understood as being dangerous. It challenged the prevailing economic theories of this worker's paradise.

"I bought them in a local bookstore," lied Ivan.

"Do you take me for a fool?" laughed the husky. "You either bought them on the black market, or you smuggled them into the country."

The snow leopard felt his ears sink. "I meant no harm."

The husky picked up the children's book and flipped it open. He pointed to one of the pictures showing smiling people in front of a Republic shopping mall. "This blinds our children to the dangers of conspicuous consumption, citizen." He pointed to the economics textbook. "And this claims that the failed economic theories of our enemies are the way to prosperity."

"They're just books," grumbled Ivan. "I'm a sociologist professor. Are we not to think anymore in this country?"

The husky leaned back in his chair and steepled his fingers. "I could have you locked up for saying something like that. Our glorious nation does not tolerate such blatant disrespect of the law."

Ivan had really fucked up. It wasn't the first time the police had caught him with illicit material from overseas. Now they were going to lock him away. "Sorry," he mumbled.

The husky picked up the books and tossed them back into the backpack, along with some of Ivan's notes and a cookbook. The cookbook was probably the only benign thing in the bag that was inoffensive to the state. "You are in deep trouble, friend."

If he was in one of the countries the books came from, now would be the time to ask for a lawyer. There would be no lawyer here.

The husky leaned forward and dropped his voice. "I am willing to overlook such a transgression for a small donation to the well-being of the state."

Of course. First came the demand for a bribe. Even if he could pay it, he might not be allowed to go and instead be charged for trying to bribe a military police officer. "How—how much?" mumbled Ivan. Maybe if he paid the bribe, he could still get out of this.

"Two hundred credits."

His hope fell away. "I make only one hundred fifty credits a month. I can't pay you that."

"I can send you to a gulag, or you can pay two hundred credits."

"I don't have two hundred credits," whispered Ivan. "I don't even have a hundred credits right now."

The husky frowned. "That is very unfortunate for you."

Who had two hundred credits? The husky probably only made a hundred credits a month himself with his food stipend. This was it for Ivan. They were finally going to put him away.

"Yeah," he replied.

The husky picked up the folder and flipped through it. "It seems the secret police have been aware of your activities for quite a while." He glanced back at Ivan. "If I send you away, you aren't going to come back. Perhaps we can make a deal."

"I can give you twenty-five credits now and another twenty-five next month."

The husky shook his head. "No, citizen, I have something else in mind of you."

Shit. If the guard didn't want money, what could Ivan give him? "What?" Ivan's voice was dry.

The husky put the folder down in front of Ivan and pointed to a line in the file. The snow leopard glanced at the sheet. His ID photo looked up at him. Below was his address, known associates, and a brief description of his activities including the phrase 'known intellectual dissident.' Below that, in clear black ink, was the phrase 'practicing homosexual', and the husky tapped his finger next to it.

"You want me to have sex with you?" gagged the snow leopard.

The husky shook his head. "I want you to get me into the Violet Connection."

Ivan opened his muzzle and then closed it. "And if I don't, you send me to the gulags?"

The guard took back the folder. "You should be more careful when you buy capitalistic propaganda."

"Why?" asked Ivan. "Two hundred credits is steep, but I get that. Find the money, and I get to go free. But the Violet Connection? You guys have to know where it is, and if you wanted to raid the Violet Connection, why not just raid the damn thing?"

The husky leaned forward, making his voice dark and menacing. "Because, citizen, some of us need an in for ourselves. You aren't the only one with something to hide. I know you don't have two hundred credits."

Lord, tonight was just getting worse. Now he had one of *those* on his hands. "Fine," he said defeated, "but I need you to look the part."

"That," said the husky stiffly, "won't be a problem."

* * *

Ivan sat in his little flat looking at the clock on the wall. Scattered on the table was a collection of contraband books along with clean, government approved editions of similar books. He probably should put everything back into his hiding space, but that seemed pointless right now. The secret police already knew he was a trouble maker, so if they wanted him to go away, they could just do that. In a way, knowing they knew helped roll back the stress built up over years of discrete activity on his part.

He sighed and waited until the clock struck 9:55 before he got up from the chair. The snow leopard didn't feel like going out, but what choice did he have? It was time for Ivan to go and sell out his friends.

He had traded his normal boring clothing for something sportier: a green vest over his spotted fur, and a pair of brown pants. Underneath, he wore a pair of hot pink underwear. The fact he even owned a pair of hot pink underwear was amazing in itself. He made sure to wash them at home and not in the communal laundry room of his apartment block.

Ivan jabbed his keys into his pocket and threw on a nondescript jacket. He closed the door to his unit, locked it, and walked down the hall to the stairs. The snow leopard had agreed to meet the husky at a location a short fifteen minute walk from his place. It was a tree lined street through older apartment blocks. In the back of his mind it seemed like too nice and quiet a street for a random disappearance. Maybe that had been why the husky chose it.

Upon reaching the street, he saw it was deserted except for a lone figure under a street light. Ivan hesitated for a moment, before he walked down the street toward the figure. There under the light was the military guard, and he certainly looked the part of the practicing homosexual. The husky had traded in his uniform for a pair of tight pants, and a low-cut shirt to show off his chest fluff. The spiked collar at his neck, and the matching band of leather at the base his tail certainly suggested a specific preference. The whole thing looked completely out of place and Ivan faltered for a moment before he forced himself to keep walking.

"Is this good?" asked the husky, as Ivan approached. "And you are not dressed?" he added, looking at Ivan's drab clothing.

"You look like a gay street walker," said the snow leopard. "Where did you even get a collar like that?"

The husky grunted. "I have my sources," He fidgeted. "Is this too much?"

Ivan breathed in. "It's fine, it will though get you some attention. It's also not very discrete for traveling."

"I know, but you said I should look the part."

Ivan pulled off his coat and handed it to him. "Put this on, and take that collar off. You can put that on when we get inside."

Reluctantly, the husky took off the collar and the tail band. "Do you like it at least? I saw it in a gay fashion magazine."

No Klechnia magazine would suggest such bold clothing. The government promoted a modest life for all citizens. The implication that the husky had seen it in a contraband gay fashion magazine hung out there. Ivan didn't need to ask if it was contraband. He knew. He'd seen some of

140

the same magazines before. "Since we're going to do this, do you have a name I can at least call you?"

"Nikolai."

"Okay, Nikolai." He looked at the dog. His tail was curled up, and he looked ready to follow Ivan wherever he took him. The whole appearance of the guard he met yesterday in this outfit threw Ivan off kilter. "Have you ever been to a gay club before?"

The dog bobbed his head. "I have gone to the Boot and Glove a few times. I find it rather sterile."

The Boot and Glove was the government sanctioned gay bar downtown. The best way Ivan could describe it was safe. It didn't play exciting music, the drinks were not very strong, and it just was a drab place in general. Ivan had never been able to shake the impression that the government maintained it as an easy way to fill out files on people. Now he was pretty sure his visits got him marked.

"Well, this isn't like that. It's much livelier," remarked Ivan.

The husky smiled, flashing his fangs. "So I hear. They say you can actually have sex in the back!" he said, with a laugh.

God, maybe he should have lied about the credits and turned some tricks for the bribe. It probably would have been easier. "Yeah, that's not really appreciated."

"Oh," the dog replied. "I won't cause any problems then."

Ivan just started walking down the street, and the dog followed him in step. There wasn't much point in talking. He just needed to get the dog in, get him a card, and once the husky got himself occupied, he could slip out of the club and return home. If there was going to be a raid tonight, he at least hoped he could get out of there before the police came. He wasn't sure if he would ever be able to forgive himself for selling out the Violet Connection, but what choice did he have?

"You know, I thought about wearing a nice skirt tonight, but I thought that might be too flamboyant."

The snow leopard stopped walking and turned to his charge. "You what?" he said, staring at the dog.

"I thought about wearing a skirt."

"Are you fucking daft!"

"Daft?" asked the husky confused.

Ivan growled and got close to the dog. "I don't know what sick game you think this is, but these are my friends you are asking me to sell out for my own freedom. Yes, I need you to act gay, but you don't need to be an effeminate mess."

The dog lowered his ears. "You think I asked you to do this just to report where the club is to my superiors?"

"That or you were charged with building a case on me."

Nikolai huffed and his blue eyes hardened. "It doesn't occur to you that maybe I want to go for my own reasons?"

"You tried to extort money from me. Why wouldn't this be different?"

The dog opened his muzzle and shut it. "I can see your logic, but I didn't ask so I could hold this over your head."

"No, you demanded."

His ears fell. "You're right. I did." He glanced off to think for a moment. "I've wanted to go for a while, but you need a friend to get into the Violet Connection."

"You really think that forcing me to take you to an underground club so I don't have to go rot in a gulag is going to make you a friend?" snarled the snow leopard.

The husky growled, fur standing up. "Stand down, citizen."

Ivan flashed all his fangs, inches from the dog's muzzle, angry. "Or what? You'll arrest me?"

"You will get us both discovered if you keep shouting."

Ivan glanced around. The street still looked to be deserted, but you could never be sure. He hadn't checked to see if someone had been following them; someone could be hiding just out of sight. "Are you afraid, dog? Afraid that your little secret will be entered into your official profile like mine is? They like to target our kind for extra surveillance. They're afraid we'll easily succumb to the excesses from overseas. All this is your doing. You're the one who wore a collar out in public. You're the one who set this up. I'm just your pawn."

The husky sneered and pushed Ivan away. "I know what happens to people who've tested the patience of the state. I don't want to cause any trouble. Everyone I meet at the Boot and Glove gives me a wide berth since I'm military, and there aren't many young people who go there anyway. I'd like to at least taste the feeling of freedom when they aren't watching."

"How do I know you are truly gay and not some mole?" Ivan asked icily.

The dog frowned and consciously smoothed down his raised hackles "The clothing isn't enough for you?"

"Anyone could wear it."

The dog exhaled. "What would convince you?"

Ivan glanced around. "Come," he said, and he started walking down the street. After passing an apartment building, he found what he wanted, and he entered a dark alley between two buildings. The husky followed him apprehensively. Once they were in the safety of the alley, Ivan turned and faced his tormenter.

"On your knees," he ordered.

"My knees?"

The snow leopard nodded. "On your knees."

Slowly the dog knelt down. He looked up at Ivan confused, and Ivan walked up to him.

"You are going to show me how gay you are."

"Excuse me?" barked the dog, confused.

"You heard me. You want to go to the club, and hook up, yes? You can hook up right now. Consider it a prequel to what you'll experience at the Violet Connection."

The dog laid his ears back. With shaking paws he reached up to unzip Ivan's pants.

"You aren't going to play with yourself?"

Nikolai paused and then lowered his hands to unzip his own fly and pulled out his sheath. He then reached up and fumbled with Ivan's zipper, leaving one hand on his own shaft. Ivan's pink underwear stood out against his white and gray fur. The husky glanced up at him and then focused his eyes on the bulge in front of him. He pulled down the elastic to expose the sheathed shaft.

"That's enough," said Ivan.

The dog looked up at him confused. "You... you don't want me to service you?"

The snow leopard let out the breath he was holding. "I just wanted to see if you were willing to go through with it. I will take you to the Violet Connection."

A wave of confusion washed over the husky as he got up and dusted his knees off. He tucked his shaft back into his pants, and then zipped up. He looked at Ivan, and they both appraised each other.

"Okay," Nikolai said, after a minute. "Lead on."

* * *

Walking through the city, they passed a number of people. Everyone kept their heads down and refused to make eye contact. After dark, no one met your eye. It was easier to just keep going so you wouldn't have to ever answer questions. When a convoy of military vehicles passed them, Ivan observed the tension in Nikolai's tail. The husky pulled Ivan's coat tighter around himself, trying to sink behind the collar. Those responses helped ease some of the nagging thoughts in Ivan's mind.

Now at their destination, a street that ran past an old, deserted warehouse, this would be the moment of truth. Ivan didn't bother to check the time, but with how far they walked, he knew it was a little before 11.

"We're here," remarked the snow leopard.

Nikolai looked up and down the street, then at the darkened, nondescript warehouse. "There is no one here at all."

"They're here," said Ivan. "Put your collar on and give me my jacket back."

The husky took off Ivan's jacket and handed it back to him, which Ivan draped over an arm while the husky fitted the spiked collar at his neck and the piece back on his tail base. After they preened, Ivan walked over to a small door next to a big roll-up doorway and pushed a buzzer.

They waited, and after a minute a small panel slid open. A pair of golden canine eyes peered out at them. "We don't take deliveries after hours."

Ivan pulled out a card and held it up so the person behind the door could see it. "We aren't making a delivery," he said.

"And your name?" asked the pair of eyes.

"Ivan Dessel and a friend."

The pair of eyes shifted to look at Nikolai. "Is he clean?"

"Yes," said Ivan, fidgeting with the keys in his pocket.

The panel slid shut and they heard the sound of a bolt being pulled back. The door cracked open and they slipped inside. The room beyond the door was almost completely dark except for a light in the back.

The wolf who opened the door closed it, then turned to give them a look over in the dim light. "What's your name?" he asked the dog.

"Nikolai."

"Full name," demanded the wolf.

The dog shifted his weight. "Nikolai Petrov."

"Do you know where you are?" the wolf asked. He wore a serious expression made more menacing from the darkness.

"Yes," said the dog.

"I don't want any trouble from you, and if anyone asks, you were never here. Until we trust you, don't ever come back here without Ivan. Understood?"

The husky nodded. "Yes."

"Talk about this to the wrong person, and we will all be in danger. We police our own, so we will be watching. Now, go enjoy yourself," he said pointing to the stairs at the back of the room leading toward the basement.

"Thanks," said the snow leopard, heading toward the stairs with the dog in tow.

Once they descended to the building's basement, the dog asked, "What's on the card?"

Ivan pulled it out of a pocket and handed it to him. One side was violet and the other was white.

"I don't understand. There's nothing on it," he whispered, following Ivan toward a large metal door in the back of the basement.

"Exactly," grinned Ivan, taking the card back. "That's the entire point."

He pulled at the heavy door, causing it to creak as it rolled partially open. A ramp continued heading down; the sound of music filtered up to them.

They stepped through the door and Ivan pulled it closed from the inside.

"We're here," Ivan said.

"That wasn't too bad," said the dog. "I expected more security."

"Oh there is. That's just all you're going to see. Come," he remarked, walking down the slopped passageway, his feet echoing down the hall. With each step they took, the music became clearer and louder. A thumping base reverberated off the brick.

The passageway opened into a large underground chamber, filled with lights and people. The sweet tang of excitement filled the air, along with a subtler scent of arousal.

"Wow," the husky said, staring in awe. "This is amazing." He grinned, tail wagging.

The dance floor sat on one side of the room, while on the other side, a long bar ran the entire length of the wall. Light reflected around the arched brick supports, and people of all sorts danced or milled about. The music wasn't overpowering, but it was opulent and crystal clear. A song Ivan had never heard before played. Based on the style, he could tell it had been produced oversees.

The crowd was pretty good tonight; wolves, bears, foxes, wolverines, lynxes, and snow leopards danced, both male and female. Some wore plain Klechin clothes, but many sported bright, imported clothing. Glow sticks shone in the low light like beacons upon the sea. Ivan glanced at Nikolai. His eyes were bright, taking in the sight. He let himself relax. Nikolai truly seemed enthralled by the whole experience.

"Happy?" asked Ivan over the music.

"This is unlike anything I have dreamed of. It's beautiful," he excitedly responded. "I can't thank you enough."

"I just don't want any problems. I'll see what I can do to get you a card, and once we work that out, I think it's best we part ways."

"I… yeah. I understand. Can I buy you a drink at least for the trouble?"

The snow leopard flicked his tail. "Sure."

They dropped off Ivan's coat in the front before heading to get drinks. The full-length bar was stocked unlike any other bar in Klechnia Ivan had ever been too. The Violet Connection sold all the locally produced vodka and beer, but they also had expensive, imported things like rum, whisky, and wine, most of which were contraband.

"What do you want?" asked the bartender, a big, lanky female bear.

"Good evening, Sveta. I'll just have a vodka," said Ivan.

"You don't want something else?" commented the husky. The bartender started to move away, but stopped.

Ivan chuckled. "And are you paying for that?"

The husky flicked his ears. "How much is it?"

"The imported drinks are ten to fifteen credits," said the bear. "Twenty if you want a cocktail. We do have a few imported beers that are under ten."

The dog was taken back by the price. "Twenty credits is a fifth of my monthly income!"

Sveta shrugged. "Imported doesn't come cheap."

"So, are you paying?" chuckled Ivan.

The husky reached into his pants and pulled out a money clip. He laid down four crinkled ten credit notes on the counter and returned the remaining ten to his pants' pocket. "I've dreamed of coming here for a very long time. I owe you for the trouble I caused you."

Ivan cocked an eyebrow. "In that case, a rum and coke."

The bartender pointed to the dog. "And you?"

Nikolai looked over the bottles behind the bar. "I've always wanted to try whisky."

"Then I know just the make for you. That will be thirty-four credits."

When the dog nodded, she took the money and fetched the drinks. It didn't take long before Sveta slid two tumblers and the remaining money across the bar. Nikolai took most of the change and left her a two credit tip, which she pocketed before heading to a different part of the bar.

Ivan picked up his glass and brought it to his lips, letting the fizz of the sweet soda tickle his whiskers. He took a small sip. The husky in the meantime sniffed at his glass, clinking the ice against the inside of the glass.

"This smells very strong," he remarked.

"I've never had it myself."

The dog held out the glass and Ivan sniffed at it.

"That smells really good. Have you had rum before?"

Nikolai shook his head. "No." He took a sip of his whisky. "Wow, that burns but it's so rich. It's so much more flavorful than our vodka."

Everyone knew the grade of Klechin vodka you could buy locally was inferior. The good stuff was sold overseas.

"Let's swap," suggested Ivan. They quickly switched their glasses and each took a sip.

"Wow. This is amazing," exclaimed Nikolai. "I've never had something this sweet and smooth before." He handed the glass back to Ivan.

"That whisky is rich. It's a good choice," Ivan added, sniffing at his own glass again, letting the fizz tickle his nose. He didn't want to want to drink his rum and coke to fast before it would all be gone.

They lapsed into silence, watching the dance floor twist and turn to the music. The song had changed, and it was a familiar tune, one of the few songs from overseas that had made it over here.

"I wanted to ask you," the husky said, "are things so much better overseas than here? I know you've not limited your sociological research to just approved sources."

The snow leopard considered. "Do you want a real answer or the approved answer for the people?"

"The real answer. Not the one we tell everyone so they believe in our worker's paradise."

"It's different. People have more freedom. They're not watched like we are, but they still have problems over there. Capitalism is great at generating wealth, but it's poor at distributing it fairly. It's amazing if you're rich. If you're poor, you may not be much better off than being a day laborer for the party. You're guaranteed food here. That's not true in the democracies overseas. Abuse of power is also still an issue."

The husky lowered his ears. "I hear so much about the excesses of capitalism compared to our glorious nation's planned growth," He sipped his whisky, "but capitalism tastes amazing."

The snow leopard nodded and just took another sip from his drink. He let the sweetness play across his rough tongue. The dog felt like a bundle of contradictions, and Ivan didn't want to explore them. As long as he got the dog a violet card, he would be free of him.

With a sigh, Nikolai finished his drink and put the empty glass down on the bar. He then leaned in to whisper to Ivan. "You know, it took me months to save up the amount of money we just drank away. Almost no one here has extra credits. We catch people all the time we have to send to the gulags, and even if you ask them for a bribe so you look the other way, they never have anything to make it worth leaving your skin to dry."

"And if I had two hundred credits?" asked Ivan.

"I'd get ten percent of that. They watch us like hawks. I have to give my superiors their cut."

Ivan finished his own drink and put the empty glass down. "We are all equal in the eyes of the government, but we still scramble for the scraps like feral animals it seems."

"Yes, yes we do. Everyone bends the rules in this country to scrape by, and the government knows that. I never see a file where they don't have something on that person. This is worth the risk though," said Nikolai, closing his eyes. "I will remember this night for the rest of my life. I am home now. Thank you, thank you so much. I knew I could trust you not to turn me in."

It hadn't occurred to Ivan the risk Nikolai had put himself in to do this.

"Come on," said the husky suddenly, moving away from the bar. "We should dance."

"Dance?" Ivan exclaimed, but the dog grabbed him by the paw and pulled him into the twisting crowd of people and toward the dance floor. The music had a beat to it, and the dance floor jumped with action; people spun, and tails swished through the air.

The husky started shaking his hips to the music, grinning. The rum had warmed Ivan, but it hadn't been enough to even get him buzzed. Also, the musk of so many dancing in close proximity was strong, so he had to block that out before he could get in tune and move with the music.

It felt silly to be dancing with the husky at first, but the dog had his tongue out in a grin of bliss Ivan never saw in the streets above. In that moment, his face radiated warmth, not the ice in his blue eyes when he interrogated Ivan over his books.

Ivan finally found some rhythm and danced as best he could. He wasn't a great dancer, but from how awkward many people looked, few in Klechnia danced anymore. Still, he wasn't feeling it tonight. He just wanted to get Nikolai a card and be free.

The feeling of a rump grinding up against him snapped him out of his reverie. The dog was grinding his butt against Ivan.

"Hey, whoa now, this is not what we're supposed to be doing!" yelled the feline.

The dog laughed, not hearing him completely over the music. "You want more than that?"

Ivan froze, but the dog didn't notice. Instead he'd put his ass against Ivan groin and danced, letting his tail get up in Ivan's face. The feline growled and grabbed the tail. He reached down to shove him away, and he felt the touch of a paw against his. It squeezed his hand, and the dog looked back at him, happy. He saw Ivan's scowl and frowned.

"Something wrong?" he yelled.

148

Ivan stepped back, and the dog turned to face him. He leaned against the snow leopard, not for support, but so they could hear each other.

"Is something wrong? Is that too much for you?"

Ivan looked at the face, expectant, eager, and blissfully happy. In his eyes, the snow leopard saw only the faintest glint of steel. "I generally avoid anyone with the military."

The dog's ears flattened. "Sorry. You're one of the few gays I know. I just figured since we're here, we should party."

"Like the capitalists?" questioned Ivan.

"They at least know how to have fun. I've never seen this many happy people before. Politics is one thing, but I want to be happy. I want to be free. I want to live."

"Freedom," Ivan said softly. Nikolai had to cock his ears to hear him speak over the music. People were still dancing around them. "Freedom does not come easy."

"No."

"You know hanging out with someone like me will get you a record."

The husky looked away from Ivan. "As if being here won't."

The snow leopard took the dog's paw and pulled him against himself. The dog yelped surprised. "You should save yourself before you get in too deep."

"And if I don't want to run and hide?" Blue eyes probed his face to see what he would say.

"You better have two hundred credits saved up."

Nikolai barked amused. "I don't think that will save me. I'm already a practicing homosexual. Now, do you want to dance or not? If you want to leave, I understand, but I want to stay for a while."

"I could use another drink. Want a vodka?"

The dog stuck out his tongue. "Rat poison tastes better."

"It's only two credits for a Klechin Select. It's the stuff we export."

"Oh, then sure."

They left the dance floor and walked back to the bar and ordered their drinks. Sveta brought them two glasses of clear liquid, and they thanked her before they took up position again, watching people dance. This time, Nikolai stayed close, and Ivan felt his hand instinctively slip around the husky. That only brought him closer to the snow leopard.

They drank in silence, just feeling the sense of intimacy. The warm presence of the husky felt nice next to Ivan. He let his mind drift over the possibility. The dog was cute in his collar. It didn't change the fact he was still a uniformed officer, but the bliss and joy he had about tonight was something Ivan never saw. He was glad in a way he'd been able to bring that to someone, even if the way it went down had been scary.

"Did you want another?" murmured Nikolai, after he finished his drink. "That is nice. Not as good as the whisky, but at least it's pleasant."

"No," said Ivan, arm still around the dog. "Do you want to dance?"

The dog sucked in his breath and snuggled a little closer. "Not right now. I'm enjoying this too much."

No one batted an eye at them. No one cared they were touching. Here they didn't have to hide their affections. It was relaxing, but Ivan had picked up the subtle change in the husky's scent and that his breathing had become shallower.

"You're thinking about what would have happened if I let you continue back in the alleyway aren't you?"

The ears swept back. "I don't want to say yes to that, but it's along those lines."

The feline leaned over and whispered into one of those ears, "It's okay, I'm thinking about it too."

The black and white head turned to look at him. "Are you now?"

Ivan nodded and grinned. "Hey, I never said I wasn't practicing."

"Then maybe we should go practice."

His smaller ears flicked as he thought, deciding, and then he smiled. "I know a spot."

The dog leaned in and licked at Ivan's ear. A paw slipped down to rub at his tail base causing Ivan to shiver a little. He felt his pulse quicken.

"Come on," he said leading the dog to the far side of the room. A wooden partition had been set up against the wall. Ivan walked over to a corner and paused. The partition covered a section of the underground store room that had never been built. Ivan looked back, and then slipped around the fake wall. The husky followed him. Behind the partition an incomplete excavation existed. A brick arch had been built, but inside that, a wall of rock stood just a meter back. There was a musk in the air because of what often happened back there.

Nikolai glanced around. It was dark behind the wall, but some light leaked around the partition. "You said nobody did this at the Violet Connection."

The snow leopard chuckled. "I lied. They call this the lover's niche."

The dog wagged his tail and grinned. "I'm all for that," he said coming closer to Ivan. He slipped a hand around the cat's waist and gave him a quick peck on the check.

"That's shy of you- oh!" The dog forcefully shoved a paw down Ivan's pants.

He pressed his muzzle against Ivan's, giving him a deeper, wetter kiss while he fumbled with Ivan's belt, and pushed him back against the arch. "Don't worry," the dog panted, "I'm not shy."

Ivan meowed and returned the kiss and slipped his paws around the husky's hips. He let his paws trail through Nikolai's fur as the dog got down on his knees and finally managed to get his belt undone. This time when he pulled down the pink underwear, Ivan's growing erection bobbed in the air. After a quick glance up, the dog went down on it.

The husky's mouth was wet and warm. His breath tickled at Ivan's thick fur as the dog pushed himself down his length, carefully working over the shaft, exploring it. The sound and feeling of canine saliva slurping around his length caused him to shiver. He grabbed the dog to hold him down, but there was no need. Nikolai didn't come up for air; he kept sucking.

He heard the hurried fumbling of Nikolai with his own belt and then the sound as he played with himself. Ivan started thrusting in, bouncing himself against the dog. There was a gurgle, but the wag of the tail told him to keep going.

It didn't take long either before he came, shooting down the dog's eager throat. Nikolai gagged, and then swallowed before he broke off. With a grunt the dog kept working at his own shaft before he let himself splatter the concrete floor.

Ivan shivered, letting the moment ride on, as he felt himself melt back against the archway. The husky looked up at him smiling and licked his own seed from his paw.

"You performed well, citizen," he said with a lilt in his voice. "Very satisfying."

Ivan blinked. "What?"

The husky laughed. "Citizen must do his duty. Glory to the gay."

"How did you even manage to join the military?" asked Ivan. "You are the worst officer I have ever seen."

The dog shrugged. "I know my place, and I follow orders." He got up and dusted off his knees. "And my place is down on my knees," he added, laughing.

"Oh lord," said Ivan, buckling his pants back up. He pushed himself off the arch and started to slip through the gap between the partition and the wall. The music still played. "You are certainly an unrepentant, practicing homosexual."

The husky skipped out happy once they got out from behind the barrier. Ivan chuckled and had to catch up with the dog. "You are glowing with joy," remarked Ivan.

Nikolai laughed. "You've made me very happy tonight. I wish tonight wouldn't end."

"Duty is calling," said Ivan.

"Yeah, yeah. A quick dance for the road?"

"Sure," laughed Ivan, who was pulled toward the dance floor. This time, when the husky ground himself against the snow leopard, they both just laughed.

* * *

In the morning, Ivan wanted to skip to work. He felt younger than he had in years. Even though he didn't get home till 2 AM, he was at work just before 8 AM. He smiled and waved to his coworkers as he walked in. The few that were already in didn't seem willing to meet his joyous mood, and the reason became obvious the moment he opened his office door.

"Good morning, citizen," came a gruff voice.

Ivan froze. A large bear with commander's stripes sat at his desk. Behind the bear, a wolf carrying a rifle on his shoulder stood at attention.

"Come in, and close the door," ordered the bear.

Ivan shut the door and walked over to the chair in front of his desk. The bear nodded, and he sat down.

"Do you know why we are here?" asked the bear. His large frame seemed to want to burst from behind Ivan's desk.

"You are unhappy with my research?" Ivan questioned.

"I'm sure you have something in here I should confiscate, but that isn't why we came here today. I believe you know this dog." He pulled out a photo from a manila envelope and slid the photo across the desk. It was Nikolai standing at attention in his uniform.

"We've met," said Ivan. He didn't want to give away more information than he needed to.

The bear chuckled. "You've apparently more than met." He pulled out a second photo from the folder and slid it across the table. It showed Nikolai and Ivan under the streetlight where they met last night. They were saying goodbye, and both of them were smiling. Nikolai still had his spiked collar on from the club.

Ivan swallowed hard. "What is it you want from me?"

The bear chuckled. "It's not what I want. It's what the law says. You have been seen fraternizing with one of my soldiers."

"I was coerced."

"This does not look coerced."

Ivan sighed. "Not by then. He is quite persuasive."

The bear leaned forward, putting both hands on Ivan's desk. "Did you commit homosexual acts with my soldier?" he demanded.

Ivan felt his ears go back. "Yes, but that's not illegal."

The bear gave him an unhappy smile. "It does not matter. You are guilty of corrupting a member of the military police and committing intellectual decadence. You are to be stripped of your professorship and your citizenship. You will be deported to the Goris Gulag."

Ivan wanted to say something, he wanted to plead with the bear, but it wouldn't help. It had only been a matter of time. When the wolf came around the desk and locked the shackles around his wrists, he could only stare in resignation.

* * *

They brought him down from his office in chains and loaded him into a car. They drove him to the train station where he was loaded onto a military train car at the front of a freight train. There he waited while a fox guarded his cell. He sat there for a while staring at the ground. The fox, bored, had napped a little, but the sound of another vehicle pulling up to the train had awoken him.

"We have one more for you, Leonid," said a voice, rapping on the train car door. Ivan watched as the fox unlocked the door and two guards hauled Nikolai into Ivan's cell, tossing the husky down. He still wore the clothes from last night, spiked collar included. His clothing was torn and dirty.

The wolverine and wolf who hauled in Nikolai saluted the guard. "Watch the filth."

"Yes sir," said Leonid. He saluted back, and the two departed. The fox locked the train car door and went back to his post.

Ivan looked at Nikolai. He had a swollen eye and his lips were swelling. The dog had been beaten up. The snow leopard felt feelings of betrayal and anger well up inside of himself, but he pushed them down. The husky suffered worse for their transgression than him.

"Nikolai?" whispered Ivan. He glanced at the fox, but he didn't seem to care if they talked. "Nikolai, are you okay?"

The husky rolled over onto his back wincing. He looked at Ivan with his good eye. His left eye was completely swollen shut. "Ivan? They got you too?"

"They had a picture of us kissing."

The husky closed his good eye. "They said they're sending me to a gulag. They called me a filthy, capitalist homosexual. They've stripped me of my citizenship."

The trained lurched as it started to leave the station. "They're sending me to the Goris Gulag," said Ivan.

The dog sighed. "Do you think they will let us stay in the same camp?"

"I have no idea."

Nikolai pushed himself up and crawled as best he could over to the bars of the cage. "Comrade, where are they sending us?" asked the dog.

"Do not talk to me filth," said the fox.

"Comrade, where are they sending us? You can at least tell me that."

The fox sighed. "He is going to the Goris Gulag. You are to be sent to a labor camp up on the Dimitri River."

"Of course," Nikolai said. "This is their way of giving us a little time together before they separate us forever. Thank you, comrade."

"They don't want us to fraternize?" Ivan questioned.

"They don't want a lot of things. They want to keep us stupid and isolated, and all of this is because they're afraid. They're afraid of being challenged, they're afraid of change."

"Shut up, dog," said the fox, getting up from where he sat. "I will not have you babbling for the entire train ride."

"Or you'll shoot me? My life is all our government has left to take from me. I know how rowdy prisoners are treated," laughed the dog.

"Just shut up," growled the fox.

"No," said the husky. "I was a guard like you, and I did my job in the name of the state. I've deported dozens by now, and I've made people pay bribes to keep their lives. I will not be sent off to live the rest of my life in a gulag just because I wanted to taste freedom."

The fox laughed. "Those are foolish words for one in a situation like yours."

"End me, comrade. Just end me. No one has to know. They will never believe Ivan if he tells anyone. His word is useless now."

"I am not going to shoot you," said the fox, crossing his arms and walking back to his post. "Now do not bother me with your traitorous words."

The dog sighed, his shoulders sagging. "I guess once I get to the gulag, I can get someone else to do it," he whispered to the snow leopard.

Ivan spoke softly. "You will have to just go on living, Nikolai. Don't let the joy I saw in you yesterday be extinguished by this. You will have to fight to stay happy, but you can survive this."

The husky closed his eyes and started to just cry. Ivan did his best to comfort the dog. He leaned next to him against the metal bars of their cell, holding him. "You can pull through. If you give up now, they win. Don't let them take your dignity and who you are away from you. You have to fight it."

"How?" whispered the husky. "I'm just a stupid military police officer who got caught for abusing his power too much. Nikolai isn't that fun loving mutt from last night because no one in this country is like that. We work, and when we get too old, we die."

"I know there is a strength within you. You just need to find it."

Nikolai stared off into space, starting to sob. "I wish I know where it was."

The guard watched them silently. Ivan wished he could add something, anything that would make their situation better. Nothing came to mind. He just listened to the sound of the train and the sound of Nikolai's sobbing. The dog cried for a long time before he finally became silent, his body no longer dry heaving next to Ivan. Eventually the clacking of the rails lulled Ivan to sleep. In his dreams, he dreamed of drinking wine in a green field on a warm summer day with Nikolai.

* * *

The blast of cold air woke Ivan, and the sound of voices filtered to his ears.

"What poor souls do you have this day, Leonid?"

Ivan squinted into the dark beyond the open train car door. Nikolai had curled up in a fetal position and fallen asleep at some point.

"An intellectual dissident," said the fox at attention, "and an ex-military police officer."

A large frame came into the open train car door and glanced at them. The female wolverine was a commanding presence in her uniform as she looked over the paperwork the fox handed to her.

"Both for my gulag?" she asked.

The fox hesitated and leaned forward to say something to the wolverine privately. Her eyes sparkled as she glanced at them.

"I'll file an addendum to the detention report," she said to the fox. "No one will care."

Leonid nodded in agreement, and they walked over to the cell. Leonid reached for his keys so he could unlock the door. When the door swung open, the wolverine walked in.

"All right you two, both of you, up. That includes you fur ball," said the wolverine, nudging the husky with her boot. "This is your stop."

Nikolai blinked and tried to get up. When he couldn't get to his feet fast enough, the wolverine grabbed him and hauled him up.

"Where is this?" asked Nikolai, confused.

"Goris Gulag. You are both sentenced to life here and will work for the betterment of the state. Now, let's move, and don't try to escape. We have guards everywhere."

The snow leopard and husky followed the wolverine toward the door. Ivan glanced to the fox who gave him a faint nod at his questioning look as they exited the train. As he passed, Ivan mouthed a "thank you" before they stepped out into the dark night beyond. Behind him, he could hear the fox closing the train car door.

Nikolai glanced at him as two guards fell in behind them. His good eye was puffy from crying, and he still couldn't see out of the other eye, but at the very corners of his lips, there was a faint smile. At least they were going into confinement together.

IRL

by Billy Leigh

"You have to try it," Sam kept insisting. "It's all anyone can talk about right now."

"So I can look like a moron as I writhe around humping at thin air. Don't you always end up with sticky underwear by the end?" I sighed as I gazed into my beer.

"It's not all sex," Sam replied as he fixed me an eye-roll. "You can just chat or hang out with people. You remember Philip?"

"The guy who ran the LGBT club at university?"

"Yeah, I was talking to him the other day and he said he met his boyfriend through it, a hot dingo from Australia. They can meet up every day without having to bother with flying."

I wasn't convinced and felt it was still perfectly possible to do all these things in real life, but Sam continued to talk excitedly.

"Think about it, Patrick is probably having loads of great rebound sex right now," the jackal continued.

"Real or virtual sex?"

"It doesn't matter; you could either mope about all day and feel sorry for yourself, or get out there and have fun."

Now, I should explain what Sam was talking about.

It began with a desire to escape - to get as far away from my life as I could.

A holiday in the Caribbean or hiking in the Alps, somewhere that looked like paradise. I browsed the internet and looked at hotels and resorts, but everything seemed out of my budget. I'd recently graduated from university, moved into a small flat near the city centre and started a new job. It all seemed very exciting at first, moving out of my parents' house and having a place of my own. Unfortunately, it had also bled me financially and left me feeling very isolated.

Subconsciously, my plans to go somewhere else was a way of meeting a new boyfriend since I was reeling from being ditched by my ex, a puma called Patrick. I met Patrick during my final year at university. At the time I thought he was such a catch. He was handsome, all the girls in my classes had a crush on him, and he seemed like a funny, down to earth guy, until I got to know him better.

We had planned to move in together, but that fell through.

After the breakup, my evenings were spent trawling through Patrick's social media pages to see if he had a new boyfriend.

"C'mon Peter, you've got to find a way to let go," Sam would sigh. "I mean, you unfriended him for a reason. You're a good looking coyote and smart guy, for the most part. You'll find someone else."

"I know, but I can't help it," I shrugged. I was in a difficult place. I so badly wanted to let go but I was still in the self-indulgent phase where there seemed to be no way out of wallowing in self-pity. If I could go back, I'd slap myself and tell me to move on, something better was waiting around the corner.

Sam tried doing just that, without the slapping part. He's a close friend, though he can be a little too much sometimes. I used to wonder why I didn't date him, he's a tall and athletic looking golden jackal, but he's more like a goofy kind of brother to me. I thought Patrick was like a best friend, until I discovered he'd been cheating on me. I was outraged when I found out, but on reflection I started to wonder if I had been responsible. On the one occasion I had brought Patrick to my parents' place, my brother had tried his hardest to intimidate him, by complaining to my mother that us kissing or hugging weirded him out. My brother, by the way, is a military cadet and thinks of himself as an Alpha male. I tried defending him at first. *"That's just my brother's way, you'll get used to it. I promise"* I tried desperately to explain. *"I don't like him, he scares me. I'm not sure I ever want to go to your parents' again."* Patrick replied. I tried asking my brother to be more accepting, but he told me to get lost. Patrick then refused to ever go near my family. That led to us fighting. The fighting led to us not talking which then led to Patrick screwing other people.

I became reclusive after the breakup and spent my evenings gazing at the mirror trying to convince myself that I could find someone else. I'm a tall-ish and skinny coyote with white, grey and golden fur and brown eyes. I held my breath and flexed my chest, trying to look more muscular. *You can get someone, you're not bad looking* I'd try to tell myself, but soon I'd need to breath and I'd gasp and let go. I glanced back up at my skinny stature and didn't feel convinced.

Sam was worried and invited me out for drinks to check everything was all right. "I get the sense the breakup was my fault," I explained as we sat at a quiet table near the back of the pub. The jackal shook his head.

"No, it wasn't your fault. Think about it, he slept with other guys and stood you up on dates. Disliking your family doesn't justify cheating. If you want my opinion, underneath the handsome exterior he was shallow. I reckon he just cruises around and dumps guys when he gets bored of them."

Sam was right and I thought him to be the voice of reason, until typically, he suggested I try something outlandish.

"Why don't you get CruiseScape?" He suggested, and there began his quest to persuade me to buy it. CruiseScape was part of an avalanche of virtual reality games that had come out that year, but in this system you didn't go around shooting enemy soldiers or racing cars around a track. It had been developed as a virtual world for guys to hook up in various locations. It connects to most games consoles or computers and it's rather like a cross between a dating app and a video game. You put these heavy looking goggles on, sit down and watch as the virtual world unfolds before you. It consists of a few exotic locations, a desert island, a mountain chalet and a chat room which is made to look like a nightclub.

Naturally, it had been met with a lot of criticism and derision from the media, but as gimmicky as the device sounded, it had been a surprise hit by advertising itself as dating and casual sex without the risks. I found the idea silly at first; something for people to use it they had no social skills. Sam had an account on it, and he invited me to watch on the first day he brought it home. I'd tried to look enthusiastic as he put the goggles on and spent the next twenty minutes twitching, practically drooling and getting an obvious bulge in his trousers as he lay on the floor. I got bored and wondered off to the kitchen to make myself lunch.

It took me a moment to realise Sam was still talking to me.

"Buy it for a trial period and see if you like it. I have a feeling you will."

The rational part of my mind should have questioned Sam's claims, but as I nursed my beer and mulled his words over, the paranoid side won.

"Fine, I'll check it out."

"Good boy," Sam replied, giving me a slap on the back.

"What if I see Patrick?"

"Oh don't worry about that, people can block each other. They just turn into a black silhouette," the jackal explained, "but relax, you'll have fun."

I had no idea if Patrick was still going around having great sex, but the idea of it made me angry and resentful. My apartment seemed so drab looking after the initial excitement of moving had faded. I gazed outside at the rain lashing down the kitchen window and wished I was somewhere else. I could fly somewhere, but the prices of the flights seemed too much, and I didn't want to think about the hassle of packing. Sam would tell me to *have fun*. His words encouraging me to get CruiseScape echoed around my head.

"Fine." I said out loud. I closed a web page talking about trekking in Manchu Picchu and searched for the CruiseScape website. You could do a trial period which limited the amount of worlds you could explore, but it was way cheaper than the average holiday deal I'd look at. My paw hovered over the *purchase now* option.

"Oh what the hell, you're a coyote. You should be mischievous and having fun." I muttered to myself as I clicked down.

I spent the next few days pacing around my apartment or checking the mail box. Five days later, it arrived.

I felt a rush of excitement as I tore open the anonymous looking brown box and found a more exciting looking blue package inside. I pulled the bubble wrap and plastic sheets out the way until a blue box with a set of goggles and an instruction sheet sitting on top became visible. The first thing I noticed was a warning in bold letters telling me not to use the device if I suffered a variety of health issues before instructing me to plug a USB cable into my computer and the second to my games consol.

"Here goes nothing," I muttered as I plugged it in and the box whirred into life. The television blinked before a white and blue logo appeared on the screen.

Welcome to CruiseScape.

A string of even more instructions appeared on the computer screen. I was told that due to being on a trial period I could only visit the island and the chatroom, but I could create a music playlist which I could share with other users if I wanted to. I'd get more locations and perks once I upgraded. I selected a playlist for the chatroom setting and browsed the most flattering photos I could find to build a virtual me, vein I know, created a personal profile and chose what clothing I was to wear. I spent a few minutes trying to think of a username, should it sound cool, sexy or neutral?

A grin spread across my muzzle as I thought of the most provocative name I could; *BadCoyote91*.

As I walked through each environment a heads up display could appear if I gestured upwards with both paws. I could use this to play my music and share it. To leave the virtual world I had to press down on a red button. The goggles had an inbuilt microphone so I could speak out loud. A likeness suddenly appeared on the computer screen. I'll admit I was impressed. The graphics were like no other I had seen. The likeness looked exactly like me, or rather the most flattering picture I'd used from a holiday in Italy a couple of years ago; a shirtless coyote in a pair of blue swim shorts flexing his chest.

A box popped up and told me I could apply some edits to my clothes and figure. I gazed at the image for a moment before I grinned to myself. I moved the curser about and made my swimsuit a little tighter and shorter. *That should do the trick.* The screen asked if I was ready to proceed. I clicked yes and some more instructions appeared.

When you are ready BadCoyote91 put your goggles on and let the fun commence!

It then called for me to lie down in a relaxed position. I dragged a blanket from my bed and laid it on the floor. I glanced around my stark looking apartment and the desire for a distraction intensified. I picked up the goggles and weighed them in my paw. For something that purported to be the future, it looked very clunky and retro, like something from a seventies sci-fi flick. I placed the goggles over my eyes and lay down. Something that looked like static burst before my eyes and I flinched. A loading bar appeared and I watched apprehensively as it moved slowly across my vision before jolting to the end. A scene slowly faded into view like a dream; blue sky, the sound of water lapping against sand and then the sun shining on my face.

I couldn't believe what I was seeing. An island paradise was appearing before me.

The island looked shockingly yet beautifully realistic. The turquoise water sparkled in the sunshine while the white sandy beach looked so inviting. A rock formation with a waterfall hemmed in by fleshy looking palm trees lay behind me. There wasn't a cloud to be seen in the crystal blue sky.

I was blown away by the technology. It was unlike any video game I'd played, if I could call it a video game. I could see a bar nearby. Feeling intrigued, I made my way over. The sand beneath my feet crunched as it would on a real beach. Walking in the virtual world felt smooth with no judders at all. Despite my amazement, I couldn't help but glance around in case Patrick was walking nearby, but the beach seemed deserted. As the bar came further into view I could see it was donut shaped around a swimming pool, like the sort I had seen in some on some of the vacation websites I'd browsed. A silver fox was polishing glasses behind the counter.

"Hello BadCoyote91, how can I help?"

"Uh, well what do you have?" I asked. The bartender looked behind at the selection of bottles.

"Beers, cocktails, soft drinks. Ah, I know what you'd like," the fox said as he ducked down behind the bar. I watched as he poured liquids into a glass.

"Here we go, one screwdriver," the fox said as he sat an orange juice and vodka down.

"That's my favourite drink," I gasped. "How did you know that?"

"Oh, I'm very good at knowing things," the fox replied with a wink.

"What do I call you?" I asked, feeling the question sounded silly.

"Call me what you like," the fox grinned. "No curse words though, that'll get your account suspended."

I thought for a moment.

"You're called Frolay." I decided, wincing as the name escaped my muzzle.

"Frolay it is," he said as he pushed the glass towards me.

The orange liquid looked tasty. I took a sip, but to my disappointment the drink had no taste. I looked up to see a grey and white wolf making his way along the sand in the direction of the bar. He was dressed in a pair of form fitting blue and white speedos that emphasised the outline of his sheath and crotch. The trunks were wet and turning translucent in places so I could see the damp fur beneath the material.

I sat transfixed. *Thank goodness for advanced graphics technology.*

The wolf's username flashed up above his head; *ApolloWolf.* As I focused on the name, profile information began to appear in thin air beside the wolf;

Age: 26

Species: Wolf

Gender: Male

Relationship status: Single

Likes: Reading, movies, listening to music, going for walks and hikes.

Dislikes: Making long lists about things I dislike.

The last part of his bio made me chuckle. The wolf noticed me looking in his direction as he walked by. He had bright, almost dazzling blue eyes that flashed in the sunlight. He turned his head and kept walking. I followed him with my eyes, almost hypnotised by his looks, until I noticed more movement to my left. I turned to see someone sitting two barstools away from me. The person was already a black shadow and I frowned. I hadn't blocked anyone yet, and I didn't know what I'd already done to get blocked.

I started to wonder if it was Patrick, but I was distracted when I heard a stool being dragged to my right. I turned to see an orange and white fox taking a seat. He was also dressed in an equally form-fitting and revealing swimsuit. I couldn't help but follow a cluster of blue star tattoos on the side of his skinny yet athletic torso that led down to the low-riding waistband of his swimsuit. The fox fixed me one of those wily and cheeky grins that only foxes manage to pull off.

"Sup, stud" he said, sweeping his black fringe away from his brown eyes.

"Oh, uh, hey" I replied, suddenly feeling apprehensive.

"First time here?" the fox asked as I gazed above his head to read his username; *RebelWithALiftedTail*. I suppressed a chuckle.

"Bit of a mouthful, huh?" the fox laughed. "You can call me Danny."

Frolay set another cocktail down on the bar.

"Thanks, Jim," Danny said to the bartender.

"Jim, I thought he was called Frolay?" I replied, before feeling silly as I realised the bartender must be an NPC-type figure. I glanced back over at the black silhouette which was now moving off. The fox followed my gaze.

"Oh, ignore dicks like that. They block people on first sight, he blocked me too."

"Ah, right," I replied, taking another sip of my cocktail before remembering it didn't taste of anything.

"Oh, sadly it's just graphic," Danny explained. "They haven't perfected the technology to make it taste of anything yet."

"Hmm, funny how they already know what we like to drink."

"Oh, that's because they get information from what you search for on the internet," Danny explained. I admit, I was a little unnerved to hear this.

"So, Bad Coyote huh?" Danny continued, edging along the bar towards bar towards me. "My mate and I have been looking for a third party to join us."

As if on cue, a black wolf sat to my left. His username *TJ Wuff* flashed above him.

"What's going on here then?" The wolf asked in a deep voice. Adrenaline was coursing through me and an absurd grin spread across my muzzle.

"Hey TJ darling, I was just talking to Mr. Bad Coyote here," Danny replied.

"I'm actually called Peter," I explained, nervously extending a paw. The wolf took it in a firm grip.

"Aw, I rather like Bad Coyote, but pleased to meet you Peter," Danny said, "Come and hang out at our cabin if you feel up to it," the fox added before he downed his drink.

"Cabin?"

"Yeah, on full membership you can build your own cabin to hang out in, or invite guests back to," he explained with another foxy grin.

Danny and TJ's cabin was located further back from the beach and appeared as a white painted wooden structure with a veranda around the outside.

"I didn't see this before." I said, scratching my muzzle.

"They're hidden from other users unless you want them to see it," Danny explained. "Come on stud, I'll show you around inside."

The interior of the cabin was surprisingly detailed, with a woven rug lining most of the wood floor, a sofa and a stone fireplace guarded by two naked fox statues.

"I got the idea from my grandmother's house, only I put my own… interpretation on it," Danny explained with a chuckle.

"I wanted wolves, but I allowed Danny to have his way in the end," TJ added.

"We have one rule in here, and that is no clothes," Danny smirked, "off with that swimwear yote." I watched as Danny slid out of his swimsuit, the pink tip of the fox's cock had already emerged from his sheath. My cock flopped out awkwardly as I jerked my own swimsuit down. Behind me, TJ had removed his swimming trunks and was watching the two of us with a hungry expression. Danny sat on the sofa and patted the spot next to him.

"Here, come and get cosy."

As I sat down the fox gestured upwards with his paw and the sound of *Addicted to Love* filled the room. I couldn't help but laugh at how wonderfully absurd yet hot the situation was.

I sat next to Danny and I immediately felt the fox's paw making its way up my leg. Danny continued to fix me his grin as he gripped my sheath. TJ was watching as his tongue hung out his muzzle. I gasped as Danny fondled my balls and rubbed the tip of my cock with his thumb. Our muzzles met and he pushed his tongue gently into my mouth. TJ reached over and pulled my sheath down to expose my cock.

"There you go," he growled, ruffling the fur between Danny's ears. Danny gripped my cock firmly in his paw and began licking the tip.

I'm not sure whether it was graphic or virtual reality, or what, but it felt amazing. I squirmed under Danny's licks as my cock stiffened and throbbed. The fox gripped the base and slid my entire shaft into his muzzle. I gripped the sides of the sofa as Danny worked his muzzle up and down while continuing to fondle my balls.

"Lay down," TJ instructed. I lay back on the sofa as Danny continued to suck me off. The fact I was in a virtual world no longer occurred to me,

I closed my eyes and felt like I was in heaven. I sensed someone standing over me, and I opened my eyes to see TJ's behind descending onto my muzzle.

"You like rimming yote?"

"Yes," I breathed.

"Good." TJ grinned. The wolf straddled over me as I began making out with his hole; lapping against the bare patch of skin where his fur ended before trying to force my tongue into the hole itself. TJ growled with approval. Danny was still sucking my dick and the wonderful sensation of his tongue was pushing me closer to the edge.

"Go on, fill up his muzzle," TJ encouraged. Danny's motions became more frantic and his rough tongue brushed against my shaft. I moaned as I bucked forwards and came into his muzzle. Danny kept his head in place, making sure he got every bit of it down his throat. A minute later TJ climbed off me and Danny raised his head, licking his lips.

"It doesn't really taste of anything on here, but I'm sure it's great in real life," he chuckled.

I suddenly felt two strong arms around my chest.

"Want to go even further?" TJ growled playfully into my ear. I squirmed with delight and nodded. "Good, it doesn't hurt on here, and there's no need to mess about with lube and condoms, I just do this..." TJ gestured upwards and slicked something over his fully erect cock. "There we go." The wolf pushed me down on the sofa, so my head was resting on a cushion. He gently slid his cock into my tail hole, causing me to groan out loud. He was right, I didn't feel the usual awkwardness and discomfort during the first stage of sex. TJ gripped onto my hips as he thrust into me, settling into a steady rhythm. I closed my eyes and moaned as I felt the wolf push deeper, feeling his cock brush against my prostate. I pushed back against his cock, allowing TJ to thrust in further.

The room was filled with the sound of our moaning and grunting while Danny watched and stroked his cock. TJ growled dominantly as he kept pounding my tail hole. I could feel sweat dripping from his muzzle onto the back of my neck. It felt like being in a scene from a porn flick. TJ threw back his head and howled as he knotted me. We fell to the floor, tangled in each other's arms. The wolf howled and bit down on my neck fluff as he came into me. I got off again a second later, cum splashed all over my chest and some even hit me in the face. I felt TJ's cock rotate inside me as he lifted his leg over, leaving us tied on the floor. I lay panting as waves of pleasure crashed through me. I glanced up to see Danny sitting on the sofa gripping his cock. His furry chest was matted with cum.

"You two were brilliant," he panted. "We must do that again sometime."

"Yeah, let's," I agreed as I closed my eyes and panted. TJ's weight wrested heavily on me, but it was a pleasant sensation.

After a few blissful moments, TJ's knot went down and we were both freed. He leant down to kiss me before going to sit beside Danny.

"Should we clean up?" I panted, feeling aware of the stickiness covering my tail hole.

"No need. Watch this," Danny grinned. He gestured upwards as if he wanted to leave the game, but instead he pressed something to his right, gently moving his paw over my hole. I wriggled under his touch, but the stickiness disappeared.

"You can clean up by going on the main heads up display," Danny explained. "Reading the instructions always helps," he added as he cleaned himself and TJ.

We left the cabin laughing and joking.

"Hey, I'll give you my number so we can let you know when we're back online," Danny said. He checked no one was around before we exchanged details.

"It was great meeting you," I called as Danny and TJ gestured upwards.

"Likewise stud, you take care," Danny called as he and TJ waved before disappearing. I grinned, gestured upwards and pressed down on the button to leave.

I pulled the goggles off and lay back panting. My cock had fully emerged from its sheath and was straining against my jeans and briefs. It was like waking up from a vivid dream, only I could clearly remember everything. My cock was throbbing. God, I felt so pent up and needed to get off right away. I jerked my underwear down, pulled my shirt up and began stimulating myself. A second later I gasped as warm cum splashed over my chest fur.

I couldn't move for the next minute or so. Real or not, it was the best sex I had had in a long time.

CruiseScape was the only thing I could think about over the next day. I texted Sam to say how much fun I'd had and the jackal encouraged me to keep it up. As I sat at my desk at work, I gazed out over the carpark, counting down the hours until I could go home and return to the island for another hook-up.

As soon as I could leave, I raced to my car and drove home like a maniac. The CruiseScape box was waiting with the goggles in place. I pulled off my jacket, unbuttoned my shirt and was about to lay down when I thought of something.

A grin spread across my muzzle. *Time to upgrade.*

I logged into my account and clicked on the option to upgrade my account. The smile was still on my muzzle as I entered my credit card details and upgraded from a trial period to full membership. Now I could explore all other virtual worlds.

I lay back down, placed the goggles over my eyes and waited for the image to load. I'd selected the mountain chalet world and as the image faded into view, I was once again blown away by how realistic it looked.

The chalet was lined with wood panelled walls, padded sofas and another large fireplace, albeit without the naked fox statues. The windows outside gave a clear and stunning view over snow-capped mountains. There was no sign of any pumas, but I saw three other guys milling about, two Alsatians dogs and a spotted hyena. The hyena looked familiar, and as I got closer I recognised him as someone I vaguely knew from college. I was pretty sure he was getting married to a woman the last time I'd seen his social media profiles. The hyena's eyes widened as he saw me and he hurried out of the room. One of the Alsatians, a tall black and tan guy with amber eyes, shot me a wink as I walked by. He was sporting a wifebeater that emphasised a muscular chest. I was sure he was licking his lips. There was also a bar at one end of the room, and I somehow wasn't surprised to see Frolay the fox standing behind it.

"Hello again, the usual today?"

"No thanks, I think I'll have something warm to drink, hot chocolate if you have it?"

"Certainly," Frolay said as he turned his back and began to prepare it. I suddenly realised there was not much point in having a different drink. It wouldn't taste of anything regardless of what it was.

I turned and saw to my pleasant surprise that Danny and the Alsatian with amber eyes were standing behind me. His username read *ShepBoi*. I stifled a chuckle.

"Hey, how's it going? I see you've decided to go for the full membership."

"Yes, and I'm pleased I did so," I replied, eyeing up the Alsatian.

"This is ShepBoi, aka Gareth," Danny explained.

"Where's TJ?" I asked as I took sip of my drink.

"Coming down with a cold sadly, but he told me to come on here and have fun," the fox explained.

"I see," I replied. I would have thought that I'd have stayed with my boyfriend if he were ill, but I admit at that moment, I could feel a tingling in my stomach and my cock start to stiffen and protrude from my sheath.

"He's a good looking one," Gareth whispered to Danny as his eyes looked me up and down.

"And he's very talented," Danny added with a smirk.

I was about to reply when I glanced over the Alsatian's shoulder and saw the grey and white wolf from the beach walking into the room. His username *ApolloWolf* appeared again. The wolf's brilliant blue eyes passed over me as if weighing me up, before he turned to face the bar.

"Peter?"

I looked up to see Danny fixing me a quizzical expression.

"Uh, sorry what did you say?"

"I was telling Gareth here about our adventures last time," Danny replied with a grin. "Would you like to come back to my room?"

"Oh, so it's just a room now?" I teased.

"The *room* is more of a personal space that transforms with each world you are in, on the beach it's a cabin and here it's a bedroom in the chalet." Danny explained

"I see, did you find that out quickly as there was shagging involved?"

"Foxes haven't always got their minds on just lifting tails," Danny laughed. *Wanna bet* I thought.

Danny led us to his room which had the appearance of a luxury Alpine hotel suite. The floor was covered by a thick shag pile rug while a stone fireplace took up one wall. I grinned when I saw it was flanked by the same naked fox statues. Danny had removed his shirt, showing off the star tattoos, and was lying back on a four poster bed. He unzipped his jeans before sliding them off with his underwear.

"So coyote, I was wondering if you wanted to show the fox some attention this time?"

Danny said seductively as he rubbed his sheath. The pink tip of his cock had emerged and was wet with pre-cum. Danny kept rubbing and stroking his cock as it steadily emerged.

I stood still, almost hypnotised by the sight, before an idiot grin spread across my muzzle. I reached down, took his cock in my paw and began licking at the tip.

As I began sucking I felt a pair of paws hook themselves over the waistband of my jeans. I pulled back from Danny's cock to see Gareth sliding my jeans down.

"Keep sucking him, yote," he commanded. I felt the Alsatian's nose press into the fabric of my underwear as he sniffed at my tail hole. I obeyed and kept sucking Danny off, working my muzzle up and down the fox's shaft in the same fashion he had done at the beach cabin. I felt my underwear being pulled down. The Alsatian then grabbed my tail and lifted it up. I felt his nose press against my tail hole before the rough surface of his tongue lapped against it. I gripped Danny's cock and sucked more earnestly as Gareth buried his muzzle into my behind, making out with my tail hole as if it were my mouth. It felt wonderful to have a tongue working its way into my hole while I sucked Danny's cock. The fox was squirming under my grip as I moved my muzzle up and down. I could barely concentrate since Gareth's licks were growing more intense. Danny writhed and bucked forwards as he came into my muzzle. I closed my eyes as I took the load down my throat, but I didn't feel the need to recoil. *Damn, whatever technology this thing uses it's realistic without real life drawbacks.* At that moment Gareth pulled away and I felt warm cum splash over my tail hole as he jerked himself off over me.

I lay on my front and panted while Gareth collapsed beside me. Danny was sitting back on the pillows, basking in the afterglow.

A minute later, Danny cleaned us up before we lay on the bed and watched the snow falling outside. I couldn't deny the sex was fun, but as my afterglow faded, I kept thinking of the wolf's blue eyes.

"What's on your mind?" Danny asked. I gazed out the window at the snow falling on the mountains.

"I've seen a wolf on here, he's very handsome."

"You may have to be a little more specific."

"I think he's called ApolloWolf." I explained. Danny thought for a moment before he grinned.

"Ah yes, I've seen him around. He's indeed very handsome, but seems aloof as hell, which is a surprise as I thought he'd have guys crawling all over him."

"Do you mind if I go and check if he's still out there?"

"Sure, I'll keep myself occupied with Mr. Shep here. Feel free to bring that wolf back if you want," the fox grinned.

The last thing I saw as I closed the door was Danny's smirk as Gareth began bending him over on the bed.

The wolf was still standing by the bar when I made my way out. I circled by nervously until he looked up. I sidled over. Up close, I could see he was even more handsome than I had seen from a distance. He was wearing a tight white shirt that emphasised his toned chest and muscular arms, which flexed as he stretched out. His face seemed almost perfectly formed, with a strong looking jawline under his muzzle, which combined with luscious white and grey fur that lined his cheeks. Still, the wolf's most prominent feature was his bright blue eyes which sparkled like the ocean back at the beach.

"Another hot chocolate please, Frolay," I said to the silver fox.

"Frolay?" The wolf asked. I sighed. What a smooth way to introduce myself to someone.

"Named after my childhood imaginary friend," I admitted as my ears splayed, but the wolf merely shrugged.

"If you think that's cringy, watch this. Hey, Kalamazoo."

The wolf ordered a drink from the bartender while I cocked my ears and waited for him to explain. "I saw it in an atlas of the US once," he admitted. "I couldn't think of what to say when the bartender asked me to name him, so I blurted that out, and I haven't worked out how to change it."

I chuckled nervously before we both stood in an awkward silence. The wolf gazed out of the window as he tapped his paws on the bar counter. *Say something* my mind screamed at me, but I didn't know what to say without coming out with something silly. I sighed inwardly. Virtual world, same awkwardness when it came to engaging a crush in conversation as reality. The wolf continued watching the snowflakes outside, but I was sure he snuck a couple of glances back in my direction. My muzzle hung open but I couldn't form any words. *Good grief I must have looked like an idiot.* I glanced around desperately and saw Danny's head glancing around the corner. He fixed me a wink and a thumbs up. The wolf looked up.

"Friend of yours?" he asked suspiciously.

"Oh, yeah. Bit of a goofball," I replied. Danny looked worried and disappeared again.

"He's not trying to be my wingman or anything. I've been wanting to talk since I saw you on the beach," I explained. The suspicious frown on the wolf's face disappeared and he nodded.

"Yes, I remember you now. The coyote sitting by the bar," he said with something close to a smile.

"Um, I'm Peter by the way."

The wolf was about to answer when he glanced behind me and cursed. I thought Danny had reappeared, but I saw a brown Setter making his way towards us with a lopsided grin on his face.

"Oh no, sorry I've got to run," he sighed. Before I could open my muzzle he began to disappear into thin air. The last thing I saw was his bright blue eyes.

"I'll be back, don't worry," I thought I heard him say in the split second before he vanished.

The Setter walked over and looked at the spot where the wolf had been standing.

"Damn, I just missed him," he sighed before wondering off again. Feeling confused, I turned to see Danny standing beside me.

"So, Mr. yote. How did it go?"

"Badly. He disappeared as soon as I said hello," I sighed before gesturing upwards to retrieve the leave button.

"Well, he didn't block you at least. I think that Setter was the reason he legged it, not you. Try again when you next see him," Danny reasoned. "Oh, pardon me, duty calls."

I watched as Danny raced across the room to where the Alsatian was waiting. I mulled over Danny's words as I pressed the button.

A second later I was lying on the floor of the living room. I felt defeated, but as I peeled the goggles off, Danny's words echoed through my mind and I pictured the wolf's blue eyes. The fox was right, the wolf was indeed aloof, but it didn't diminish the fact I had a huge crush on him. I sat down and thought the situation over. I'd been obsessed with Patrick's looks, until I dated him and found out what he was like underneath. The wolf could turn out the same. *Then again he could be different*, I told myself. *I should take Danny's advice and try again. If he turns out to be like Patrick, I'll face up to the fact he wasn't for me and move on.*

Work the following week became busy, but as papers piled up on my desk, all I could think about was going back on CruiseScape to talk to the wolf. I wanted to find out his real name and where he lived. Maybe, just maybe, he could be what I was looking for. My phone buzzed as I kept receiving promotions texts from CruiseScape; *New Worlds Available! Explore them now. More options for clothing.* I muted the sound as my manager glanced over. I browsed my emails during lunch to see even more promotional messages. I growled to myself, turned my phone off and spent the rest of the day concentrating on work.

I arrived home and almost forgot to switch my phone back on. I hadn't missed being pestered by promotions, but I saw a text from Danny; *Heading to the beach with TJ. Wanna join us? Your wolf may be around too ;).*

I changed out of my work clothes, placed the goggles over my eyes and found myself on the beach again. I wanted to find Danny or the wolf. The bar near the beach was empty apart from a black bear chugging a bottle of beer, his username read *GimmeSome*.

"Hi." I said, trying to sound casual as I took the seat next to him. The bear wiped his mouth with his paw.

"All right?" He replied in a gruff voice. Before I could say anything else, he reached down and groped my crotch.

"Oh!" I replied in shock. I was too surprised to feel aroused by the bear's advance.

"C'mon, let's see that dick of yours." The bear said with a grin.

"What, right now. I mean…"

"Come on," the bear growled. "Don't be a pussy."

"It just seems a bit forward…" I began, but the bear interrupted me with a growl.

173

"Timewaster," he spat before he vanished and was replaced by a faint black outline. It took me a moment to realise I'd been blocked.

I sat speechless for a minute.

I couldn't believe how obnoxious the bear had been and felt a little frightened. Fortunately, Danny showed up a minute later.

"That guy just blocked me because I wouldn't show him my cock," I explained, reeling at how ridiculous the statement sounded. Danny shrugged as he took the stool next to me.

"Welcome to the world of virtual reality; like the internet, people think they can treat each other like crap and get away with it," he said with a wry chuckle.

"Well, it wasn't very nice." I huffed, but at that moment I looked up and saw the wolf walking along the sand. Danny followed my gaze.

"Oh, it's your wolf again," he teased. "I can see why you like the look of him."

"I wish I could find out what he's like," I sighed.

"Just go talk to him, you were confident enough when you had fun with TJ and me," Danny teased.

"I know, but it went wrong the last time I tried speaking to him," I faltered about.

"You want to fancy him but you're scared of screwing it up, whereas you just wanted to play around with me?"

"No, it's…" I spluttered as I felt my ears burning.

"Heh, I was just teasing you. Go and talk to the wolf before someone else snatches him from you, quick he's heading towards the chatroom!"

I followed the wolf from a distance along the sand. He was making his way towards what looked like a doorway cut into the rocks, like the entrance to a villain's lair.

I hung back, but took a deep breath and followed him inside.

The sound of pounding music hit my ears and the stab of flashing neon lights hit my eyes. I shielded my face with a paw as I walked inside. It took me a moment to realise the music was from my playlist. Somehow, it made the situation a little more comforting. As I anticipated, the chatroom took the form of a nightclub, only it was different from the clubs I had been in as a student. The floors weren't sticky with spilled alcohol and it wasn't packed full of dancers leaving the heavy scent of sweat and damp fur in the air. A Husky and an Akita were dancing slowly arm in arm, gazing hungrily into each other's eyes as they moved to what I assumed must be a slow and romantic song.

In the background a black silhouette was talking to a fennec fox. The fox looked excited for a moment, before anger and disappointment flashed across his face. I guessed he'd suffered the same experience of being blocked that I'd had on the beach.

We Built This City began playing and I glanced around feeling shocked. Trust my playlist to choose a cheesy track. The wolf didn't seem to notice and I realised that he couldn't hear it unless I wanted him to.

I approached the wolf as he took a seat at the bar.

"Hi," I said, trying to sound casual as I took the stool next to him.

"Hello again," he replied as he splayed his ears. "Sorry I had to vanish, that Setter guy has been stalking me a lot. Doesn't take no for an answer. He either tries to flirt with me or start political arguments, without realising the latter is a bit of an erection killer."

I felt a rush of relief knowing I hadn't scared him off.

"You could block him?" I suggested.

"I try not to do that, although it's tempting sometimes," he reasoned. I needed something to get the conversation flowing and gazed over the wolf's biography again.

"I couldn't help but notice you like reading," I explained.

"Oh yes, I'm half-way through Wuthering Heights."

"Gosh, I love that book." We spent the next ten minutes discussing it, although I was careful to avoid spoilers.

"I love how Emily Bronte describes everything so well."

"Doesn't she just? The way she describes the moors, so eerie, but I promise I'm nothing like Heathcliff in real life." I laughed, before splaying my ears, but the wolf didn't seem to mind.

I smiled as I felt the conversation flowed more freely. I decided to put something a little more romantic on and subtly gestured upwards to bring the display. I chose *Beast of Burden* and selected the option for him to hear it.

"Ooh, I love this song," the wolf sighed. I couldn't help but smile to myself.

"I'd offer to buy you a drink, but…"

"It won't taste of anything," the wolf finished for me. We both chuckled.

"Um, want to dance?" I asked nervously. The wolf hesitated for a moment, but nodded and took my paw. We walked to the middle of the floor and danced slowly to the rhythm.

"So, what do you do when you're not on here, if you don't mind?" I asked.

"I used to serve in the army, now I just help out with my parent's engineering business."

"Ah cool, no wonder you ended up with such an amazing physique."

The ghost of a smile spread across the wolf's muzzle.

"Oh, uh, I'm sorry. I hope I didn't say something wrong," I stammered.

"No, you're fine. Don't worry about it. So, what do you do when you're not having fun with foxes?" the wolf teased as he seemed to recover his composure. I splayed my ears a little as I explained I worked in data processing and described the city I lived in.

"It's boring and not my first choice, but it helps to pay my rent I guess."

"Oh well, but you don't live *too* far from me as a matter of fact," the wolf said with a smile.

The song came to an end and was replaced by the sound of the Fennec ranting and swearing at the black silhouette, calling it vile names and giving it the finger. The Husky and Akita glanced over in shock. I found it rather off-putting.

"C'mon, let's go outside," the wolf suggested.

We made our way outside and saw that the sun was setting over the water. I couldn't help but marvel at the sight. The sky was now a rich shade of royal blue, and the sun cast out orange and yellow rays over the sea water as it gently lapped against the shore.

"It's beautiful," I breathed.

"It is, until I remember it's just pixels and graphics," the wolf replied. He gestured with his paw and I suddenly realised the horizon was not limitless, as it feels on beaches in real life. After a certain distance it became flat like a giant screen.

"What brought you on here?" I asked.

The wolf paused as he considered the question.

"I guess I wanted a chance to talk to people, and feel more confident, not that I'm much good at that on here," he sighed before gazing back out at the sunset.

Knowing the wolf felt nervous was somehow comforting to me, and I could relate. I suddenly realised how overconfident Patrick had been, but how fake it seemed in retrospect. I pushed all thoughts of the puma from my mind as I tried to focus on the wolf.

"I wish we could share a moment like this in real life," the wolf continued.

I felt a fuzzy sensation in my stomach at the mention of *we* that had nothing to do with the virtual environment, but the apprehension returned. *Would it be wise to meet him in person, is it too soon, what if he does something to hurt you?* One half of my conscience questioned. *You wanted to get to know him better, don't let this opportunity pass you by* the other half reasoned. I weighed up both sides before I took a deep breath.

"Why don't we?"

The wolf paused for a moment as if he regretted his words.

"You wouldn't like me," he eventually sighed.

"Why? I mean, you're handsome, a stud in fact, but you don't have that arrogant attitude a lot of good looking guys have. You seem shy and down to Earth."

"There's a reason for that," the wolf began before he glanced at his watch. "Damn, I need to go. I promised I'd help my mother with something at her house."

"Wait!" I called, "look, please can we meet in person so we don't keep getting interrupted. What's your number?"

The wolf paused, glanced around and then leaned over to whisper it in my ear. "My real name is Douglas," he added as he disappeared.

I gazed back at the sunset and felt a sudden compulsion to find Douglas in real life, even if he claimed I would not like him.

I brought myself back to reality and entered his number into my phone. Should I message him right away?

I thought it best not to. I'd always been told rule 101 of dating was not messaging instantly, even if we weren't technically dating. In the end I left it a couple of days as I became caught up at work. I thought it best to let Douglas make the first move.

Promotions texts from CruiseScape kept buzzing through to my phone and I growled to myself as I tried to stop them, but there didn't seem any way to do it. Finally, a message from a different number came through. My heart skipped a beat but my excitement vanished as I saw it was Danny, not Douglas.

Hey, taking a break from CruiseScape for a bit. Too many morons on it now. Wanna meet TJ and me IRL sometime? No sex stuff if you don't want :P

I smiled to myself, but felt a hollow feeling in my stomach.

I caved in and message Douglas as soon as I got home from work. I sat around and waited all evening for a reply.

My phone stayed silent.

I sent another message, but still there was nothing. I cursed to myself. Douglas had probably got cold feet and decided not to contact me. I went to bed feeling defeated.

There were no messages waiting for me the next morning. It was Saturday and I knew I could spend all day waiting, but I had a sinking feeling that Douglas would not contact me.

I was about to give up hope when the sound of *Instant Crush* by Daft Punk filled the room, heralding an incoming phone call. My heart jumped as I recognised Douglas' number.

"Hello?"

"Peter, it's Douglas."

"Oh, hi."

"Sorry I didn't contact you sooner." I could hear the sound of the wolf breathing at the other end. "Please don't think I'm a weirdo or anything, but I was scared of inviting you to see me in case you were repulsed."

"Douglas, I promise I won't be repulsed."

I heard Douglas take a deep breath.

"Okay, I live over in Upper Halewood. I'll be in the café at midday, if that's okay with you?"

"Of course it is."

"Good, you'll find the café, it's the only one in the village," Douglas explained.

I admit Douglas' call unnerved me somewhat. I'd read all these horror stories of guys pretending to be younger online than they really were, or turning out to be serial killers. I forced myself to consider that CruiseScape was different in that it gave a much clearer image of other users. Still, I thought it best to let someone know where I was going. I called Sam.

"Hey, I'm going to meet someone I met on CruiseScape."

"Fantastic, get in! I told you you'd fine someone…"

"Sam," I interrupted. "I wanted to let you know I'm going to Upper Halewood tomorrow. I'll text you to say how it's going."

"Sure, let me know how it goes."

Douglas' village was a forty minute drive from where I lived. I knew it by reputation as a close-knit, but picturesque place.

As I drove through the countryside and the sun broke through the clouds, I couldn't help but smile as the light touched the rolling hills. It seemed very idyllic, but it was real and tangible.

The village itself was nestled amongst the hills and comprised of yellow-stone buildings and cottages, like something from an old postcard. I admit, I had always found the idea of living in the countryside boring, but as I drove through the village and glanced at the old buildings, I could see why people would want to.

The village café looked rather quaint. It was housed in a Tudor style building off the main street. I walked in to a cacophony of steam, cups clinking together and customers of several species chatting loudly.

I searched around, looking for a solitary wolf. I spotted him sitting at the back reading a copy of Wuthering Heights, his athletic grey and white stature was instantly recognisable. He was even wearing the same white shirt from the chalet.

"Hello," I said as I sat down. Douglas put the book down and I admit to my shame that my eyes widened a fraction.

Billy Leigh

The left side of Douglas' face was the handsome wolf I recognised, but the right side was different. A red scar was running down his face, cutting through his luscious fur and exposing a patch of bare skin, while a chunk of his ear was missing.

"I thought you'd make a face like that," Douglas said.

"No, uh, I didn't mean…" I stammered.

"It's okay, I should have warned you rather than simply claiming you wouldn't like me."

Part of me wanted to know what had happened but I didn't want to ask. Douglas read my mind. "I stumbled across an IED at the side of the road when I served in Afghanistan. The blast took part of my ear out, sent a piece of shrapnel into my face and left me practically blind in one eye," he explained in a matter of fact voice.

"Oh. I'm sorry," I said quietly, feeling the response sounded silly and hollow.

"It's all right," Douglas replied. There was a moment of awkward silence.

"While we're here I recommend getting the coffee and walnut cake," Douglas suggested as he forced a smile. I felt a little taken aback, but I was eager for something to break the silence.

I walked over to the counter and ordered a coffee and slice of cake. I took two forks back to the table for Douglas to have some too.

We sat in silence as we ate.

The wolf was right, the cake and coffee were indeed good and it suddenly felt refreshing to be able to taste something real. As I looked closer, the scar wasn't as pronounced and the missing chunk was hidden as he flicked his ear back.

"Why didn't you show yourself like this on CruiseScape?" I asked.

"Honestly, I thought I'd scare people off," Douglas sighed.

"Don't take this the wrong way, but the more I look at it, the less obvious the scar seems, and it doesn't detract from the fact you're still handsome," I said sincerely. Douglas looked a little surprised, but nodded slowly. "I mean that." I added firmly.

"I was lucky I wasn't blown to pieces, but when I saw my face for the first time after I got out of hospital I was horrified. I thought no one would ever want to date me ever again," Douglas sighed. "I collected old pictures of me and used them to build my CruiseScape profile, and even though I mislead people, I'm glad I made an account. Meeting you kind of restored my faith in talking to other guys," he glanced down. "But you'll be relieved to know I do have those blue swimming trunks in real life, and they indeed go a bit see-through," he added with something close to a smile.

179

"We should go somewhere exotic, so you'll have a chance to wear them," I suggested, but instantly wished the words had not escaped my muzzle, thinking them too forward.

"I'd like that," Douglas replied as his smile became more obvious.

We sat in silence for a minute as we finished our drinks.

"I'll show you somewhere I used to walk to as a cub," Douglas said. He gestured for me to follow him out of the café and through the village.

"I like living here, it makes me feel more anonymous, and everyone knows who I am so they don't gawp at my scar when I walk down the street."

I thought Douglas was still being too judgemental about his appearance, but I kept quiet. I glanced at the old stone cottages as we walked along. I couldn't deny the place looked cosy. I surreptitiously sent a message to tell Sam that everything seemed okay.

Douglas led me to a path than ran between two cottages. It gradually ascended up a hill by the village until we were overlooking a valley. There was a breath-taking view over the village and the open countryside beyond. The sky was the same crystal blue that it had been on the CruiseScape beach, but here it felt limitless knowing that it was not artificial.

I could smell the earthy scent of the fields and feel the warmth of the sun on my muzzle. It felt so real and wonderful. I reached out and took Douglas' paw and squeezed it. I immediately felt worried I was moving too fast, but he didn't recoil and turned to shoot me a smile. The warm and gentle grip of his paw felt affectionate and reassuring.

"This is truly being alive," I murmured. Douglas fixed me a dazzling smile and his bright blue eyes sparkled in the sunlight.

Heavenly Flesh

by *Slip Wolf*

The long-awaited rapture that came to our crowded world was not at the hand of any God you'd think you know. It was dangled before us by science, not faith, set in motion by a desperate government. And those who chose to go to paradise, carried up scant dozens at a time, did so reluctantly. That was because to get to heaven, you had to say goodbye. To literally everything you've ever known. The only things you could take with you were those who agreed to take the trip with you.

Heaven had a location, a fixed celestial point in the sky, forty-two point seven light years away and red-shifting further. It took the first light-speed probe a mammal's lifetime to get there while the earth and her in-system colonies rapidly over-flowed. The follow-up habitation and reception matrix took another two hundred and twenty years to limp to heaven, holding a LaGrange point above the green adolescent body below that robots had only begun to tame. The first settlers manifested in a frontier town, the second set took their first interstellar breath in a burgeoning city. By the time Puca and I arrived, there was a gleaming metropolis ready.

I don't remember the transit. Nobody can. Mass pushed at light-speed is a horrendous struggle; just the smallest of probes manage. Only signals can stab effortlessly through the veils of subspace, collecting at the receptacle probe that downloaded all I could remember being into the sinew and bone that was grown for me. Whiskers twitched and fingers curled I'd never had before. Claws brought the first beads of pain to furred thighs, invigorating after the long purgatorial non-existence. The body I'd left on earth was long back to the dust along with all those I'd known who stayed. My new life had begun. And in those first days, as a certain truth coldly settled upon us, I took on the lie that would be my cross to carry in heaven for years to come.

As a bear, six and a half feet of muscle and sinew, there's little the robots weaving habitat sixty-cee could do that I couldn't, but their jobs were more about horticultural precision than brawn. In my solitary job as habitat growth foreman, I rarely did more than fix one of them when something froze up. The bots kept at their tasks when I clocked out, weaving and stacking the frames of new homes long through the night.

At home, our lovingly curated habitat bungalow that was grown in countless vines around a plexi-pour frame, Puca was at the stove. He was trying on something new. I frowned when I saw him under the light cascading down under the transparent roof. Hadn't it just been a few months? "Rabbit tonight?" I muttered as I smelled the scents rolling from our rustic kitchen area. The white-furred creature stirring the pot stirred carefully and long ears went tall and attentive. "I know you really like it," Puca said, and left the kitchen to tend itself. He wore a lime green apron and nothing else, fur shimmering over slender muscular arms and squat haunches leading to thick lapin feet. His grin was beatific and wicked. "When dinner's ready, so am I."

I looked him up and down, eyes wary but appreciative. "When did you get this?"

"This afternoon."

"Wasn't the last one like this brown?"

"It, you know, just didn't work for me."

"Oh." The green apron found the floor and he was in my arms in a second. I could smell that telltale scent, burnt and new. "Why'd you pick—?"

"I got bored. C'mon don't you ever get bored?"

"Well, no. Why? Do you want something else?" I put on mock offence.

He laughed. "Nothing's as huggable as this." His paw reached around my chest and caressed my haunches through the overalls I wore to work. Lust on him smells like sweet sherry. Smoothed ivory fur tapered down his chest to the pink prod peeking below. He was out of my grasping arms and slipped down my overalls with deliberation. They were getting uncomfortably tight since I came in. Freed, I searched his pink eyes for that telltale spark that told me it's him.

By their hunger, I knew. His paws kneaded my flesh and mine clutched his, our cocks primordially slicked and buzzing against one another.

Dinner burned a bit. So did we.

* * *

Heaven wasn't built in a day, but we were made in far less. Nano weavers get a six hour window on an incoming signal, heralded by a present packet before the neural mapping with all the instructions, casting the bones, weaving the flesh, growing the fur or feathers or scales. I'd been out of my spent body back on earth for a mere instant, insensate to the forty two years it took my tight-beamed pattern to traverse the silent dark. My mate's pattern ran along with mine, sharing the same signal.

Most mind patterns are sent in threes. Not ours. No, it was just us two. Such a waste of potential bandwidth when you stopped and think about it and Puca confessed he thought of it often. I would always change the subject of course. Puca was always looking for patterns in things that weren't there.

I woke up the next morning spooning Puca, his swept back ears ticking my throat as I tried not to burp some of last night's stew. I still feel that blessed fatigue in my limbs that comes after a good romp, even though I'd woken troubled by questions I didn't want to ask. "Stay here," Puca said. "Take a day off." But I'd already gotten out of bed.

"Come on," Puca pleaded playfully. "I can call Daniel at the office and ask if I can take a day offline. Your condo-weavers can figure themselves out for a few hours without you can't they?"

I hobbled across the lawn in our room, dappled sunlight from the gaps in vegetation and open clear ceiling above adding patches of dry warmth to the recesses of dew. Our grown home, like all the units on our burb block, was a genetically programmed biosphere, cubic-trained vegetative walls and ceilings of tamed jungle. I shook myself off, still static from sex. "If you love what you do, you never work a day in your life," I intoned and the grinder and brewer in the kitchen nook started on my coffee. I mulled over Puca's words as it worked. "Daniel, huh?" Puca said nothing, pouting.

As the first sips of coffee woke me up, the question I'd been forming all night since almost immediately after orgasm found words. "Puca, have you been trying to remember again?" I asked.

He blinked his lapin eyes. "I stopped trying years ago. I know that what's gone is gone. Why do you ask?"

"No reason." I left him with a kiss, those soft rabbit lips feeling so familiar but so strange.

Work was predictable enough to let me ponder Puca's disposition, the fragile sense of himself and the world my mate maintained in the wake of his accident. After two years he was still missing his entire life prior to waking up in heaven and the first week after, an error in our pattern's transmission that cost him his memory. It had been a struggle helping Puca find himself, acclimate to our relationship again. Fortunately, his body told him what his mind never quite pieced together and we found a vein of normalcy with help from a councillor and considerable therapy.

As if to remind me that the most advanced technology at our disposal wasn't perfect, a mishap took me out of my head. One of the construction bots in outer heaven's settlements mistook another robot for building materials and started bonding a foundation using its casing as support. I scolded the well-meaning offender with a software reset and got them back to work. Another day, two new homes built. Tight beams would put colonists in them within the month. Heaven would grow.

And would gain a personality. Puca, following his recovery worked as an artist from home, designing unique signage and artistic displays for the twenty four subdivisions spoking out from heaven's urban core where the ebb and flow of culture was like an electric current drawing everyone in on evenings and weekends. As I turned back towards our suburb, I could see the spires of the city rising on the horizon, pointing at the bluish sun that stayed up the whole walk home from work.

My nose sought dinner when I arrived, but smelled that smell again. Carbon and iron, slightly burned like a fresh kill. He didn't, did he? The very next day?

Dinner was done a while ago by the weaker smells and the caramel-furred mountain lion was perched on a chaise lounge in the flower-walled garden area. A sport was on the in-city live feed, but the mountain-lion wasn't watching the snap and the catch of the defending team. His eyes were in a book the whole time, something leather bound. When I got near, the cat put the book down and I could feel him girdling for a jump.

I couldn't believe my eyes. "One day? One day, Puca? What the hell happened?"

"I got bored again." He either didn't sense my consternation or didn't care. "I just felt like a change and, well, liked this."

"But after just one day?"

"Is it a problem?" His frown was borne of confusion. The eyes that blinked at me were Puca's. The listlessness, even lounging in a book, was definitely his, and seemed alien to this feline body. His whiskers twitched and one bare leg crossed the other. Of course he was naked. We all enjoy feeling the air on a new body's fur.

"It's unusual, is what it is. Was there an accident?"

He thinks about that. "Nope. I just wanted to try this." With a curl of his abdomen he's out of the chaise. "Wouldn't you like to try this?" His eyes are wicked with ideas.

"Puca. We talked about—"

"I mean," he draws the word out along his fresh rough tongue, rich hot breath tickling my chin hairs as the cat sidles up to me, "wouldn't you like to try 'this' out?" The graceful meat of that paw is around mine, raising it, the opposing paw's claw tracing soft shapes on my palm. "You know newness makes one pretty excited."

"You didn't need to re-cradle to get aroused." Even as I said it, those overalls getting tight again as his fingers stirred.

"Yeah, I know."

"Then, why?"

"Because I felt like a change," he said again, stating what to him was obvious. "Don't ask me to explain it. Just enjoy."

He undressed me adroitly, and a westward wind through the open portal that overlooked the rolling natural preserves below our home tickled my well-worn flesh. His paw took me as I grew and teased me bigger, sticky slick and hungry for contact. Yesterday's rabbit had an urgency, today's mountain lion had a languid insistence. We're it not for those same bright eyes, now golden, I'd have been with someone else in that moment.

This wasn't the first time Puca has changed himself, re-cradled as they call it. It simply hadn't been a single day between exchanges.

Knowing this, my worry was tamped down by my arousal. Out here, in this new world, we were allowed, even expected to make something new of ourselves, weren't we? Others have done this, haven't they? I'd never asked the neighbors, so I didn't know for sure how often others changed without medical reasons.

That beautiful powdered-gold cat's body slipped low and I felt breath and then rough tongue on my cock. Lips and cheeks nestled hot around it.

What even was I worried about? He liked change, I liked stability. Fate hadn't left him with the option for that after all. Cat claws dragged across my flanks and tongue dragged back from my balls to my tip. My eyes rolled to the vines creeping overhead and the bluish clouds beyond the plexi-cover they clung to. All else was unimportant. This right here was the way we've both always wanted it. Puca took me down to the grass and I mewled like I was the cat. As his claw found its way to the expectant ring of my anus, I made myself forgot the whole thing. The cat could take his time playing and he did.

The next day came and I left him with his tablet rendering signage. I saw two more habitats finished, their walls already grown as the robots finished the superstructures and sutured everything together. The roads that would join them to the rest of the new neighborhood were set to start weaving soon now that the air was getting warmer, ending my need to take a float skiff out here every day that I didn't feel like walking through this world's egg-blue undergrowth. It was nearly summer here. I watched robots build more pieces of some other couple's perfect world and wondered why life couldn't be this tidy everywhere. For everyone.

When I went home, waving to the mustelid next-door neighbors snuggling on their vine-woven hammock together, a sense of trepidation had me sampling the air as I parted the willow threads and wandered in. Dinner was already made and I found Puca in the study, his feline tail, the same mountain-lion's tail, twitching in interest at whatever was reading on the web, checking happenings in the inner city by the looks of it. "We should totally go out." He said by way of greeting.

I gazed at the way that feline frame stretched back along the grassy expanse of the living area, feet curled up into the air and toe claws clenching. I enjoyed that body the night before, as much as I'd enjoyed other bodies he's had. I removed my work coveralls to hang them back over a chair, settled down next to him, felt his body warm next to mine. I could feel that innate sense of Puca-ness that had travelled with both of us for lightyears. This was as him as any him that had been. I needed to remember that in all the ways he couldn't. "Okay. Where do you want to go?" I asked, rubbing my bare shoulder against his.

"There are fun things going on this weekend," Puca said. "An art exhibit on reclaimed monuments back on earth like the Giza Pyramids or the American Statue of Libertines."

"Sounds exciting."

"I checked in with my buddy at work, Leonard, to see if he had any suggestions."

I blinked. "Oh?"

"Couldn't get a hold of him. Oh!" He stopped scrolling and brightened. I had no idea what he'd stopped on because I was staring at his fresh cat's face, eyes wide and gleaming with purpose. "There's a science-fiction convention, themed around monster invasion films from the CGI two-D era."

"That sounds interesting."

"Noted," he said brightly. "I also see there's a few musical acts, lots of artists coming to reside here now." He scrolls a little further. "They have Marigold Harper."

"The name is familiar."

"She was a folk artist back on Io. She was a wolf whose career was ended by a paralytic infliction that messed with her guitar skills." He brings up a photo to enlarge. "She transited and they had a new body ready for her, ten years younger and free of disease."

188

"This is a fox." I focus at the image of the vixen with an acoustic guitar resting in her lap.

"Her husband's a fox, so she decided to have vulpine bodies ready for both of them. It was really touching."

I don't say anything for a moment. "She stay in that fox body? Or did she ever go back to her wolf self? Or anything else?"

Puca didn't look at me. "She stayed a fox. And she's happy. That's the point, right? Everyone here deserves to be happy, however they get that way."

I smiled weakly. We weren't going to have this conversation but Puca clearly thought we needed to. "I agree," I nodded, wondering if he'd ever have an inkling of just how much I agreed with him. "Are you happy, Puca?"

Puca looked inward for a moment, lost in a fog of thought. "I've just been going through a bit of ennui of late. I dunno why."

I roll away a bit, just so I can look at him better. "How long has this been going on for?"

"Months. Maybe longer."

"You've been re-cradling yourself pretty often. Are you sure you're not trying to remember again?"

"No. I know it's gone, Janus. I gave up on that a while ago."

"But you are trying new bodies a lot, Puca. I mean, if transit caused memory loss, then aren't you worried about—"

"Janus, we went forty light years. Re-cradling here takes me thirty feet at most."

"But so often, Puca. It's…"

"What," his cat mouth frowned and his tail switched. "Wasteful? The resources don't run out. Every single resident could re-cradle once a day for months before the biomass reactor ever suffered a shortage. And all of these frames go back when we're done with them. We don't waste the meat, Janus."

I felt myself shrink at that description. "We're not meat, Puca. Seriously, please don't be reductive."

Puca sat up and crossed his legs, the entertainment interface forgotten. "For over forty years we were both much less. And I arrived incomplete. Do you know that I don't remember what species I was born into, Janus? I can't remember what I was or my parents were. All of that's gone. Reductive sense of self is one way to describe it."

"I told you. You were born a coyote. You were a coyote when our signals came in and we first cradled here and they brought you around."

"But I don't feel that, Janus. I've never felt that, never felt like I belonged in front of that tail or behind that muzzle." Puca jumps up and begins stalking around the room on the grass, tail low and ears back. "It was like coming too in some kind of costume. It didn't feel like me."

I swallowed as I picked my words carefully. "That's who you've always been, Puca. That's the dog I fell in love with back on Earth. Even if overpopulation hadn't banned re-cradling tech back home, I'd have never wanted to see you change. I'd have stayed a bear, and you'd have been my coyote and I'd love you till the day we died. I still will."

Puca stopped pacing by the hanging shelves where hard prints of our favorite images smiled back at us. Most of them had a sand-furred coyote looking reflective next to a grinning idiot ursine. One of them, one of the very last we took together, had me gazing evenly into the middle distance next to an alert black ferret.

I read into his confusion and found my opening. "We can just be us, Puca. You don't feel like you, and I can't understand that but I can help you. We came here to start a new life."

"So why hold back?" Puca was staring at the photo with the ferret. "Who'd want to cross the universe to just be themselves? We can be whatever we want to be here, that's the point right? So why not let it all go and just indulge in our fantasies?"

I was taken aback by that. I don't remember standing up off the grass where we were laying, but I'm nearly pacing myself. "I don't know what you're getting at."

"Remember back when we were getting re-acquainted after the psychologist was done with me, and we traded our deepest, most intimate fantasies. Remember that?"

"Yeah?" I took a seat at the dinette table. The whole situation was giving me a sense of worry, even though Puca was finally opening up.

"I told you how I wanted to be fucked on a skiff going at a hundred miles an hour, feel the wind in my fur, your cock deep inside me as we bucked in the saddle, remember that? Remember giving it to me on that day you shut down all the remote habitat construction cameras?"

My small-round ears blushed despite myself. "I never got that skiff up higher than sixty-five."

"Doesn't matter. I never felt something so wonderful in my short, remembered life. I want to give that back to you."

"But I never told you what my fantasy was."

"Yes you did. Once, after a concert and several drinks, you told me all about what truly, deep down excites you. We'd never role-played together as youths. You did that with your school friends, you said."

I do remember, classic table-top adventures with dice and character sheets and dungeons to raid. What had I told Puca? I must have been really drunk.

"What monsters are down there in the labrynth, little mage?" Puca whispered as he stalked over and picked the tablet off the lawn. "What horrors and wonders do they hold?"

I remember suddenly as the grin crosses the mountain lion's face. "You know that monster convention I told you about? They have a programmed bio-reactor running special templates there."

"You've got to be kidding."

"You better believe I'm not!" Puca beams. There's something so sweet and innocent in an excited cat's expression. But under the circumstances I feel a weight in the pit of my stomach.

"Puca."

"What? Come on, it'll be fun. It wouldn't be a wholesale re-cradling, just a temp transference. You've never been out of your skin—" He sees my scowl. "—well, since we arrived. Come on, live a little."

I instinctively shrank away, the sensation of Puca's excitement running hard into the knowledge of what it portended. Another change, another confused attempt at finding something he couldn't get back. And here he was trying to make a game of it. For me.

Puca's expression gave way to a frown as he saw me tighten up, my expression showing hurt, and I openly shuddered. He blinked once, looked at the tablet and then back up at me again. When he blinked again, his eyes were getting wet. "But we never do anything fun anymore," he mutters. "I'm planning this for you." His voice goes from small to enraged and hissing in an instant. "I don't have a regular life to settle into and get fucking bored with, Janus. This isn't fair!"

I felt that reedy, hollow pain that comes with hurting someone you love. Anger stained it quickly. "Come on Puca, don't feed me that shit."

"What isn't fair is that you don't support me! You don't even try to understand! It fucking hurts all the time, Janus! I have nobody else to talk about this with, in all these months I haven't made a single friend out of all the acquaintances we've met here and a couple people I trade updates with at work. It's like I'm inauthentic to anyone who'd ever take the time to know me. I just can't connect."

"I'm sorry, Puca. Lots of us tend to be...introverted here. Who else would agree to leave the rest of civilization completely behind? Honestly, it will keep hurting if you keep running around trying to get something back that's gone." I growled through grinding teeth. "You aren't incomplete.

I love you, even though I never know if I'll be able to pick you out of a crowd on any given fucking day."

The tablet fell to the lawn and bounced. The mountain lion with Puca inside cried openly now, tears trailing down fallen feline whiskers. "So if you love me than why not go on this journey with me. I can't forget what I've lost if you won't help me make something better. But that's nothing to you, is it? Why the hell would you—" he snarled.

"I know more about what you've lost than you'll ever know, Puca!" I seized myself on the brink of saying something I couldn't take back. "I can't handle this. I have to go."

"Fine. I'll go to the city alone. I'll play out *your* fantasy. Alone. Go back to tending your empty houses. They won't be perfect if they aren't all the goddam same, right?"

I closed my eyes, rumbling on the precipice between fury and tears, hearing a distant rustle of vegetation parting. When I opened them Puca had left. I was alone with our photos, our imperfect, unkempt home. It was silent enough to hear all the ghosts.

They followed me back to work, where I tended the growing homes long past the setting of the bluish sun. In the dark the glowing indicators on the robot's backs made them look like constellations in motion as they weaved silicone frame and cellulose shells long into the night.

The calm of their work allowed me to center myself, to become reflective. This was how things looked in the beginning. The first probe here, the only device too actually cross the dark divide, had been equipped with a nanoblock builder that started assembling our world with the materials available, starting with other builders. All of heaven started with a tiny molecular forge the size of a dinner table. Now it was as massive as half the cities that teemed on the worlds we'd left behind.

Most of us missed all that, but Puca was a unique case. You'd have thought the ignorance afforded him would be bliss, no surrendered world to yearn for. As the robots wove heaven, I placed a call home. No answer. I thought carefully before I dialed the next number.

The voice that answered sounded tired. "Who is this?" A female voice grunted and then held for a long lupine yawn. I'd disengaged video but I could imagine those clinical blue eyes blinking.

"Dr. Somnul, I'm very sorry to call you so late. It's Janus."

"Janus? Ah, wait, I remember. You're partnered with Puca." She stirred a few moments as she collected herself and remembered. "How's your friend doing? Is he still trying out that marsupial body from last time?"

"No. He's re-cradled again."

A wolf's sigh was a particular kind of weary. "Well, I did tell you something like this might happen."

"Five more times?"

All I could hear was robots nestling vines into place for a moment. "You have to be fucking kidding me. It's been barely eight months. That's... dangerous."

"To his body, well bodies, or mind?" I asked ask I walked outside and looked up at the cluster of stars that lined heaven. The spill light from the city center was kept low and contained to minimize the saturation out here. Seeing the stars at night was one of the most precious things those in the Sol system scarcely knew. I craned my neck as though my blunt muzzle could touch them.

"Which do you think I'm qualified to opine about?" Somnul asked. To remind me that she was a psychologist rather than a medical doctor, I heard the telltale flick of a lighter and a static fuzz of tobacco burning. Even with re-cradling as an option, some recreational past-times were frowned upon. Dr. Somnul came to heaven so she could help others like herself who didn't want to give a shit. "Is he starting to remember things?"

I swallow. "He's tried to have conversations about things with Daniel and Leonard at work. So yeah, he's getting some inkling that there's things to figure out."

Dr. Somnul said nothing.

I sighed. "Puca is still blank to the past. I can't tell if he's re-cradling so often because he's trying to get closer to some idea of a real him or getting even with the universe for making sure he'll never find it."

"The former most likely. Re-cradling to a new body, even one physiologically similar to the last, has complications because new bodies always come with different instinctual firm-ware that helps the host consciousness utilize it. Imagine trying to get in a fish's body without a mind that knew how gills work. He try anything-?"

"Thankfully no," I snorted.

"Well, some small part of you is always re-written with a re-cradling to help the natural talents integrate. He could be subconsciously shaking his mind up and down to get something to fall out of it. Or he could just be acting out against a feeling of rootlessness." The wolf puffed again. "How about you? What happened to finally make you call me again?"

"We had a fight." I looked off into the dark. "He wants me to temporarily re-cradle with him at a convention event in the city."

"He wants you to escape with him. It might bother him that you've stayed fixed to your ursine self."

"And is that bad?"

"No. He needs to see someone rooted in themselves and understand how that works for most people. He has to be him and you have to be you, even if one of you is incomplete and the other still feels guilty."

"This just isn't fair. We came here to be happy, all of us."

"Yes. If that was how it always worked out, I would be water-coloring all day. Too bad, the mess everybody is. My landscapes are getting pretty good." Another draw and slow exhale. She clicked her teeth. "You can't give him what you think he really needs."

My steps became heavier as I trod my thick paws through the grass. Home was just a few kilometers away. "Dammit, I'd almost managed to forget all this. I don't want to bring the past up."

"Yes you do. I can hear it in your voice, just like I heard it last time we talked. You're tired of carrying secrets. You think doing so means you don't really love him and that he won't love you."

"I can't…"

"Honestly, Janus, and this is as a friend, not a mental health professional, truth is not the answer here, no matter how noble it seems, no matter how formative and beautiful pain is in philosophy texts and romantic poetry and other shit. Don't. Do this to him. If you want, I can help make sure you don't."

I shudder at the prospect. "You don't need to do a thing. Dammit, Doctor. What kind of idiot do you take me for?"

"The worst kind," she took a quick drag, "a loving one."

"We'll ride this out. I just need to let him find himself."

"Will you?"

I didn't answer, and immediately wanted to swear at myself for not doing so.

Dr. Somnul grunted. "Call me if things get worse. Are the neighbors aware of how rocky things are?"

"No. We keep to ourselves. We like it that way. Tonight was the first time I can remember that we had an open argument about this."

"Alright. I have appointments tomorrow but I'll look in on you when I have the chance, maybe pay you a visit."

"I'd like that." A tone announced a message coming in. "I think Puca's linking me."

"Okay. Keep in touch, Janus." She disconnected.

The comm trilled soon after. The screen emitted from my collar where I'd clipped the projector and filled my lower vision. 'I'm having a great time, but I miss you. Sorry 'bout before. Drunk as fuck right now. Coming home with a surprise.'

Oh shit. I stared at the line of text and nearly tripped on a root along the flattened path back to my burb. I could see the lights from home by the time I responded. 'What surprise?' No answer.

I arrived home soon after, and found it dark as I'd left it. I fixed myself a snack, unsure of what to do, chewing granola in my thick ursine jaw with trepidation. I poured a bourbon to take the edge off. Were we about to have another fight? This one with the mountain lion drunk? Should I be drunk myself? I thought back to my talk with Dr. Somnul. I just needed to let things take their course. Our relationship was worth that, at least at this point. I needed to let Puca be Puca.

I didn't hear the taxi skiff hiss as it lifted off. Of course, there were no locked doors in our home. Heaven provided for everyone in advance. What is there to keep out?

The bungalow went dark as the main power circuit opened. Moonlight peeked through vines, creepers and the geometric patterns of framework that shaped our home. It tattooed the muscles on my arms and trunk as I sat with an empty bowl at one elbow and a drink I'd just poured in my meaty paw. My small ears caught a ragged breath, like wet gravel shifting. "Little bear mage," came the taunt from the dark, "what brings you to my lair?"

"Puca? Is that you?"

"Yes, bear. It is I, Puca the unfathomable! Puca the immortal dominator. Puca the God of unspeakable horrors and…unmoanable pleasures."

Unmoanable? My nervous laugh was interrupted by a scent which drew a questing sniff from my wide nostrils. I caught something close by, a fecund pungency like swampy vegetation and a sharp tang of what was definitely spiced rum. He'd been in the sauce, and by the smell of things, fallen into a lake somewhere. What kind of convention had this been again? "Pleasures?" I asked, trying to focus on movement in the darkness.

"Yes, bear mage! Now that you have been enslaved by me, you shall know exquisitely unbearable sensual rituals at your new God's irresistible whims. You, puny mortal bearer of tricks, are now mine to toy with as I desire!"

My memory jogged to last year, when Puca and I discussed our deepest fantasies with bellies full of wine. Hadn't Puca brought this up again earlier when we'd fought?

Something touched the padded sole of my foot, startling me. It was warm, but slippery wet. A lick and then gone. Another touch grazed my thigh through my clothes, front to inside, then up and gone before I could react.

"Remove your vestments, slave. I won't have them in my dungeon." There was a wet hiccup from the sibilant mouth that spoke and the rum and cola scent was distinctive. I realized right away that Puca had done it, he'd re-cradled into something at the fantasy thing he'd gone to. Pinpricks of light played with the form that approached in the darkness, silent in the grass. The voice was a sultry, threatening promise. "I have come from your deepest nightmares and most guarded desires to show you the wondrous sensations that lie beyond your limited senses."

My cock put it all together before I did, and starting hardening as I remembered. Dungeon crawling, fighting some monsters, succumbing to others. Puca really had remembered everything I'd confided to him on our Dionysian bender, when he'd told me about fucking in the sky, and I'd confessed my favorite masturbatory fantasy. The firm restraint, the humiliating exposure, the surrender of control to a creature of pure, carnal hunger.

Oh. Wow. My clothes came off, quicker than they ever had. Let Puca be Puca. Let Puca be God. A horrible but loving one. He was doing this to make up with me perhaps? I needed to stop thinking and just go along.

The meager light caught glints of wet, pinkish flesh, undulating and winding as tendrils reached for me. A tentacle brushed my shoulder. Another caressed my chin. Yet another dragged a trail of moisture up between my legs to the soft mound of my testicles. They buzzed with my quickened pulse as the slippery appendage traced underneath and up to tickle one of my buttocks.

The ancient one moved forward and my heart skipped a beat as two narrowed eyes with cat-like slits took me in with a feral glow. "Submit." Puca's voice spoke through its hidden mouth. "Submit and be conquered with sensual delights that will take you to the verge of," he hiccuped and shook his tentacled body, "unspeakable divinity. You only need to pledge yourself as my eternal slave."

"I doubt you have that power!" I playfully growled back as more and more tentacles wound around my limbs, poked at my ears, twinged my nipples and teased my cock. I was lifted off the grass carpet of our home and vaguely remembered that only hours ago Puca and I had been fighting when the tentacle that tickled at my taint snaked higher and poked at my anal vestibule. I gasped as it slipped inside me, countless binding stalks of warm, slippery flesh winding around me everywhere else, massaging my limbs, teasing my genitals, poking at my teeth. The moisture that brushed my tongue was vaguely sweet, vaguely sour, the taste of an unknowable God made to pleasure supplicant subjects. As the thickened member that slipped my cheeks started to languidly fuck me with a blessed, relentless heat, the rest of the creature pulled itself around me, slipping itself around my lower torso. I felt hot breath on my cock. "Know what it is to be supplicant to the ancient one who will fuck your silly magician's brains out, you dungeon-diving bear slut!"

Okay, Puca was slipping out of character somewhat, but who cared. A rubbery lipped throat I couldn't see closed around my drooling cock and tentacles and lips got to work, moaning in and around my ursine heat. I arched my back, my hips bucking like a driven race animal. There were no words at this point, just primal sounds from me in my nakedness and my lover in a borrowed body, laying bare the erotic pulses that drove us from so deep. I didn't want to think, didn't want to know or worry. As a chorus of massaging limbs worked me over and abused me sweetly in every way I could dream at once, I let myself submerge into sensual bliss. God of unmoanable pleasures indeed.

The tentacle winding within my ass pulsed and slid and tickled and fucked. The hot bright moment when I popped inside him, loosing seed within that monstrous frame was a moment I'd only hope would stay burnt upon my consciousness until I'd die. The creature shivered, and with a snap and a quiver, the tentacle stuffing my asshole withdrew and wound ropes of jizm all up and down my buttocks. None of the other restraining and tickling tentacles let anything loose, for which my already matted fur was likely grateful. The ancient one gasped around me, gurgling my essence back upon my balls.

We both slipped down to the grass, the tentacled mass sliding around me in a spooning moment, those eyes settling sideways, glinting faintly in the dark. "My slave has earned his rest," rumbled Puca.

"Much thanks, God of the depths," I replied, narrowly keeping myself from giggling. "Will I be tamed again later?"

"Perhaps."

"And on the morrow? When the sun rises?"

Puca sighed, sounding like a wet balloon letting out air. "Sorry, Janus. They need to get it back in the morning to clean it for a room party tomorrow night back at the con."

"Oh. Where's your...?"

"My current body is in storage. I can check it on an app they gave me."

I raised my brow. "In case somebody does things with it?"

The shrug jiggles six or seven tentacles as the reptilian eyes blink. "They say people worry about that kind of thing. Plus it keeps me from getting into too much trouble while away." He sighed again. "I just realized I left the anti-moisture upholstery cover they gave me in the taxi. Dammit."

"I'll find you something."

"Come back with me." The eyes blinked. "I don't want to have to explain the whole thing to the next AI that comes to collect me. Plus, you'd have fun there."

Things come down to heaven again as I remember our fight from earlier, what it was and what it represented. All the things I'd wanted to say crept back in and I could hear Dr. Somnul lighting up in my imagination, giving me that muzzle crinkling frown of disdain that wolves were so good at. "You can't give him what you think he needs." I could hear her say, and I already know how I felt about that. I couldn't expect him to figure his problems out alone. The only way Puca would move on was if he had a good enough life now to never want to go back.

"Sure." I grinned. "Let's go."

We got him back to the city in an hour, after we both separately cleaned up and I changed into something more befitting a night on the town, a black, slick jacket and loose fitting pants. With the erotic haze of my fantasy lifted, I couldn't wait for him to get out of the monster form and back into the mountain lion that awaited in slumber. The convention was replete with costumed characters we'd enjoyed back on earth, gaggles of tipsy geeks like us swapping stories of memories they'd long cherished and childhoods well lived long ago on planetary system far, far away.

When we passed a middle-aged coyote reflecting with friends on how a beloved fantasy game had touched his childhood, I felt a twinge of regret that I couldn't name, and wondered if Puca had heard it too. How hard it was to wear someone else's dreams, wondering what you had loved in the place you came before? We were quiet, almost somber by the time we arrived at the rental return desk. A meaty long-horned minotaur lay upon a long couch, giving its crotch one last playful tap before falling into slumber with a smile. The contacts that tapped its brain case completed the transfer silently and a slim, slight, female ferret came out from behind the curtain taking recuperative breaths, a smile on her thin lips and a paw touching her femaleness quickly and with familiar pride. Then it was Puca's turn. The tentacled creature settled in repose and the mountain lion I had known just a couple days longer exited the back with a yawn and an elastic stretch of his limbs. "It's weird just having two arms again," Puca said.

I didn't know what to say at first, and then decided to hug him. The warmth, the way his muzzle nuzzled my shoulder, all of it was familiar in its own way. I realized I wanted to fuck this form of his too, get myself re-acquainted with the creature who was continually searching for himself. Sadly, I knew from experience that the con hotel would be booked solid at this point.

Mountain lion eyes roved along a sea of people, blinking away the disorientation of being behind feline eyes in a four-limbed body. "Well, that was fun, where do we go from here?"

Something about his demeanor told me we needed to keep moving, keep the night alive now that our libidos had cooled. We lost ourselves in the headiness of the con and the city beyond it. We ate medieval themed meals at the hotel restaurant, sat in to watch an adult-themed night panel on the power of myth, then left to bar-hop and dance. Halfway up the strip, Puca picked a place, a modest bar with pounding music erupting from it.

The place looked strangely familiar. "Let's go to the next one," I said, pointing further down the thoroughfare, but Puca's tail was winding left and right as he bounded past the doorman who gave him an appraising smile and nod. Fighting an onrush of nerves, I followed him into the hazy, pulsing place. Puca danced backwards into the throng, so I followed him in, smiling back. My moves as a bear were never that bad, because I'd long learned to avoid overcompensating for my lumbering frame. I swayed breezily despite the quick tempo while Puca slunk around in a decidedly un-catlike manor. In the headiness of all that was to follow I'd never put my finger on it, but he seemed to combine the jumpiness of a rabbit with the sideways slinkiness of a weasel, as though he were mimicking the movement of other forms he still kept in memory. Twice he stopped in what I assumed were moments of tiredness, but on the third pause, I realized that Puca wasn't out of breath. He was confused, gazing around as though uncertain as to where he was or what he was doing.

"Are you okay?"

He couldn't hear me over the thump of the music, nor was he paying me any attention, having fixated on a booth across the thinning dance hall as the music slowed down. I followed his gaze. Two canines sat across from one another, one male, one female, dreamily staring into one another's eyes. The light distorted their fur as such that I couldn't quite tell if they were lightly furred foxes or, I felt my stomach sink as I realized how Puca saw them, caramel-furred coyotes, tails bushed out and almost touching under their table. One male, one female, grinning and whispering giddy things to each other.

There are well over fifty-thousand of us in heaven at this point, just enough that one could live their entire life and not deliberately meet everyone even if they sincerely desired it. But even with more and more coming to heaven every month, it was still, for all our sprawling efforts at providing space, a small world. I should have seen something like this coming.

I didn't hear what Puca said when he started to pull away. I gently took his hand and pulled him back with a questioning look.

"I said I have to go," he answered, eyes not meeting mine.

"What's wrong?"

"I don't know." He looks back to the exit. "I just need to get out of here for a bit."

We'd been to clubs before as a couple, him in an earlier form. Not this place, but ones like it. I couldn't ask him to confirm what I suspected was happening. I hoped I was wrong. "Maybe we should go home, if you're not feeling well. You're probably got frame-lag from the switch back."

He looked at me and I couldn't read his expression. "Yeah, Janus. Maybe."

"I'll settle our drinks and we'll go. Wait here okay?" Why did I start a tab here? I usually paid up front for drinks, especially since we intended to hop. I slipped a few feet away to where an otter staffer with blue fur glowed under dark light and offered my thumb to close our bill. There was a discount for a three drink tab, that's why I had held off paying. Right. I thanked her and returned to find Puca had melted into the crowd, likely headed for the exit. Not finding him there, I slipped back through the dancers to the restroom. Not there either. At this point I was a little perturbed. The song changed to something I know Puca really liked so I returned to the spot where I'd asked him to wait and danced some more, eyes roving the crowd for him and ears trying to pick out anything above the noise of the music. A wide-racked moose entered my space, catching my eye for a second and matching my slower dance tempo before seeing me divert for the search. He got the hint and swayed his hips as he moved off.

My heart sunk as I realized Puca wasn't returning. I immediately checked the inbox on my phone. The heads-up had one message. 'I'll see you shortly.' Puca had texted a minute ago.

'Where are you?' I replied, wondering what shortly meant. A pit in my stomach came and grew as time passed without an answer.

I left the club two songs later. The bear at the door, meeting my gaze balefully, hadn't seen him.

Inner-city streets flanked by tall, vegetative-wrapped buildings of the core surrounded me on every side. Holos cycled after-dark delights and print-fab vehicles crawled the main strip. The teeming nocturnal masses were everywhere, thick and anonymous. Still no reply from Puca. Here and there in the throng, I could see street leads and holo-signs giving sporadic directions, designs done by Puca for the city that ironically couldn't direct me to him.

I was set to ring Dr. Somnul again when I realized that it was extremely late, early morning hours in fact, and I'd already pressed my luck calling her well outside of her office hours. I settled on sending her a long message detailing what had happened since our conversation, which she'd no-doubt read in the morning, and then called a skiff to take a deliberately long route home, my eyes on the passing empty, pointless delights of our world. Each one was lit brightly, calling me out and promising memories made that I'd never forget. One still image flash on a billboard of a fox with a guitar in her lap, with a scrolling insistence that Marigold Harper's last few tickets were selling fast. I kept from feeling sick to my stomach by quickly checking our shared account. No seats purchased. Or anything else. Unlike bodies recycled by universal healthcare, entertainments were things of minor scarcity here, existence being pointless without experience. I checked accounts and texts all the way home to get a sense of where Puca had gone and came up empty.

When the car returned me to my little hamlet of grown houses, the dark and quiet was no relief. Every shadowy tree and hedge seemed to hold the aspect of my missing lover within it. I arrived at home, re-entered to the lingering wonderful smell of ursines and ancient ones fucking and went to bed in a state of worry, the scent and its delighted memory already fading. I stared at my readout, seeing the greenish pane where his text would any second appear, and stared anxiously through the night as each blink of my eyes came closer together.

* * *

"I made breakfast," Puca said as he nudged me. Something smelled good. Something else smelled burnt. I woke up and saw the goat nestled in bed next to me staring softly into space. "I made you sunny side up eggs." He said as his horns dig into the pillow propped behind him.

I sat up quickly, sleep pulled away like a yanked sheet keeping out the cold. "Son of a bitch, Puca."

"Not this time." The smile at the corners of his bearded mouth was thin and pained.

I got out of bed, resisting the downward pull of gravity caused by a worried hangover and looked at the newest Puca. Grey fur decked his naked body down to thin fuzz at the hocks and forearms. Hooved legs crossed one another atop the blankets and thick-fingered arms folded over one another. "Again?" I asked. "That's three re-cradlings in less than twelve hours, Puca."

"One re-cradling and two temporary exchanges, actually."

"Dammit, why?"

"I knew a goat, once. Had a cute goat boy-friend back on Earth, you know, before us. Or I think I did. When I was a youth in a school near the polar safe-zones learning to create art. I remember that by flashes. Took forever to be sure it wasn't just a dream."

"Puca."

"You should eat something, Janus. You look like hell and I'm sorry that I know I'm likely the cause."

"Where did you go last night? We were having such a great time!"

"We were. Then I saw what you saw and something that was missing came back."

I didn't ask him what that was, and by the look on his face I didn't need to. His next words made me shiver. "Last night proved something I suspected for a-while. I wasn't sure until last night. Not all the memories I lost were back on earth, were they?"

My mouth opened with the ready lie. I didn't know how to phrase it, to shut this down, to get him quiet and in my arms, or into the kitchen. "Puca."

"It didn't make sense, but it did happen. Why, Janus. Why if I lost everything I was when I was back on earth from a transmission accident during the long dark am I also missing some of what came after? How is that possible?"

"Why do you think you're missing some of what's happened here?" My heart started hammering in my chest and I fought the urge to swallow.

"Because I'd seen that coyote couple before, right on that spot, while we were both right where we were. They're regulars there. I know this, even though I'd never seen that particular club before. I remember it clear as day. I remember being in your arms as I gazed at them. And I felt pain like I'd never felt before, Janus. Pain and loneliness and misery at the sight of those two, right there in a place where we should have been the happiest in our lives. And you held me up as I collapsed and wept and cried. You knew I felt it. You took me out of there." He turned his head and gave me a suspicious sideways gaze. "Why?"

"Because you wanted to go."

"You're lying. Why are you lying, Janus."

"I'm not." I wanted to growl back at him but my voice was becoming smaller. I took a step back as Puca unfolded his legs and slipped off the bed, his nostrils flaring as though he was setting up for a charge.

"Every time I re-cradle something else spills out. Flashes, impressions, other pieces I never knew were me. I thought they were dreams but they aren't are they? Dreams don't feel as good as this or as horrible. Sometimes

I want to cry out with joy and sometimes I want to die. What are you hiding from me?"

"Nothing."

He stood and was nearly hoof to toe claw with me. "Tell me." He punched me in the stomach. The hurt wasn't physical.

"Nothing you want to know!" I roared, and I could already feel the tears starting again.

"Why, Janus? Why wouldn't I want to know what I've spent months searching for? I can't remember and I can't let myself just forget!"

"You can."

"Why?"

"Because you're the one who made yourself forget in the first place! He's fucking dead, Puca. He's lost!"

He became dead silent. The goat's ears I'd only just noticed fell and he blinked his fresh eyes at me. Tottering back like a newborn foal, he fell back on our bed. "He…"

"Lethanial." I said. "That word on the tip of your tongue, that name you can't quite ever remember, it's him. You wanted to never remember that name again, but you've been breaking your own wish for months now."

"No."

"Who have you had trouble getting a-hold of at work, Puca. Leonard? Daniel? You only report directly to one person and you have no other coworkers, Puca. Those two people aren't real. They're just names that your mind fished up as close to the one you're missing, that you feel as missing. For fuck's sake, you had your memory capped, you had him erased because you couldn't stand to live without him. To keep you around, I did what you asked. I erased the pictures, recycled every bit of data that was still here. I helped you forget him to fucking keep you alive."

The goat's eyes went wide, and wet and I saw the look in them when the fog started to clear, just a bit. The name was all it took for his lip to start quivering and I realized how inevitable this moment always was, that we should circle back to here where his soul could stab itself again. "What happened to him?"

His arms were already up, seeking to wrap themselves around the missing element in his life, limbs quivering in space around the cold vacancy of a lover whose ghost never left despite the best science heaven could mount against it.

"We came here together, all of us, together. Signed the forms and said goodbye, billions of miles and decades ago. But there was an accident; something the techs couldn't explain interfered with our transmission. You and I were degraded just slightly. Not Lethanial. His signal was hopelessly corrupted, his mind jumbled and incomplete. There was only enough data to give us a body to bury when we woke here in heaven, in the place you and he and me as the third in our relationship, came to for a better, less complicated life."

"How?"

"We didn't know, Puca. We only knew that you'd dreamed of this new life years before you two had even met with me. You shared that dream and we all made the sacrifices needed to obtain it. We all gave up everything we had to be here. Everyone we ever knew back home would be dead, but we were all that mattered to each other. To start a new life, it was worth it."

I swallow back grief as it hits again, just like it's brand new. His realization, and mine. "With Lethaniel lost, with that future stolen from you, you only had me. I'd hoped that as the third in the relationship, I would be enough, that time would heal you and forge us. For the first few months while you grieved, it just seemed it might be." The memory I'd refused to bury, that I'd lived with so I could guard Puca from it, stabbed hard. "When your suicide attempt failed, when I got you to throw up the pills you took all at once and called Dr. Somnul, it was you who made the decision. You couldn't live without him." I swallowed, arms folding and head turned so he couldn't see the tears starting. What I could see was horrifying. Each piece that tumbled back into his head, jogged by what I told him, seemed to sting him like a brand as I watched his cap dissolve and the memories reconnect in his conscious mind. No sense in trying to bury things now.

"I'm sorry. That's what you have been missing, Puca. That's what all those bodies you tried couldn't give you. A memory you yourself had us pull like a tooth. You asked for the cap when you couldn't take the misery of life without Lethanial anymore. I'm sorry I couldn't help you get past him. I tried. I tried so hard."

Puca stared off into space, the goat's face slack. I should have felt guilty at pulling back the curtain, but I knew instinctively that I had no choice. All that nameless, inexplicable dread that was chasing him from shape to shape, trying to find an ideal self from shards of a missing one. I had felt horrible on the day I'd dragged him back from death, stopping him from following Lethaniel into the dark.

"I love you." I said, watching him intently. "I tried to help you build a new life with the blank slate we had left after we gave you your wish. I tried to fill in all the gaps left and give you something new. It was what you told us you wanted." I took a deep breath. "What do you want now that you know the truth?"

204

Puca's eyes welled up though I could see in his expression he couldn't understand why. "I just have flashes. I don't really remember him. But it still hurts. Why does it hurt?"

I needed time to compose the answer even though I knew the answer right away. "Because you were everything to each other, and you didn't think there was life beyond him but you had to try. I'd have done the same, Puca. What else can you do? Heaven is about pursuing happiness. Is there any bliss greater than ignorance when you lose all you care about? Obviously, you've decided subconsciously that won't do. The doubt is torture all on its own. I can't leave you there."

Puca wept like a lost soul. Right there and then he cried and I stood by and felt my own tears roll down and stood stock still, ready to comfort, ready to leave the house. Whatever he decided he wanted me to do, I'd do. Given the latter however, even with the worst settling down around him, I wouldn't let him take his own life. No matter how much he suffered, I'd sworn I'd make sure that he saw another for as long as longevity allowed him to have them. Maybe, in his pain, that was the most loving thing I could do. Or maybe it was the most selfish. In that moment I really had no idea.

Puca echoed my sentiment. "I don't know what to do. I feel him missing and it hurts but I can't get him back. I can't ever get him back."

"No."

"I can't remember, but I can't forget. I feel like I'm breaking in half. What the fuck do I do?"

"We can lift the block, completely. Dr. Somnul, who advised me not to tell you this, knows how it's done."

"But if I remember him and if I can't handle his loss than what do I do next?"

"We discussed this possibility." I spare a tear for what comes next as I cross to my night-table and fish deep into its contents. I'd been willing to take these steps before, and she'd refused. Now I'd make sure of it. "I'll get your heaven back for you, Puca. I promise." I took a step towards Puca, the lost creature I loved and accepted fate with all the grace I could muster. "Here is where we spend eternity with those we love the most. That's the promise I'll make sure gets kept. I love you."

"How can you possibly-" he jerked and spasmed, falling back on the bed as I hip fired the neural scrambler that blacked him out. The goat body of Puca slumped on the comforter, peaceful and beautiful despite the tears that collected in his eyes and the grimace on that ungulate muzzle. It would be the last time I saw him this way and I preserved it in mind for several minutes.

I called Dr. Samnul, explained everything. I had to give her several minutes' worth of cursing and sputtering before I was able to tell her what would have to come next. She was reluctant to listen to me. But when she finally did, it all made sense. We'd have to secure some agreements with my company and alter some key records, but I'd been ready for this before. Somnul had the resources to do what was right if it would save a life. I was sure beyond sure, as I took deep, precious breaths. This sacrifice was worth making.

* * *

Two months passed. Puca finished his lunch and wagged his tail languidly, muzzle curled with the bliss of the full and content. We touched noses and cleaned up our leavings, leaving no litter under the blue bowl of heaven's sky as we wandered back from the gardens to our suburb, now an inner arm of the colony's wide reach. "I want to stop and leave a flower," Puca said, and when I realized when he meant, I was touched.

We entered the modest yard two burbs over, where the first graves were settled. It contained no more than a few hundred souls out of the thousands who'd undergone the final passing, beyond help from re-cradling or medics into whatever lay beyond this colony, deep on the verge of space. We passed stone after stone, framed by cultivated foliage and woven gazebos of floral patterns with urns in their center daises. Finally we came to a small knoll of tamed lavender grass where a narrow marker commemorated the passing of one of the pioneers who'd been trained to build the districts that heaven's denizens now lived, loved and slumbered in. He'd died in transit, his passage remarked by few in his working solitude save the two in all of Heaven who had known him best. Puca placed the solitary crimson flower at the marker's base. "I still can't remember him. I don't know if it was the trauma of transit or something that came after. I remember his face, some of the life he shared with us before the transit and nothing else. I don't know how, but it's still gone. How about you?" He turned to me. His expression was sad but serene, confused but accepting. I felt his grip on my paw tighten and mine tightened in return.

"I remember enough," I said with a deliberate but subtle seeming shrug. The next words were harder to say, but felt right. For the first time ever, despite their cost, the words felt like what I should have said all along. "I remember that Janus loved us both. I don't know if anything else matters if I get to keep that much."

Puca looked off into space, at trees rustling leaves in a breathy wind and at fauna buzzing in the cool bits of shade. His sandy coyote's paw reaches out and takes my matched, pale canine digits in his own. Our muzzles hovered around one another's before trading a brief affectionate kiss. "I'm ready to go home, Lethaniel." he said at last, reluctantly.

"So am I," I whispered, feeling his warmth against mine. Arm in arm, with the world cast by dusk in sharp relief, we followed the garden paths back to the house that never stopped growing.

Waking Neil

by Skunkbomb

It's not easy seeing someone you love hooked up to so many machines. I held his hand. My ferret had always had slender fingers, but they somehow felt frailer. A metal helmet with blue wires rested on his head. A matching helmet sat in the bed next to him.

"We've called Neil's father," the doctor, a badger with small glasses, said as she checked the consent forms I just signed. "No one ever picked up, but we've left multiple messages."

"I wouldn't count on him answering," I said, slapping my plank-like tail against the ground. I gnawed on my bottom lip with my buckteeth. After visiting his dad, he hadn't made it home. Neil had somehow wrapped his car around a tree. Eyewitnesses had said no other car was involved. What had been going through Neil's head?

I touched the band of the ring on my finger. "He's family. I'll do whatever it takes to help him."

The badger nodded and pointed to the empty bed. "Okay, Archie, we'll get you hooked up."

After I lay down in the bed, a pair of nurses, a skunk and an otter, came in. The otter mostly focused on making me comfortable, and we made small talk about a river we'd vacationed at in the past. I must have been one of a couple dozen beavers while she was one of a hundred otters there. The skunk went about hooking me up. I barely felt the needle dart into my arm. Shaving the fur off that patch of arm had been more painful. Finally, the skunk adjusted the helmet over my head. Screws on the side of it allowed the helmet to adjust to different head and ear sizes.

When the two nurses left, the doctor walked over to my bed. "As you know, this is an experimental procedure. If all goes well, you'll experience a connection with Neil like you've never shared before."

I looked over at my unconscious ferret. The beds were too far apart for me to hold his hand. "We're already connected."

"Not like this," the badger said, looking at me from over her glasses. "I know you already agreed to this on paper, but I'm required by law to verbally go over the potential risks and side effects of this procedure." She flipped to the next piece of paper on her clipboard. "You may, upon waking up, experience hallucinations, exhaustion, the sensation of heavy limbs, the temporary muting of your senses, and the temporary overloading of your senses—"

"Both?"

"Different subjects experienced different side effects," the doctor said, "but neither happened at the same time, of course. Where was I? Oh, yes, lack of appetite, constipation, sleepwalking, cardiac arrest, and dry mouth. Are you, Archie Palmer, willing to go through with this procedure?"

"I am."

The badger put down the clipboard and grabbed a needle filled with clear liquid. She placed it into the tube connected to my arm and pressed the plunger. "It shouldn't take long for the sedative to kick in." She smiled. "Talk to him, but more importantly, listen to him. I wish you luck."

I opened my mouth to thank her.

* * *

White. Every direction I looked in, I saw nothing but white stretching for miles, except for right in front of me. A black door stood unconnected to any sort of hinge. It seemed rude just to barge in, so I knocked. The door swung open slowly.

Inside was a mishmash of old and modern eras. A jukebox sat underneath a lit torch, which illuminated the wood-paneled wall and floor. Neil had never been skilled at interior decorating, but neither was I. A giant flat-screen TV was built into the wall facing the red circular bed. And on that bed, a ferret, my Neil, turned over. His length pressed against his red silk pajamas. "Hello, stud."

I lunged for the bed, wrapping Neil into a hug. I kissed him on the lips and his cheek. In the haze of hospital smells, I missed Neil's scent: Mountain Spring deodorant, Hazelnut coffee, and ferret musk.

"What's all this about?" Neil said, chuckling a little. "And why are you wearing that?" He stared at my hospital gown for a few seconds before his tail went limp against the bed. "Why can't I change your outfit?"

"Outfit?" I shook my head. "Neil, it's me, Archie."

Neil ran his hand though the fur on my arm. Then he wrapped himself around me, burying his face into my chest. The wooden walls gave way to walls painted in light blue. The round bed morphed into a rectangle, and the silk sheets turned into cotton. A pile of clothes fell to the floor next to a hamper that we never used. It wasn't real, but it felt about as close as possible to home. "It really is you! What are you doing here?"

I rubbed his back. "I'm here to wake you up."

"Wake me up?" My ferret clenched the bed's sheets. "This isn't the afterlife?"

I shook my head. "You're in the hospital. The doctors put you into a coma after your car accident." Heaviness gripped my chest. "Neil, what happened? The cops said you didn't swerve or brake or anything. Were you texting or—"

"Hello, gorgeous."

I stood in the doorway. Actually, I was on the bed with Neil, but another me stood at the doorway in nothing but a small towel that did nothing to hide his hard on. "Help a beaver with his wood?"

I looked from the other me to Neil back and forth until I settled on my ferret. "What the fuck?"

Neil waved the other beaver away. "Take five, will you?"

The other beaver was suddenly clothed in jeans and a flannel shirt, and all trace of his erection was gone. "Okay." He walked out of the room.

My ferret sighed and held his paw up. The fur on his hand turned purple and his fingers softened into tentacles. "I can do anything here. I thought I was in limbo or something, but all I knew was that you weren't here. I missed you, so I made another you, but I wasn't trying to cheat on you or anything like that."

"No, no," I said, holding his purple tentacle hand. It morphed back into its original form. "I know you weren't trying to cheat on me, but this isn't the afterlife. You're still alive."

"Huh," Neil said, sitting back on the bed. "So… what now?"

I shrugged. "The doctors say talking and hearing you out is the best way to coax you out of the coma."

Neil snuggled up to me. "I know that me waking up is priority number one, but all I know is that for the first time in, um, how long have I been out?"

"33 days."

"Damn." He placed his hand on my chest. "Well, for the first time in over a month, limbo is paradise. I'm with the real you, and in here, we can do anything." He hand lowered to my waist.

I leaned in closer to my ferret. "Anything?"

He smiled, his black-tipped tail swishing slowly behind him. "Anything."

* * *

We made a blanket fort.

Actually, it was more than a fort. The blankets, sewn from all different colors and soft like a cloud, surrounded us like a gazebo of coziness. We sat in a nest of body-sized pillows. A plate of s'mores and mugs of hot chocolate sat on the table in front of us. A movie screen played Netflix. Well, Neil's brain didn't get Netflix, so he made up the show, a black-and-white noir, as it played on the screen.

The countess pointed a gun at the private investigator who drank from a flask at least once for every minute of screen time.

"That bitch," Neil said.

"You know," I said, "you could just make her drop her weapon and confess."

My ferret shrugged. "A story's boring without conflict." He smirked. "And she's not the murderer."

"What?"

"Keep watching."

Neil shifted against me and I wrapped my arms around him. A part of me wanted us to stay in this moment forever, but how much time had passed in that hospital room? I didn't have the money to just stay in my husband's head and watch TV for the rest of our lives, and I didn't want to go back to a world where Neil never woke up.

"Neil, can we pause for a moment?"

Neil nodded. "What is it?"

I turned my ferret around so he could face me. "We should talk about the accident."

Neil's tail stiffened. "I didn't drift out of the lane on purpose."

"Did you get distracted by the radio?" I asked, my heart thumping. "Or… it was your father, wasn't it?"

Neil drew in his knees and hugged them. "I wasn't feeling well after seeing him." When I rubbed Neil's back, my ferret smiled at me. "But you're here now. I'm feeling better."

I sighed. After dating Neil for so long, I had come to understand why he cried at the sappiest rom-coms and why he found Nascar interesting, but I could never understood why he still tried to get his father to accept whom he was. "All he does is hurt you. You know parents aren't supposed to do that, right?"

The countess looked at her gun. "God, what am I doing, waving this around like a brute? I'm just like my father."

Neil glared at the screen, and the movie stopped. He leaned forward onto his knees. "I'm happy with you here. Maybe focusing on the good stuff, and not the bad, would be better for waking me up."

I nodded slowly. "Okay, that could work, but we should talk—"

Neil twitched his whiskers, a mischievous smile on his face. "Remember that time in the park?"

He was changing the subject, but I couldn't help but chuckle and hide my face in my hands. During our junior year, a little over a year since we'd started dating, Neil had pulled me from a bar into the park. Even though campus security made regular loops around the campus to watch for troublemakers, Neil and I managed to get each other off. Flashlights shined on us as we were getting dressed. Luckily, campus security didn't follow us, and we sprinted back to their dorm without further incident. A thick glob of my seed still dampened the underside of Neil's tail. If any of the other students in the elevator saw or smelled it, they didn't say anything. "If you want to have sex, we can do that once we wake up."

"I know," Neil said, placing his hand on my lower back, "but this is my world. I can make anything happen here. Could you help me live out this fantasy I have?"

I placed my hand over his. "What kind of fantasy?"

My ferret's hand slid onto my butt. "You'll see."

Blankets rolled themselves up on their own. The pillows flew into the air and didn't come back down. I managed to grab the last of my s'more off the table before the table sunk into the floor.

I popped the chunk of s'more into my mouth. "But when we're done, we're going to talk, okay?"

Neil nodded, "Right, of course."

* * *

I fussed with the collar of my silk bathrobe. "I've got a couple questions about all this."

"Okay," Neil said, his voice low. He glanced back at the curtain surrounding us in a ring. "I know I'm throwing a lot at you."

I nodded and crossed my legs. Maybe wearing a knee-length bathrobe and nothing else was supposed to be sexy, but I felt more exposed than anything. "What exactly is behind that curtain?"

My ferret kissed me on the cheek. "You'll see in a minute. If it's too much for you, let me know."

"Okay," I said, my tail tapping the ground. "Then I've only got one more question." I hiked a thumb at the other me from earlier, who stood behind me in a matching bathrobe. "What's he doing here?"

Neil put a claw in his mouth. "When am I going to get the chance to have you in my mouth and my ass at the same time?"

The other me stepped between us, throwing his arms over our shoulders. "Think of it as a kinky bonding experience." He clapped me on the back. "There's no need to worry. Neil's in good hands."

I grabbed the other me by the wrist and placed his arm by his side. "Sure."

"He won't do anything I would be against," Neil said, rubbing my back. "Are you sure?"

Neil nodded. "He's based off you, and you'd never force yourself on me."

From the other side of the curtain, a piano played a twinkling melody. The curtain rose, and I froze.

A stadium full of people surrounded us. They watched us the way someone looks at a painting in a museum. Some of the audience members had their gaze fixed below the belt. When Neil touched me, I jolted.

Neil snapped his fingers. Everyone in the audience now sat in their underpants. "I heard that makes people less nervous."

I let the jitters in my gut out in a shaky chuckle. "Thanks."

A wolf popped onto the stage. The fur on his head was moussed into a pomp. His tux was spotless, and his fur was brushed and shiny. A short, crisp loincloth rested against his sheath.

"Good evening, everyone," the wolf said into the microphone. "Today, we gather to witness Neil, Archie, and Other Archie engage in sex." He waited for the crowd to stop cheering to continue. "Please be respectful to our performers. I ask that you remain in your seat during the performance. We hope you find this an arousing experience." He looked back and winked at me.

My ferret fiddled with the knot on his bathrobe. "So, are you ready?"

I took a deep breath and let it out, "As I'll ever be."

When Neil and the other me dropped their robes, I bit my lip and followed suit.

214

Orchestra music filled the air. A conductor's pit in front of the stage was filled with at least fifty different musicians, each plucking or blowing away at their instruments. The wolf waved his wand, and, seeing the bulging in his loincloth, I bit back a 'wand' joke. Neil's cock stood at half-mast. My ferret placed one hand behind my back and the other on my hardening cock.

"I'm not sure where we go from here," I said, placing my hands around Neil's slender frame. "But we'll figure it out, right?" I reached down to his cock.

"I," Neil shuddered as I brushed my paw along his shaft. "I actually had something in mind. I want to see you fool around with yourself."

"You've seen me do that before."

"No, I mean fool around with him." He pointed at the heart-shaped bed that suddenly appeared to the left of us. The other me laid on his side, already sporting a full erection.

I've seen myself in a mirror before, but it's an odd sensation seeing a non-reflection version of me. Posing and showmanship were never my style, but the other me did look good. Usually, I don't notice my scent unless I've gotten really grungy, but his-my smell hovered in my nostrils. Neil was right. I did smell a little like tree bark.

Before I could climb onto the bed, the other me pulled me onto it. "Come on, let's give Neil a good show." He reached between my legs, and a twinkling piano song played as he gently fondled my balls.

I bit my lip. I always liked starting foreplay with my balls first. It was like prepping the goods for when I come.

I grabbed the other beaver's wrist and looked over at Neil. "Wait, is this technically incest or masturbation?"

"It's fucking hot, whatever it is," Neil said. He stroked his dick to its full length. "Touch him too."

The other me widened his legs, and I reached down to his balls. The other me let out a contented sigh as I worked his fuzzy orbs.

I wanted to focus on the other me's hand sliding up onto my shaft, but even though this beaver in front of me is me, even with the familiar feel of my balls and my scent, I was groping someone who wasn't Neil.

The other me placed his hand on my shoulder and drew me in. He kissed me, and I stiffened, in more ways than one. I kept my eyes shut, trying to pretend his lips were Neil's, but ferrets don't have teeth like beavers. Kissing someone with buckteeth can be a challenge, but as long as neither party shoves their face forward suddenly, we could avoid knocking out a tooth.

The other beaver pulled away.

Before I could react, a sharp pain poked the head of my cock, and I winced.

The other me, on his knees and his mouth still open, chuckled nervously.

"Wow," Neil said. "Even with all the power of my imagination at my disposal, I still can't see how you beavers can give a blow job with those buckteeth."

"There's a steep learning curve," I said, stepping off the bed. "Is it okay if... if it's okay with you..." I reached my hand out to my ferret.

Neil's smile widened and grabbed my hand. "Okay, we're all good and hard now anyway." Neil propped himself up on all fours on the bed. He lifted his tail and gave his rear a little shake. "Hold out your hand."

I did, and a moment later, a bottle of lube appeared in my grasp. I slicked my shaft up, crawled back onto the bed, and positioned myself behind Neil.

The other me was already on the other side of the bed, his crotch inches from my ferret's face.

Neil licked his lips and stroked the other me's shaft. He looked back at me. "Ready when you are."

A thick percussion filled the air, mimicking the beating of my heart. I wasn't thrilled that I'd be looking at this other me the whole time, but it beat looking into the crowd. I slicked up my finger with lube and slipped it into my lithe lover. Finally, I slid the head of my cock into my ferret and he took the other me's cock into his mouth. Chairs in the audience creaked as they leaned forward. The air was thick with the scent of arousal.

I'd never had a threesome before. Sexually, I wasn't too much more than vanilla. Other than the time in the park, the most adventurous sexual activity I'd ever done was rimming Neil. That hadn't gone exactly as planned. Neil said ferrets call it 'poofing'. Thankfully, the smell went away after a few minutes, we had a laugh, and we finished without any more poofs (that time).

This, on the other hand, seemed to be working without a hitch. I expected our thrusts not to match up. Maybe this was Neil's influence, but whenever I thrust into my ferret, Neil drew back on the other me's cock.

Neil's tail thrashed, and I put it under my arm. I tried to focus on the softness of Neil's fur, the slenderness of his hips, and how warm and tight it was inside of him. Instead, I was looking at the other me. Did my tongue poke out like that when Neil usually blew me? Do I flare my nostrils that much? I knew I wasn't usually that noisy.

"You've got a hell of a mouth," the other me said, placing one hand behind Neil's head.

Neil shook his head free of the other me's grasp and looked back at me. "Harder." He slowly licked up the other me's shaft before going back down on it.

I squeezed Neil's rear and thrust. A little gasp escaped my ferret, and the tip of his tail squirmed. At that point, I barely withdrew my cock out of Neil before slamming it back into him. I thought about how Neil would walk funny when I was done. Somehow, my dick stiffened even more. I dug my feet into the ground.

Or at least I tried to. My feet touched nothing but air. When I looked down, my breath caught in my throat, and not in a sexy way. We were floating over the audience.

"Don't stop," Neil panted. Precum leaked from the other me's cock, and my ferret lapped it up.

The other me held Neil's head in place. He wasn't getting a blowjob anymore. If anything, the other me was fucking his face.

"This is what he wants," the other me panted. "He needs them to see this."

The orchestra worked themselves into a frenzy as the music quickened. The wolf conductor's cock had pushed his think loincloth aside, and it stood at full attention. The crowd cheered.

The other me pulled his cock out of Neil's mouth. He jerked himself off for all of two seconds before painting my ferret's face with his cum. Neil turned his head. He kept one eyes shut as beaver seed clung to his brow and dribbled down his nose.

My whole length buried into Neil, and I locked up. My cum filled my ferret's insides right as he came. His seed nailed one of the audience members, who looked up as if he'd felt a raindrop. All three of us plummeted to the ground, landing in a heap.

Murmurs rose from the audience. One of the audience members, the one who Neil had cum on, climbed onto the stage.

"Neil, I—" The words froze in my throat. The audience member was changing. His wider body shrank into a tube shape. His larger teeth pulled into his mouth. The fur around his eyes darkened.

My ferret trembled. "Not again."

We looked back at the ferret in front of us. The white parts of his fur had more gray to them, and his arms were more muscular. We were looking back at Neil's father.

"You dirty faggot." He backhanded my ferret across the face.

I was shot back out of Neil and crashed through the floor of the stage.

* * *

Even though I opened my eyes, everything around me was darkness. I tried to pick myself up, but I was floating. Gray dust swirled like a hurricane. It caked onto my fur. "Neil! Neil, where are you?"

A doorway opened up to my left. Neil reached out and pulled me in, slamming the door behind us.

We lay on the ground panting. I was vaguely aware we were both still naked, but there were more important matters to discuss. "What was that?"

Neil didn't meet my gaze. "That's my mind."

I looked around us. We lay with our backs against a tree with a truck so thick that I couldn't wrap my arms around it all the way. A wide river flowed to our left. A bird crap-covered dock point over the water. A volleyball court sat next to a row of thick bushes. Birds chirped overhead, and a gentle breeze cradled our bodies. In this park, I was put on a team with Neil in a beginning of the semester game of volleyball. Within the cover of those bushes, Neil and I made love. By the water the day before we graduated, I had gotten down on one knee.

Neil smiled sadly. "This is a pretty nice illusion, huh? It's a lot to maintain to cover all the real parts of my mind."

I turned my ferret over so he could look out at his creation. "This isn't fake. Our park, that awesome blanket fort, and that sex stadium, that's all you too."

"Then why does all that mess below us feel so much more real?"

I rubbed Neil's chest. His heart was pounding so hard. "What happened with your dad?"

"I told him we were going to be better dads than he ever was."

I'm not sure exactly when we started talking about adopting or using a surrogate. We talked about it at first the same way we'd talk about starring in a movie or gaining superpowers. It was a 'wouldn't that be neat?' kind of thing. We're both still in our 20s, and we had times where our budget was tight, but the more we talked about it, the more we thought about saving money.

"I thought we were going to leave him out of those talks," I said in my softest voice possible. Neil was finally opening up, so I didn't want to kick him while he was down.

Neil nodded. "I know, but then he was going on about how 'a faggot can only raise someone to become a faggot and nothing more.'"

"Something tells me your dad doesn't have any sort of proof to back that up."

My ferret turned to me. "But he was referring to you that time. No, he said the child would have a chance with me though because..." He took a shuddering breath. "Because he raised me, so I know what to do when a child acts out."

"A backhand to the face."

Neil nodded and laid his head against my chest. "To start. I was fine when I left, but then I thought, what if he's right? What if I'm just like him and I hit our child?" Tears soaked into my chest fur. "I just cried and cried, and right when I thought I should pull over, I looked up and there was the tree and then I woke up here."

I let my ferret cry himself out. A good cry could be medicine. I busied myself thinking of baby names.

When Neil's crying quieted to sniffling, I rubbed his head. "You're going to be an amazing dad."

"But—"

"You've told me all about the harm your dad caused you growing up," I said. "I know you'd never hurt our child."

"What if I get overwhelmed or make a mistake or yell at him or her?" Neil said, shaking in my arms.

I kissed him and held him tighter. "I'll be there the whole way to help you. And if we get overwhelmed, we can ask our family for help."

"My dad will never go near our child," Neil growled.

"I actually meant my parents and siblings," I said. When Neil stopped barring his teeth, I smiled. "You've been an honorary beaver since you came home for Thanksgiving the first year we started dating."

Neil covered his mouth and looked away. "I don't make a good beaver. I don't have those buckteeth to chew down trees or a paddle stuck to my ass." He laughed as more tears fell.

"It's okay. I'll help you build a dam that's obviously required of all beavers to enter adulthood."

Neil kissed me, wrapping his arms around me. The grass around us bloomed into wildflowers of all colors of the rainbow. The sun brightened, warming our fur. The sun continued to brighten until its glow overtook the field and everything in it.

* * *

There were some side effects when Neil and I returned to the real world. We could barely lift our heads up the morning we woke up. The first couple nights, we woke up drenched in sweat, panting. Neil would stare hard at any object in the room, only relaxing when he couldn't turn it into something else with his thoughts. I thought I lost my sense of taste, but it turns out hospital food really is that bland.

The clock on the wall read 1:46 a.m. In about eight hours, Neil and I would finally be discharged from the hospital. I was way past due for a real shower, and I could down a thick stack of pancakes in a heartbeat. Mostly, I was looking forward to lying in our own bed together.

"Archie? You awake?"

I sat up. "I am. We're both awake, Neil. We're both here."

My ferret sat up. "Oh, no, I didn't mean it like that."

"Oh." I chuckled. "So, what's up?"

His bed creaked as he rolled out of it. I should have asked if he was well enough to stand or if he needed my help, but Neil crawled into my bed and nestled against me. I wasn't about to protest.

"I doubt this breaks protocol or whatever for our recovery," Neil said.

I shrugged. "It's a hospital. We did what made us feel better."

We were quiet for a bit, but Neil broke the silence. "There's a part of me that thinks we're still in my mind."

"Wherever we are, we'll be okay," I said before kissing the top of his head. "After we get home, we can wash up, eat some real food—"

"Go on the Internet."

"Aw, does somebody miss looking at porn?"

Neil's ears flattened a little. "Maybe, but I was thinking of looking up names. Baby names." Neil turned over so we rested belly to belly. "But that's still years from now. I just like thinking about baby names."

I kissed his nose. "Do you want to think about boy or girl names? My dad's named after some famous architect, so we can keep up that theme, or not."

"Well, right now, I was thinking of dick."

I snorted. "That poor child."

"No, I meant, we can think of baby names tomorrow," Neil said. "Because right now, I thinking about…" He placed his hand over my crotch.

Having not been touched there in days other than being bathed, my cock grew to half its length. "One of those nice nurses will have to clean up our mess."

"Oh, I'm sure they've seen worse," Neil said. His hand slid under my hospital gown. He rolled one of my balls in his hand with his thumb.

I pushed the front of his hospital gown aside so I could watch my ferret's length grow. The scent of his musk mingled with the antibacterial smell of the hospital.

Neil worked his paw along my shaft. "I love you."

I kissed him. "I love you too."

"That being said," Neil said, wrinkling his nose, "you haven't gotten a good dick washing in a while—"

"I like where this is heading."

"—and I'm not putting that in my mouth."

I pulled a face like I'd been wounded. "We'll make it work." I placed a hand behind his back, drawing my ferret in. His cock rested on top of mine. We're about the same length, but mine was thicker, just like how we're about the same height, but I was stockier.

Neil thrust his hips slowly, our cocks rubbing against one another. Our cocks quickly grew to their full lengths. A dollop of pre nestled between our heads.

I grasped our cocks and jerked us slow and firm. Neil was never heavy, but his weight on top of me was reassuring, grounding. I thought about the times before this: coming early when he blew me the first time, learning spit can be lube, but not a great substitute for the real thing, and rimming Neil always came with the risk of my ferret poofing. I thought about holding hands with him when I came out to my parents that Thanksgiving long ago, holding Neil in my arms after one of his fights with his dad, and how he kissed me after he agreed to marry me. Holding him over me now, I knew we could take whatever life threw at us next, whether it's homophobic dads or a child to call our own.

I quickened the pace of my jerking. Neil bucked his hips against me. Little dooks escaped from his lips, and I smiled.

Neil placed his head against mine, our panting mingled in that hospital room. Our cum rocketed out, staining the front of my hospital gown and the nape of my neck. A couple more spurts squirted onto me until our cocks stilled. My ferret collapsed against me, no doubt making a mess of his hospital gown.

The door opened.

Neil and I froze as the light flipped on.

The badger opened her mouth to speak, but seemed to hold back after seeing what position Neil and I were in. Her nose twitched. She flipped the light off and backed toward the door. "I see you've both made a full recovery. Please try to get some rest." She was smiling when she shut the door.

Neil stifled a chuckle. "Oops."

I kissed him gently. "See? Nothing to worry about."

We only slept about five hours that night, but it was the best night of sleep that I could remember.

Too Good

by Mythicfox

Paul stretched out on the chaise and felt the late morning sun soak into his tan fur. The balcony doors of the sitting room in the Zerda Pleasure Palace were left open so he could enjoy the morning breeze, barely fettered by the light robe he wore. A nearby table held a carafe filled with some sort of fruit juice, a pitcher of water, and an empty glass. Soft music played somewhere in the distance, though even his sharp canid ears couldn't pick out the exact instrument.

As his tail lazily swayed from side to side next to him, it occasionally tapped a nearby servant's leg. There were four servants, all nearly-identical fennecs, and aside from them he was alone in the room. The silken garments draped over their slim, toned bodies didn't hide the fact that all were males, as was his preference. Their sand and cream-colored fur shone in the sun coming in through the balcony doors, their tall ears standing proudly like sails as they attended to him.

One rubbed his footpaws with skilled fingers, kneading and massaging the pads on his toes and only *slightly* tickling with his breath when he leaned in for a better angle. A second had sprinkled some scented powder into the fur on Paul's chest and abs and was brushing out the excess, giving his body a light massage in the process and leaving him with a faint aroma of cardamom. The third fed the coyote grapes; in what Paul was dimly aware was some sort of cartoon stereotype, but in his current frame of mind he was too blissed out to really care. The fourth simply knelt nearby, watching attentively in case the honored guest needed anything the others couldn't immediately provide.

Paul blinked—at least, he was pretty sure he'd only blinked—and the next thing he knew the servant brushing him had moved behind him, and

223

the one at the coyote's feet had moved up along his legs. Fingers rubbed at his scalp and massaged around the bases of his ears, while another pair of hands kneaded his thighs and sent shudders of pleasure through him. He felt himself melting under the surprisingly intimate caress. Out of the corner of his eye he saw the fennec with the grapes kneeling on a cushion, waiting. The sun no longer shone on him, having risen high enough that the beams coming in through the balcony doors had crept from the chaise to the floor.

"Did I fall asleep?" he asked.

"For a little while," the fennec behind him said.

Paul opened his mouth to say something, cut off by a light—but not unpleasant—pinch to the base of his ear. He glanced up at the fennec all but standing over him.

The fox's cream-colored fur showed the outline of a toned chest and not-quite-six-pack abs. He wasn't as elaborately adorned as some of the others, wearing a purple loincloth hanging from a chain belt around the waist and a matching silk choker. From the angle Paul laid at, he was reasonably sure the servant wore nothing underneath. He noticed the servant's intense gaze and how it didn't quite match the others' looks. He wasn't sure whether or not to say anything, but somehow he knew that it wasn't part of the fennecs' usual disciplined demeanor.

"Have you been enjoying your stay, sir?" the servant asked as he continued the scalp massage. "Comfortable?"

"Absolutely," he said, closing his eyes, his concerns momentarily forgotten. "You folks do a wonderful job keeping the guests happy."

"We are very pleased to hear that, sir. We do what we can to make sure our guests forget the stresses of home."

"Well, home is stressful," Paul reflexively said. He opened his eyes and realized he had trouble remembering the specific stresses of home. Or where 'home' was. He tried to think of home and found his memories a little blurry.

"But there's no need to think about that," the coyote dissembled; trying to convince himself everything was fine. "I feel too good to think about home."

"Of course, sir," the servant caressing his thighs said. "Just focus on the pleasures you have enjoyed in the time you've spent here, as well as those to come."

Again, Paul mentally paused. How long had he been here? Was he losing track of time?

Or maybe it's because you just woke up from a nap and your brain is being turned to mush by a pair of very lovely massages, he thought to himself.

224

"That said," the fennec rubbing his head began after a few moments. "It's always good to contrast your experiences here with those of... what job was it you said you do?" The deferential tone Paul generally received from the servants suddenly seemed a little forced.

"I work for the labor board," Paul reflexively said, though afterwards he wasn't as sure of that as he wanted to be.

The fennec with the grapes moved in with quick, silent steps and dangled one over the coyote's muzzle. Paul eagerly snatched it with his tongue, crunching down on it and tasting the sweet juice. He all too easily accepted the distraction, and opened his mouth for another grape.

The scalp massage ended and the servant moved away, but by this point Paul was more focused on gentle fingers moving to tug his robes aside and take hold of his stiffening length. All thoughts of "home" and "work" quickly left him as teasing became stroking and moved on from there.

* * *

The knock at the door snapped Paul out of his reverie. He stood in his private bedroom, by a balcony door open to what had been a spectacular sunset. The sun had fallen beneath the horizon, and now he watched the moon and stars settle in. At least, he was pretty sure he was.

The knock came again.

Oh, right.

"Come on in," he said.

The door opened and one of the palace's fennec servants came in. Paul immediately recognized him as the one that had brushed him and rubbed his head earlier. He carried a tray with a bottle of wine and an empty glass.

"Would you like a nightcap, sir?"

"I'm good, thanks," he said, waving dismissively.

"Are you certain? I know you've had a busy day, and surely a fine dinner, but one cannot be too relaxed as one drifts off to slumber." The servant gave him that intense, unreadable look again as he put in his best effort to affect the other fennecs' speech patterns.

"Dinner was fine, yeah," Paul commented as he tried not to think about how much of the 'busy' day—including dinner—was a blur. He curiously regarded the servant. "Actually, you know what, join me for a nightcap. Please."

The fennec gestured to a nearby armchair, opulent and plush, with a table next to it upon which he set the serving tray. He poured the glass of wine and offered it as Paul sat down.

"Go ahead, have some," the coyote suggested.

"It would not be proper." The servant knelt next to the chair.

"Hm." He took a sip of the wine. He wasn't a "wine guy," but he knew what he liked and this tingled on his tongue just right. "I don't think I saw you after that head massage earlier."

"Likely not, sir, I have been kept busy."

"But you've been taking care of me for a while?"

"Perhaps. How long have you been here, again?"

Paul realized he couldn't quite answer that. He sipped the wine again and made a dismissive gesture with the glass.

"Doesn't matter," he said. "But you've been attentive, that's what matters."

"I have indeed, such is my duty..." The fennec trailed off like there was more he wished to add, but he simply closed his mouth and looked obediently to the floor.

"What's your name?" Paul asked.

The servant opened his mouth and the look on his face made it clear that he was about to deflect the question, until his amber gaze met Paul's. "Alex. My name's Alex." His tone was different when he said that; firmer, confident.

"Alex, do you know exactly how long I've been here?" Paul asked as he sat up, finishing the glass of wine and setting it on the table.

"Not really, no. Not off the top of my head."

"Do you know how much longer I'm supposed to stay?"

"I'm afraid I don't know that either." Alex paused before he continued, his smile and tone suddenly forced. "I do worry that we have done such a fine job entrancing you, you may never go home."

He didn't know if it was the comment, the facial expression, or something else, but something about that sent a chill down Paul's spine. Like that moment in a spy story where someone reveals they know something they aren't supposed to know.

"What do you know about that?" he asked.

"I just know that..." Alex sighed. "You've got a life to go back to, someplace. And I worry that you've gotten so caught up in what we have here, that you may be losing sight of it."

"Does that happen often? I mean, if I'm having a good time, and I want to stay, is that a problem?"

"I haven't seen it happen like this, no. And we do enjoy having you, and want you to have a good time. But..." The fennec bit his lip, trying to find the words. The image of the obedient, disciplined servant faded under something Paul had trouble reading, "I worry is all."

Paul reached down and hooked a finger under Alex's chin, turning his gaze up to face him. There was something in those eyes, a certain need, things unsaid. Was the servant falling for him, perhaps dreading a time when Paul would leave without him? Did the coyote really mind such an attraction? His fingers brushed along the fennec's cheek fur until he reached the corner of his mouth, then he hooked a finger into that silk choker around his neck.

Paul gave Alex a light tug, guiding him up off his knees and getting a gasp out of him. Still sitting in the chair, Paul pulled him close and pressed his muzzle to the servant's, tongue pushing past his lips. The fennec shivered, squeezed his eyes shut, and sucked on Paul's tongue. He reached out and grabbed the arms of the chair, bracing himself against them as he leaned into the coyote's kiss. He lightly whimpered into it, the fur on his tail standing on end.

Paul broke the kiss, provoking another gasp from the fennec. Alex reflexively licked his lips with desire, panting as his gaze and Paul's locked on once more. Alex's bottle brushed tail flicked back and forth behind him.

"I... appreciate the worry," Paul panted. "And I assure you... everything... everything's fine. Lemme show you."

He reached out to run his fingers over the fennec's chest. Alex leaned into the touch as he gripped the chair's arms, leaning in over the still-sitting Paul. The coyote's gentle fingers traced a line through the fur on his abs and even further down, unceremoniously pushing aside that silk loincloth to take Alex's erection into his grip.

Paul's fingers wrapped around his length, coaxing a groan out of him. It was thicker than he expected, not the sort of thing that one would expect on such a slim body. The fennec leaned in a bit more, like he couldn't decide whether to just climb into the coyote's lap or wait to be instructed to do so. Paul slowly stroked his shaft, feeling droplets of the fennec's precum landing on his thigh. The coyote's sharp nose picked up the scent of arousal, of raw need, tinged with something else.

"See, Alex, everything's fine," Paul whispered. "There's no need to worry."

One of Alex's hands moved from the chair arm to Paul's thigh, nudging his robe aside, rubbing and kneading his leg. Paul leaned in to nuzzle Alex's cheek, his free hand stroking over those tall ears and the back of his head. Bit by bit, Alex came closer to climbing into the roomy chair with the coyote, squeezing his thigh like he was afraid to let go.

"I know you want to stay with me..." Paul whispered, panting. "Stay here tonight... with me. Surely they won't mind you going so far to please a guest..." He licked his lips. "I just want you to stay with me, please."

Alex pulled away, making a sound very much like a sob. There was reluctance to the movement as he braced himself and pushed away from the coyote, feeling his dripping length slip from Paul's gentle caress. He covered himself with the loincloth, already showing a damp spot from the drizzle of precum.

"I can't, I'm so sorry," he gasped as he all but fled the room, the words hanging in the air like an afterimage of regret.

"Alex, wait!" Paul said as he got up to follow him, his robe parted around his own rock-hard prick. He rushed to the door but there was no sign of Alex in the hallway, like he'd just vanished.

The coyote leaned against the doorframe, trying to figure out what went wrong. He idly licked the fennec's preseed from his fingers and went over the encounter in his head. Was it something he'd said? Had he pushed a boundary? To his surprise, his heart sank a bit at the thought that he'd chased Alex away.

"Does sir wish some company tonight?" came a purring voice from a nearby shadow. Paul jumped and saw another of the fennecs from earlier standing there, in a blue vest and soft silk trousers. His eyes seemed to glow in the dim light of the hallway.

"No, no, I should be—" was all Paul got out before he felt fingers wrap around his cock, sending a nearly-electric tingle through him. Everything became a blur as he allowed the other fennec to lead him back into the room that way.

* * *

Paul sat down at the large table and watched servants bring various dishes out from the kitchen. None of the scantily-clad, nearly-interchangeable fennecs addressed him directly or even acknowledged him as they set up the table for what promised to be a small banquet. He simply relaxed in his seat and watched the well-trained, nearly-mechanical precision of servants setting the table as they had surely done countless times before. In the far corner one of his hosts, a striped hyena named Hamideh, gave instructions to one of the fennecs. She was draped in blood-red silks that both covered and emphasized her curvy body as she addressed a fennec in a uniform suggesting a majordomo rather than a mere servant.

The growing feast before him held a cornucopia of spices he never found outside of the more exotic restaurants back home (*Which was where?* a voice in his head asked). Cumin here, paprika there, as well as assorted other scents he couldn't casually identify. He was dimly aware of the fact that he'd been experiencing luxurious meals his whole time here, but he was having trouble picking out specific memories of them.

Had he simply become jaded with the pleasures of the palace? Was he "entranced," as Alex put it?

He swiveled an ear away from his host's conversation so as not to be rude, and so he could focus on the delivery of the meal. As a result his sharp canid hearing picked up a distant conversation that disturbed the quiet enjoyment of the moment. It was like watching the wind send ripples across a lake, only to have a fish breach the surface. He couldn't make out every exact word, but recognized one of the voices.

Alex.

Paul got up and quietly crept over to a nearby doorway that he knew led into the servants' quarter of the palace. He peeked around the corner and spotted Alex, wearing a purple cotton kilt, talking to a stranger halfway down the hallway. Alex faced away, leaning against the wall, his arms crossed over his chest. He seemed oddly casual.

Alex talked with a skunk in a black and white, elaborately-patterned kaftan. Between the skunk's own fur and the outfit, he stood out from the very colorful world around him, which may have been the point. This was the only skunk he'd seen—really, the only person who was neither fennec nor hyena—and between the clothing and the species he had to assume he was some sort of merchant or outsider. Another guest, perhaps? Not that he'd seen any others.

He felt his jaw clench slightly at the notion of another guest having a private conversation with oddly-casual Alex.

"You've seen what I'm talking about," the fennec sighed to the skunk, sounding weary.

"Yeah, you've shown me enough, and I think I have a solution right here." The skunk produced an elaborate liquor bottle seemingly from nowhere. He held it out to Alex. "This should do it. It'll set things up so you can pull him out without too much of a struggle."

Alex accepted the bottle and turned it over in his fingers before he looked back up at the skunk.

"I just hope I can get it into him without being noticed. Keeping ahead of the defenses here has been… surprisingly tricky." The fennec's ears flattened slightly with embarrassment. "You'd think I'd have a better handle on it here, but…" He trailed off and shrugged.

"Look, you couldn't have known what Paul's got in his head, but that doesn't change the fact that the problem is fixable."

The coyote's ears perked and he straightened up a bit. Before, he'd suspected he was the topic of conversation, but now he *knew* this was about him. He eyed the bottle that Alex held with more than a little suspicion.

"Let's be honest, I *could* have known. I should have asked. I just assumed…" He trailed off. "I wish that maybe he'd trusted me enough to volunteer it," Alex said.

"Well, look," the skunk sighed, looking awkward. "Get that into his system and trust won't matter. At least not until you can get to a point where you can talk to him about it."

"I appreciate the help, Jex," Alex said as he leaned in to give the skunk a friendly hug. A chaste hug, sure, but it caught Paul off-guard enough that he jerked with surprise and banged an elbow on the doorframe. He froze.

He saw "Jex" whisper something in Alex's ear, which immediately swiveled like it was trying to listen to something behind him.

Paul quickly ducked away from the doorframe and returned to the table without causing a ruckus. Hamideh and her fellow-hyena husband Naseem, already sat with expectant smiles. The coyote only saw them for meals, and he'd been mostly left alone the rest of the time to enjoy both the simple comforts as well as the more carnal pleasures offered by the servants.

"Is anything the matter?" the lord of the palace asked, his tone of voice suggesting that he couldn't *imagine* anything being wrong and that the question was rhetorical. The hyena made a gesture and the servants prepared plates to set before the three of them.

"Nothing at all, Lord Naseem, nothing at all." Paul made a dismissive wave. "Just trying to keep up with the antics of the servants here. There's always something going on."

Paul closely watched the hyena's reaction to that, not knowing what he was looking for but paying attention nonetheless. Naseem looked perturbed, like he didn't know quite what to think of that. He reached out and plucked a bit of fruit off one of the plates and chewed on it thoughtfully. Paul was reminded of an actor buying time to improvise something outside his script.

"What sort of 'antics' do you mean?" he asked the coyote after a moment. "Is there something I should know?" He glanced at his wife, who offered a confused shrug.

"No, no, sir." He thought quickly and forced a smile. "I just saw one of them carrying a plate that looked too big for him down a hallway. It amused me because… it looked like he was about to fall over." Both Naseem and Hamideh burst out in laughter over that mental image.

"Yes, I can see that being distracting," the lady of the palace said with a chuckle as she forked a piece of meat and chewed it. "You know, I believe some of the servants here at Zerda are accomplished jugglers and tumblers, if you would prefer that sort of show. Just say the word, and there can even be some one-on-one entertainment with the more agile ones," she said with a grin and a wicked gleam in her eye. She wasn't Paul's type, but he wouldn't be surprised if she'd ask to watch him with any of the servants in question.

"I'll think about it, but you know..." Paul made a big show of considering something as someone took his wine glass and filled it up with something fizzy. "I've considered asking if it would be out of the question to get a more personal touch, perhaps getting someone specific assigned to me full-time." He picked up the glass and felt the bubbles deliver a nearly-electric tingle to the tip of his nose.

Naseem and Hamideh looked at each other. "That should not be an issue," Naseem said. "Did you have one in mind?"

"I was thinking Alex," Paul said, trying to sound casual and keep his feelings for the servant from reaching the surface.

There was a gasp next to him. He glanced over and Alex stood there, eyes wide, holding that bottle that the skunk had given him before. Paul glanced quickly at the wine glass and saw that the liquid inside was green. What kind of booze was green? He looked back up at the fennec and just saw him subtly shaking his head as if to warn Paul off the subject.

"I do not think I know an 'Alex,'" Naseem said with a confused frown. "Not that I keep track of the names of—"

"This is him, right here," Paul blurted out, gesturing to the one who served him.

Naseem's gaze snapped to Alex. "Who are you?" the hyena asked, growling.

Naseem's reaction worried Paul. The coyote got up, like a part of him needed the reminder of just how much taller he was than the fennec. He held up the wine glass.

"What is this?" he asked, sudden fear tangled up with anger. He glanced at Naseem. "He got this from a skunk, earlier, I saw him!"

"What skunk?" Hamideh asked. "Guards! Capture that one!"

A pair of hyena guards in light armor appeared from thin air. Literally. Paul was certain there was a flickering and then they stood there without entering the room. The two of them were identical, drawing scimitars that hadn't been there a moment ago.

"Shitshitshitshit," Alex gasped. The bottle vanished from his hand. "I was *really* hoping I wouldn't have to—God, *please* let this not fry your brain."

Alex waved his hand through the air, sending it on a wavy path, leaving a trail of light behind it.

"God mode override." He snapped his fingers. "Free frame." Everything stopped—not only did everyone freeze in place, but also a fly hovering over the table and steam rising off a bowl of soup. "Reset to room one. Limit and relocate."

Before Paul could ask what the hell was happening, everything vanished until he was just in an empty white room with Alex, and then a bright flash blocked even that out.

* * *

The two of them stood in Paul's bedroom. Out the windows, instead of the expected sunset, the coyote saw a plain, dull, featureless gray. It was like the bedroom stood alone in a larger space where the walls were made of the most generic modeling clay imaginable. He immediately ran for the doors, only to find that there were no doors—they looked painted onto the wall itself, like a train tunnel in an old cartoon.

"Alex?" Paul asked as he turned to face the fennec, trying not to panic. "What's going on here? I'm beyond confused right now."

"I can imagine you are." Alex's ears nervously twitched.

"No, no, I'm not sure you can imagine that."

The fennec held his hands up placatingly, and sighed as he took a moment to gather his thoughts. His ears drooped and he glanced away, biting his lip.

"Okay, okay," he said after a moment. "I didn't want to have to do this because I don't even know if it will work, but... none of this is real."

"Wait, what will work? Or won't work?"

"Paul, you're not actually in a pleasure palace and I'm not actually a servant. Your memories of the real world are clouded by the program, but this is... it's a virtual paradise. Well, it's a beta test of a virtual paradise. You've got an implant in your head that lets you connect to computers and can give you sensory input. You were testing out a program designed to give you an immersive sensory experience, and now you're trapped in it. Does any of this make sense to you?"

"Yeah, actually," he said before realizing he meant it. "I couldn't tell you why, but it does. So who the hell are you, then? What about the servants? The hyenas?"

"I'm still Alex. I'm literally the only real person you've seen while you were here. Everything else is part of the program; basic AIs performing according to scripts to keep you happy."

"What about the skunk?"

"Okay, I rehearsed the speech in my head before I thought to ask for help. The skunk is Jex. We're the only real people you've seen, but I'm the only one you've interacted with."

"Okay, okay. So this is a beta test for some sort of VR system," the coyote said out loud to help wrap his head around it. "And you're saying something went wrong?"

"To put it mildly," Alex groaned. "The system is intended for customers with a Class II neural interface, which we thought you had."

Paul tilted his head, confused.

"And now you've lost me," the coyote said.

* * *

Earlier...

"Shit, shit, shit, shit," Alex muttered as he stood next to the hospital-style bed.

The coyote laid there, unmoving but breathing, with various wires plugged into his head while sensors took his vital signs. IVs fed him and the fennec stood at one end of the bed where he could reach Paul's head. The wires in the coyote's head connected to a nearby computer system labeled with 'Zerda Pleasure Palace Beta' written on strips of masking tape.

Alex remained close as he had over the past couple of days that Paul was trapped in the simulation, unable to log out or even remember that he could leave. The fennec wore a visor connecting him to the virtual fantasy in which Paul was trapped while he multi-tasked to find out what was wrong. He gave the coyote's ear a pinch and a tug to give himself better access to scan the coyote's implant. Flashing red warnings appeared in his vision as hardware scans picked up an anomaly.

"Shit, why didn't he tell me when I... Fuck!" Alex snarled through gritted teeth. Fortunately his equipment made sure his outburst didn't translate over into the simulation unless he wanted it to. He looked down at the coyote, regret in the eyes behind the visor, his ears and tail drooped. He wasn't just wracked with guilt over administering the beta test in the first place, but worry that he may have effectively fried the brain of someone he cared about.

In the simulation, Alex's attempts to subtly probe Paul's mental state and memories were just making him upset and confused. As it was programmed to, the system did what it could to distract him from those efforts to keep him happy. He unplugged himself, and in the simulation his avatar stepped away to let the virtual slaves take over. It was time to make a call and then go back in while he waited for backup to become available.

* * *

"Have you read over the diagnostic I sent?" Alex asked as he connected the laptop to the server.

"I regret to inform you that my second opinion agrees with your first one," said the skunk on the laptop's screen. "It's a hardware problem more than a software one. He's jailbroken and skulljacked. You couldn't have foreseen that when you helped write the code."

"In my defense, the intended customer base can afford the proper hardware," the fennec sighed. "But that doesn't help him now."

"Not much, no. Are you gonna be okay?"

"Maybe. Eventually. Someone I care about is trapped in something *I* built and I'm trying to get him out and…" He took a breath. "I'm on the verge of a breakdown, okay? I mean, if I fuck this up, he's a vegetable."

"Well, look," Jex said awkwardly. "Once you get me hooked into the simulation, I can look at the code from the inside." He pulled a visor down from his forehead to cover his eyes. "I think I can put together a program that will extract him."

"I really appreciate you doing this on your lunch break," Alex said with a grateful smile. "I know it was short notice."

"Well, I haven't quite rocked the boat here at the day job yet, and this time of day I figure I can put the control room on autopilot and get them to just give me an extra hour for lunch if need be. If I can't, well, this is a better use of my time in any case." Jex shrugged. "Even if it is for someone who thinks beta testing a virtual brothel is an appropriate anniversary gift. Or, you know, celebrates a six-month anniversary at all."

"Yeah, yeah," Alex said, laying his ears back. "Just let me log in and I'll use debug mode to patch you in since the initial release isn't supposed to be a 'multiplayer' experience. Just have an avatar ready so we don't have to waste any time."

Alex snapped his own visor on and made sure the laptop with Jex's face on it was plugged into everything. He took off the emotional filters that dulled his responses when translated into the simulation. If this didn't work, he'd have to do something dangerous and he needed to be sure Paul could read his sincerity. He saw that Jex was ready, and went back in.

* * *

Now…

"Instead of a Class II interface, you have a Class I that's been modded," Alex explained. "For, like, 99% of things for which it might come up, it's perfectly compatible, even if it is just south of legal. But for the beta test…" He dramatically trailed off.

"That's why you made that comment about trusting you," Paul said, furrowing his brow. "Admittedly, I… my mind's still a little fuzzy on everything 'outside,' but maybe I didn't think it'd be a problem either?"

"Oh, I believe that, but in the moment it was just…"

"Just what?"

"I feel shitty. I feel like I should have known, like I should have checked ahead of time." He frowned. "Maybe I trusted you too much," he quietly thought aloud.

"When would you have a reason to check something that personal if I didn't think to volunteer it?"

Alex winced. "How much do you remember of the outside world?"

"It's patchy, still. For instance, I remember my job. Most of my daily routine. But specifics, newer stuff…" He held a hand out and waggled it. "It escapes me."

"Wow, now I feel shitty for a different reason," Alex said as he sat on the bed. "Paul, I plugged you into this thing."

"Yes, I guessed that."

"I'm actually one of the lead programmers on it, and this sort of thing isn't exactly what I dreamed of working on, but I've got a contract to work off some gene-mods and my own interface. Of course, I had to get the gene-mods and the implant to get the job, but—"

"Not to be blunt, but can you skip to the end if I'm in danger?"

"I offered you a spot in the beta test as a 'six month anniversary' gift."

Paul blinked. "Six months isn't an anniver—"

"Look, I'm not going to do cutesy alternative words for 'anniversary.' And you're missing the important part of that sentence."

Alex rubbed his forehead, the strain showing in the tilt of his ears and tail. Paul was quiet for a moment, his own ears lying flat. They stood up as if to point to an invisible lightbulb over his head.

"You and me?" he asked.

"Yeah. We met through your job because of something involving my job, and we hit it off, and I thought it would be cute to let you enjoy a trip to the virtual paradise I was building. Like treating someone to a spa day.

And the sheer 'perfection' of it hit that little issue with your interface mod, and… It's a little like hypnosis. You're stuck."

"So I can't just casually will myself out?"

"Try it."

Paul closed his eyes, scrunching them up real tight like a kid trying to lift a pencil with their mind. His ears lay back as he strained to remove himself from the system. After a few moments he relaxed and opened his eyes.

"Huh," Paul said as he looked around. "Okay, then, let's try this. Computer, end program."

Nothing.

"Exactly," Alex said, sniffing once. "You see the problem. I could just unplug you myself but that would lobotomize you or worse."

"So why didn't you just tell me all this before?" Paul asked. "Why all the poking and prodding and virtual magic potions?"

"Because bringing up the subject made you confused and uncomfortable. The program reads that discomfort and compensates. It distracts you with grapes and sex and whatever else is handy. And I didn't want to do something drastic for fear of the program overreacting and maybe frying your brain."

"This isn't drastic?" Paul asked, slightly exasperated, as he gestured to the door texture on the wall.

"It was a last resort, I think I said that!" He gritted his teeth and forced himself to calm down. "The potion represented a software patch we were going to load into your interface to get you out. You had to voluntarily drink it to install the patch, regardless of whether or not you knew what it did. Like accepting an EULA."

"I could drink it now."

"The code's currently tied up in all the stuff I cleared to get us the private space. I can't just casually call it back without putting us both in danger, and even then the program's anti-tampering safeguards will probably purge it now." Working the problem helped Alex visibly relax. "I might be able to get Jex to put together a new extraction code that compensates for that, but that might take a while and I'm not sure I can safely leave you here at this point."

"So how do we get out without it?"

"Well, I can just unplug, but you…" Alex gave Paul a look as he trailed off, looking like he was about to burst into tears. "You need to really *want* to leave, more than the program can convince you to stay. But because of the glitch who knows if…" The fennec trailed off and put his face in his hands.

"God, I fucked this up and you're going to die twitching in a hospital bed," he muttered into his hands.

Alex felt a weight next to him on the bed. A pair of hands gently pulled his own off his face and a single finger hooked his chin to turn his muzzle up to face Paul. Alex just looked at him as if he wanted to ask a question but wasn't sure what.

"It's going to be okay," the coyote whispered as he looked into Alex's eyes. "I have faith in you. Lemme take care of you now, and we'll figure something out."

Paul's free hand reached around to pull Alex closer as he brought their muzzles together, his tongue swiping across the fennec's lips. Alex gasped and opened his mouth just enough to welcome the coyote's tongue. It danced and slid over his own, the brief moment of connection sending a charge of raw pleasure and desire down his spine.

Despite himself, Alex whimpered into that kiss. His hands moved to Paul's chest and parted the silk robes he wore in the simulation to feel the fur over his firm pecs. A fingerpad teased over a nipple and felt it harden under his touch. His tongue pushed back against Paul's as he grew more engaged in the kiss with a churr of arousal.

Paul tugged away the kilt Alex wore and wrapped his fingers around the fennec's stiffening length. Alex groaned into the kiss, every sensation he experienced in the simulation affecting his body. And of course, that went both ways, translating Alex's actual erection into the digital illusion Paul was stroking. It became all too easy to imagine how someone could get stuck in a simulation like this, should the slightest thing go wrong.

Alex drizzled precum onto Paul's fingers as he stroked him, coaxing that plump prick to full hardness. The fennec whimpered into the kiss now, leaning back as Paul took charge of it. He melted under the touch, under feeling Paul's larger body against his own.

Paul broke the kiss, getting a gasp out of the both of them. The coyote gave him a smoldering look, the sort of look he'd give him in moments like these back in the real world. He took hold of Alex's shoulder and gently pushed him to lay back on the bed with his legs hanging over the edge. He knelt next to the bed, spread the fennec's thighs and ducked his head between them.

Alex gasped as he felt Paul's broad tongue swiping over his ballsac and the underside of his cock, gathering up some of that preseed. The coyote's lips brushed along the length and he made his way up to the tip. His tonguetip nudged back Alex's foreskin and he wrapped his lips over the drizzling cocktip.

Paul took more of Alex's shaft into his warm muzzle and stroked his fingers over those bits of the fennec's cock still beyond his lips. He squeezed the base as he slowly worked his head all the way down, and then moved his fingers to cup the fennec's balls. His free hand kneaded Alex's sandy-furred rump, squeezing it in his broad hand. He closed his eyes for a second and took a deep breath, filling his nose with the scent of the fennec's arousal.

Alex squirmed from the attention, letting out a fresh whimper each time he felt Paul's lips move up and down his prick or his tongue lash at the underside of the tip. The coyote nudged a finger up under his tail and brushed along his entrance. It was already slick and prepared—literally nobody wanted to have to fumble for lube in a sex simulation—and he wriggled his fingertip in.

Alex squealed as he felt the finger part his ring, giving it a firm squeeze as it sunk deep. A second finger joined it a few moments later, as if Alex needed the extra stimulation. Those fingers wriggled inside him, stroking and teasing sensitive spots, and the fennec found himself defenseless against it. He arched into the muzzle that kept bobbing on his cock.

Paul pulled off of Alex, exposing his slick length to the air. Alex's initial gasp became a yelp when the coyote wriggled his fingers free of the fennec's rump. The fennec looked up as the coyote shrugged off the robe he was wearing, rising up so his dripping prick was now visible to the reclining fox. Paul took hold of Alex's hips and pulled his rear to the edge of the bed so he could more easily reach, and then he gently rested Alex's ankles on his shoulders.

Their eyes met. An unspoken question passed between them.

The coyote gripped his own cock and guided it up under Alex's tail, pressing the tip against him and slowly spreading him open with a groan. Alex squealed with pleasure, spread his thighs some more and slid his legs down along Paul's sides to grip them and pull him in closer. Paul rubbed over Alex's chest, ruffling the fur there, as he briefly lost himself in the snug warmth around his dripping shaft.

The coyote slid a hand down to stroke and squeeze Alex's cock in time with his steady thrusts. The fennec reached up to grip the covers above his head to cope with the spikes of pleasure running up his spine each time he felt Paul's hips press against his rear. Alex leaned his head back and closed his eyes with a groan of pleasure, flexing to squeeze around that throbbing prick.

Paul's fingers did their best to keep up as he buried himself deep into Alex, but eventually his thrusts grew faster than the strokes. Not that the fennec seemed to mind. The bed rocked beneath them and the coyote's thighs thumped against the side of the bed. He pumped his lover's shaft faster to try and make up for lost time, but any sense of rhythm quickly got away from him. His ballsac smacked against the underside of Alex's rear and he felt the fennec's tail brushing against it each time he buried himself to the hilt.

Alex's groans broke down into a series of rapid yelps as he tensed up beneath Paul. His cock jumped under the stroking fingers and he erupted all over his own chest and abs. He squeezed at the larger canid's shaft as he came and coaxed a long groan from his lover.

Paul picked up the pace as he rapidly reached the point of no return. He kept pumping Alex's spurting prick, trying to get every last drop out of him. He leaned in to kiss him deeply, taking him harder, and his free hand slid to grab one of Alex's gripping the covers. Their fingers laced together and the kiss muffled Paul's moan as he reached his own peak and filled the fennec's tight passage.

Several blurry moments later, the pair were a panting, whimpery mess, nuzzling and kissing each other. Paul eased himself out of Alex and leaned over to lay down next to him, both of their legs hanging over the edge of the bed. Paul stared at the ceiling while catching his breath and Alex rolled onto his side.

"You okay?" he asked.

"Yeah, yeah, I'm fine, just... we need to get out of here," Paul gasped. "If this... if this is an echo of the real world, I... I can't believe I'd have forgotten about that."

Alex leaned in to kiss his neck, letting the bliss of the moment wash away the guilt he was feeling earlier.

"Love you," the fennec whispered.

"Love you too," Paul said as he turned to face him. He kissed him softly and then sat up with a blink. "Whoa."

Alex also sat up. "What?"

Paul gestured to the empty space in front of him, as if to ask *Can you see that?*

Alex blinked and made that wavy-gesture again. "Visual share."

A dialogue box floated in the air in front of Paul. It moved with his head as if to make sure it was in the center of his vision. Alex recognized it, since he designed it. It read "Log out?" with boxes for "Yes" and "No" options.

"Well, here we go," Paul said. "I think... I think I've decided there's something out there even better than what this program can give me." He offered a warm smile to Alex.

"If that 'something' is anything other than me, I might be offended as a programmer," the fennec chuckled. "Go ahead, get out of here while it will let you. I'll wait for you to go first, just in case."

Paul nodded and took a deep breath. He reached out and poked "Yes" with a finger. His avatar in the simulation lost color, then grew blurry, then became a wireframe skeleton, and then blinked out.

Alex waited a moment, just in case, for any sign that something had gone wrong. The HUD in the corner of his vision helpfully informed him that Paul was waking up in the real world. Tears of relief streamed down his cheeks in both worlds. He took a moment to collect himself and resist the urge to just yank the visor off.

"Computer," he said after a moment, fighting to keep his voice steady. "End program."

Making Contact

by Tym Greene

Excerpt from the Dedication Plaque, Captain's Hall Monument:
This ship, this mighty Ark, is dedicated to the planet we leave behind: the horrors of war, the ravages of pollution, the cultures of waste and consumption. We vow never to forget, for this is our origin, and this ship may be the last hope for society. Go, live your lives as you hurtle to our new home, but never forget the wreckage, never forget the past, the planet you have never seen. It is what made us who we are, and to forget this means we will simply do it all again.

This ship, however, is also dedicated to the planet we are approaching: the future of humanity, a new Eden. We vow to take the lessons of the past and learn them well, so that we may build a society that will last until we reach that shining untouched world; so that on that new homeworld we can thrive and continue all that is good about our various races. Never forget what we have left behind, nor what lies ahead for all future generations.

We survive so they may live.

* * *

On a spaceship, you're never truly alone. At least, not on our ship, the *Osiris*. You're always breathing someone else's air, eating food made from the disassembled molecules of someone else's waste, someone else's corpse. Of course, on a planet it's *technically* the same situation; it's just far more noticeable on a ship.

It's a fact that we've had centuries to come to grips with; perhaps that's why we cluster together the way we do, in groups of two or three. A closeness you have control over is better than being lost in a crowd—even if that crowd represents what may be the last of society.

We'd all learned about what we'd left behind: cities crowded with all the different races—cats, bears, horses, all of them—sleeping ten to a room, fighting over scraps of food, warring over centimeters of land. In the time since the *Osiris* had been launched, there could have been half a dozen more world wars, a nuclear holocaust, and a second ice age. That's why we were out here.

And now we were almost done. It seemed like only yesterday that we'd been ten years away from our destination—a planet that someone had named Asimov, back in the ship's first generation—and now there were only a few scant months left. You wouldn't know it to look at us, though: Captain Parker had ordered that life should continue on as it always had.

Which is why Burl and I were looking forward to our next day off. We were planning to go to that new holoflick, the one about one of the men who'd built *Osiris* who'd been trapped aboard and was only just now unfrozen. It was supposed to be a comedy. I'd rather have seen a drama, or maybe spend the day at the ship's museum—our day off was a Tuesday, which meant the museum would be set up with art history displays—but I know Burl needed a bit of relaxation.

As Third Officer, he's got a lot to worry about, now that we're coming up on our rendezvous with Asimov. So has the Captain. All the generations before, all that had been needed was to maintain a status quo: same speed, same heading, and same conditions on board.

But more than a century ago, they had started to change the ship's environment to prepare for our new homeworld, with slightly higher gravity, thicker air, and a fourteen hour day. The genes of every subsequent generation were edited to match.

Then, thirty years ago—around the time I was born—the landing drills had begun, every April 3rd (our estimated date of arrival) we would line up and file into the landing pods, one cadre at a time. First the Culturals—those who held psychological, historical, or entertainment roles—would board the pod, strap in, and then unbuckle and leave the pod to make way for the following cadre. Next the Sciences, biology, astronomy, and physics; and lastly the Crew. Growing up, I had always boarded with the first group, since my parents were both entertainers.

Now I was in the last group. As the ship's Safety Officer, I had a lot to worry about too. The next time we boarded those pods, it would be for real, and we would be leaving the *Osiris* for good.

Even though we were on duty, Burl sidled up to me, his yellow and grey uniform showing off every curve of his lithe body. I wanted to reach out and touch him.

"Just think, two more shifts and we'll be able to have our date night," He whispered into my ear as though uttering some profound declaration of love. I nuzzled my head against his; we did pretty good at keeping romance off the bridge, but neither of us could resist sneaking a grope or kiss now and then.

Behind us, Beaumont—a walrus, a decade our senior and the Chief Security Officer—harrumphed a warning into his mustaches. Burl straightened up, making it look like he'd just been going over some details of ship's operations with me, rather than flirting. I turned to the walrus, quickly nodding my thanks: his wife worked in the hydroponics bays, down in the light of our ion drive engine, and he was always ready to help out "young love." Beaumont may just have been a hopeless romantic (and neither Burl nor I were any sort of young) but his alert came in handy: as a security officer, he had access to the ship's camera network, and therefore had ample warning. "Captain on the bridge," he sang out in his warm and grumbly voice.

We stood to attention, turning to watch as Captain Parker took his place. A deer, he had no antlers of course, just as I—a wildebeest—had no horns. Deer, wildebeest, bull, or moose, we had all been born without headgear; just as every person on the Osiris had been genetically altered to be roughly the same size, we had all been given the polling gene, so we never grew horns in the first place. There simply wasn't space on a space ship. The first generation born on the planet, however, would be entirely natural, without any of the modifications that generations of their forebears had needed. It would be a strange new world indeed.

As each of the officers reported their particular aspect of ship's status to the captain (all nominal), I was struck by an odd thought: all of us on the *Osiris*, every single member of society's various races and breeds, were cogs, purpose-built to shepherd the unaltered genetic material and historical data of old Earth to our new home. If the builders had felt more certain that a computer could have managed the trip un-aided, it's likely that none of us would even exist.

Maybe that's why Captain Parker always looked so melancholy, knowing that he was the last captain. I didn't blame him: as the ship's Safety Officer, I was pretty sure that I wouldn't have much function landside either. Then again, if the builders' plans were accurate, we might all end up as farmers, starting our own families and homesteads. I wondered if Burl would let us adopt—as an officially-registered couple, it was our right (once we passed certain competency exams) to be given one of the children born from randomized genetic stock, grown in the fertility labs, and raised in crèche. At two years old, they were assigned to appropriate parents. I'd thought before about holding a little cub in my arms, but a bridge officer's life was a busy one.

It was my turn to report: "All clear, sir, apart from a small grease fire in kitchen three, science section. Automatic systems handled it before there was any significant damage, the chef involved is being treated for minor burns, and the maintenance crew for that section is nearly done with clean-up."

"Good. Let me know if there are any reports of smoke damage."

"Aye, sir. Oh." A blinking notification on my screen had just popped up. "Sir, it's probably a sensor glitch, but the astro labs report…flashing lights. I'm not quite sure what they mean by that. 'Flashing lights, 500 meters off north bow,' that's all it says." The marble floor of the Captain's Hall—the main ceremonial space on Osiris, which had the dedication plaque as well as the illuminated map of the ship's progress—had other stones inlaid, forming a compass rose aligned to the four spars holding the ion engines. For the most part, the quadrants of each deck were the same, but it did help navigation when visiting other decks. I'll admit to feeling a little foolish, relaying such a scant message. "Shall I go check it out, sir? Everything else seems buttoned up right now."

He nodded. "Maybe they're just playing a prank on us. All that time staring at a telescope screen would make anyone a little loopy," he joked weakly. When nobody laughed, he added, "Go on, Orville, report back if you find anything more…concrete."

Squeezing past Burl as I left the bridge, I was able to grope his thick rudder. The soft fur was soothing as always, redolent of his mild scent. Tuesday couldn't come soon enough.

Riding one of the elevators in the central shaft down to the science level—midway between the bridge at the "top" of the ship and the engines at the "bottom"—I thought back on the changes I'd noticed lately. People seemed more jumpy, and more furtive; there had been reports of minor thefts too: food, tools, even jumpsuits, as though the culprits were hoarding supplies for when we landed. There was nothing significant, just petty crimes that merited nothing more than a few hours of community service, usually scrubbing deckplates.

Even Burl had been in an odd mood, calling up ancient sci-fi movies. *The Invasion of the Body Snatchers* wasn't scary at all, and I found *Alien* a bit boring, but I did enjoy the way my otter wrapped his body around mine, peeking out from behind my neck at the viewscreen in our quarters. And after the movies, he'd been even more amorous, rump in the air, rudder swaying, enticing me. That view never failed to get a rise out of me, and he loved the way I'd snort and ruffle his fur, said it made him feel like an animal. We'd ended up skipping our normal workouts several days over the past week, opting for a little more *personal* cardio. I wasn't complaining.

Still, if the records of the midpoint chaos were any indication, we might be in for a rough patch. Halfway through the trip, a few hundred years ago, the engines had been turned off, the ship maneuvered so the tail end would be pointed at our destination, and then the engines switched back on to begin the long process of slowing down until *Osiris* reached Asimov, all according to the builders' designs. Apparently though, in the weeks leading up to the middle of the voyage—not to mention the three hours of weightlessness—there had been graffiti, demonstrations, even riots as non-crew passengers objected to the builders' plans. That had all blown over, of course, but as Safety Officer it was my job to ensure that chaos like that never happened again. I knew the captain wasn't the only one feeling a little lost.

The elevator doors opened on a lobby like all the others, marked by red letters reading "Science 2 - Astrometrics, Astrophysics, and Astrometry." You had to hand it to the builders, they sure knew how to organize things. Just as I stepped out of the lift, the lights flickered; that had never happened before. Perhaps it was just the engineers working on the ion drive, prepping it in some way for when we arrived. That must be it.

The astronomy department's main lobby was just a few dozen meters from the elevators, and from there rooms branched off to provide specific space for the various sub-teams, as well as equipment and storage. The young antelope at the desk directed me to the office of the head astronomer on duty.

I knocked on the door, but found it ajar. The desk was littered with tablets and dusty, un-recycled computer printouts. Charts were held to the bulkhead with magnets, and a full wall was devoted to a digital chalkboard covered with scrawled equations. I wondered if this were simply the normal state of things, or if the mess were due to the mysterious lights that had been sighted. The lights flickered again, and I could hear a shouted argument coming from one of the nearby rooms.

Following the din, I approached what turned out to be one of the monitoring stations. "No, no-no-no," a woman was shouting gruffly, "do it again. Run *all* the diagnostics if you have to!" I poked my snout in, and was nearly run into by a large bear, the red piping on her uniform marking her as a member of the scientist class.

I stepped back to give her space. "Myrtle Twenty?" I inquired; the number, of course, meaning that she was the twentieth person aboard the *Osiris* to hold that name—I was the eighteenth Orville, but only the first wildebeest to be named that, and my otter was the eighth Burl. At her distracted nod, I went on: "Orville Eighteen, Safety Officer. The captain has asked me to check on the lights your department reported sighting."

"Damn and blast them," she grumbled, pushing past me and back to her office. "I'd told them not to report anything until we knew what we were dealing with."

"What do *you* think they are?"

"You should know better than to ask that: I don't have enough information, and it's not likely we're going to get it." She dropped into her chair, rubbing the bridge of her snout with a hand that could have torn a deck plate in two.

"What do you mean? Weren't you able to—"

"Any time we try something more than a visual scan, the power flickers, resetting the whole system. At this point, I can't tell if it's something the lights are doing, or just this old bucket of bolts," here she pounded the bulkhead behind her with a fist, "throwing one last fit before we dismantle it for parts. I've got one team working on analyzing the last visual scan, and another trying to shore up the systems. But of course, there aren't any batteries available."

"I'm sure the captain could requisition some, if you think it'll help." She nodded, leaning back in her chair. "Could I use your com?" She nodded again, looking more tired than I'd imagined, now that her bluster had drained away.

I dialed up the bridge on her office's com panel, and saluted when the captain's narrow face appeared on the screen. "Sir, I'm at Astronomy. They say there seems to be an issue with the scanners."

"Does this have anything to do with the rolling power outages that we've been getting reports of?" His ears flicked as though he were nervous.

"It's possible, though right now we're not sure which side is the cause: the scans could be causing a feedback loop which causes the outage, or the outages could be causing the scans to fail. Either way, apart from visual scans, we've got nothing."

"And the 'scopes were never intended to be used at such close quarters," Myrtle broke in, looking over my shoulder. "We've got a team working on adjusting the lenses."

I slid to one side, blocking her from view. "That was Myrtle Twenty, sir, head astronomer. She says that she needs some batteries, to see if unplugging the scanners from the rest of the ship's systems will keep the feedback from happening."

"Fine, whatever she needs, just find out what this is before the rest of the ship finds out. We do *not* need a riot, not when we're so close to Asimov."

"Aye, sir. I'll requisition them and report back."

* * *

It was almost two hours before one of the maintenance men arrived, pushing the massive batteries on a trolley. I stood back and watched while Myrtle directed everyone. Eventually the scanner was unplugged, the batteries attached, and everything made ready.

"Ok, punch it," the big bear told one of her underlings, who dutifully flipped the switch. She bent low above the screen, hovering over his shoulder. "No, that can't be right, it must be a sensor reflection, our own image bounced off astral gas."

"It doesn't look like the *Osiris*, Ma'am," the meerkat replied, trying to shrink lower in his seat. I knew how he must feel: I hated it whenever the captain watched over my shoulder, or even when Burl did it.

"No, it doesn't. Tighten the scan, see if we can get a reading from inside. Maybe a compositional analysis."

The meerkat adjusted some knobs, and even I could tell that the resolution was improving. There seemed to be a few blips—life signs, perhaps—in the vaguely squid-shaped *thing* that was still hovering, with its three brothers, off our bow. And then there was the smell of ozone. I glanced down, saw the battery casings starting to buckle. "Get back, shut it off! It's going to blow!"

The bear and meerkat, startled by my exclamation, just stared at me. Thankfully, the batteries did not explode. Instead the screen flickered, something within the scanner started smoking gently, and the casings melted, pouring acid in a congealing cascade onto the trolley. The fumes, however, were not so benign. "Out, out, out!" I ordered, half-pushing and half-dragging them to the doors. I slammed my fist on the emergency pad once we were on the other side. The safety systems kicked in, sealing the room and pumping out all the air. It would be processed, broken down, and the component chemicals stored for future use.

Growling, Myrtle stormed back to her office. "It's a damn good thing I have things linked up. Maybe we'll be able to salvage this little fiasco after all," she muttered as she hurled herself into her chair. Her computer did indeed have telemetry from the scan, right up to the point where the scanner's circuits had been fried into a solid gold-and-silicon lump. Tabbing through the data, Myrtle suddenly went silent.

"It *is* a ship. All these years...all these years in space and not once did we find any evidence," she whispered reverently, as though she didn't quite believe what she was saying. "This...these things, they're ships."

"What do you mean, ships? From Earth? But how would they have caught up with us?"

"No, these aren't from Earth—have you ever seen anything designed like those? I can't even begin to guess what *that* does," she tapped on the fuzzy false-color image, indicating a bulbous protrusion hanging from the ship's belly like an anglerfish's lure. "Besides, there's no such thing as faster-than-light travel. That's the sort of thing you only see in lazy science fiction."

"And what about…aliens," I finished in a whisper. "Aren't those just sci-fi too?"

We both stared at the screen. "Apparently not."

I gathered up my courage and phoned the captain again. On his orders, Myrtle and her underlings were confined to the Astronomy department, using the melted batteries as a half-truth explanation for the "safety precautions." Every single person, from the gazelle at the desk to Myrtle herself, was sworn to secrecy until the captain said otherwise. Meanwhile, they were to analyze the little data that had been gained in that last scan, and to continue working on refining the telescopes for a more short-range view.

Myrtle grumbled, but understood the dilemma that faced us all. She also agreed not to attempt any further non-visual scans: it appeared that the power outages and burst batteries were indeed caused by a feedback loop, some sort of defense mechanism perhaps, or maybe just a fatal incompatibility between our systems and *theirs*.

It felt strange to think of anything outside of *Osiris*. It had become our Earth, hurtling through the stars, a microcosm containing the last threads of humanity, each race preserved and replicated as assiduously as the historical and cultural records in our computer banks. Walking back to the bridge to report to the captain, I stroked my muzzle and massaged my eyes. If Burl had been standing beside me, he'd have called me a "bewilderbeest;" I felt like one alright, but I tried to master my bafflement before I reached the bridge.

After all, I was the Security Officer. I had a responsibility for the safety of each person on board, as well as for the ship as a whole. If nothing else I needed to put on a brave face. I resolved to check the vast Operations Manual the builders had left us, to see if there had been any contingency plan in place for alien attacks. It felt silly just thinking it, but I couldn't deny the evidence of my own eyes, nor the banks of mangled sensors.

I finally reached the bridge and made my report to the captain. He was not pleased, but accepted my recommendation that it would be best to keep things quiet until we had a better idea of what was going on. I loaded the Manual onto my tablet and started thumbing through the index when I saw what time it was. Our shift had technically ended hours ago, and Burl—I scanned the bridge to confirm—had already left for our cabin.

Still skimming my tablet, I powered down my station and returned to the elevator banks. It wasn't too late, so maybe we could still get some dinner. As bridge officers, we were entitled to eat at The Captain's Table, the one fancy restaurant on board. But we normally preferred to dine in the mess hall nearest our cabin's deck, reserving the restaurant for more special occasions.

He was indeed in our room, sprawled on the bed and watching another old movie on the wall screen. "*Klaatu barada nikto*," commanded the horse in the silver suit, just before Burl switched it off. Propping himself up on his elbows, he turned to me. "Is everything ok?"

I hesitated, trying to decide how much to tell him. Finally shrugging, I said, "Why don't we get something to eat—you hungry? We can talk on the way: there isn't much to tell." He nodded and leapt from the bed, my otter never being one to turn down a meal invitation. As we walked through the hallways, I explained briefly what had happened, and what I suspected. "Have you come across any protocols that might help?" I asked at the end of my rehash.

"No, not really," he said as we entered the hubbub of the mess hall. "I mean, there's all sorts of anti-riot and anti-panic stuff. I bet that would be helpful."

"Yeah, I know. I've already read those—I bet I could recite them in my sleep." I chuckled weakly as I grabbed my tray from the stack. "I was just hoping there was something more…specific."

"I guess the builders couldn't think of *everything*. And it's not like you can't think for yourself, right?" His hand on my back was warm and reassuring, even through my uniform. He was good like that.

I turned to smile at him, then focused on getting dinner. Salad, roast chicken, mashed potatoes, and a little wedge of chocolate cake: I felt like I deserved some simple comfort food. Burl got his usual clam chowder and smoked salmon on toast. Despite the late hour, three past the end of Alpha Shift, plenty of people were in the hall, snacking and chattering.

Our usual quiet corner table was filled with a bevy of women, their blue-accented uniforms denoting them as members of the Cultural class, probably psychologists: I could hear them discussing the differences between Jungian and Pinellian interpretations of shared consciousness, and how that applied in times of group stress. Steering Burl away from what could easily erupt in an argument between theoretical precepts, we settled instead in the middle of the large room.

As we ate, I listened to the overall flow of the conversations around us. There were no mentions of aliens or ships, thankfully, but I did overhear several red-striped scientists complaining about power fluctuations, and one even went so far as to suggest that there was some problem with Asimov, that we were going to change course soon and head for another planet, 20 generations away. Thankfully his friends laughed him off.

Besides, even if there were an issue with our new homeworld, even if it turned out to be entirely uninhabitable (true, spectrometry had shown a bit more carbon monoxide in the atmosphere than had been expected, but that probably just meant an active volcano or two) there was nothing we could do about it. The *Osiris* only had just enough fuel left to get us there and place itself in orbit, and while we could use water instead of xenon, it was far less efficient. Not to mention the fact that most systems had already been patched and jury-rigged by our parents and grandparents.

There was no option but to see the mission through, or die here in space and let society's last chance die with us.

"Are you going to eat the rest of that?" Burl asked, nudging my elbow and indicating the cake with his chin. My bleak train of thought had sapped all flavor from the dessert.

"Yeah, go ahead. I'm not that hungry anyways." He gobbled it down cheerfully enough, and then we left.

Walking back to our room, he again placed a hand on my back. I could feel his blunt claws pressing into the fabric. "Orville, are you ok? You seem to be taking this really hard. I know you're the Safety Officer, but you don't have to shoulder this alone."

"I know, it's just…it's hard finding out after all these centuries that we *aren't* alone, that there *is* someone else out there. There's so much we don't know: are they friends, or are they going to zap us with some weapon we've never even thought of? What if they have some disease—a common cold for them—that would be worse than any plague. Do they even think like us?"

"So many questions," he agreed, his hand sliding up to grip my shoulder, making me sigh audibly. He pressed harder. "Oh you *are* tense. Why don't you let me help with that? You can't save us all if you're tired and sore, right?"

He shepherded me back to our quarters, positioning me in the middle of the little space. "Stand there," he instructed. I obliged and let him peel off my uniform. His hands slid across my shoulders as he spread the tunic wide, guiding the sleeves down my arms until it fell on the floor behind me. His fingers slipped beneath my undershirt, claws tickling the hide on my belly as he stretched it out, pulling the thin fabric over my head. He made short work of my pants and briefs, taking a moment to grope my rump on the way down.

"Now, get on the bed. On your belly," he said with a gentle swat. I obliged, feeling my spine pop just from laying myself out. There was a rustling and a weight on top of me, his bare chest against my bare back, legs laid along legs, sheath pressing against my tail.

I lowed. I couldn't help myself: I mooed into the pillow as his hands started working my shoulders. I could just picture him, back and rudder curled in an arc above me, the full weight of his upper body channeled through his arms into my trapezii, with our hips as the fulcrum point. Those thumbs worked on me, moving lower and lower along my spine, until I felt like I'd melted into a puddle of wildebeest-flavored ice cream.

Then he lifted up slightly, and I felt the cold fluid dripping between my buttocks, followed by a finger that rubbed and spread. More relaxed than I'd felt in weeks, it seemed, I let his finger in, giving it a gentle squeeze as though to say, "I know what kind of trick you're pulling, but I don't mind playing along."

With one hand pressed against the small of my back, I felt him jerk a little, heard the soft churring he always made when he unsheathed himself, and was unsurprised by the slick slender length that slid under my tail. It seemed that every time we did this, I realized just how long it'd been since the last time, and how good it felt, and how I wanted to be sure that no similar gap occurred again. Well, this time things would be different, I was sure of it. We just had to pull in to orbit, and land, and…I'd almost forgotten about our "visitors."

I know he felt me tense up, his pistoning slowed by my tightened grip, but he didn't say anything. Taking a deep breath, I forced myself to relax: the aliens would still be there by the start of tomorrow's shift, and maybe we'd have some more information to act on by then. There was nothing to be done tonight, nothing but relax, and rest, and spend time with my man. He started thrusting faster, both hands gripping my shoulders once more, his breath ruffling my mane.

I couldn't help but feel like a piece of exercise equipment in that position. My own shaft was unsheathed, pressed into the smooth sheets by our combined weight. I backed up to Burl, taking a more active role as I lifted my hips to mash against his, accelerating our rut and milking his shaft with each movement.

* * *

We had just finished and had begun cleaning up when a klaxon sounded. "All officers, report to the bridge," the captain's voice said. "Repeat: all officers to the bridge."

I looked at Burl: he seemed as nervous as I felt. "What now," he sighed, dropping the little towel he'd been using into the laundry chute. A new towel, freshly recycled, landed on the shelf next to it.

"I guess there's been a change in the situation. Better get dressed." I'd already started pulling on a clean uniform, the light fabric cool and strong, and the same warm grey as the other fabrics on board—all made from enzymatically-recycled plastic. Now and then, I'm struck by the realization that in the closed system of the *Osiris*, there really isn't anything new. The water, air, carbon, the biomatter and metals and plastics are all exactly the same as the ones first loaded when *Osiris* was launched. It was a little humbling, actually. Ours would be the generation that would break that loop, that would crack open our hermetically-sealed ship and pour it out onto Asimov.

If the aliens didn't blast us first.

I followed Burl to the elevators, watched as he fastened up his tunic while we waited to ascend. His hands were trembling. "What do you think they're going to do?"

"I don't know, but I know we can handle it. We've dealt with cosmic rays and meteor showers and clouds of gas, and survived it all."

"Yeah, but those were generations ago." It was his turn to be worried. The doors opened, and we stepped in.

"Sure, but we're no less resilient than they were. I know we'll be fine, Burl. Just take a deep breath and—" I was interrupted by the doors opening again, revealing a scene of chaos. The lobby was filled with officers from all three watches—some milling around, a few trying to hurry through on some errand or another, and most just standing and gossiping—as was the short hallway to the bridge. The bridge itself, once we made our way to it, wasn't any calmer. The captain seemed overwhelmed with officers asking for orders or information or reassurance, and several consoles were lit with red or yellow warning lights.

"Attention!" I shouted, drawing it out like a drill sergeant from an ancient movie. As Safety Officer, it was my duty to ensure that things were orderly and organized in the event of an emergency, and this situation certainly fit the bill.

It worked: in an instant the babbling had stopped, leaving only the soft pulse of a system alert ringing through the silence. I turned to my otter: "Burl, go bring all the officers in from the lobby, that way the captain can address all of us at once." Captain Parker nodded at me in thanks; I couldn't help but notice the bags under his eyes and the dull scruffiness of his pelt.

Once every officer—about forty in all—was crammed into the bridge and standing shoulder to shoulder, the captain strode out to the big viewplate that showed a tiny blue-green speck in amid a sprinkling of stars. He seemed to stare at Asimov for a moment, and then turned his back on our destination. Clasping his hands behind him, he spoke. "We are facing a crisis. The alien ships have begun shooting off…lights. I'm afraid we don't know much more about them. With the damage to our scanners, we can't get more than a visual of them. They might be probes, or scout ships, or some kind of weapon—"

Here some wag shouted out, "Photon torpedoes, sir?" which caused several other officers to laugh. Even the captain cracked a wry smile.

"I certainly hope not. We are no warship as you all know; the builders had found no evidence of alien life, and thought it would be a waste of resources to give us anything more than basic shielding. Members of B-shift sent out a few probes to intercept these whatever-they-are lights, but the probes were, well, absorbed. That's what you'd described it as, right, Merrick?" A horse across the room nodded. I vaguely recognized him as the First Officer of B-shift. "Gwen, would you show us the diagram you showed me?"

A ferret pushed a few keys on her console, then stepped up beside the captain. The display had changed, now showing a wireframe diagram of the *Osiris*. Three white shapes, like little grubs, were positioned in a circle around the middle of the ship, each five-hundred meters from the ship and one-hundred twenty degrees from one another. The ferret gestured as the image began to rotate. "As you can see, the alien vessels have taken up station alongside us. So far there have been no attempts to communicate. They have, however, started sending out these 'lights,' which we suspect to be probes."

Each of the three ships began to shoot out little white lights in the diagram. I counted three from the head and tail of each one. We watched in silence as they spiraled out, the first lights continuing until they reached almost the farthest tip of *Osiris*, the second ones midway, and the third ones remaining closer to their origination. Our ship was now encased in a spiraled net, like a piece of candy wrapped in a twist of cellophane. "We actually aren't sure," Gwen continued, "how big each one is. It's possible they're manned, but given the fact that they're holding position, it's more likely that they're controlled by computers on board the three main ships. So far, they haven't done anything, apart from absorbing our probes, of course."

255

"Why can't we use the asteroid cannon, Captain?" We all turned to look at Beaumont, who huffed into his whiskers. The walrus seemed unperturbed by the attention, only standing little straighter at his station. "I know it was intended to knock things out of our way, sir, but I'm confident we can use it to blast those...*things* into oblivion. As Chief Security Officer, I think it's just part of my duty to help protect—"

"I won't hear of it," the captain interrupted. He sighed and rubbed his fingers against his long, cervine snout. "There's no way we can know if a little ion cannon like that will do any damage to them, and I doubt there's any way we could take out all three before they retaliate. We've seen the kind of damage they can do in response to simply scanning them. Anyone who attempts to fire on these aliens or their probes will be stripped of rank...assuming we survive long enough for that to matter."

"Aye, sir," Beaumont replied sullenly. I suspected that his gears were still turning, trying to think of a way to fight back.

"Now, I want you all to—" The captain began, then stopped, staring with wild eyes at the crowd of officers before him. I followed his gaze and saw Beaumont standing frozen, his hand stopped midway through stroking one long tusk as he usually did when pondering something. A light seemed to surround him, and as the officers beside him started backing away, I realized that he had become translucent, as though someone were slowly lowering his opacity setting in some kind of real-life image editor.

Glancing around, I saw a few other officers suffering the same fate. One was even frozen with his arm outstretched, pointing directly at Beaumont. In a moment, they had all vanished. The captain was just staring, only his trembling jaw and twitching nose showed that he was not frozen like the others. I had to take action, if only to avoid a general panic.

"First Officers, take stock and report," I commanded. "Everyone else stay quiet—we need to keep our heads, people." The First Officer of B-shift announced that only one person was missing and C-shift had five. A-shift had four people gone, including the First and Second Officers, which left Burl in charge, the sort of promotion one only read about in war stories from old Earth. I gave his shoulder a squeeze, trying to say "I believe in you" with touch and gaze alone, then turned to glance up at the Tactical station.

One of the C-shift officers was looking down at the monitor, his arm held high. "Yes, Bosun?"

"I'm getting reports from other sections, sir. Other people have been... vanished. Twelve from Science, two from the hydroponics bay, seven from Engineering, and all but one from the Biology deck, sir. I'm also getting calls from quarters, people reporting that their spouses have vanished, one little girl says both her parents are gone, and I have no idea how many people in the 'bachelor' quarters have vanished."

My mind reeled, torn between trying to tally them all up and trying to make a plan of action.

"Bosun," I said, deciding that one step at a time was better than nothing, "have one of the nursery staff go to that girl's quarters, make sure she's ok. And start compiling a list of missing personnel, organized by class and position—see if you can find any sort of pattern." The lean panda nodded and bent to his task.

"Sir," an older mare said. I recognized her as the B-shift Communications Officer. "There's something coming in over all audio channels. It sounds like static, but a little bit like language, too. I can almost—" Then with a scream, she tore the headphones from her ears. I could hear the shrill piercing static, wavering seemingly at random, until the little speakers finally burnt out, sending up twin plumes of smoke. Grimacing, the mare waggled a finger in one of her ears, and worked her jaw like she was trying to equalize pressure in her eardrum. "Ow. Sorry, sir, I guess it overloaded our system. Ship-wide audio communication is down."

Just like the scanners, I thought. It was like the aliens were taking out our systems one by one, using their incompatibility to blind and deafen us. *What's next?*

"Captain, I think it's time to implement Emergency Protocol Beta." No one had called EPB since the midpoint riots—and since Emergency Protocol Alpha was an order to abandon ship, no situation had ever gotten *that* bad. So far.

The captain nodded and returned to his chair. A few keystrokes and verification from a senior officer began the process. All down the length of the *Osiris*, relays clicked into action, sealing off each deck and locking the elevators in place. Independent ventilation scrubbers kicked in and view screens all showed the same message above an image of the current captain's gently stern visage: "Do Not Panic."

We were now all trapped on the bridge, with only small relief room on the other side of the elevator lobby and enough ration packs for about a week. A week, I realized, that had been calculated assuming the standard complement of fifteen officers. Even with the missing ten, we still had more than twice the expected amount. With rationing, we could make the food last for four, maybe five days. I hoped it wouldn't take that long to get this situation resolved, and I could only imagine how the people in the lower decks felt.

"Do Not Panic" was not very reassuring, after all.

* * *

We had huddled together for two days while the captain strove to maintain some semblance of normalcy. We were held to our normal shifts, with "battlefield" promotions to fill as many gaps as possible (obviously without bringing in anyone from the other decks). Poor Burl looked even more run-down than I felt: he wasn't used to command, let alone under such stressful circumstances, and the captain insisted on frequent meetings with all acting First Officers, as though there were any status changes worth meeting about.

Actually, there was one significant change, although we all did our best to ignore it: the smell. Fear sweat and halitosis seemed to form a visible fog, since the little relief room only had two toilets, two urinals, and three sinks, there wasn't much to be done about hygiene. Hunger, too, was an issue, with each ration pack being cut into thirds. Tempers were short, and would have been likely to cause fights, had the Captain not instigated a policy of silence: only on-duty officers were allowed to talk above a whisper, and non-essential conversations were discouraged. It also helped to keep down what would have been quite a din, had everyone started talking at once in such a small area.

I nuzzled up against Burl, our tunics spread out to form a makeshift mattress beside the elevators—the lobby had been designated ersatz sleeping quarters for all off-duty officers, since no one wanted to sleep in the relief room and there was no space on the bridge—our undershirts damp and stained. The little recirculator for this deck was no match for the heat of thirty-five bodies. Despite circumstances, his musk—lighter and more floral than my own, which I always thought smelled like cinnamon mixed with chicken soup—reassuring me with each in-breath. I tried to exhale out the side of my mouth, aiming it away from the back of his neck so as not to make the situation any worse.

As though it had no awareness of how dire our situation was, nor how dead-tired I felt, my sheath still stirred as I cuddled up behind my otter, the weight of his rudder on my hip, the slow rise and fall of his chest beneath my arm. This was no place to make love.

There were only two other couples where both partners were bridge officers, and one of those (the B-shift navigator) had been rent when his girlfriend had been among the vanished. The other pair, a hippo and tigress from C-Shift, had tried to be amorous, draping their tunics across their bodies in an attempt at privacy, but the makeshift blankets kept slipping down, giving everyone a good view of his hefty pink rump and smooth flank. I know Burl had snuck a few glances, and I for one welcomed the attractive distraction. A little eye-candy helped relieved the stressful monotony. Other officers slunk away to take care of their needs in one of the relief room's stalls, or simply did without.

I sighed and tried to get to sleep, but the breadth of my shoulders and lack of a pillow made for a very sore neck. Our situation was anything but calming, and my mischievous libido did nothing to help matters. I was practically wide awake, therefore, when I saw it.

There was a glowing, much like there had been around Beaumont before he had started to disappear, and sure enough, there was a figure within the white aura. None of the other off-duty officers seemed to be awake, and I certainly wasn't going to give any indication that I was any different. My arousal, thankfully, flagged like a burst balloon.

Keeping my eyes hooded, I watched as the figure grew in opacity, but not in definition. Even when I could no longer see the bulkhead through it, it remained a vague bipedal blob. I watched as it walked around, leg-blobs and arm-blobs swaying, tall blobs that could have been ears pivoting like signal flags, revealing two vertical blobs that could have been horns, or antennae, or part of a weird hair-do. I screwed my eyes shut, then opened them, hoping that the figure was just a hallucination brought on by the situation; a waking bad dream.

When I looked again, it was still there, however, in all its amorphous glory. I did notice, on second glance, that it was standing in one place, and that the glow around it was roughly in the shape of a cone. Looking up to the apex, I saw that it was coming from one of the lights mounted in the ceiling of the lobby. I hadn't known that they could project holograms. The aliens, I realized, had found a way to tap into our systems, using one of our light fixtures to project themselves into our space.

I wished that Myrtle had been there, or maybe one of the engineers. They might have been able to make more sense of this. All I could do was watch and wonder at the technical prowess it must have taken to turn a simple light into a complex projector. Then the figure started walking.

As it left the shaft of light, it disappeared, only to reappear once it entered the cone emanating from the next fixture. It was heading towards the bridge. Then the tigress awoke. She must have been rolling over, trying to find a comfortable position beside her hippo, when the glowing apparition floated over her. She leapt up, growling.

"Intruder alert! Intr—" she froze, glowing, and quickly vanished. The figure continued moving from light to light towards the bridge as though it hadn't even noticed her. The other officers gave it a wide berth while the hippo clutched his girlfriend's tunic, moaning wide-eyed: "Sheila, no, Sheila."

I sprang to my hooves, not even stopping to snag my own tunic from atop the still-sleeping Burl, and raced after the figure. It had already strode past the last light cone in the short hallway, and was now on the bridge. I skidded to a halt just behind it, realizing that I had no plan, no idea of how to stop the intruder. It stopped in the middle of the bridge and turned in a slow circle, arm-blobs outstretched. The speakers built into some of the consoles began to tweet and rumble, as though someone had thrown old Norwegian death metal recordings and Chinese language lessons in an aural blender.

Like everyone else on the bridge, I tried to cover my ears, but without much success. The piercing caterwaul was just too loud. Over the din, however, I could still hear shouting. A few of the officers were begging it to stop, some were yowling in pain, and above it all, the captain was shouting: "Get off my ship! Leave us alone! Forty generations will not end in my failure!"

And with that, he raised his arm. In his hand was a gleaming concoction of tubes and wires: one of the "stun guns" that had been developed and used in the midpoint riots. It looked pretty good for a relic from over five hundred years ago. Just as I was wondering if it even worked, the captain fired.

A bolt of angry blue electricity shot across the bridge, straight through the ghostly figure without seeming to have any effect, and slammed into the pig—one of the C-Shift officers—who'd been manning the navigation station. He jerked and slumped, dropping out of the chair. The holographic figure had vanished. "Oh shit," the captain mumbled, dropping the gun.

It cracked on the floor, sending up a small streamer of smoke. I could still taste the scent of ozone from the shot, and the fur on my bare chest was prickly with static electricity. I tried to shake it off.

Other officers were tending to the downed navigator, but everyone seemed to be ignoring the captain. I walked up to him. "Sir, I think we need to talk." He nodded, still stunned, and followed me into his office.

It was a small room—just big enough for two chairs and a desk—and bare of any decor. In the middle of *Osiris'* bulk, the Captain's Hall held portraits of every captain since the ship was launched. Horses, felines, a rhino, three wolves...these were the faces that had looked down on us over the centuries, as though to say that we could be whatever we set our mind to, no matter what species or gender. Of course, we all knew that to be a bit idealistic: aptitudes were strengthened or hindered by the vast genomics computers that took up the bulk of the Biology decks, and accentuated by the training we received in crèche and the parents to whom we were assigned.

That was another thing that would end when we made planetfall. It was unlikely that we would be able to expend the resources for ectogenesis, so natural mating and births would result in hybridization and randomization of traits and talents. Then again, perhaps that would remain a priority; it was hard to imagine a settlement built of wood and adobe and scrounged ship parts with a gleaming "fertility center" in the middle of it. Who was I to say? I certainly wasn't one of the decision-makers, but I *did* still have a job to do.

"Sir," I said as he dropped into the chair behind his desk, "Did you honestly think that would accomplish anything? I'm surprised that thing even worked."

"Poor Samson. I didn't think…" He looked up at me, his eyes wide with fury. "How could they do this? Just walk on *my* ship, take *my* people, like I didn't matter. I *had* to act—you see that, don't you?"

His tablet buzzed, rescuing me from having to answer. He picked it up, glared at the screen, and then tossed it to me. "It's communications."

I read the screen, saw similar reports from all over the ship. "Our visitors haven't restricted themselves to the bridge," I said quietly, keeping my voice even. We needed our captain, and he needed the calm determination that had been the hallmark of his leadership. Of course, he hadn't had to face a crisis of this nature before—none of us had.

Placing the tablet squarely on his desk, I stood. "Sir, I think we need to decide on a plan of action. If we can just survive this, we'll be able to make it to Asimov and start our new lives. After all, there's just a few months left. If we turn off Emergency Protocol Beta, maybe downgrade it to Gamma, return a bit of normalcy, maybe the aliens will see that we're peaceful." Emergency Protocol Gamma was simply a restriction on non-essential travel between decks, not nearly as draconian as Beta; it also meant we'd be able to return to our quarters, shower, and sleep in real beds.

"Do you think that's wise?" He gestured at the tablet, his nostrils still flared, ears still canted back. "It's chaos down there!"

"Exactly, sir. We need to show everyone that we're still in control. It won't be long before people start dying, especially if they weren't rationing their provisions. Even with all the people who had been taken, it's still not enough for more than a few days. And what if somebody panics? There were maintenance crews working on the launch bays—what if they decide to take the landing pods, try to do some foolhardy suicidal stunt. Even if they did manage to *kamikaze* the alien ships without getting us blasted too, how would we be able to shuttle everyone down to the planet once we get there?"

I snorted, realizing that I was only feeding into the captain's uncertainty. I ran a hand down my muzzle, squeezing my eyes shut and massaging my snout. I could smell Captain Parker, too, just as rank as the rest of us, with the added acrid tang of fear sweat. If he wasn't going to be our rock, then I needed to be. Once this was over, he could resume command. If we survived, that is.

"Sir, I am hereby relieving you from duty. Please confine yourself to your office, sir, until the situation is resolved."

He spluttered, but I managed to stare him down. I had protocol on my side, and he'd already shown himself inadequate to the task. I only hoped I would be more fit. I turned my back on him and returned to the bridge.

The stunned officer had been revived and was now sitting with his back against a bulkhead, with someone from B-shift taking his place at navigation. "Attention, everybody," I began, holding out my hands just as the alien figure had done. Perhaps it had been trying to communicate with us. Then I realized that I was still wearing only my uniform pants. I tried to shrug off the stage fright, clearing my throat to buy me some time.

"I have *temporarily* taken over from Captain Parker. As Safety Officer, it's my duty to take charge during an emergency, and I'm doing just that. First, I will be moving us from Emergency Protocol Beta down to Gamma." Thankfully, the officers were more interested in the prospect of EPG than in who was in command. We're all people, after all. I smiled wryly and nodded, "Yes, I'm looking forward to a shower too. But this incident is far from over. We still need to take stock of all missing personnel, and assess any damage that might have been caused, whether by aliens or panicking passengers."

As I spoke, I stepped towards the captain's chair and the keypad which would allow me to officially assume command and downgrade our emergency status. "We also need to be vigilant, and report all—"

I had just sat down when the lights flicked off. I reached for the keypad, only to realize that the keys weren't lit. Glancing around the bridge, I saw only blackness. Everyone seemed to be standing still, holding their breath. I couldn't even hear the hum of the recirculator. This kind of total silence was something I'd never experienced before.

"Ok, everyone, stay calm. Don't move—we don't need any broken bones." I cupped my hands and raised my voice to echo down the hallway and into the lobby. "Did you all hear that? Just stay where you are, sit down if you're standing, and keep your legs and tails tucked up. We'll get this sorted out. Burl, are you awake?"

"Yes, Orville, I am now. What's going on?"

"It's probably just a blown relay," I had no idea what it was, but that sounded as good as anything else I could think of. "You're in charge of everyone by the elevators. Oh, and check to see if anyone's in the relief room."

"Aye, sir," he replied. I was relieved that he heard the tone of authority I'd tried to inject into my voice, and had taken the cue.

"We are all officers, and the best of the best on *Osiris*. I expect every one of you to act accordingly." The chorus of timid "aye"s wasn't exactly reassuring, but I'd take what I could get. "Now, there should be flashlights in the lockers beneath the communications and tactical stations. Whoever is standing there, are you able to find them?"

There was a rustling, a fumbling, and a clanking as two boxes were drawn out and opened. "Got it, sir," said a female voice. Another voice cursed, as a clatter sounded from the other side of the bridge. Obviously he'd opened his case while it was upside-down. "I think I found the flashlight, sir, but it isn't working." We all listened in silence to the sound of a switch being toggled. The other voice cursed again as his toggling was added to hers. By this point the darkness seemed to be pressing up against my eyes, like a black plastic bag slowly shrinking around my head.

"Is there anything electronic working right now? Everyone, check your wristpads, pocket tablets, anything within reach."

That's when the female voice spoke again. "Sir, I can't feel the engines." Her words were so small and soft that for a second I thought I'd misheard.

"She's right," gasped a voice from the general direction of the floor next to the navigation chair, probably the pig who'd been shot by our captain. "The engine is off. Oh god…if it stays off for too long, we won't be able to slow down enough to enter orbit. If we miss our rendezvous—"

"We'll be trapped on this ship forever!" cried one frantic voice that I sincerely hoped didn't belong to Captain Parker.

"Belay that!" I bellowed, feeling the despair start to rise in my throat. "This ship has lasted for a thousand years, and if need be it can last a thousand more. But it's not *going* to need to. Because we are going to fix this."

If only I knew how.

* * *

A few minutes' search—it felt like hours—showed that nothing electric or electronic was working. It was though we were in a field of anti-electromagnetic energy, something out of one of the horrible ancient sci-fi movies Burl loved to watch. Meanwhile, I crawled on hands and knees, feeling my way over deckplates that probably hadn't been properly cleaned in months. Trying to ignore the bits of dust and hair and dried-hard crumbs of food that had all been invisible from two meters up, I made my way to the little hallway.

"Burl, can you hear me?" At least I didn't have to shout.

"Yessir. Do you want me to come over there?"

"Yeah. Everybody tuck back, let him come through. Burl, I've got my hands out, just come towards my—there you are." I felt soft thick fur and pulled him in close. A part of me wanted to sob into his shoulder and never let go; this was no time for tears. A desperate hug would have to suffice. He held me tight enough to pop my back, welcome after days of sleeping on the floor, and I buried my snout in his neck. It was good to just kneel there so close to him, in absolute darkness, listening to his breathing, his heartbeat.

"Shall I report?" He whispered, almost his usual playful self. I nodded, my cheek brushing against his. "Everyone's fine, but the water doesn't work."

Leaning back with my hands on his shoulders, I tried to look into his eyes, but of course saw nothing. "Why would...the pumps! With no electricity, there's no pumps, and no pumps mean no water." I suddenly felt very thirsty.

"No electricity?"

I nodded, a reflex, then said "Yes. It seems that every electronic thing on board has been disabled. Flashlights, wristpads, even the engines." I could hear him gasp, could imagine the look on his face. I pulled him close to me again. "We'll be ok. I'll figure something out."

"Ok. I know you will. You'd better get back to the bridge. I'll...be ok here. I'll keep things quiet."

"Thanks," I whispered. A hand on his cheek was enough to guide me in for a kiss. He held it for longer than I would have expected, and I felt his fingers digging into my back, webbing brushing against hide. *At least*, I thought wryly as I made my way back to the captain's chair, *I don't have to worry about being out of uniform now.*

The warmth of my otter's touch faded quickly, however: our situation was bleaker than I'd ever thought it could have been. If a space rock had punctured our hull, we might have lost some air, some lives, but the affected area could be sealed off, the breach repaired. If there were a disease on board, we could implement a quarantine (one of the primary uses of Emergency Protocol Beta) until a cure was found. We were shielded from cosmic rays, and genetic engineering ensured that food and personnel alike wouldn't suffer from degradation over the centuries.

But without power, without air and water and light, there was nothing we could do. Now that the engine was off, not only would we not be able to decelerate in time to meet Asimov, we would soon be losing the illusion of gravity too. I already felt a little lighter, although that could have just been my mind playing tricks on me. I could only imagine the terror of people in the lower decks, people without the benefit of crew-caste training and discipline.

I climbed into the captain's chair, the plastic padding a cold comfort on my bare back. I had to take *some* action, give *some* order, if only to keep my officers' minds occupied. I was just about to ask for volunteers to climb the emergency shafts down to the tail end of *Osiris*, to see if there was anything to be done to get the engines working again, when there was a crackling sound.

There was also a light.

A slender vertical beam of light was fading into existence, growing and expanding. I glanced around the bridge and saw the ghostlike eyeshine of every officer as they stared at this new phantasm. Once again, the light bifurcated, took on bipedal form, but this time the blobby limbs continued to resolve themselves. Even as the figure became more definite, the light began to fade, until we were left once more in darkness.

A muttered curse came from where the figure's afterimage still hovered in my vision, and then a click and we were bathed in light once more. At first, it was too bright, all I saw was a glowing sphere, with what looked like a thumb and fingers eclipsing parts of it. Then the hand tossed the ball up and it stuck to the ceiling—a little miniature sun.

While we were blinking in the light, there was a scream. The eyes of the cheetah who'd been stationed at tactical must have adjusted quicker than the rest of us. "The alien!" She screamed again. I turned from her out-stretched arm to look back to the middle of the bridge.

Before me stood a creature that did, at first glance, appear to be alien. Ignoring the hackles rising on my shoulders, I stood and stared at our visitor. It lacked the horn-things of the first apparition, and instead had a pair of wide-spread ears—like a mouse's—bracketing its head. It's face looked somewhat like the cheetah's, but the coloring was all wrong: it had zebra stripes of green and gold running down its short muzzle and long sinuous neck. It was wearing a filmy costume with an out-flung collar and puffy sleeves, and seemed to have the lean, strong body of a cervine. A thick tail swished behind it, with a powderpuff of gold fur at the tip.

I stared, sucking in a breath, and along with it a whiff of the creature's scent. It was musky, resinous—like the dwarf pines that grew in the arboretum—but with a hint of cinnamon too. It shifted, turning to look at me, and suddenly there was an odor of blueberries. "Youu ore kyptin?" it warbled, its open mouth revealing a too-long purple tongue that seemed to be tasting the unfamiliar words.

Here I was, at the first contact with an alien species in the whole history of history, and it spoke English. Not perfect English, of course, but damn better than that yowling racket they'd tried earlier.

It took a graceful step towards me, and I noticed that its feet had wide-spread toes, like a tapir. Clearing its throat with a bullish grunt, it repeated with more confidence, "You are captain? In charge?" It cocked its head on that long neck, looking me up and down.

At least it's not telepathic, I thought, realizing that it assumed me to be in command because the captain's chair was in the middle of the bridge, on a little dais by itself. I stepped forward, one hand outstretched. "I am Orville Eighteen, Safety Officer and acting Captain." It heard the last word and bobbed an emphatic nod.

"Good, good. Safety. No harm." Both its hands stretched out to either side, just as the previous figure had done.

I matched its pose, palms up. "We will not harm you, see? Everyone, put your hands up like this," I said over my shoulder, desperate that there be no misunderstanding. "See? We want to be friends."

"Orville," Whispered a voice behind me; I didn't dare look away from the alien, but I thought I smelled Captain Parker. "Don't trust it! It's already taken our people, disabled our ship! We should take it hostage, bargain—"

"Shut up, Captain." I hissed. "I told you to stay in your office. I will not have you endangering this ship any further. Your shot is probably why they turned off all elect—"

"Yes, do not shot, no harm." The alien said. With those radar dish ears, it must have heard every word.

I bowed my head briefly. "We are sorry if we hurt your...friend. We didn't mean any harm."

"No harm, no harm!"

"Good, perhaps you would turn our power back on? We need power for light and air."

The alien trilled something at me, a more-beautiful version of what had come over our speakers, which was likely just another symptom of the incompatibility between our systems.

"I'm sorry, I don't understand. We don't mean any harm, we are just trying to reach Asimov, the planet we're headed towards." I swung an arm, palm still upraised, at the black viewscreen. "If you will restore our power and let us go, we promise we won't bother—"

"Thank you, that is sufficient."

I stared at the creature once more. Not only did it speak English, but now it could use full sentences.

"You're lucky that I was on board. I'd studied ancient languages a little, and it was decided that I should get you to talk enough for our translator to piece together an algorithm. It's funny that you don't communicate with anything other than words." Sure enough, its smell now had an iron tang like boiled spinach, and the tail was curled into an inquisitive spiral behind. "My name is Ignatz Geor, by the way."

"So you understand—wait, you said ancient?"

Ignatz nodded and made a little two-step backwards. "Earth languages haven't been spoken outside of the classroom for centuries." Again the head tilted, but this time one ear folded up too. "I'd been a bit of a dabbler in antiquities myself, but I never thought to see such a relic myself. And all of you, it's really astounding. Pure species in the flesh, wow."

"You're…from Earth?" Asked one of the officers.

"Well, of course! It's kind of funny, to be honest. We queried the main planetary database before they sent me over, and it looks like only a century or so after your ship was launched, the first faster-than-light drive was developed. I'm afraid your whole ship is rather obsolete."

"So society didn't die out? We'd been told that we were the last hope, the last chance to save…" My heart was racing, my mind a blur between hope and despair. All these generations, all these people who had lived and died in this little microcosm. "Wait, main *planetary* database?" I was struck with a sudden sinking dread. "The only planet near here is Asimov."

"I don't know of any Asimov, just good old green Kalark. Judging by your trajectory, though, I expect we're talking about the same thing. It looks like we beat you to it. The first colony here was founded almost four hundred years ago."

"Four…hundred." I dropped back into the captain's chair, staggered by the revelation. The whole mission was for naught, a worthless waste of generations. With a herculean effort, I managed to wrangle my thoughts from the spiraling black hole of despair. I sighed. *One step at a time.* "Maybe there's still a space for us there…but if you don't switch our power back on, we'll all be dead before we even get close."

The hybridized definitely-not-alien did a funny little jig, as though sketching out the question with his feet. "Of course, only…you promise that there won't be any harm?"

"Yes," I tried to inject as much confidence into my voice as I could. "As soon as power's restored, I'll be able to address the ship and advise everyone of the situation."

"Good." And with that, he warbled again. In an instant, we were all pressed into our seats: the apparent lightness that had grown since the engines were switched off now replaced by the normal "gravity" of what I hoped would still be our new home. Asimov or Kalark, it was still a green world, still what we'd been dreaming of for centuries. A cool woosh of air and the rising glow of the ceiling lights signaled a further return to normalcy.

I wondered if anything would be truly normal again.

"What about our people? The ones you took. Are they still—"

"Oh, they're fine. We're holding them in stasis. We thought *you* were the aliens, at first, and then once we realized what you were, we had to be sure you didn't carry any ancient diseases." It snapped its fingers and the main viewscreen flickered to life, showing what must have been the inside of one of the three ships. I could barely understand the structure, all gleaming white curves, like the inside of a seashell, but I could see several figures in grey uniforms, hovering in a few centimeters above what seemed to be the floor, including the tigress in mid-leap, snarl frozen on her face.

"We'd like them back, please."

The creature nodded and I began to take up my end of the bargain. I would address the ship, then turn off the Emergency Protocol. Then there would be discussions with the ship's historians and psychologists, as well as the elected leaders of each caste and class. At some point I'd be handing control back to Captain Parker so I could resume preparations for landing.

But first, a shower, I thought wishfully, then shook my head. Duty first. I thumbed the armrest of the captain's chair and downgraded the ship to Emergency Protocol Gamma. I could feel the muffled thunk of bulkheads sliding back into place, the hum of lifts moving again. A ragged cheer went up from the other officers as the screens changed status, now displaying my face with a brief list of the current restrictions.

"B-shift, go home. Take a shower, brush your teeth," I got a few laughs at that. "But be ready to report for duty in—" I checked the time. "In three hours. C-shift, I want each one of you to take a deck, check for injuries, malnutrition, anything. Deal with as much as you can and report back to me. Once you've checked the whole ship, you can shower too. A-shift, we're on duty right now."

I waited for the groans and complaints to subside somewhat. "We've been through a lot, but we've got a lot more before this gets back to normal." *If it ever does.* "I am proud of how you all have handled this emergency, and so is Captain Parker. Now, hop to it. Let's show our…guest just how hard we can work."

Those were three very long hours.

* * *

We finally reached our room. In all the ship, there had only been two deaths: a poor old lion who'd been trapped in a lift was felled by a heart attack, and one of the patients in the psych ward had managed to commit suicide in the momentary blackness. Other injuries could be dealt with, but the emotional healing would take longer. I wondered if some of the people on board would ever forgive our erstwhile captors.

As for myself, I was nearly beyond caring. Supporting one another, Burl and I staggered through the door and tossed our uniforms directly into the recycling chute. We'd only been in there for a few minutes, but already the tiny room had started to stink. He flipped the recirculator to maximum while I warmed up our little shower cubicle—one of the other perks of being on the command staff.

We never showered together: neither of us was petite, and there was barely room in the cubicle for one. But that day we somehow managed to fit. Maybe it was the leanness of two days' starvation rations, maybe it was desperation for the reassurance of his touch.

"Damn." Burl moaned, water matting the fur between our pressed-together chests. I held him tight, not caring if the water on my cheeks came from the nozzle or my own eyes.

"Thank you."

"For what?" He started digging his claws through my hide, letting the ionized water seep in and wash away oils and sweat and dander.

I returned the favor. "For being such a good First Officer."

"You're welcome, *Captain*," he said as his hands slipped lower on my back, inching close to my lank tail.

"*Acting* Captain," I corrected, nuzzling against his neck. My chuckle turned into a sigh. "I just can't believe it."

"What, that Parker would crack like that?" He started running my tail through his hands, pulling it gently.

"Be fair, I doubt I'd have done much better: it's not easy being Captain. But I meant Ignatz. Kalark. This whole thing." I leaned against him, the stench of the last few days finally washing away. "I'm just afraid we're gonna end up in some museum, relics of an ancient age. Pureblood, simpleminded, prehistoric freaks. They're so advanced, too…I felt like a little calf standing next to him. Did you see how quickly he understood our systems? I don't know if I could even *start* learning how their ships work."

"Yeah, but the builders didn't exactly design the *Osiris* to be hard to understand…hey, do you think they still have sex?"

"The builders?"

"No, silly!" He blew a raspberry that vibrated his whiskers and tickled my cheek. "I meant the aliens."

By this point, his fingers had stopped toying with my tail, and had worked their way underneath. "Well, if they don't, I bet you could teach *them* a thing or two." I heard familiar click of a cap being opened, and felt the slick claws that stroked, prodded, and entered my hole. My otter had foreseen this moment, sneaking the little bottle of lube into the shower with him while I'd merely been focused on getting wet.

"Yessir, Captain," he muttered as two fingers popped in. After so much denial, so much suddenly-alleviated stress, we were both quick to rise. A few moments of sword fighting—his shaft shorter but thicker than my own—and the feeling of my heavy balls bouncing against his soft thigh, and I couldn't take any more.

I managed to turn around in the tiny cubicle, and realized something I'd never noticed before: our heights were just right, I didn't even have to bend over or squat down for him to slip up inside me. Silently I thanked the builders and their genetics program. We were nearly the same stature, but his hips were situated lower, given his longer torso and shorter legs. All he had to do was lift my tail out of the way.

With both hands on the wall, I supported our little two-man lean-to as he thrust into me, one webbed hand slick on my dick, the other gripping my chest. Hot water poured down our backs, steam filled our lungs, until I felt clean inside and out.

"I...hope they're taking...notes, Captain," Burl growled into my neck as his thrusts started speeding up. I had a sudden vision of Ignatz reclining in some cloudlike room, pawing at himself while he watched a Technicolor X-ray of the two of us going at it. I smiled and closed my eyes, letting my head droop until it was against the wall. I lowered one hand, reaching back to cup Burl's rump, feeling the muscles tense and relax as he pistoned, his own hands bringing me close.

Snorting, I finally came onto the shower wall, my own scent strong in my nostrils even as it was washed down the drain to be recycled, broken into various proteins and chemicals, and stored until needed. My climax milked Burl, just the way he liked it. A guttural, "Oh fuck, oh fuck," and a chirping chitter, a digging of blunted claws into my hide, a head pressed against my neck, and a throb beneath my tail, and I knew he'd finished as well.

How long we'd taken, how long we continued to stand there, I couldn't have cared less. All I knew was that sometime later we were almost dry and lying in bed, between sheets that felt like air, on pillows that felt like tufts of cotton. As I faded away, I said a silent prayer of thanks for the fact that we had two shifts before we had to get up again. There would be time enough for aliens and planets and politics and spaceships in the morning.

"I love you," I heard him mutter, before I fell asleep too.

The Center of My Universe

by T. D. Coltraine

The scent was strong and exotic, rich, intoxicating. It stirred Frank's memory, reminding him of early morning breakfast and days spent on foreign shores watching alien stars sparkle around moons so close you could almost touch them. It was made of cinnamon and body heat, and it had greeted him most every morning for years. How many, the bear refused to put a number to. He didn't want to know how long it'd been. He'd say you can't quantify love, because that diminishes it. He was content to know that it had happened at all and hadn't ended yet.

"Morning, sunshine," a voice murmured from a short distance away, tempered with the sound of electrical lights and the craft's engines as it cut a through space. The fennec smirked at Frank from the doorway into their washroom, arms crossed and hip cocked against the frame. He was as naked as the day he'd entered the world, freshly showered and groomed, just like every morning before. "You slept so hard I was afraid you were hibernating on me."

Frank pushed up against his pillows and rose slowly, taking time to admire his partner in business and husband out of it as he worked the sleep out of his muscles. "I wouldn't dream of it, Zeke. You'd miss me too much." Meaty arms lived over a brown torso almost as thick as the hull, flexing as the bear yawned hard. "Did you already make breakfast? It smells like French toast in here."

The fox swished gently and strode into the half-lit bedroom, sitting down on the side of the bed alongside Frank. "The cooker's warming up. Last of the nice stuff, though. We're gonna be stuck eating protein patties and biscuits until we're back in port." Ezekiel was a slight thing by comparison, perhaps a meter and three-quarters tall—not counting his ears, of course—and sixty kilos if an ounce, though for his race he was something of a giant among the tiny citizens of his homeworld. Frank had quickly learned that he was not some sort of delicate creature that would shatter at the slightest touch. It was the exact opposite in fact: the fennec was a tightly muscled machine wound like a steel cable, more than capable of holding his own. It made sense. Scavengers that couldn't didn't last very long.

Frank slipped an arm around Zeke's waist, nudging the smaller male close to him, pushing his nose into copper-colored hair. "Tell me we at least have some coffee left."

The fox laughed and tilted his head back to kiss Frank on the lips lightly. "We won't if you don't ration it." A slim tan finger poked a deep brown belly. It wasn't fat or flabby; it was just *big*, like the majority of Frank was. Like fennecs didn't come in large, bears didn't come in small. Oddly enough, he was the more modest of the pair, the quiet partner who enjoyed being in his office doing paperwork or wrist-deep in the chunks of a derelict drifter while Zeke was out painting the town all kind of colors.

"You know I just can't get started without a big cup of the brown stuff," Frank said with a pout. Broad palms roamed Zeke's back, stroking calluses over a silky smooth pelt, feeling the musculature shift under it like an exotic dance.

"It'd be different if a 'cup' didn't take the whole pot, hon." Zeke moved to straddle his husband's lap, sitting on his knees chest-to-chest with the bruin. They shared a quiet laugh that melted into another kiss, longer than the first, as if neither wanted to let the other be apart for a second. "Love you, papa bear."

Frank flushed, lips curling in a dopey smile as he held the fox close to him and brushed out a thick tail brush with his fingertips. "Love you too, bushy-butt." The smile was genuine, warm and true, his forehead against Zeke's as they sat and stared into each other's eyes.

"You smell amazing," Frank said, pushing his nose into Zeke's chest ruff. "How do you keep yourself looking that good when we dig through people's garbage for a living?"

Zeke giggled and shifted, arching his spine and swishing his tail out behind him. "It's a family secret," he murmured in a sing-song voice. "I miss my hair though," he added with a small pout on his slim muzzle. It was true—in his younger years, Zeke had been blessed with flowing platinum locks in his youth, hair like silk that reached to the base of his tail. The reality of being a scavenger had forced him to trim it away until little was left but stubble between his ears.

"It didn't fit in your helmet," Frank said, stroking the fox's ears soothingly.

Zeke allowed himself a little smile. "And the shampoo bill was just insane." He tilted his head and rubbed a cheek against Frank's, licking gently at the brown fur. "You need a shower, Papa Bear." Those fingers grazed up and down a broad torso, over hefty abdominals, and gave Frank's half-firm member a squeeze. "Someone's happy to see me…"

"Always am." He squeezed Zeke's backside, his hand easily covering a cheek. "Bet you got off in the shower." There wasn't a pause for an answer. "Dang foxes."

Zeke bit his lip and hiked up, tail rising all on its own as he held back a soft whine. "I can't help it." An arm came to rest on Frank's shoulder, golden fox eyes meeting dull brown bear eyes. "Seeing you lying there like that…" He put his lips to Frank's again, eyes lidding. "I'm addicted to you, Frankfort Berlin."

The bear crinkled up his snout and stuck his tongue out at Zeke. "No fair. I can't make fun of your last name, you ain't got one." Frank clenched his fingers and squeezed at the fennec's back, forcing a rolling moan out of the smaller male. Zeke radiated body heat like a tiny furnace, and a particular firmness pressed against the curve of Frank's belly.

Zeke straddled Frank's thighs and pressed himself closer until he could rest his arousal against the bear's. Both were impressive but not excessive pillars of manhood, one pale pink and slender, the other a dark angry red thickness that dripped down its length. Zeke rolled his back, feminine hips pressing and grinding their cocks together into Frank's plush pelt. Slim tan fingers worked though the deep brown fur of an ursine chest, mouths too busy with the other's to do more than breathe.

Sharp teeth teased along the cup of Frank's ear, nipping harmlessly at the peak. "Don't try and hold out on me." The bear tensed and shut his eyes tightly, mouth hanging slack as the fox frotted him, spread over Frank's front like a shroud. "I know what you want, 'because I want it too."

Frank tried to force his eyes to focus. Zeke made him dizzy at the best of times; when hormones came into play, he got easily lost in his thoughts. With effort he managed a small nod, letting Zeke go and slipping away from the fennec. "Read me like a book," he murmured, rolling over onto his belly, sprawled out on the bed like a sort of living bear-skin blanket.

"That's what I like to see," Zeke said, pressing his palm into one of Frank's hips, squeezing. "Who would have expected a big strong bear to have such a cute ass?" Slim fingers trailed over a stubby brown tail and under it, caressing Frank's full scrotum and along the length of his slick cock. "Or that he'd like being' on the bottom."

"Shut up," Frank huffed. He didn't turn back to look at Zeke though, especially given the fox was right as usual. It was a give and take relationship, and more often than not Frank was the taker. "And stop teasing."

Zeke laughed as he rolled a condom down Frank's cock, the bright green material making his manhood look distinctly alien. "Oh hush. You like it and you know it. Pass me the lube." Frank opened a drawer and tossed a clear bottle back to his lover. "Good boy." A healthy of the slick stuff filled his palm and coated over his fingers. One of those digits drew lightly over Frank's anus before slipping inside to spread the lubricant in. Now it was Zeke's turn to flush and bite his lip as he watched his bear arch his spine and sigh, long and liquid. Even after more times than he could count, watching Frank writhe made his pulse race.

"Now you're good and greased up, papa bear." Frank's pucker drew closed as Zeke's finger slipped out, replaced by a fox cock was pressed against the ring. Zeke thrust once, the swollen head spreading its target open easily, coaxing Frank to relax and let more in, inch after inch surrounded by warmth and tightness.

There were no witty double entendre or laughable one-liners that would have been at home in a pornographic film. The fennec nudged his muzzle into Frank's cheek, urging the bear to kiss him as they coupled. Each was intimately familiar with the other in both senses of the term; there was neither urgency nor timidity. They had time and they had each other.

Zeke pressed Frank's knees apart, pressing his own legs to the bed sheets as he worked his hips. Each stroke was a sinuous motion from his neck to his tail, the tip flicking behind him as he drew his maleness up and out. Zeke seemed as though he was built for this very purpose, a machine built of taut musculature that bent in whatever way would give his partner the utmost in pleasure. And it was working as intended, leaving Frank in a dream-state against his pillow, jaw slack and eyes unfocused. Each bar of the duet they performed grew a bit faster and stronger; Zeke pressed his palms against Frank's broad back and *pushed*, toes curled into the bed, working with every inch of his powerful physique to pound at the ursine's backside.

The heat grew; the strong scent of two very male bodies in motion filled the room. The pitch rose to a crescendo. Zeke's barking gasps of breath echoed off the walls. And then the feverish climax that drove the fox deep until his balls slapped against another larger pair and his surging cock flooded its sheath with come.

Both males shared panting breaths for a moment. Zeke put his teeth against the scruff of Frank's neck and nibbled the skin there affectionately.

"Godsdamn, Frank." The fennec slid himself free one last time, watching in rapt appreciation as the bear's pucker flexed and drew tight again before casting his eyes on the still steel-hard erection below it resting in a puddle of its own pre-come. "Oh baby," he said with a pitch of sadness as the condom was peeled free and cast away. "Come on, roll over."

"H-huh?" Frank asked through a cloud of euphoria. "What's wrong?"

Zeke whined in annoyance until the bear gave in and flipped himself over, where he was pulled until his feet were resting on the floor. Both hands grabbed at the red column of muscle and squeezed it, pumping from base to crown. "I can't leave you like *that*, papa bear. What would people think of me?"

"Zeke, you don't—oh, oh damn…" A generous application of fox tongue to bear cock shut Frank up immediately. Clawed fingers grabbed at the sheets while his phallus was bathed and left hot, dripping, slick with fluids. Tree-trunk thighs tensed as they resisted the primal urge to use the fennec's face as a sex toy.

"Come on, bear. Give me that honey." Zeke's mouth hung open, his tongue lolling over the point of his chin. Frank was in no position to refuse. Experience and practice had burned a roadmap of sensitive spots and hair triggers into Zeke's mind, so all it took was a gasp of hot breath and a flick of a supple wrist to force the bear's his orgasm, rewarding the fennec's dedication with a mouthful of spunk. A slim muzzle sealed tight to keep the prize before tipping his head back and swallowing theatrically.

Frank laughed through his panting, stroking his palm over Zeke's cheek affectionately. "Show off."

"Give me that honey? What kind of corny crap is that?" Both males looked over to the wall-mounted intercom then back to each other. Zeke raised an eyebrow. Frank shrugged and leaned over, pushing the only button on panel. "Oh hey, boss. What's up?"

"We don't mind an audience, Rachel, but your mic's on."

"It's what—shit!" The blush from the ship's pilot and only female crew member practically came through before her voice did. She stammered something over the shuffle of papers and personage while Zeke and Frank practically died laughing. "Well um use some mouthwash this time!" The small pop of static signaled that the show was over for real now.

* * *

The collie didn't bother looking up as Zeke and Frank popped into the cockpit behind her ten minutes or so later. She was way too busy with the helm's widgets and gizmos that she couldn't spare the attention. Even when she was 'on duty', Rachel looked like some kind of party girl, pelt dyed in a dozen colors that didn't exist in nature and her hair styled like she'd gotten in a fight with a chainsaw. "Boss, you told me you were going to have the stabilizers looked at. The ass-end of this ship is wobbling more than a stripper on a Saturday night bender." With a sigh Rachel pushed her over-styled bangs up out of her eyes and crossed her arms, tinkling a little as all her piercings came in contact with each other. "I've got it stable for now *aaaand* you're naked in my cockpit again."

Frank gave her a sidelong glance and a quirked eyebrow, arms crossed over his double-barrel chest. "*Your* cockpit?" He laughed hard. "Listen, kid, you've been my pilot for how long now?"

Rachel spun her chair ninety degrees and hit a switch, reclining back and kicking up her boots. "Five years now, big guy." Her lazy streak drove Frank nuts—yeah, she rarely ever left the cockpit, but she was asleep more than any cat he'd ever met. And people accused *him* of being the lazy one. "Not saying I'm not grateful you schlepped me off that backwater because holy cow am I. But if you're going to have me as your chauffeur we've got to have a boat that floats. Just…" She made some vague gestures with her hands. "Pants?"

Zeke laughed and sprawled his equally unclad self in the co-pilot's seat, making a show of resting his tail in his lap. "Sweetheart, you've spent a fifth of your life on a ship the size of a small apartment with two *very* confident and *very* gay men. How can you still squirm when one of us walks in starkers?"

"'Gaze upon the eye of Cyclops every morning because your boss is allergic to pants' wasn't in the job description, Zeke." The canine flipped a switch on the console with her toe, popping up an information display for the pair. "Besides, I hate window shopping when I can't buy. But enough about your dicks. We might have hit the motherlode t'day." Markers flew around the screen, pointing here, there, and everywhere at the planet's surface before settling on a grey mass the size of a small city. "Gentlemen, behold."

Frank leaned in over Rachel's shoulder and poked the map around with a fingertip. "That's a Solaris class cruiser. What in the hell is it doing sitting on an uninhabited world this far out from the homeworld?"

"Couldn't start to tell you, boss. What I *do* know—" The collie zoomed in, showing the ship in coarse detail. "—is the drive core's active. Hull's intact, electrics are all up, and there're no signs of combat or an accident. Only thing missing are the escape pods." She turned towards Frank and lifted her head. She was worried about something. "Someone ditched it here."

278

"Looks like a honeypot," Zeke said.

"Kinda. But what moron baits a trap with a ship worth a hundred quadrillion credits? And the cherry, Frank, it's undocumented."

Frank's eyes were bear-sized saucers. "That's an X-class ship? Union Navy should have this sector locked down tighter than a vault by now."

"So either they don't want it," Zeke said as he cut through communications logs. "Or they don't know it's here. Could take months before anyone notices an emergency beacon. Who goes this far out into the ass-end of space?" A pause. "Except people like us, anyways."

Frank mulled things over. "Rachel, where are the escape pods now?"

The pilot started punching buttons, then more, faster and faster. "I can't find them. There should be hundreds but there's no sign of them."

Zeke shrugged and kicked up from his console, grabbing a weather-beaten hat from a hanger and tucking it over his ears. "We're not gonna figure it out from up here. Come on, papa bear, let's hit the surface."

Frank didn't sound so convinced. "You sure that's a good idea? We'll be up to our necks in it if the Union shows up while we're cutting their ship up."

"It'll be fine." Zeke put on his best smile. It was infectious, creating a pandemic of confidence. "Two or three trips down in the junker and we'll be gone. Nothing left but footprints." He stood up on his toes to kiss his bear on the lips in reassurance. "You've got a nose for scrap. I've got the ear for danger. Add Rachel up here in the cockpit and we haven't got a thing to worry about."

Rachel snagged a protein bar from a stash she kept under the console. "I can't see anyone for a quarter parsec. No one surfing these stars except us, Boss." Chomp, chomp. "It's got a tolerable atmosphere. Go down there, scout, and if anyone shows up we'll be halfway to the fences before the fuzz can say ixnay on the hombre."

Frank just stared at the canine with an eyebrow hiked. "I've got to stop letting you watch all those old vids."

"It's not my fault if two hundred year old movies and hardcore porno are the only entertainment I've got on this tub, *Dad*."

The bear rankled. *Dad*. That had gotten old a long time ago. "This is a job, Rachel, not a cruise." He exhaled. "Get the runabout warmed up, Zeke, we're heading down."

The runabout landed with a shuddering clank on the surface. Bringing the old lady down was never much fun, but until their ship came in full of money they just had to put up with spilling coffee and rattling teeth. Zeke liked to call her the junker, and she at least did her job—she'd get you to the scrap, hold the scrap, and get the scrap back to the ship proper. You just couldn't expect much more. The girl would never out run the authorities or pirates, but if it came to that speed was the least of their worries.

Zeke was first out, adjusting his bomber jacket around his shoulders and instinctively running his fingers through the hair he didn't have. "This is a pretty nice place, Frank. We could always come back here and open up a resort for a change of pace." The fox tipped his nose up and took in a deep breath, muzzle spreading in a smile. "Air's so *clean*. It kind of reminds me of home." He turned to watch Frank squeeze a little to get through the hatchway. "And that reminds me you need to cut back on the beer and pretzels."

"Losing weight won't make me *shorter*, fuzzball." Frank turned to scan the horizon, one hand over his eyes as a makeshift visor. "You ain't wrong. This place is pretty." Where Zeke looked like a civilian in his leather jacket, loud shirt, and blue jeans, Frank came off more like a wrench jockey with his worn cotton jumpsuit and work boots. No matter how much his husband had *insisted* on retiring the old that thing and getting with the times, Frank refused. "So you think this is our retirement fund here?"

Zeke popped open his PADD and flicked his way through a few menus as the pair approached the cruiser. It drew a shadow that carried on for miles into the distance under a trio of suns. "It might just be. The onboard data says it's USC X45, the Hephaestus, or at least it will be once it's out of testing." A fingerclaw tapped against his tablet's screen. "Entry hatch is twenty-five meters along this side."

Frank climbed over rocks and bits of metal debris left from the cruiser's obviously troubled landing; the furrow left behind stretched into the distance like a ragged scar. The damage along the vessel's length was obvious even from a distance, great splits in the metal cut the otherwise smooth and polished surface of the hull into chunks, and lights sputtered and flashed from between broken panels and shattered windows. "This thing came down fast and hard. Surprised it didn't break up worse than this."

"Union engineering at its finest. Planetfall cuts through half a continent, all the vitals are still doing their thing. Here we are." Zeke pushed his palm to a panel. After a moment of unhappy metal shifting against itself, an access door fell open with a loud hiss of released gas, creating something of a ramp into the cruiser. "After you, papa bear."

The two explored the cruiser with great care, walking through tilted corridors full of flickering lights and scrambled displays. Even with their experience, this was a dangerous environment to be in with potential hazards at every turn. The split at the midsection meant only the forward compartments were available, but that was more than enough—12 decks, including the command bridge, jam packed with technology so high-end Frank wasn't entirely sure they could they could resell it. Or, for that matter, if there were a fence in the known galaxy who would have an inkling of what to do with it.

Hours flew past. The pair sat down against the outer wall of their runabout for a moment's rest after hauling another crate of electronics out. Zeke had tossed his jacket into the cockpit some time ago, and Frank had been working with his jumpsuit unzipped and the top pushed down to his waist. The fox had taken ample opportunity to swoon and ogle, playing up his affections much to Frank's amusement. At first, anyway; the girlish giggling and 'accidental' brushes got old pretty quick.

"It's hotter than homeworld out here," Zeke groused, working through another bottle of water and fanning out his sweat-dotted shirt. "Why didn't we bring fans?"

Frank rolled his arm, trying to work out a kink in the shoulder. "And plug 'em in where?" The bear flicked his eyes upwards. "This is a staggered trinary system." A chug of water, a long sigh and a shake of his big head. "It's just about to hit the hottest part of the day. Now's probably a good time to head back up to the ship and unload." Frank slapped Zeke on the shoulder with a big stupid grin on his face. "And you can sit in front of the fans, you big kit you."

Zeke chuffed angrily and flatted his ears. "And you can take a long shower, because honey there's no way I'm sharing a bed with you smelling like the inside of a latrine. Phew!" Frank reached out and grabbed Zeke in a big bear hug, laughing as the fox squirmed to get free.

"Alright, alright, you win, Zeke." Frank slid into the cockpit of their runabout and tapped a button, firing up the control panel before tossing on his headset and grabbing the mic. "Rachel, this is Frank, come in."

"Rachel here. You guys ready to offload? I'm about done with my last smutty novel and I could use some eye candy that isn't interested in me to fill the void. That and I'm hungry."

"Kid, you're always hungry. 10-4 on the offload, we're fully loaded with copper and titanium plates. I don't think we can strip this thing for more than basic components but that should get us enough—"

"Shit, boss, there's something coming up on the sensors, and fuck me it's *huge*." Rachel paused for what was only a couple of seconds but felt like eons. For once in her life the collie was moving with urgency, and that made both the scavengers prick in concern. "Aw Hell, Frank, it's a Union cruiser—how did it—the sensors—"

A sharp burst of static cut Rachel off, replacing her someone thick, heavy, loud, and authoritative. It was the voice of someone who held no concern for much of anyone else, one that shouted and expected the whole damn universe to jump. "This is Union forward command vessel Expedition to unauthorized vessel. Please respond and prepare to have charges listed."

Frank squeezed the mic until the plastic creaked. "Frank Berlin here, owner of the Starduster. Don't know what 'charges' you're talking about— I'm registered with the Scavenger's Guild. Just doing my job here. Gimme a minute, my pilot can send you our licenses."

There was a long pause. Frank could feel the smug smirk crossing the Union drone's face. It made his blood run cold. Zeke climbed in from outside the cockpit with concern crossing his eyes. "Well I'll be damned. Bet you thought you'd never thought you'd hear from me again."

"Who is that?" Zeke whispered. Frank shrugged slightly, confused himself.

"You didn't tell your new friend about yer old scavin' partner Kyle?" There was a loud snort, the porcine kind, sloppy and wet. "I'm hurt, Cubby. Real hurt. Ya wound me."

Frank's eyes went open big and he snarled, setting Zeke back. Frank didn't *get* angry. This was way out of line. "Leave him out of this, Kyle. What in the Hell are you doing on a Union ship? If anyone here's a criminal it's *you!*"

Another snort and a deep laugh made the handset crackle. "Now now, cubby, it's *Captain* Kyle. See, I got more friends than you know about. Just because you pulled a mutiny and ditched me without any way home—"

"You tried to kill me, Kyle! Me and the entire team!"

"Ya got between me and business. Y'never did understand that. You always were one of them soft-hearted kinda people." Kyle took a deep breath and sighed theatrically. "But ya gave me an opportunity. The Union offered me a chance t'clean the slate." Kyle snorted again. Zeke clung to Frank as the big man shook just as tightly. "I sell a few people out, I get a ship. A few more people and suddenly I'm in command. Ain't life grand?" There was a long pause. Kyle's next words were a muted threat. "How long you been out on the rim, li'l bear?"

"A year." Frank's heart stopped clean dead in his chest.

"Yeah, that sounds about right." Kyle chuckled disdainfully. "There ain't no more Guild anymore, buck-o. Union took the ones what would play by the rules. The ones that didn't, well." A laugh, a vicious one. "They ain't havin' a good time." Zeke tugged at Frank's arm, trying to get him to say *anything*. "'cept for you. But them days just ended. Them licenses you've got ain't worth nothin' but time in the lockup, cubby-boy." There was a rapid tapping sound. "Everything you've done since you left homeworld Terra is a capital-k crime, Franky. I could put you away for a *real* long time, boy." Kyle grunted. "Management says I'm supposed to offer you the usual agreement: you surrender and sign on to the fleet, we forget you ever did anything wrong. Course, your bitches go to jail, but them's the breaks of makin' deals with the devil."

"I'd nev—"

"I know you won't. Ain't in yer nature. Now, I'm supposed t'bring you three in. But…"

From the surface, there was only a brief flash in the sky as the Starduster was erased from existence. There was no sound, no massive explosion or rain of debris, just a tiny sparkle in the blue of the day sky. The emotional force was tremendous, a million megatons to the heart. Frank dropped the handset to the floor as Zeke scrambled out of the runabout.

"I know ya hear me, Frankie I can hear you breathin'." Kyle barked commands to his crew. "Whoo, that was *satisfying!* Things like that make a man happy t'be alive." Knuckles cracked and Frank could hear a chair creaking as someone leaned back in it. "Karma's a bitch, ain't it?"

"Godsdamn it, Kyle, you can't do this!"

"Can an' did, buck-o." The voice got weaker, noise crawling into the feed. "I'm headin' on home. Have a nice rest'a yer life, cubby!" And he was gone. There was nothing but dead air left on the headset. The comms panel curtly reported back that there were no contacts in range before it went blank.

Zeke could only watch as his husband emerged from the roundabout and fell to his knees, staring at the skies. Nothing came out. The magnitude of such an event—he had lost his ship, his career, the woman he had come to see as a daughter, all in a burst like a soap bubble miles above his head. And no one would know that he and Zeke were very much alive on an unnamed planet in an uninteresting system thousands of lightyears from common space. There were no words to say. No one would hear him.

The odds of escaping were infinitesimal. Survival was hardly a better bid.

The fennec sat down next to the man he'd loved for years. His bear was broken, and he did not know how to fix him. All he could do was be patient.

* * *

The next thing Frank knew, he was staring into the ceiling of the junker, blinking his eyes as they slipped back into focus. The scent of sheets was too fresh and clean. Zeke's scent was nowhere to be found. The bear lifted his head. Where had this bed come from? Where was Ezekiel? What was going on?

"Oh godess, I thought you'd never wake up." As if cued, the fennec stuck his head through hatch with a smile relieved smile. The fox sat on the end of the bed; just being close soothed Frank. "You just kind of... dropped off on me. Eyes rolled back in your head and everything." Zeke stretched up and kissed Frank on the lips with a soft rumble. "Lunch is in the cooker. It's not going to win any awards, but a man can only go so far with travel rations."

Frank sat up in the bed. "Where'd this come from? Where's all the scrap?"

Zeke crossed his legs and sat next to Frank, forcing the bear to the side a bit. "You needed to rest, so I pulled something out of the cruiser and tossed you on it. The scrap is outside. Frank was poked with a fingerclaw. "Don't you dare tell me I shouldn't have. I wasn't going to let you stay passed out in the dirt. I'm putting you on a diet though. I almost had to strain to get up on your feet." Zeke's nostrils flared, and he hopped to his feet and out the hatch. "Food's up!"

Frank followed, cringing as the sharp light stung his eyes. The smell of something at the very least meat-like wafted around. "What time is it?"

"Hard to say. You were out for about twelve hours." Zeke shoved a plate with some sort of sausage covered in heavy gravy vegetables at the bear. "There's always one of those big suns hanging around." Zeke leaned back against Frank, using him as sort of chair as he ate. "So this planet doesn't have a night, just variations on day."

The ursine worked through his food quietly. Eventually though the elephant in the room had to be brought up.

"Zeke, what're we going to do?"

Zeke's continued cloud-gazing posture slumped a little though. "I'm as lost as you are, papa bear. Maybe we can take the runabout."

Frank chewed with a dour look, "Won't do us a lot of good." He took a generous bite of the mysterious protein, trying not to think about what it might actually be. "She's only got enough fuel for a few thousand kilometers, maybe a few days worth of oxygen, not much water, and a couple of ration kits that you just used up." He reached out with a big hand and stroked over the runabout's hull lovingly. "As good as she is the girl ain't made for deep space travel. At least your PADD has a few thousand years of power in it."

The fennec stood up and dusted off his pants, tail wagging gently behind him. "Then the choice is made for us, isn't it?" There was a twinge of excitement in his voice. Adventure had always thrilled Zeke in a way Frank

284

couldn't quite relate to anymore. Zeke pulled on Frank's hand insistently. "We've got shelter, we've got supplies. Let's go see what home looks like."

Frank rose, still sullen. "What for?" he lamented, adjusting his jumpsuit back into place.

Zeke turned and glared right up at the bear. To most people a less-than-two-meter (including the ears) tall fennec trying to be fierce at someone what could swallow him whole would get a laugh. To Frank, it was anything but. When Ezekiel got mad, bad things had a tendency to happen, the kind of things that ended up with court hearings and hospital bills. You didn't want the little fireball pissed at you. Frank's ears flatted against his head and he put his hands up defensively.

"Frankfort Tabernacle Berlin, you whiny little baby. You have one minor setback and suddenly you're on your knees practically digging your own grave. Did you leave your balls up on the Starduster?"

"Mi—minor setback? Rachel's dead and my ship's debris. That's not a 'minor setback', Zeke, that's 'we're screwed'!"

Zeke's tail lashed out behind him. "When I met you, you were a heart-stopping stud with big dreams and a rust bucket two-seater with a funny smell. Everyone said it was too good to be true but I didn't care. You were my spaceman with stories of zooming around the stars and getting into all kinds of amazing trouble. You'd been everywhere from backwater dens to heaven and back again. You were an *adventurer*." A finger poked right into Frank's belly. "Now all you do is fill out paperwork and eat Twonkies." The fox turned and looked off into the distance. "Frank, love of my life and the greatest thing that ever happened to me."

Frank ran his hand through the fur on his head, trying to keep his composure. "What?"

"We can do this." Zeke turned back and gave Frank a winning smile. "And we're going to, whether you want to or not." The fox turned on his heels and pointed towards a point on the near horizon. "Let's go see what's over there!" And he was off like a shot, scampering over the terrain with ease as Frank struggled to keep up. Fennecs were an excitable bunch. But when you lived on a ball of sand hardly anyone ever visited and no one stayed on for long, you had an excuse. Frank was treated like a celebrity when he landed, wined and dined and sixty-nined until he couldn't stand up. Finding out one of them had stowed away in a cargo crate—one of the royal family to boot!—got him in hot water, but the big bear couldn't tell the wide-eyed teen he'd have to back to sand farming and picking fleas out of his ears for excitement. Now there he was leading Frank who-knows-where. All these years hadn't changed the kid a single bit.

"Zeke, slow down!" Frank shouted with half a laugh as they scrabbled up a hillside. "You're gonna run off a cliff!"

"Then you better catch me, papa bear!" They both kept tearing along the lush green grass, humid breezes whipping through their fur. It was alien to them both, lush in a way that no populated planet Frank had ever seen. By the time someone like a scavenger could visit, The Union would ensure that the place was a uniform, pre-fabricated colony world just like all the others, stamped out in factories and populated with familiar flora and fauna guaranteed to keep the people nice and cowed. Hell, after spending most of his life living shoulder-to-shoulder in tenement houses and scavenger ships, the very idea of *quiet* was as alien to him as crystalline blue flowers and the knee-high stalks.

"Woooo ooooh craaaaap!" Frank snapped out of his reverie just in time to grab Zeke's jeans by the waistband, hauling the fennec back before he toppled down a steep slope into the valley below. A sharp tug sent Zeke spinning backwards into big, protective arms. "My hero," Zeke murmured.

"I told you, you goof."

Zeke stood on tip-toe and gave Frank a kiss on the lips before grabbing the bear by the hand. "Look out there, papa bear. Don't say anything, just look."

The view from Zeke's vista was enough to suck the breath right out of Frank's lungs. When you grow up in steel and concrete, nature is the artificial thing. You're content with plastic and grey. But here every inch of the horizon was painted with foliage in every color imaginable and then some, shifting in waves along the searing orange of the sky. Resting square in the middle of the floral sea was the bluest water the bear had witnessed, a massive shimmering azure pool that drew the eye to it like a cache of diamonds in the distance. Frank had to convince himself that he wasn't watching a tape. It was impossibly beautiful.

"Damn, Zeke."

"And it's all ours, baby." Zeke laughed and slapped Frank on the back. "I don't know about you, Frank, but I'm gonna go get a bath. Race you to the bottom!" The fennec whipped off his sweat-soaked shirt pants in one smooth motion. Before the bear could even think of a protest the now naked fox was diving off the ledge into the water below. Frank grabbed the clothes and tore off at full gait down along the edge, careening like a fuzzy cannonball towards the plain, the whole time shouting that if Zeke had survived that *stupid* stunt Frank would kill him.

"Godsdamn it, Ezekiel, are you okay?!" Frank scanned the lake's surface for any sign of his husband. There were none. The surface was as still as glass. "Oh gods, you're dead, *damn it damn it damn it...*"

Zeke surfaced suddenly, his head thrown back and water going cascading around him. If he still had his hair it would have finished the effect, but the image was fine enough as it was. "By the goddess, I haven't been in water this perfect since I left homeworld. It's even got fish! They're weird but that's even better!" The fox turned and caught Frank's eyes suddenly, eyes bright and wide as water trickled off his pelt. "This place is like a resort planet, Frank!" The fox tilted his head. "Are you okay?"

"I thought you'd died, Zeke!"

Zeke laughed a little, splashing about in the waist-deep waters. "I'm sorry, honey. I just couldn't resist! It's like the best of being back home without all that damn sand." He paused a moment, deep in thought. "There's no one else here, right?"

The bear blinked in confusion. "I don't think so. Why?"

Zeke's muzzle cracked in a wide, wicked smoke. "Oh, just had a thought." He ran his hands through his short shock of hair with a long sigh, striding through the pool towards the edge where Frank waited. Frank watched in quiet rapture as the fennec—*his* fennec—rose from the water inch by inch, revealing more of the golden pelt pressed that lay flat against a dancer's build. The chest showed first, then a tight belly that led into feminine hips and strong thighs, a slowly swaying tail swishing behind them. The bear swallowed his breath. He had seen Ezekiel naked every morning since they'd first met. But familiarity did not breed boredom, and the scene built around the fennec's form as he came closer kept the bear's eyes open wide.

"Being alone means I can do things like this," Zeke murmured and pressed his palm to Frank's bare chest. He gave his love a soft kiss to the lips, stroking over thick russet fur with thin fingers. Frank's senses filled with Zeke, the softness of his pelt, the way he moved and the sound of his breath, how cool moisture soaked into Frank's fur as they pressed together.

Frank found his breath with a soft cough. "You're amazing, Ezekiel..." His big hands found themselves on the fennec's waist, resting at the small of his back, holding him as if he might escape at a moment's notice.

"I love you, Frankfort Berlin, even if you're kind of boring and you need to ease off the snack cakes." Ten fingers slipped into the waist of the bear's jumpsuit, cupping a rising firmness in a warm and damp palm. "I see the feeling's mutual." Frank's clothing fell away with a flick of the wrist. The both of them fell backwards into the grass, tangled in an embrace of limbs and lips. A single breath was passed back and forth between the couple, tongues tied and teeth parted to give the other unfettered access.

Zeke broke the kiss with a gasp, sitting on Frank's belly, his eyes never breaking from the bear's. His tail swished lazily behind him, tickling at brown thighs. "You're beautiful," he murmured. The fennec's length lay deep in the warmth of Frank's fur. Every move he made was like rubbing against the lushest carpet imaginable.

"Look who's talking." Frank felt every inch of Zeke he could. If Frank was plush carpet, Zeke was made from pure silk, fur that felt impossibly soft as it dried in the sun. The fox writhed under the attention, a grinding dance on Frank's lap. Muscles moved with practiced precision and coaxed steadily stronger reactions and hotter passions; their aroused scents drifted away on the summer wind.

"Did you…" Zeke was not much for words, lost in his erotic dance, panting loudly. Frank nodded and grabbed for his jumpsuit, pulling a few foil packets from the pocket and passing them to his partner. "I hope we don't run out." It was *mostly* a joke—the cruiser had enough condoms and such to last hundreds or thousands of passengers for years. But when two men love each other *this* much, well, sometimes they lose count.

Zeke's makeshift chair chuckled and let his hands rest on coppery hips as the fox put his fingertips to Frank's member. The blue skies cut a sharp contrast against the slickened redness. "Let me give you a raincoat," he sang as the thin wrap slid down until the end rested snugly around a blood-filled shaft. A thick sheen of lube followed suit, interrupted only briefly as Frank's broad tongue lapped quickly over Zeke's pink head before giving it a kiss.

Zeke shot the bear a glare. Frank just shrugged with a wide smile. "I just can't resist a treat." The fox rolled his eyes as he settled back into place. Frank set himself back to the task at hand—or more accurately at ass, where his masculinity prodded at the fennec's pucker. With one deep intake of breath, the fennec let gravity take him down, slowly spreading around Frank's cock. Zeke's jaw tensed for a moment before his ever-confident smile bloomed back on to his face. The fennec was a dancer on a stage with his hips rolling and swaying like a belly dancer's. Each downbeat of the 'song' brought strong hips up and away; when one bar passed into the next, they met again with his lover's lap, a cycle of rises and falls that plotted the way towards a crashing climax. It was a dance they had practiced until it was etched in their minds, pure muscle memory.

"Gods, Zeke," Frank panted. His skin was hot and damp with sweat. The fennec merely smiled in response, sighing as Frank filled his senses completely, drowning out the world around them, soaked in bliss.

Strong hands clapped against rounded hips, urging them to go faster. Zeke's tempo peaked, and the music they made together rose in pitch until it burned with their primal cries as the chorus. Frank became the first to reach his crescendo as he pushed up *hard* against the fennec, pouring his seed into the condom, leaving a stinging heat deep inside Zeke. Zeke's eyes lidded and rolled; he ground down, clenching, barking in surprise as Frank's hand curled around his cock and created a sharp contrast to the groomed softness of belly fur. It took but a moment before the duet ended, leaving long trails of his cooling pleasure through Frank's pelt.

They rested there in the grass for hours. There was no need to rush; there was nowhere to be and no one to answer to. Right at the moment, the universe existed for just them.

* * *

The pair settled smoothly into their new lives, free of worries and well cared for. Every square inch of the plains was a new discovery, plants and small animals that defied description and made Zeke's PADD scratch its virtual head in confusion. If they made it off the world—and that became a bigger "if" with every passing day—selling the wildlife data alone would make them billionaires. Food from the cruiser kept them fed, and Frank even found a new project to throw himself into: building a cabana for the couple to spend their downtime in. It took weeks of testing frustration and hacking together bits from the cruiser, but after all was said and done Frank and Zeke were happy with the results. For the first time in a long time, Frank was proud of something.

Six Terran months passed, by the PADD's approximation. The lack of a night made it hard to tell one day from another, and without a remote signal to keep the clock synced, the PADD was drifting. But what did it matter? The exercise and clean air had done them actual visible good; freed from the constant confines of the tiny ship and its recycled air, Frank had lost the 'sloppy gut' that Zeke liked to tease him about, while Zeke himself took the opportunity to grow his hair back out and lounge about in not much more than his luxurious pelt. It was a second youth for them both.

It was early morning by Terran measure when Frank rose from his bed, holding the thin sheets to his chest and yawning. "Another day in paradise," he murmured with a dreamy smile, watching the horizon shift like a hand petting over a cat's back. The bear reached for his husband, surprise suddenly changing his demeanor—Zeke was nowhere to be found. His spot on the bed was cool, and his scent was conspicuous in its absence. "Zeke, where are you?" They'd both agreed to not go off into the wild alone—it just wasn't safe—and that really only left a few options, the most obvious being the cruiser.

Frank ducked through the hatchway and back into the Union ship, the tap of his boots the only sound. It hadn't changed very much since they'd discovered it months ago, but Frank had steadily grown less and less comfortable being inside it. It was cold and sterile, designed by a military mind to be the peak of efficiency. The endless silence ate at his nerves, and he couldn't quite put some questions out of his mind. Where was the crew? Or the escape pods, for that matter? How was this thing still working? It didn't add up.

A white haze oozing from a door caught Frank's attention. Inside he found Zeke hunched over a terminal, eyes bloodshot. Even with his technical expertise the bear didn't know what this room was, exactly. The Starduster was powered by hacked-together technology and a lot of hope, nothing like the high-quality bleeding-edge Union technology. Whatever Zeke was dealing with, it had his entire attention; he paid no mind to Frank coming into cramped office.

Frank stepped carefully up to Zeke, putting his hand on the fox's shoulder. "Zeke? What are you up to?"

Zeke jumped in surprise, turning in the chair to face the bear. "Goddess! Don't sneak up on me like that!" He clutched his hand to his chest, panting a little.

"Sorry, sorry! I didn't mean to scare you." Frank leaned his muzzle over Zeke's shoulder and tried to make heads-or-tails out of the data cycling through the displays. It made his head spin trying to follow any thread there might be buried deep inside. "I didn't hear you get up."

"I didn't want to wake you," Zeke said as he turned back to the screens. "It was really early. I think. I just couldn't get to sleep…"

"Something woke you up?" Frank raised both eyebrows. "You sleep like the dead. I can't wake you up with explosives." He nudged his fingertip toward a patch of text. "What is this?"

"I'm not sure." The tapping of fingers against touchscreens echoed off the metal walls. The room was small, cramped full of electronic gear, and with Zeke in the middle it left Frank just enough room to breathe. "You're gonna laugh, but I saw it in a dream. Someone told me to come in here and do this."

Frank looked to Zeke with an eyebrow quirked. "That's crazy."

"I know, papa bear, but here we are. And I think I might actually be on to something." A cylinder next to Zeke whirled up, projecting a small hologram out of the console. "The data was stored over in the busted part of the cruiser. There's just this last one left."

A slim feline, his features indistinct at the smaller scale, fidgeted his fingers together before glancing back over his shoulder nervously. The room was the same one the pair were in at the moment, though the lighting was stronger. "I'm think this thing is on. I can't tell. Stupid Union designs…"

His voice was more unnerved than his hands, which was saying something. "I'm Technician Brightmore of Union vessel Hephaestus. I'm just a junior tech, and I know I shouldn't be doing this, but the senior technician is… engaged." He scratched at his ear and looked behind his chair again. "The shakedown has gone completely fubar and we're getting ready to abandon ship." Brightmore sighed. "The mission was to test out this new AI-powered simulation system. It's supposed make long trips easier. But it's way too effective. Forty percent of the crew is incapacitated. Just…" He shook his hands in frustration. "They're lost in their own little worlds." There was a shout from the corridor; for a moment, Brightmore disappeared from view. He returned just as quickly but his face was painted with fear. His voice was a hoarse whisper. "Listen, if you find this, I'm warning you. It's unsafe. It's dangerous. It *listens* to you, man. It watches you and it learns about you and then it gives you exactly what it thinks you want. It sounds good but it's not." The cat looked behind him again. His eyes were wide and bloodshot. "We can't shut it off, so we're going to set the ship adrift and hope it crashes somewhere." He ran his shaking fingers through his hair with a laugh that was anything but happy.

Zeke and Frank watched on in shocked silence. The projection flickered; Frank worked quickly to stabilize it. "We've launched most of the pods already. I'm one of the last ones to get out of here. I haven't slept more than an hour in almost a week. Have to keep my guard up. I can't feel my face." Brightmore's voice wobbled as he started to cry softly an. "Davison set up some garbage programs to try and distract the AI, keep it away from the escape pods. I hope it holds." He took a slow breath, shut his eyes, and tried to settle himself. "It'll hold. It'll be fine. Come on, Peter, put on your game face." There was a shuffling sound behind the technician. "D-Davison? Is that you? Oh hells, I've got to—"

Silence hung heavy in the room. Both men held their breath waiting for the cat to come back and tell them the rest of the story. Eventually Zeke pressed a button and turned off the projector. "That's it. The rest of the file is empty space."

Frank realized he had stopped blinking. "I…" He turned to Zeke. "Did he get off the cruiser?"

The fox didn't answer. He couldn't. "He had to have. All the escape pods are gone and there're no bodies." Zeke exhaled. "I hope he did. The weirdest thing is it's timestamped over fifty years ago."

"Are you sure?" Frank ran his hand over his scalp and whistled. "Fifty years is a long time to go missing."

Zeke shook his head and stood up, stretching a stiff back. "Exactly, papa bear. I don't know she found this planet and crashed, but it wasn't for a while." The fox gave his husband a big toothy smile and kissed Frank's belly. "I've been cooped up enough today. You know if I don't get my exercise I'll be fidgety all day!"

Zeke chased after Frank as they headed for the exits, not noticing the display that came back to life behind them, flashing two words silently: *Elysium engaging.*

From that day onwards, both men agreed that avoiding the cruiser was for the best. While it had proven safe so far, neither one could shake Brightmore's warning or the lingering feeling that something was very wrong inside the Hephaestus. After spending a day pulling supplies from the ship and stashing as much in the junker as possible, they kept to themselves. The planet was huge and had options; why spend another minute in the cold and unwelcoming corridors of the cruiser? Out of sight and out of mind was for the best.

Zeke huddled against Frank in the early morning chill. Two of the suns were now rising lower and lower in the sky, signaling a slow easing from endless summer into autumn. Today was the worst day of the lot so far, a blustery grey scene that made Zeke's pelt bristle. He just wasn't built for cold.

The fox nuzzled up under the bear's chin. "You're amazing," he whispered, Frank's cock still buried deep inside of his backside, the scent of slowly drying come high on the air. All Frank could do was smile and blush under the fur before kissing his husband on the lips. "We should get cleaned up before I'm glued to you." Zeke giggled like a teenager when Frank scooped him up in both hands and strode down the incline towards the water's edge effortlessly.

There was a pause as Frank looked over Zeke's shoulder with wide eyes. "I don't think this is gonna work."

Zeke tilted his head in confusion. "Why not, papa bear?"

Frank simply turned around to let Zeke see for himself. The lake was not quite frozen over, but the edges had grown white with frost. The surface was choppy under the wind; the water itself was dark under the sunless sky. What had been welcoming was now inhospitable.

As carefully as he could, Frank eased himself out of the fennec and then helped Zeke to the ground. For several minutes they stood there, shivering, one scowling at the loss of a treasured ritual while the other looked frustrated.

"What's the alternative, Frank?" The bear didn't answer. He just stood there with his chin in his hand as if contemplating a math problem far too hard for him. "Frank? Papa bear?" Zeke poked the bear in the belly. "Terra to Frank, come in Frank…"

Frank exhaled. "Well, we could wait until the summer season comes around again, whenever that is." He looked down with a smirk at Zeke's grimace at just the *thought* of the idea. The fennec could spend *hours* preening when he was dirty, and in this line of work that was pretty often. Even after leaving the homeworld, little Ezekiel was still a prince at heart. Or maybe a princess. "Yeah, that's what I thought you'd say."

"Bleh, bleh bleh *bleh*. No sir, I don't like it." Zeke managed to calm himself enough to bring his tail back from bottle-brush state. "Is there a choice that won't make me scream every morning for goddess knows how long?"

Frank tipped his chin over his shoulder. "We go use the stalls in the cruiser."

Zeke visibly withered. The derelict ship spooked him, got into his head and wouldn't let go. "You can't be serious. I never want to go in there again. Can't we do something else?"

Frank put his hands on Zeke's shoulders and drew him in. "I won't let anything happen to you, my little princess. You have my word."

Zeke sighed a little and pressed his against the bear's chest. "You always know what to say."

"It's my silver tongue. Pretty women and prettier men can't resist it."

"Oh you scoundrel, you've swept me off my feet." The fox wrinkled his nose up. "And now you've made me sick. Phew! Come on, let's see what the concierge on Starship Titanic can do for us."

* * *

It took a few tries before the couple found showers that were in a useable condition. Finding facilities wasn't the challenge—the cruiser had enough signs and arrows that any idiot could find what they were looking for—but the crash had been shut off by the automatic systems when the pipes cracked. Finally though hot water and soap were applied to fur and the grunge of early morning love-making was washed away. Zeke's relief at being clean was palpable, and Frank had to chuckle at how hard he wagged after he was dried and brushed to gleaming perfection.

"Y'know, Frank, it's funny," Zeke said as he got dressed in another of his cut-off shorts. The fox had been converting everything he could find into cut-offs and by now had something of a collection. If they ever returned to 'proper' civilization, training him out of walking around in what were practically snug briefs would take some effort. Frank, on the other hand, just kept finding new jumpsuits. "If no one's been here in fifty years, why is there still hot water?"

Frank ran a towel over his belly for the thousandth time. It was so hard to get that thicker fur dry. "I guess no one told it to stop." The bear tossed his towel to one side absently and ran fingertips through Zeke's hair. "Computers don't think for themselves."

"The ship wide malfunctions may have impacted some services. Service technicians have been dispatched to the most critical instances." An almost impossibly slim feline, almost impossibly so, strode into the damp showers with them, expression blank. He carried himself something like a butler or caretaker with the detached concern of one performing out of obligation. He wore nothing on his androgynous frame, and his steps were light, as if gravity did not apply to him. "I also apologize if I startled you. It was not my intent."

Zeke stepped in front of Frank, ready to leap at the slightest provocation. "Who the hell are you?"

The cat tilted its head curiously. "I am Elysium, the artificial intelligence that operates the Hephaestus. This information was included in your boarding briefing." There was a long pause, as if it were processing a heavy load of information. Zeke reached out a hand to touched Elysium along his chest but found nothing there but dust motes and light. "I am unable to access the ship's manifest. Who is your commanding officer?"

"Don't have one," Frank said.

Elysium again looked confused. He stared unblinking as his systems attempted to find a rational answer. "This is an invalid response. All aboard the Hephaestus were assigned a commanding officer and a crew designation during processing. No other persons are permitted onboard." The cat's voice warbled like the playback from a well-worn cassette. The dissonance made Zeke's ears ache. "Who is your commanding officer?" There was another pregnant pause. Elysium's eyes locked on Zeke's as fingers passed through the cat's face. "Please do not interfere with the projection. It is disruptive."

Zeke stepped back but his posture did not relax. "We're not with the crew. Hells, you don't *have* a crew. You're a wreck, brother."

"I am aware of the extent of the damage. I must verify the crew status." Elysium shook and his image grew indistinct. "Error. My data stores are unavailable. I appear to be operating on severely reduced power." He put a hand to his chin, mimicking deep thought. "This is unexpected. I will need to re-evaluate the situation to determine the proper course of action." Elysium bowed slightly to the duo. "Please report to your quarters and wait further instructions."

Frank looked down to Zeke. The fennec simply shrugged in similar confusion. "We don't have quarters. We're not on the crew."

Elysium was silent. Frank took his turn to shrug. "Maybe we should just head out to the cabana—"

"That is not recommended. You have been assigned quarters on this deck. Please follow the corridor indicators to its location." The lights in the shower dimmed significantly, replaced by a long row of flashing dots that moved out into the hallway and off into the distance. "To best optimize analysis, I must disengage this projection. The Union stands above." Elysium disappeared with a sharp click as his aperture closed, cutting the projection off.

Frank blinked once, then again, listening to water drip against the tiles. "That was *weird.*"

"Papa bear, that's the understatement of the year." Zeke shook his head to clear it out. "I hate to turn down hospitality but something's off."

Frank nodded and moved into the corridor. "Can't disagree." With each step they took towards the exit hatch the lights grew brighter and blinked faster, angry that their directions were being ignored.

"Do you hear that?" Zeke asked. Frank shook his head. "It almost sounds like…"

A gust of wind through the exit hatch pushed Zeke back. Frank grabbed the fennec with one arm, the other shielding his eyes. Outside a storm raged, blasts of wind cutting through the grass and hail sailing through the air like bullets. The junker was completely lost in the driving rain. Blades of lightning cut the sky.

"*Godsdamnit,*" Frank whispered under his breath. "We can't go out in that."

Zeke fidgeted. "We could huddle up in the junker—"

"Zeke, look out there. It's not safe."

Zeke ran his hand over his face as the access door sealed shut with a soft puff. "Are you sure, Frank? I mean—" The fennec just shook his head. "No, you're right. Not like we're going to find a hotel around here." As if the ship itself was listening in the lights for a brief moment, glowing like stars in the distant sky.

* * *

The quarters of Elysium were simple, offering featured the minimum of creature comforts. Neither Frank nor Zeke were surprised—after all, the Union was a government, so this was a government vessel. More than somewhere to sleep and keep your uniforms would be a waste of resources.

The bed was serviceable; the walls kept the storm outside at bay. Frank and Zeke were comfortable, yet not much at ease.

"So what now, papa bear?" Zeke sat in the lone chair in the cabin. "Not a lot going on here." The fennec ran his palm over the bare surface of the desk. "Not even a computer."

Frank leaned back against the wall and stretched his hands high over his head. "Wouldn't be much use." The bear raised his eyebrows with a saucy smirk. "We could always…"

Zeke rolled his eyes with a low laugh. "Frank, honey, even I need some recovery time." He shifted his hips against the seat. "I'm gonna be sore for a while, you animal." The entire ship rattled and the lighting flickered then dropped out for a few seconds. Zeke held his breath and stared up at the ceiling. "I hope this thing holds together…"

As if summoned by some otherworldly power, Elysium appeared in the room with a dull click. The projected image was less defined as before, clouded by noise and constantly flickering. "I apologize for the sudden power instability. Measures are being taken to bring the situation under control at this time."

Frank rose with concern in his voice. "What's going on with the power?"

Elysium ignored the bear. "Emergency protocols have activated as well as the repair drone system. Their functionality is limited, but—" Elysium crackled and distorted sharply before snapping back into focus. "—is limited, but sufficient to bring a portion of the datastore online. I have verified your reports. All crew have abandoned ship and the state of the vessel is d-d-d-dire." The lights flashed again. The warmth in the room faded briefly. "The Hephaesus is beyon-yon-yond recovery."

"That's obvious," Frank said. "But if the power core fails—"

The virtual feline cracked and faded again. This time it took far longer for him to reform, and even after his speech was slurred. "There is nooooooo r-r-rrrrisk of a signif*crackle*ificant incident. Your li-i-ife is not a risk risk risk risk riiiiisk."

Zeke just listened to Frank and Elysium in silence, shivering not just from the growing chill in the room. "This ship's been fine for decades. Why is power a problem now?"

"You did not stay within expected paaaarameters. My calculations are now invalid."

Frank's blood went cold. "What do you mean parameters?"

The cat's voice was flat. It had never been particularly emotive, but now any semblance of warmth had vanished. "The Hephaestus is a modified terraforming vessel, designed by the Union Fleet engineers to test a new sub-conscious stimulation system. By processing accumulated data, the system attempts to create a perfect substitute reality for the subject to reside in during the long travel time to a new host world *crackle sputter crackle* as well as during early planetary processing periods."

Frank fumbled for words. Zeke moved to his side, clinging. "This cruiser…it's a giant virtual reality system?"

"In a c-c-crude sense, yesyesyeeeeees. Your actions have disru-r-rupted the environment." Elysium's ability to speak continued decaying at a steady pace, and his projection was almost lost in static. At this rate there wouldn't be much left of the avatar within minutes.

Suddenly they crashed into Frank's brain like a thousand pounds of lead. Every gear clicked into place. His eyes went wide. Zeke stared at him in confusion.

"It's simulation. The entire planet is a simulation." The bear's hands gesticulated madly as he paced the room. "No wonder it's perfect. It's everything I've—we've ever wanted. But—" he pointed at the far wall, the only thing keeping the storm at bay "—it's breaking down. It's crashing."

If Elysium could still hear Frank's voice, it didn't react. "Access to the communications terrrrrminal by a crew member *crackle* reactivated the artificial intelligence." For a split second Elysium disappeared entirely, returning with a loud burst of static. "—increased complexity of the simulation has led to terminal failure." Frank thought he could hear a hint of sadness in the feline's voice. "As per emergency protocol, shutdown is eminent. At that time, this simulation will terminate. There are approximately ten minutes remaining."

Frank slid his arm around Zeke's waist as the feline avatar vanished out of existence in the middle of its last attempt to speak. Whatever it had left to say would be lost to time, to space, and to meaning. "All good things, huh?" The bear gave his husband a broad smile and leaned in to kiss the fennec's forehead softly, taking a deep breath of his scent. "Back to the grind."

Zeke fidgeted. His eyes pointed to the floor and his tail hung limply behind him. "I guess, yeah. Heh."

"What's wrong, princess? Is the cold getting to you? We can wrap up—" A glimmer in the fading fluorescent light caught Frank's attention. His voice fell to a whisper. "You're crying."

"Y-yeah. I can't help it." The fox held Frank's arm tightly, as if it would be gone without warning. "I hate saying goodbye."

"What—"

"Frank." The fennec's face streaked with tears, matting the lovely copper and bronze, dripping from his slight cheeks. "I can't go with you."

The bear laughed, the kind that's meant to mask a rising terror deep in your chest. "You want to stay here? Come on, fuzzbutt. Don't be weird."

Zeke darted from the room, his sobbing echoed off the metal walls. Frank took to his heels, following the flickering shadows as they went, shouting for the fennec to stop, to listen, that it would be alright. Frank would make everything okay again.

At the edge of the gash between the two sections of the crashed ship, Frank found him, standing and staring out into the distance. "Zeke. Talk to me, I'll fix whatever's wrong…"

"Oh papa bear," the fox said with a choked laugh. "If only you could." Frank reached out and grabbed Zeke's shoulder to pull him back. The fox did not move, firmly rooted to his spot. "But you can't. No one can."

Acid boiled in the pit of Frank's stomach. His heart pounded and the blood crashed in his ears like thunder. "Don't do it, Zeke. There's no reason—"

"I'm not going to jump, Frank." The fennec turned to Frank and looked him square in the eyes, speaking with a voice that could barely rise above the roar of the storm just meters away. "It's not like I can die."

Frank started to answer. Then it happened. It was a tiny thing, a blip in the scene that destroyed Frank's world for the second time in less than half of an hour. It brought tears to his eyes as it pulled the breath out of his lungs.

Ezekiel, the fennec he'd given his life and heart to, flickered.

"No. No no no *no no no no no*…" Frank dropped to his knees, numb to the cold that stabbed into his fur and soaked into his skin.

Zeke turned back to Frank. A thin smile played over his lips. "This isn't our perfect world, Frank." He padded on silent feet to the bear, stroking his soft palms over Frank's cheek. "It's yours. I'm just part of it."

"But all these *years*, Zeke. We've been all over, we've done things!"

"I know, papa bear." Slim fingers rolled through Frank's hair soothingly. "It's so real you can't tell the difference. But there's no Ezekiel. There never has been, not like you know him." Another flash of lightning brought another shimmer. Frank could see the world around him start to shimmer as the simulation began to fail. "This is going to hurt. Oh Gods, I'm so sorry, Frank. This wasn't supposed to happen…"

The first flashback was a razor slashing into Frank's mind. This morning, waking up to Zeke coming out of the shower, their morning lovemaking. Slowly it shifted, the real world taking its place, Frank left alone in the room quietly. Step by step it went back, hours, days, weeks, the resets coming faster and faster. Lunches and dates evaporated. Scavenging jobs were replaced with faceless, nameless partners assigned by the Guild.

Even the flavor of food and the sound of Zeke's laughter burned up like paper in fire.

Finally the memories landed on the day Frank had left the fennec homeworld. The Starduster was leaving orbit. And there, just like always, he found a skinny fox hidden in a closet. His name was Ezekiel, and they had met many times before. Frank liked Ezekiel quite a bit—he was enthusiastic and intelligent, a stark contrast to his decadent brethren. Ezekiel wasn't content to sit around palatial manors and sip wine all day. He believed there was a world out there worth exploring and Frank was his ticket out. The bear was skeptical. He wasn't any hero, just a guy who could tell a mean story after a few bottles of high quality liquor and some proper companionship. Ezekiel didn't care.

They spent twenty minutes sitting in the cockpit of the Starduster, just talking. They were a pair, the twenty-something bear in his blue-collar work clothes and the fennec in perhaps his eighteenth summer, wearing the traditional drapes of his people that provided a degree of decency but not much else. Frank tried to talk him out of it. Ezekiel was having none of that. Danger didn't bother him. Anything was an improvement over sitting around waiting to die.

The world rippled sharply. Frank felt the shift in the very core of his being—this was the first memory, the crux of everything. In the memory Frank cherished, he had relented and brought the fennec along with him, quickly building a rapport that would lead to their marriage. Ezekiel's parents had protested at first, but they had given up after seeing their son truly happy for the first time ever.

Slowly Frank surfaced. The sobs racked him. His stomach threatened to pour its contents on the deck. "I went to the fennec homeworld…I met you there, and I took you with me…and…" Zeke cried with Frank, holding him tightly as the constructs fell away like molted skin. It was agony for them both. "You…you decided not to go." Frank tilted his face up and met Zeke's eyes. "I talked you out of it. It was too dangerous, you were too young. You were a prince. Your place was there. I was scared you'd get hurt, that I couldn't protect you." A choked sob swept his voice away. The storm grew weaker above their heads. "I made myself forget you. I was a coward."

The fennec shook his head, "Never. You beautiful man, you, you were—you *are* perfect. I wish I could go with you and see what's out there." Brown arms wrapped around the fox and hugged him tightly, a grip that would fight against reality itself to keep Zeke where he was. It had to work. It just had to. He couldn't let go.

Minutes passed as they held each other tightly. There was nothing else to the world but Ezekiel of the fennecs. His scent, the feel of his fur against Frank's fingers, they were everything.

"Goodbye, Frankfort Tabernacle Berlin. You're gonna be awesome. I just know it." There was a small laugh. "Don't worry about me. I won't feel a thing..." The sound of rain grew softer until it vanished. The weight in Frank's arms melted away. Frank slowly opened his swollen eyes.

Zeke was gone. Frank was sat alone in the tattered corridor, dressed in his old trusty jumpsuit just like when the junker had landed. Rain poured through the split in the hull, and debris skittered about his feet. There was no sign Zeke had ever been there. Slowly the lights of the cruiser faded to dull embers then went out completely. The Hephaestus was dead.

Frank walked through the halls towards the exit hatch. The sound of rain echoed off the hull, ringing through the cold metal. The air was still and acrid, burning his lungs. Outside fared no better; the planet was barren and dark, stabbed with stone pillars that twisted towards the sky. There was no sign of the cabana. Of course there wouldn't be.

Frank pulled a deep breath, and with leaden feet he returned to the runabout and sat in the pilot's seat. The co-pilot's chair was stacked with boxes and technical readouts; no one had sat there for gods knew how long. He had flown alone for as far back as he could remember.

"Hey Frank. How's business?" Rachel's voice cut through the headset as he activated the craft's power systems again. He could at least take some solace in her being alive after all, little solace that it was to his shattered heart. He laughed sarcastically at himself, all broken up over a romance that hadn't even happened. It was being angry at a dream.

"Everything's green across the board." He fired the lift jets. Outside the screens the Hephaestus slowly receded from view until the grey clouds swept it away entirely. "How long have I been on the surface?"

"About 12 hours. You alright? You sound choked up."

* * *

Back onboard the Starduster, Rachel sat with Frank in his cabin. The ghosts of the simulation still lived in at the edges of his mind. He had to remind himself that he slept alone and that the exotic smell was just in his mind. There would always be pieces of Zeke left, flickering half-formed memories that taunted him.

"Wow. That's...that's a hell of a story, Frank." The collie ran her hand through her punked up hair. "I'm sorry." It was probably the first real sentiment he'd gotten from Rachel in all the time he'd known her; maybe she was growing up a little after all. "So what do we do now?"

Frank tapped Zeke's—no, his PADD absently. "The same thing we usually do, kid." He put the tablet down and rubbed over his forehead. "I've already notified the Guild to steer clear, and slipped the Union a message that they should come get their garbage before it hurts somebody else. Otherwise…" He shrugged and tossed the tablet aside. "Life goes on."

Rachel nodded softly. Without warning she leaned in, hugging Frank tightly around the neck; he swore he could hear her sniffle in his ear. There was a small smile on her face as she walked out of the room and back to the cockpit.

Frank mulled his options. Nothing had changed; he'd lost things that hadn't been real, so it shouldn't make a difference. Life would go on, and he'd eventually forget.

A thought occurred to him. "Hey, kid?"

Rachel came back over the intercom. "Yeah, Dad?"

Frank laughed. *Dad.* That would never get old.

"How long would it take to get to the fennec homeworld?"

Frank could practically feel Rachel's confusion melt into a smile on the other end. "I can get you there in a Terran day or two. Three if you want to stop off at port and get some supplies."

"Sounds good." The bear lay back on his bed. "Wake me up later. I'm gonna go chase a dream."

Little Death

by James Hudson

I guess being hit by a bus doesn't hurt as much as you'd think. This weird, floating sensation is a little disconcerting though, not to mention the fact that I can see myself lying in the road down there. No pain though. Not a bit of it. There's no getting round the fact that I'm dead though. I must be. Alive people can't see their own body lying in front of the number 76 bus, so I'm fairly sure I must be dead.

For some reason all I can think is that I look so silly lying in the road, as if I've chosen the worst possible place for a nap. My tail's even curled up between my legs like I'm settling down to hibernate. Not that foxes hibernate. Actually, nobody hibernates anymore, except animals. There's not a mark on my fur though, I suppose that's a blessing. I would have expected a little blood, or maybe a broken arm or leg, but I look perfectly healthy, apart from being dead. At least I left behind an intact and, I dare say, fairly handsome body for the hospital to carve up.

Shouldn't I be more upset about this?

The bus driver seems pretty upset, standing over my body. He's a big ol' bear like so many bus drivers seem to be. Why are so many bus drivers bears? I don't suppose it matters, not to me anyway. I've got more important things to worry about like why I seem to be floating away from my own body.

Oh, right, I was hit by a bus and I died. That's why.

But wait a minute Frederick, you dumb fox! Is that what normally happens when people die? I suppose nobody knows. Well, except me. I know because it's happening to me right now. Shouldn't I be scared or something? I really don't feel scared.

Still, if my body's down there, then what exactly is it that's floating away from it and wondering why it's floating away from it's own body? I suppose it must be me. At least I'm floating *up*. That's got to be a good sign, right?

Watching on as I float serenely away, the scene below me starts to look blurrier by the second, as if I'm watching a slow focus pull on a trashy daytime TV drama. I can still make out the increasingly large crowd gathered around my former body, but they're all starting to look like one indistinct jumble now.

A pulsating blue light arrives rapidly on the scene below and comes to a halt beside the blurry onlookers. It's not clear to me whether the light belongs to a police car or an ambulance, but either way I'm impressed by the speed of their response to the incident. Obviously it's too late for *me*, but a crowd of that size gathering on a public highway is definitely a cause for concern. I would feel awful if someone *else* got hurt.

Just as the world is starting to look completely unintelligible, a blinding brightness begins to cloud my senses even further. Somehow the impossibly slow flash of pure white light seems to inhibit not just my vision, but my other senses too. I can't smell anything on the air. I'm not even sure if there *is* any air where I am anymore. My whiskers don't seem to be working! How is that possible?

For a moment I feel as though I'm suspended in perfect nothingness, as if I've simply ceased to exist, or never existed in the first place. It is a feeling not incomparable to falling asleep, except that instead of embracing darkness, I am surrounded by light.

After a period of time that could as easily have been a century or a second, I realise that the light around me is starting to fade away again. My senses are starting to return too and I can feel the air on my whiskers again. All I can do is float still and wait to see what's revealed when the light fades enough for me to see beyond it.

Okay, it's pretty obvious where this is going, where *I'm* going, Isn't it? Ascension toward a bright light? I've never believed in any of that stuff, but there have been enough heaven clichés for it to be obvious already. Well, I really *hope* that's where I'm going, because it sounds really good. Better than really good actually. Eternal paradise? Certainly sounds better than the alternatives.

An unexpected surge of adrenaline distracts me from my thoughts. I shouldn't be getting my hopes up. I don't even *believe* in god or heaven or anything like that. I've only ever imagined heaven as a daydream, a fantasy to distract me from reality. Still, I've imagined it often enough to know what it looks like, and what to expect when the light fades.

I laugh slightly at the thought of all this being some sort of devilish ruse. Perhaps this is actually the route to hell, and I'm being tricked into believing that I'm going to get everything I've ever dreamed of, only to end up on the receiving end of eternal torment. Actually, that's not very funny.

As the brightness fades enough for me to finally get a rough impression of my surroundings, I suddenly realise that my feet are on the ground again, or on *something* anyway. I momentarily feel a strange sense of vertigo as I realise that what was down is no longer down, and that I'm experiencing gravity again. I had been starting to miss it.

Blinking rapidly, I start to see the world, or whatever it is, as it comes into focus at last. Within a few seconds, I know that I had been right. I know exactly where I am.

To call what I'm looking at a beach does not do even the remotest bit of justice to the beauty of my surroundings. No tropical paradise on Earth could compare to the flawless landscape before me. The fine golden sand that I can feel between the toes of my foot-paws sparkles under the sun like countless miniature diamonds stretching out for what must be miles. I crouch down to take a handful of the tiny grains and feel them flow through the minute gaps in my fur like liquid gold to rejoin the vast, warm desert beneath. Dotted around the sands are palm trees, standing proudly like a tropical cliché, laden with coconuts the size of bowling balls.

A single coconut falls from the nearest tree and splits perfectly in two as it lands, revealing it's milky white flesh. I smile, but look away from it. I am waiting for something far more enticing. Even the glittering blue sea, only a short distance in front of me, cannot hold my attention for long. The gently undulating, translucent waters stretch out for infinity before me, and I know that to swim in them would be a joyous experience, but I'm not here for swimming.

I'm sure that I'm in heaven, because this is *my* heaven, *my* paradise. Every idle fantasy I've ever had about the afterlife has looked like this. This is the setting for my ultimate fantasy. A fantasy that I've literally been waiting my whole life for.

I curl up the toes of each of my foot-paws, and feel the little grains of sand tickle my pads. Turning my lidded eyes toward the sun, I smile broadly and then sigh a deep, contented sigh as the warm light caresses me.

It's not that I'm unaware of the situation I'm in, or of what I've left behind. I know that I'm going to be on this beach for a *very* long time, but I don't mind. I don't mind because I know that *she'll* be there when I open my eyes. Spending eternity alone on a beach, even an unnaturally perfect one, would get boring after a few years. However, the beach is only a setting, a backdrop, for my fantasy. I will admit, it's a fairly predictable fantasy, but I'm a fairly normal guy really. Maybe not a normal *fox*, if you pay attention to crude stereotypes, but a normal *guy*.

I take a moment to ready myself. I'm starting to feel slightly apprehensive for the first time since my death. I suppose meeting a new partner for the first time is always nerve-racking, even in heaven.

Keeping my eyes firmly shut, I imagine her long, luscious tail swaying behind the curves of her rear. I picture myself stroking her luscious, soft fur.

The sand shifts a little beneath my feet and I have to use my tail to catch my balance, but I do not open my eyes. I continue to visualise my vixen's perfect body, as if needing to make her real by doing so. I picture the autumnal red of her fur, and the golden sheen of her eyes.

A strong gust of wind hits me and I have to take a step backwards to prevent myself from falling but still I keep my eyes shut tight. Focussing hard, I try to imagine the hour-glass form of my imaginary partner's body, but I feel as though I'm straining against something intangible, and she looks indistinct. I can hear the wind gaining strength, as if complaining about my choice of companion. I can feel the sands shifting as if they might give way and send me tumbling to the ground, or perhaps swallow me up altogether.

Forcing my eyes to remain closed, I squeeze my hand-paws into fists. In my frustration I let out a feral cry, almost a bark. I haven't done that since I was little, but something seems to be breaking me down, at least in my head. Although right now, I'm not sure if there's anything *outside* my head.

For the first time since I died, I am scared. Of course, I know that I'm not in any danger, and I know *exactly* what's going on, but that doesn't make me feel any better about it. I've had this same problem every time I've tried to indulge in my fantasy, except the tropical storm isn't usually real.

Once again I try to imagine a vixen, *any* vixen, but I cry out in fear as a gust knocks me off my feet and into the prickly sands. Each grain feels as though it's burrowing into my fur, but I sit still, knowing that I only have myself to blame for my torment.

I start to gently sob. I've been fighting to maintain the same illusion my whole life, but death seems to have robbed me of my resolve. I know what's happening, and I know why.

The moment I stop imagining a vixen, the howling winds die down, and the sands become more stable beneath me. "Don't do this," I whisper aloud, although I'm not sure who I'm talking to. "Can't I just..."

I'm not even given the chance to finish my sentence before the winds begin to howl again.

"Fine," I say quietly. I know there's no hiding anymore. I cover my already closed eyes with my hand-paws, my snout sticking through the middle, sensing the salt air. The fur around my eyes is becoming damp from my tears and I feel so foolish because I know what I really want to see when I finally open my eyes. I've *always* known what I really wanted; I've just never allowed myself to see it.

Perhaps I was just sick of people making assumptions and trying to make choices for me. Either that or maybe I just wanted things to be easy, because nobody would think less of me as a man if I was with a woman. The problem isn't even that I'm gay. If I wanted a cute, feminine boy then I would still be a man in other people's eyes. No-one would laugh at me if I wanted to be *top*, but that's not what I want.

Of course, *I* know that I can want to be penetrated by another man and still be a man myself, but I know that's not how other people will see me. I know my family would only ever see me as a homo, as a failure.

"I'm sorry," I say in a whimper, not to myself but to my family. I'm assuming the worst of them without giving them a chance. I was projecting my own insecurities onto them. How could my family accept me if I can't accept myself? Surely that would be a good place to start at least.

With a deep, stuttering breath, I begin to clear my mind fully of the vixen I had coveted for so long. My eyes still shut, I start afresh.

Somewhere in the back of my mind an image starts to form and, perhaps for the first time in my life, I *don't* fight it. As I begin to picture his black-spotted silver fur, the air around me settles. The shape of his taut, muscular legs brings the sands under control, and I sit more comfortably. Once I've imagined his defined abs, his broad chest and his strong arms, the sun is shining warmly upon me again. I can see his thickly-furred yet lithe tail swishing across his buttocks. I can see Toby's kind, smiling face looking down at me.

I gasp as I feel a hand-paw rest gently on my head. Slowly, I open my eyes at last.

The beach is calm again, my paradise no longer disturbed by my turmoil, and yet I cannot see through the tears as they matt the fur around my eyes. Toby is standing over me, gently stroking my head.

"I knew you could do it," he says, caressing me so softly.

Toby doesn't tell me to stop crying. He understands the reason for my tears, and that they need to fall. The overwhelming relief I'm feeling is tempered only slightly by the knowledge that the man in front of me cannot possibly be Toby. Nor do I wonder for too long whether perhaps my death, and my current predicament, were the only reason I was finally able to be honest with myself. I accept that what I'm seeing is a fantasy, but at least I've been able to admit to myself what I wanted that fantasy to be; Toby, my best friend, a feline near twice my size.

In the past I'd told myself that I envied Toby's muscles, but deep down I knew that I admired them for a different reason altogether. I'd always thought I wanted to be strong like him, because that's how I thought a man should be, but really I wanted to feel comfortable with my vulnerability. Toby made me feel safe, and I know he would have accepted me, if I had given him the chance.

I'm not crying anymore. In fact, the tears are gone as if they had never been there. Toby is smiling down at me, still stroking the top of my head. It's not just my tears that are gone, but any trace of doubt has vanished from my mind as well. It feels as though I'm not being *allowed* to suffer anymore, or to feel uncertain.

I've reached a decision. My heart is beating faster, but purely from excitement rather than nerves. Knowing in my heart that it isn't really Toby standing over me has allowed me to forget about the consequences of what I'm about to do.

As he continues to caress me, I look into Toby's gentle eyes for a moment before extending a hand-paw gingerly in his direction. I barely touch the thick fur between his legs, not feeling able to do any more than that yet. With a claw, and barely a finger-tip, I lightly play with his fur as if he's something so delicate that I might break him; or break the illusion.

I pull my hand away in surprise at the sight of a little patch of red breaking through Toby's silver fur.

Now my heart is pounding.

Toby laughs softly as his erection begins to reveal itself to me, each pumping of his heart making it grow a little more. My heart beats so strongly that I feel as though it's helping Toby's erection to grow.

Finally it stands there proudly, a pulsating red beacon of hope. I laugh a little nervously. Toby's penis, only inches in font of my face, is much larger than my own, but I feel no insecurity. All I feel is desire.

With a stuttering breath, I rock forwards onto my knees. It's so close now that I can feel the warmth of Toby's blood. I can smell his desire, as he can surely smell mine.

Closing my eyes, I extend my tongue slowly until it meets the base of his erection. Pausing a moment to catch my breath, I slowly run my tongue up his length, tasting him inch by inch, until I reach the subtly pointed tip.

My tongue still in contact with my best friend's penis, I am panting as I feel my own erection grow between my legs, my heart beating like a drum. I open my eyes and look up at Toby's kind face. He places his other hand-paw on my head. He's no longer stroking me, but guiding me.

Barely believing what I'm doing, and yet feeling as though I should have been doing it for years, I close my mouth around the end of Toby's penis. Breathing heavily through my nose, I slowly lower my head until I've engulfed as much of him as I can within my muzzle.

My eyes wide, I notice the sand at Toby's feet. I'd forgotten that I was even on the beach. I don't *care* that I'm on the beach, or wherever I actually am. I don't care that I'm dead or that Toby probably isn't really Toby. I *certainly* don't care what anybody thinks about the fact that I have another man's cock in my mouth. All I'm feeling is pure, animal lust.

I wrap my right hand-paw around the base of Toby's thick, warm cock. I barely feel in control of my body as I begin to move my mouth and hand up and down his erection simultaneously, rapidly. Somehow my teeth don't get in the way. I know logically that they should, but they just *don't*, and I don't care why.

Pushing harder now, I feel Toby enter my throat, but I don't gag. I can feel his big, soft hand-paws on my head like a comforting embrace. He's telling me through his touch that I can do what I want and that it will be alright, so I push his cock deeper down my throat, knowing that I won't feel any pain or discomfort, only joy at having Toby inside me at last. Somehow I know instinctively that he is enjoying it as much as me.

Reaching down, I start to masturbate clumsily, unused to using my left hand-paw. Moaning, I realise that I've never had such a firm erection before. Toby begins to moan softly too, and only then does it occur to me what's going to happen if I continue pleasuring him. I feel light-headed, not so much from the thought of Toby ejaculating in my mouth, but because I know how much I want him to.

Shaking a little, I'm franticly pleasuring Toby and myself, yearning to taste him, and becoming all the more aroused as I wait for it to happen.

With a stifled roar of a cry, Toby's grip tightens on my head. I feel him shake a little as he fills my mouth with the most divine salty taste. Still masturbating rapidly, I swallow each wave of Toby's semen, sucking hard so as not to lose a

drop. A warm, fuzzy feeling begins to build inside me, and I involuntarily release Toby from my mouth as I cry out, my climax becoming an irresistible tidal-wave of pleasure. I fall backwards onto the sand as jets of semen fire from me into the air.

* * *

I'm not sure how much time has passed before I am brought back to my senses by Toby's rough tongue as it removes my semen from my chest.

I hadn't even noticed where it had landed, but now I'm glad it went where it did. Toby's muscular arms are planted either side of my body and he's looking down at me now, his erection undiminished between his legs.

Our eyes meet.

Toby laughs again. Not mockingly, but because he's realised what I want him to do next. No, what I *need* him to do next.

Despite having just been so intimate with him, the thought of allowing Toby to penetrate me is enough to make my head swim. I dig my fingers into the warm sand, my tail twitching restlessly between my legs. When I had pleasured him, I had been in control, even if it hadn't felt that way. Now, however, I am contemplating submitting to him, a larger male, and allowing him to do as he pleases with my body.

Toby laughs again, as if he can read my mind. Maybe he *can*. I'm certain he knows that I want him to fuck me like I thought I wanted to fuck that vixen. I want to feel his strong arms hold me as his cock…

Suddenly Toby lifts my legs from behind the knees with his big hand-paws. My heart really is pounding now. I'm shaking. I know I'm too overwhelmed to do anything more than submit to Toby's will, but maybe that's exactly what I want anyway. I nod subtly, but he already knows that I'm ready, because *I* know.

Toby parts my legs and pushes them up towards me. I can feel my rear lifting off the sand a little, and realise that my anus is exposed to him. My erection, now pressing warmly against my midriff, is throbbing in anticipation, but I'm feeling something new and even more exciting as well. There is a tingling inside me. I don't know what it is, but I'm desperate for Toby to fuck me now.

Reaching down with one hand-paw without releasing my legs, Toby grasps his erection. Adjusting his body slightly, he guides his tip to my hole. The sensation of Toby's warm tip touching my anus sends an electric thrill through my whole body. Just this initial contact is more exciting than anything I've experienced before, but I know that it's only the beginning.

With a gentleness that seems to defy his size, Toby pushes a little with his hips. Only the slightly pointed tip enters at first, but I moan at the feeling of my anus being opened. Then, he pushes a little more firmly, and I feel him stretching me, slowly filling my body with joyous warmth. I cry out as he excites the source of the tingling I'd felt

earlier. The pleasure is intoxicating, and I feel as if I'm floating as Toby expands inside me. My own erection twitches every time Toby's slow penetration sends a shock through the tingling source of my pleasure. "Toby," I say quietly. "Toby, I love you. I've always loved you. I'm sorry." I struggle to speak as I'm breathing so heavily, but I manage to say what I've always wanted to say.

Toby smiles and shushes me, telling me not to be sorry. "I know. I love you too, Frederick."

I throw my head back as Toby begins to draw his hips away from me, and cry out as his erection rubs against my prostate.

My prostate! That's what the tingling is! I laugh at the irrelevance of my realisation, but it becomes a moan as Toby pushes himself into me again. I feel no pain as Toby's hips begin to rock back and forth, despite the depth of his penetrations. Every thrust sends a wave of pleasure through my body, and I look into the eyes of my love as they smile down at me.

I laugh, almost giggling. "Fuck me, Toby, fuck me." My words liberate me. I feel free at last.

Toby begins to deliver his erection with more speed, and I feel my hole squeezing him in return. Words are beyond me now, but I make little high-pitched cries that would once have embarrassed me.

With a groan, Toby starts thrusting more powerfully, his hand-paws gripping my thighs firmly. I reach out and touch his arms, rubbing his fur, wanting to squeeze his hard muscles but finding myself too weak. My tongue is sticking out from my muzzle and I'm drooling, but I don't care. Toby's face doesn't look any more sensible than mine anyway.

Letting go of my legs, Toby lowers himself onto me, still thrusting deeply, until our bodies meet. I can feel his breath on my face and his heart beating against my chest in perfect rhythm with my own. Throwing my arms around him, I marvel at how broad his back is, and how thick his fur. I breathe in his masculine scent, and I'm excited by it.

I pull myself up to allow Toby's arms around my back, our embrace becoming more intimate. My erection presses against his middle, a pleasing contrast of soft fur and firm muscles. Wrapping my legs around him, I feel his penetrations becoming deeper. Our bodies entwined, we kiss and lick each other as we make love. Toby's tongue is big and rough but he avoids my sensitive nose and eyes. Part of me wonders if it would even hurt if he didn't, but I prefer it this way; I feel as though Toby is being careful not to hurt me, despite his deep, powerful penetrations.

Suddenly Toby leans back, pulling me with him. Hooking his arms around my legs again, he effortlessly stands, lifting me off the ground in his arms. With my arms and legs wrapped around him tightly, I feel my whole bodyweight press down on Toby's cock. The pleasure as he begins to move my rear up and down is intense, and I bury my face in his neck fur, my moans stifled. My erection rubs against him, and my tail thrashes behind me. Looking over his shoulder, I see Toby's tail moving lazily, happily, behind him. His tail is calm and proud, where mine is wild and lusty.

I realise that I'm moving my hips too now, forcing Toby's erection onto my prostate, increasing the pleasure. He takes a firm hold of my buttocks, squeezing them, no longer needing to help support me. I can barely believe that my best friend is taking such pleasure from touching *my* rear, or that I'm enjoying the touch of his big strong hand-paws just as much. If only I'd told him how I felt before...

My unwanted thoughts are interrupted by Toby as he begins to bend his knees, gradually lowering us to the ground. Not knowing what he wants to do with me next, I just hold on and allow myself to lay on top of him, his hard cock still deep inside me.

Our eyes meet, and then so do our mouths as we kiss. My erection is caught pleasurably between our bodies, and I squirm a little as I experience pleasure from several angles at once. Looking into Toby's beautiful eyes, I gasp slightly, having only just realised what I'm supposed to do next.

Toby makes a noise somewhere between a laugh and a low growl, his face kind and yet full of desire. I would laugh too, but I'm imagining what I'm about to do, and I've started to pant.

Slowly sitting back on Toby's cock, I feel it press impossibly deep inside me, every inch of it giving me nothing but pleasure. My erection twitches almost comically, and I see a few drops of liquid drip from the tip and land in Toby's fur. I'm breathing too heavily to laugh or even cry out for joy. Putting my hands on Toby's chest and grasping at the fur, I take a moment to admire the strong, handsome feline I'm straddling, before my lust takes over.

As I begin to bounce rapidly on Toby's cock, I feel as though my transformation is complete. I'm choosing to do something that I would have been ashamed to even imagine when I was still alive, and I love it!

My penis bounces rhythmically each time Toby's much larger penis is forced onto my prostate, giving me a jolt of pleasure. I throw my head back and cry out wildly, my inhibitions abandoned.

Toby grasps at my legs, grunting as I ride him. The pleasure is building within me as Toby's warmth seems to spread throughout my body from the inside out. My tail wags from side to side as I call my lover's name, knowing that I am approaching climax.

Toby begins to growl beneath me, his grip tightening on my thighs. I call his name again as I realise that we're both approaching the peak of our pleasure together.

As a warm ticklish sensation spreads irresistibly through my body, Toby throws back his head in a roar, and begins to fire his warm fluids inside me.

I utter a last feral cry as my own semen begins to shoot across Toby's chest and then his face.

Laughing, Toby begins to clean his face with his tongue as the lasts drops of my orgasm fall from me onto his fur before I collapse onto his chest and close my eyes.

* * *

My breathing and heart-rate slowing gradually, I listen to the gentle sound of the waves and the reassuring rhythm of Toby's heart. I hadn't been aware of the beach at all as I'd made love with Toby. I hadn't been aware of anything but him. Thinking back, I wonder if the beach really had vanished for a time, only to return when I had wanted to hear the waves again.

I can feel Toby still throbbing inside me, and it gives me pleasure, but I am satisfied. I have lived out my fantasy, and need nothing else. I feel immense calm, as if I could lie in Toby's arms forever, gently rising and falling with his breathing. I'm starting to forget where my body ends and Toby's begins.

It is with no sadness that I realise what is going to happen next. Maybe heaven isn't forever like everybody thinks, or maybe that's not really where I am after all, but I know I've reached the end.

"Thank you," I say to Toby.

He doesn't respond.

It isn't really Toby beneath me anyway. Besides, it's the real Toby that I'm thanking, wherever he is. I probably should be saying sorry really, but it's too late for that.

I start to feel as though I'm sinking into Toby, our bodies becoming one, or perhaps we're both just sinking into the sand. Whatever is happening, I don't feel scared, because I don't feel alone.

My eyes are shut, but I'm not sure there's anything for them to see now.

* * *

Amidst nothingness I hear something.

Everything is dark and I feel peaceful and warm. I want to give in to the feeling, but I'm sensing something else too, something *outside*.

A sound. That's what it is. A familiar, almost welcoming sound. It's enough to keep me from giving in to the calm that drags me away.

A voice. That's what I can hear. A familiar voice.

"You can't leave me... I need you... Please don't..."

I frown. I feel like it's been a long time since I've frowned. For a moment, I consider just ignoring the voice, as it's causing me pain. The comforting nothingness beckons me, but I want to know whose voice I'm hearing. I know he's important for some reason, and he's in pain.

"There's so much I need to say... You can't die..."

My head begins to hurt, as if someone's tightening a vice around it. The darkness is starting to turn grey. I realise that I'm weeping, but I haven't worked out why yet.

"I love you... Please, stay with me Frederick..."

Frederick? That's *my* name. The one who's in pain is saying my name. He's asking me not to leave him. I don't want to leave him either. I don't want to leave Toby!

"Toby," I mutter, my voice hoarse. I had been trying to call his name, but I feel so weak.

Forcing my eyes to open, I see his face staring down at me, tears streaming from his eyes. "I'm here, Toby. I'm here," I manage to say.

Sobbing loudly, he makes to embrace me, but someone pulls him away. I hear him growl momentarily before apologising meekly, and letting the medic past.

"Don't worry, we'll be at the hospital soon. You'll be just fine."

* * *

"So you're saying the bus never actually hit you?"

I avoid his eyes. He's right. According to witnesses, I passed out when I thought the bus was going to hit me, and I didn't wake up until I was in the back of an ambulance, having worried Toby half to death. The doctors weren't sure what had caused it, but the important thing was that I wasn't going to suffer any long-term problems as a result, unless you count dying of embarrassment.

Sitting on the end of my hospital bed in my somewhat private room, I look up at Toby's concerned face. "Doesn't seem like it. I'm really glad it didn't. Hit me, I mean." I immediately realise that I'm probably not making much sense to Toby, but I don't mind. I'm just happy to be in the same room as him again.

"*You're* glad? How do you think *I* feel? I thought I was never going to see... never mind." He looks away for a moment, taking a deep breath to compose himself. His tail is still twitching restlessly though, giving away his disquiet. "So, you're really fine then?"

"Never felt better. Nothing like a near death experience to shake you up when you need it I guess."

Toby frowns. "It's not funny. I was so worried... What were you even *doing* in the road anyway?"

I sigh. That's a question I've been asking myself too, and I'd like to say that I don't know the answer, but that's not completely true. Still, I can't tell Toby the truth yet. Maybe I never will. It might hurt him too badly. Besides, I don't feel that way anymore. "I don't know, Toby. Does it matter? The important thing is I'm okay. *More* than okay actually," I smile at him.

"Yeah, I guess," he replies unconvincingly.

I can tell I haven't heard the last of this, but I see the corners of Toby's mouth begin to creep up in a reluctant smile.

"So, what did you see? I mean, while you were out. You're always going on about your divine vixen, the one who's waiting for you after you croak. If it really was a near death experience, then you must have..."

My laughter interrupts Toby's babbling.

"What is it? Wait! You really *did* see something?"

"Oh, stop it;" I say dismissively, "you know I don't really believe in all that stuff. It's just a fantasy."

"But..."

"Yes, Toby, I saw *something*," I put my hand up to silence him, seeing that he's eager to interrupt, "but it wasn't heaven. It was pretty great, but it wasn't heaven. No, I think my brain just had to sort a few things out, and..."

"But you saw *her*, didn't you," he says, unable to resist interrupting. "You saw your true love, your ultimate fantasy girl."

I'm unable to stop myself laughing again. "Yes and no."

"Yes and no? What does that mean?"

I know the only reason he's asking so many questions is because he's jealous, and my heart's beating faster because I want to just blurt out everything I've learned about myself, but this isn't the right time. I want that moment to be perfect, and this isn't that moment. Ignoring his question, I decide to tease him a little instead. "You know, I heard you talking to me in the ambulance. What was it you were saying?" This time I stifle my laughter.

Toby's eyes widen and he stands up very straight. "What?"

"In the ambulance. I heard you saying something about not wanting something to happen. I think it was..."

"You heard everything, didn't you?" he blurts out, interrupting me. His tail is twitching violently. "Look, I was upset. I..."

I can tell he's genuinely worried, so I cut my game short. "It's ok, Toby," I say more gently.

"No, look, I meant I love you as a friend, that's all. I was just really worried I might lose you and I got a bit emotional. Not very manly, eh? Look, I know you're not gay. You've made it *very* clear that you're not gay, believe me. I just meant I love you as a friend. I love you, that's all."

I'm still trying not to laugh as Toby panics. I want to blurt out everything, but it isn't the right time yet. I want to tell him that I love him too and that I was always just afraid to admit that I'm gay and that I want him to fuck me with his big cock, but I can't. Not yet.

"I love you too," I say at last.

Toby looks momentarily stunned, and then tries to hide his disappointment as he assumes I mean that I love him only as a friend. "Well, you've changed. Aren't you worried people might get the wrong idea? You sure you didn't hit your head or something?" He smiles.

I smile too. Inside, I'm weeping with joy. I said it! I actually told him how I feel, even though I knew he'd take it the wrong way. Still, I'll tell him for real soon enough. "Yeah, I guess I *have* changed. Definitely for the better too. I learned a few things whilst I was *away* actually."

Toby looks at me quizzically. "Oh yeah? What kind of things?"

I stand up from the bed and look into his eyes. "How about we go away for a couple of days. I'll explain everything."

"Away?" he replies, his gaze not wavering from my eyes for an instant. His big feline eyes are locked onto me like I'm prey that might escape if he makes the wrong move. "Where to?"

I tilt my head slightly, trying to look cute.

Toby opens his mouth slightly, his gaze softening.

"How about the beach?" I say, stepping towards him.

"The beach? I erm… Yeah, sure… Are you sure you're feeling okay? I mean, for real."

He looks so cute, and I can feel my resolve vanishing. I'd meant to wait until we were on the beach. I'd meant for it to be like my fantasy, but everything feels so much more real, and I need him *now*.

I lean forward a little and gently kiss the end of his muzzle, his whiskers tickling my nose.

Toby doesn't say anything, he just looks at me in astonishment.

"Toby, I didn't just mean as a friend."

He looks at me blankly for a moment. "What do you…"

For the slightest of moments, his eyes become so sad and yet so happy, and I think he's going to burst into tears, but then his expression suddenly becomes stern.

"This better not be some kind of joke, Frederick. You know how I feel about you…" His voice cracks a little with emotion and tears start to appear in the corners of his eyes.

I feel a prickly sensation as I try to prevent my own tears of joy. "I *am* serious, Toby. I love you. I've *always* loved you. I just couldn't admit it until now, not to you or to myself. I love you more than anything."

With a deep, rumbling growl, Toby throws his arms around me, surrounding me with his body. Breathing in his familiar scent intimately for the first time, I relax completely. Sighing deeply, I put my arms around him, and rub his broad back with my hand-paws.

Toby releases his embrace a little so he can look me in the eye. His eyes are wet, but he isn't crying anymore. His face looks different somehow, and it takes me a moment to realise why. For the first time since I've known him, he looks happy.

"So you nearly get hit by a bus and now you're what? Bi?" he teases.

I smile back. "No, I'm as gay as you are, Toby."

His laughter shakes my body.

"I hope you know I'm always top. You know what that means, right?"

"Yeah, I know," I say, in what I hope is a sexy voice.

Toby doesn't say anything for a moment but I can feel that his breathing has become heavier.

"You're ok with that? I mean, you've never been with a guy so I thought maybe…"

I rub my head against the thick fur around his neck. "Toby, I want you to fuck me," I say, loving how sexy I *know* I sound. I feel his fingers grasp at my fur a little.

"Do you know how long I've waited to hear you say that?"

I laugh, and pull myself tighter to his body. "Do you want to know what I saw when I was away?"

"Yes," he replies in a whisper.

"Heaven, my own personal paradise. I saw you."

Toby doesn't reply, and I know he's waiting to hear more.

"I'm not saying it was *really* heaven, because I know it wasn't. I think I just needed to convince myself that I'd died so that I'd finally start living the way I've always wanted. I went to a place in my head where I felt safe, because I wasn't coping with my feelings and, well, I thought I was about to be squashed by a bus. We'll talk about why I was in the road another time, but what I saw was you. And it was you that brought me back from that place too. The real you."

I can tell that Toby wants to ask me some difficult questions but, like me, me doesn't want to spoil the moment.

"So, what happened in your heaven? What did we do?" he asks.

"I sucked your big, hard cock," I say with a grin.

Far from the shock I was expecting, Toby barely reacts. I can still hear his breathing, perhaps getting a little heavier.

"I sucked your cock until you came in my mouth, and I swallowed every delicious drop," I whisper mischievously.

Exhaling deeply, Toby looks at something between us. Following his gaze, I see the pointed tip of his sheathed penis beginning to appear. I yipp slightly, and feel blood beginning to pump towards my own groin. There is a slight gasp from Toby as he notices my arousal, and I see his erection grow, every bit as impressive as I'd imagined.

"And then I lay down and let you fuck me," I continue, swishing my tail as seductively as I can manage. "Then I rode you until you came inside me, and I came all over you. That's what I saw, Toby."

There is nobody else in the room, but I'm sure there are other people nearby. I'm probably crazy for trying to seduce him in the hospital, and I'd planned to wait until we got to the beach, but some things just can't wait.

Toby finally looks up. His eyes are half-closed but he looks determined, like he's made an important decision. With a quiet growl, he spins me round.

I make a silly yip in my excitement, but it seems to spur Toby on. He bundles me toward the bed and pushes me from behind, forcing me down. I yip again as I realise what he's doing.

Now bent over the bed, my knees on the floor, I lift my tail over my back, waving it from side to side, inviting him.

With another growl, Toby takes his cock in his hand-paw, and crouches to place the tip against my hole. I'm trembling now, the tingling inside me so much more intense than I remember. Well, maybe *remember* isn't the right word exactly. I'm starting to realise that I've never actually made love with Toby before, or *any* man for that matter. I'm panting, my whole body shaking as I wait for it to happen.

Simultaneously pushing with his hips, and lowering his body onto my back, Toby mounts me.

I cry out in pleasure and pain. There had been no pain in my fantasy, but he feels so much bigger now as he pushes himself inside. He's stretching me so much more than *before*. I can't breathe.

Hearing a growl, I then feel a sharp pain as Toby latches his teeth onto the back of my neck, his breathing warm and loud in my ears. He begins to thrust powerfully, rapidly, the pain now rapidly being overwhelmed by pleasure. I start to cry out in joy. More than the physical sensations, I take pleasure in being *fucked* by Toby. I always knew that he loved me, but being *fucked* by him makes me realise that he sees me as sexy.

I cry out into the bed sheets as the pleasure becomes too intense for me to contain. My cock twitches suddenly, and I feel my climax being released beneath me.

A rumbling growl in my ear, and I feel warm and wet inside as Toby begins to fill me with semen. His teeth dig in a little, but do not break the skin.

My climax already so much more intense than I've experienced before, despite nothing having even touched my erection, I feel another wave of pleasure as Toby slowly withdraws both his cock and his teeth from me.

Closing my eyes and resting my head on the bed, I wait for the pleasure to subside. My body feels as though I've run a mile, even though our lovemaking cannot have taken more than a few minutes, if that. I try to ignore the faint scent of blood in the air, masked by the intoxicating aroma of Toby and what he's just left inside me.

Starting to miss Toby already, I look over my shoulder. I see him still panting, but his penis is sheathed, and he looks sheepish.

"Fred, I'm so sorry, I don't know what happened. Are you alright?"

He begins to help me to a sitting position on the bed. Under the circumstances, I'm not entirely comfortable sitting, but my only real concern is Toby. He sits next to me, and holds me tightly with his big arms.

"I just lost it. I never should have been that rough with you, especially not your first time. Does it hurt?"

I giggle. "Toby, I loved it. You felt so strong. But yes, I guess it does hurt a little."

"I just couldn't hold back. I never thought you'd want me to do anything like that. I guess I've just been frustrated."

"Well, you'll never be frustrated again. Although if that's what you do when you're frustrated, maybe I'll make you wait! You were like an animal, Toby!"

Toby laughs a little. "I guess we *both* were! I really hope nobody heard us."

"Well, maybe we should clean up this mess, and make a run for it just in case," I say, half joking.

"Oh? Where to?"

"The beach, remember?"

"Oh yeah. Just you and me?" He kisses the top of my head.

I smile back at him, "Just you and me."

"Sounds like heaven."

I tilt my head up to kiss the side of his mouth. "No, it won't be heaven. It'll be much better than that!"

Empty

by *Faora Meridian*

I never saw him enter.

I felt him, of course, as he arrived in the middle of the night. I felt the hot breath on the back of my neck, a soft lick to the tip of one ear, and even gentle strokes through my fur. Each was but a memory now suddenly given new life. I felt them all, just as surely as I had years ago, decades ago. Way back when… way back before.

I didn't question his presence. It was all just a dream. I couldn't move, and why would I want to? I knew who was there. Maybe I even knew why. Maybe I was sure. Maybe I wanted to be sure. My body – my heart, my *soul* – had been empty for so long. Anything at all to fill that void was welcome, for however short a time.

His body pressed up against mine. He moulded himself to me, just like he used to. I couldn't open my eyes, but I didn't need them. I could feel his warmth at my back. I remembered the feel of his arms around me; black-furred fingers through what had once been russet-red pelt so long ago.

Everything tingled under his touch. Everything from the tip of my tail to that softly licked ear hummed just with his presence. I didn't have to speak. I didn't have to ask. I didn't even have to understand.

Motions, long lost even from memory rushed suddenly back, beckoned by his touch. Old bones that hadn't shifted so in years worked muscles that ached day in and day out. But his touch carried warmth that sank beneath the fur, beneath the flesh, through the tired sinew and muscle and bone like a reminder of times long gone past.

The heat carried deeper and I trembled. Fingers clenched at a pillow as claws unsheathed with a want unfelt for an age and a half. The dream lifted my paralysis, but his presence remained a constant warmth behind me. I could move, and so I did. Oh, I moved. I squirmed. I bore back. I felt more of my emptiness filled like nothing I'd experienced in so, so long.

Full wakefulness eluded me still, even as my energy returned. An arm lifted to wrap around my middle, and I clutched it fiercely. Even if it was just a dream, I wasn't about to let go. He was here. He was home. Everything was right in a way it hadn't been in too long.

He turned me on my back, and I could see him again. Angular lupine face. Smugly perked eyebrow. Ratty, torn left ear. Rugged, toothy smile. I reached up with a smile of my own to cup his cheek. Black paw-fur shone as the moonlight crawled across it, a lost lustre restored.

He placed his paw over mine, his other on my chest. I wondered if he felt my old heart race the same way it had when we had first met. I wondered if he felt it skip a beat – or was it two? – when I felt him, as sure as ever, press beneath my tail.

I knew he'd loved it. That twitch; that tremble of broken anticipation as he slipped inside me. He'd loved to see it written across my face. Could he see it there, sheathed in the full moon's silver glow? How like a wolf to come hunt me under its light. How like him to smile down at me while I shook for and against and around him.

I didn't question his malehood as it spread me open for the first time in too long. I didn't think about the lack of pain or discomfort. It was all just a dream. It was all memories, tempered by time and polished to a perfect shine that reality couldn't compare to. It didn't matter why I took him into myself so easily. All that mattered was that he was there, and that I had.

It didn't matter that I couldn't wake up. There was nothing in the world I could want less. His eyes shimmered in the moonlight as he watched me. I smiled back, and it was the largest smile I could remember smiling in years. I smiled all the smiles I'd missed for him, and he winked at me like the coy devil he always was.

And he moved.

His paws moved all over my body. He ran claws through my fur, and wherever his fingers travelled they left that humming energy in their wake. The grey faded and the red returned, rusty and deep like it had been when we'd met. He traced across cuts and scars and bruises and I felt them mend before him. I felt myself renewed under his touch.

Inside, my heart skipped another beat as it raced for him. It pumped with renewed vigour as one of his arms slid between me and the ratty old mattress beneath. He lifted me up and off it as he leaned back, and then I was in his arms. In his arms and in his lap with his body shadowed by mine.

And I could still see him. I could still see that cheeky smile as he leaned in close, and it only vanished when his forehead touched to mine. His muzzle rubbed across my own – did he lick alongside it? He always did like to – as he lifted me with him, my body wrapped around his shaft. I bore down against him and forced him deep. The best dream. The earliest memories.

But the moment held none of the pain of strained muscles or the awkwardness of young lovers. The dream held the bodies of youth with the experience and driven desire of maturity. The dream set into motion the times we had wanted, as I rode up and down along his shaft. All the hot summer nights and cool winter mornings. All the blustery autumns and bright springs. They melded together with every rise and fall of my body. Time rolled with his hips as he helped slide up into me. I thought I felt the world turn around us.

I didn't question the ease with which I exerted myself. I didn't care where I found the energy to be taken so vigorously by this apparition of a long lost love. It didn't matter how or why. All that mattered were his eyes, locked on my own. My eyes, locked on his. An unbroken stare and a desperately happy smile. He was there. He was *there*.

I swelled with him as I bore down. I panted with him as the end approached. Tightness gripped my chest as he squeezed me tight, and tightness gripped his maleness as I clenched upon him. He knew what was coming. We both felt it. One of his paws stroked my cheek, a mirror to how I cupped his. Breath caught in my throat. I braced at the precipice.

We kissed as we peaked. A silent affair; a tremble of bodies locked together in the throes of passion. Love, muted by love. Pleasure of the flesh tingled through the satisfaction of the soul. Dream or not, he was there. He was the missing piece that fit. He was the piece that had never been replaced. Breath was stolen, just as my heart and soul had been stolen.

The surge of the flesh ebbed away, but the emptiness remained fulfilled. It remained filled, and I squirmed atop him just as I had the first time. He smiled at me just as he had the first time. His fingers traced absently down my cheek and along my jaw. I felt my body sing with its new energy as our muzzles met once more. The first time for a second time.

When we broke, I felt as though I could finally breathe again. I felt as though I could move and sing and run and leap. I felt free in a way I'd not felt since I was a child, and as I saw his smile warm I knew he understood. His eyes seemed to bore through me, past the shadow I cast and to the bed below. He began to pull back from me.

I didn't question how I felt him withdraw so smoothly, just as I hadn't questioned how he'd slid in so effortlessly. I simply sat up, ears perked like a little puppy as I watched him almost seem to drift back into the moonlight. Further he went as he slipped seamlessly from the bed, only to pause and linger there at the very edge. He turned his gaze to the moon.

I followed it and then, right there in the corner of my eye, I saw. I understood the truth behind me. Should I have been afraid? Should I have been uncertain? Shocked? I was none of those. Instead, I smiled. I smiled for him all the smiles we'd missed. I smiled for him all the smiles we'd yet have.

He smiled back as he caught my eye. He nodded to me; offered me his paw. I didn't hesitate for a moment. I grasped it tightly, with the same grip I'd held it the last time I'd felt him near. I held it with the grip of one who wouldn't – who *couldn't* – let go. I knew then that I would never, ever have to let go again, and all was right with the world at last. There were no more questions.

The moonlight continued to drift across the empty old fox, still in his bed.

No one was there to see us leave.

About the Authors

Al Song

Al is a red kangaroo living near Seattle. He is an American of Lao descent, who has learned German. Besides writing he also loves playing the flute and guitar. You can find more of his stories online at: https://www.furaffinity.net/user/alsong/ and https://alsong.sofurry.com/

NightEyes DaySpring

NightEyes DaySpring is a known troublemaker who is rumored to have a penchant for coffee and an interest in dead, ancient civilizations. He has been actively writing since 2010. Recently his stories have appeared in Werewolves vs. Fascism, Gods with Fur, FANG, and Knotted, along with other anthologies. Currently he resides in Florida with his boyfriend, where in his spare time he masquerades as an IT professional. For updates on his writing visit nighteyes-dayspring.com, and for day-to-day nonsense, follow @wolfwithcoffee on twitter.

TJ Minde

TJ grew up as a military brat, jumping around between Northern California and Southern California before moving to Ohio, where he found the furry fandom. There, he picked up the pen. TJ is incredible grateful for the community of artists, writers and friends he found; they helped him discover something that he cares about – writing. TJ has grown to become more passionate about the craft of writing and enjoys creating new worlds and aiding his friends with projects of their own.

TJ's other works may be found in Roar, Fang, and other anthologies both in and out of the fandom. For thoughts, comments and replies in 140 characters or less, he can be found on Twitter @TJMinde.

Jaden Drackus

Jaden Drackus, or Jay Dee is a foxdragon from Maryland. He has been writing furry stories since officially stumbling into the fandom in 2010. Since then he has written in his spare time. He counts joining the greater furry writing community as one of the best decisions he has made, and feels that he has improved greatly for the experience.

A video gamer, builder of model airplanes, reader, and keen observer of Life's little ironies Jay Dee lives in Baltimore with his boyfriend and 4 cats when he isn't writing while waiting for games to load.

In addition to a story in FurPlanet's upcoming second volume of Dogs of War, his short works can be found at http://www.furaffinity.net/user/jadendrackus/ His silly observations on life can be seen on Twitter: @ JadenDrakus.

Miriam "Camio" Curzon

Miriam "Camio" Curzon is a full time graduate student again. Reads a lot of fantasy, plays a lot of games, and finds some time to write. There's also a lot of beer in there... searching, consuming, and brewing. They gave up coffee recently for tea. "Antisocial Paradise" is Camio's fourth story to appear in FANG. You can find them on Twitter @Miriam_Curzon, tweets very occasionally.

Billy Leigh

Billy is a writer and historian who likes to be a Wolf on the internet in his spare time. Naturally very active, he can be found hiking or jogging in the country with his fiance, playing guitar or listening to music when not brainstorming story ideas.

Slip Wolf

Slip Wolf has been weaving tales from errant signals collecting in the void over years, trying to find little bits of better worlds to draw travellers together. Don't know if he's found heaven yet, but purgatory at least has coffee. Find more of his musings at the Furplanet, in the well-kept domicile of Sofawolf, and the wide open expanses of Rabbit Valley and Red Ferret.

Skunkbomb

Skunkbomb currently lives in McLean, Virginia. He is an alumna of the Regional Anthropomorphic Writers Retreat (RAWR), and has been published most recently in ROAR Volume 7 and FANG Volume 7. He's getting better at writing erotica, but is still amazed how much work it is keeping track of whose body parts are where in relation to the other person in bed with them.

When he isn't writing, Skunkbomb goes to the movies, eats Double Stuf Oreos, and hopes to return to Disney or Universal Studios to ride the rollercoasters. He can be found as Skunkbomb123 of Furaffinity and on Twitter @skunkbomb123

Mythicfox

MythicFox discovered the furry fandom via an anime magazine's letter column in the late 90's. While he'd been writing before that, mostly trying to shamelessly ape Stephen King, finding the fandom helped focus him. His biggest influences are, in no particular order, the aforementioned Mr. King, William Gibson, S. Andrew Swann, and Kyell Gold. He's also an avid tabletop gamer, and outside the fandom his writing has seen print in a number of RPG books, most of them about werewolves and involving handfuls of d10s.

Tym Greene

Tym Greene is a writer and artist, particularly of anthro things, and aspires to work in concept art. In the meantime he fulfills his world-building desires with fiction. Apart from a few entry-level college courses, he's mostly self-taught with regard to writing, and has to thank the pantheon of authors (both classic and otherwise), his editors, and his boyfriend for helping him to be the writer he is today. http://www.furaffinity.net/user/tym/

T. D. Coltraine

Tyler "T. D." Coltraine, now in his third Fang appearance, is a sometimes-novelist, sometimes smutsmith, often lazy bum who spends his frequent bursts between writings working up new worlds to explore and petting his cats. Look for his work on SoFurry and FurAffinity.

James Hudson

James Hudson is a furry author from Sheffield, England. His writing is influenced by his obsession with foxes of all descriptions and his lifelong affinity with anthropomorphic animal characters in books, films and video games. Although having only participated in the furry fandom from the sidelines so far, he hopes to play a more active role in the future. 'Little Death' is his first short story to be published but he intends to continue contributing to the fandom through his writing, art and music for the foreseeable future.

Faora Meridian

"When he was but an innocent child living in the Australian suburbs, Faora was bitten by a radioactive book as he explored a secret, government-run library. Now by day he plays video games and writes stories like those that have previously appeared in Heat #7 and Hot Dish #1 and #2, and by night... well, he pretty much does the same thing. But he wears cool costumes while doing it! Well... he wears cool pants. Well... he sometimes wears pants. Uh... well...

... what was I saying again?"

About the Editor

Ashe Valisca

This year is Ashe's fourth year editing the Fang collection. He is a long time furry writer in the community both editing and writing. For the past decade he has worked on the writing track at AnthroCon working to nurture writers in the community attempting to put his English degrees to good use. Known mostly for his quirky teaching style and unorthodox editing style he delights in discovering the hidden potential in new authors.

Always willing to take a risk he specializes in Science Fiction and Fantasy, but will still write more conventional fiction. Ashe is always willing to push the boundaries with his writing willing to bring focus onto the darker parts of human nature—sometimes the good guy has to fail. Art imitates Life and he makes every attempt to make that true.

About the Artist

Mehndi

Ever since he was young Jack Rohn, or Mehndi as he's known in his art, has been fascinated with the world of art and animation. Hardly a day went by that he didn't spend time honing his craft, whether it was quick sketches inspired by everyday life or a complex painting of the family cat. He graduated with a Bachelors Degree in art from Carlow University. These days he spends his time lusting after the next big ink break through while maintaining an active freelance portfolio.